I0599678

Cover design: KiwiCoverDesigns

Beneath the Strokes

CONTENTS

Author's Note

This is the second book in the LIES WE BELIEVE series, but each book is a standalone, and it is not necessary to have read the first book, WHAT HURTS THE MOST, before reading this one.

In this book, you will find flawed characters, themes of mental health and guilt, and open-door spice.

CONTENT WARNING:

Talk of attempted suicide, bullying, low self-esteem, thoughts of dying, death of a bird, and depression.

The following are present, but not described in detail: extreme poverty, alcoholism, and a drug-addicted parent.

Playlist

BLUEBIRD by Miranda Lambert
ELUSIVE DREAM by Rain City Drive
BLANK SPACE by Taylor Swift
BEAUTIFUL CRAZY by Luke Combs
GO FIND LESS by Riley Roth
SOMEONE TO STAY by Vancouver Sleep Clinic
PEACE OF MIND by Max Aubrey
BUTTERFLY EFFECT by Tenille Arts
LOVE ME NOT by Ravyn Lanae
BROKEN by Seether [feat. Amy Lee]
THROUGH HELL by Melrose Avenue
I AM NOT OKAY by Jelly Roll
RUNAWAY TO MARS by TALK
CAUGHT UP TO ME by Alana Springsteen
YOU ARE THE REASON by Calum Scott
ANGELS FALL by Breaking Benjamin
BLUE SKY & THE PAINTER by Bastille
SURVIVE by Lewis Capaldi
SHE'S GOT THIS THING ABOUT HER by Chris Young
STARGAZING by Myles Smith
FOLLOW YOUR ARROW by Kacey Musgraves
DAYLIGHT by Shinedown

1

NOTHING ELSE GOING ON

I freeze, leaving my underwear dangling around my knees, and my eyes bulge like a cat's at the ring glittering in the moonlight. A thin gold band with an oval-cut gem, not quite a carat, and who knows if it's real. But it doesn't matter; it's perfect.

"Marry me," Brian says from the leather car seat beside me. His blond hair sticks up in all directions from when I had the locks gripped in my hand just moments ago.

Unable to handle the romantic haze in the air, we escaped the wedding we attended as guests, invited out of obligation; my sister's boyfriend's mom is the bride. The country love songs softly playing while couples held each other close, the glow of the lights wrapped around the pillars, and the flush on our cheeks from the champagne built until we were bursting with need for each other. Along with our need to make things more exciting.

"What do you say?" Brian asks.

Brian and I met over a year ago at a local bar where his metal band poorly played a set of covers. His dimples and drumstick-wielding arms called to me like a whale singing to its mate, and I've had a blast with him ever since. Well, mostly.

Just like today, he's always available to accompany me to whatever family function or dinner I'm forced to go to, and he's always up for sneaking off for a quickie to liven up the night. It would be nice to know I'll never be alone again or forced to scramble for a last-minute date, so my answer should be yes.

And I already know exactly what I want: a small, backyard wedding, only family and a few friends in attendance. I'll walk with Dad down the aisle to *On My Way to You* by Cody Johnson, and the eyes of every guest will fill with tears. Once it's time to exchange the rings, I'll hand my bouquet to Cori, my fraternal twin. She'll stand between me and my best friend, Danielle, both wearing short, dusty-blue dresses. I'll step in front of Brian, and we'll declare our love for each other before turning the music up loud enough to elicit a call to the cops.

We'll eat catering from the Mexican restaurant down the street, drink from an open bar, and dance on Mom and Dad's patio. We'll cut into a homemade cake with simple white frosting and flowers surrounding the bottom, with a cardboard Mr. & Mrs. stuck in the top.

And the timing couldn't be better. Cori's now in a serious relationship with the perfect man after dodging a snake, and things have settled down after spending the last year building a business together.

So why am I hesitating?

My relationship with Brian has ridden a roller coaster lately. In love one day, definitely broken up the next. Any time he and I are in our 'hate you' stage, I keep Cori company at our grandmother's old house, where she's been living for the past year. Half of my stuff is still there from when he and I broke up a few weeks ago.

"Sage?" Brian asks, caressing my cheek.

I open my mouth to shout my acceptance, but the doubt of my family members rings through the silence.

Two weeks ago, at a family dinner, my younger and dumber brother, Spencer, said, *'I'll give it a month before you're back at the farmhouse.'*

My older, married, and supposedly mature sister, Stephanie, snorted. *'I give it two weeks.'*

'Give me a break, relationships are hard,' I snapped.

'Sure they are, sweetie. So was softball, so was college, so was that job answering phones...' Mom went on for a while, listing everything I've quit in my life, before dropping it to comment on Cori's weight again. And Dad shoveled food into his mouth, knowing any contribution to this conversation would result in having to explain himself at that family counseling Cori's been dragging our parents to.

After we got home from that dinner, my mouth found Brian's before the front door was even closed, wanting to silence the thoughts before they grew roots. Truth be told, it wasn't just my family's doubt in our relationship making me queasy; the ride was losing its thrill.

We laid in post-coital bliss, skin sheening with sweat, when I said, *"Tell me that will be the last time, Brian. The last time that we make up."* Obviously, I couldn't stop us from breaking up if we truly weren't meant to be together, but a decision needed to be made: either we stopped playing around and buckled our seatbelts, or we hopped off the ride entirely.

"I can't exactly promise that, but I'd like it to be," he said.

I sat up then, gasping, with the sudden solution to my problem. *"Let's get married."*

He narrowed his eyes before a slow smile crept over his lips. *"That's funny, right there."*

"No, seriously." I put my hands on his shoulders. *"Why not? You love me, don't you?"*

He nodded. Hesitantly, but still.

"And I love you. So let's do it." I've often been told that I don't think before I act, but I do. I just don't spend too much time *over*thinking, allowing the opportunity to pass by me.

"I think you had too much wine at dinner."

"Come on, Brian. Everyone's always telling us to choose a lane. You're my lane."

He pulled me down to lie on his chest once again. *"Let's sleep on it."*

When I woke up the next morning, I figured he was right—we needed more time before taking that step. I certainly didn't expect a proposal this soon, given how he reacted. And with a ring too, instead of a twisted condom wrapper or something.

Have we had enough time? Could we make a marriage work if we struggled as hard as we did when we were dating?

Screw this.

I know what I want. Maybe that changes faster than the Texas weather, but I'm flexible and confident. And no one is going to take that away from me.

"Yes!" I jump at him, clashing my lips to his. He slides my underwear from where it still rests around my knees, and we began round two.

WHEN WE FINALLY PRY OURSELVES AWAY FROM ONE ANOTHER, WE return to the party. The reception is held in the groom's airplane hangar, a metal building on his property where he normally stores his planes. It's not the most romantic venue, but the maroon fabric wrapped around the rafters and the white floral centerpieces do wonders for the atmosphere.

Brian heads to the makeshift bar, a fold-out table covered with bottles, for celebratory drinks, and I walk across the room. I spot Mom and Cori, itching to tell them the news now. Cori will smile and immediately jump into wedding preparations, perfectly unbothered as long as it doesn't affect her directly. But Mom will sigh and tattle on me to Dad before giving every excuse as to why I'm making yet another stupid decision.

With that image at the forefront of my mind, I approach them from behind, deciding to save the announcement of my engagement for a more appropriate time. Like maybe after I'm already married.

I wouldn't want to steal Elaine and Jonah's thunder anyway. They've been in love for years and kept it a secret from Cori's boyfriend, Nick, until the news accidentally came out. Today is for them.

But that changes when I overhear Cori, unaware of my presence. "Getting married isn't everything. It's not for everyone. Who knows, Sage and Brian have been working through their issues. Maybe they'll last this time."

Mom snorts. "No, they won't. Sage can't commit to a hair color, let alone a man."

Reflexively, my hand goes to my dark red hair. I like to color it according to the season or important events in my life. It's always taken color well, something not a lot of people can say for theirs, and I like to take advantage of that. But something as trivial as hair color shouldn't be a criticism, and certainly shouldn't have my stomach sinking.

Fuck it. I don't have to announce it to the whole room, just these two women discussing my love life like they have any say in the matter.

I step between them, pushing them apart, and hold out my left hand. "Is now a bad time to tell you we're engaged?"

As expected, Mom's head falls into her hand. "Oh, Sage. Please tell me you're not pregnant."

Cori, the peacekeeper and confrontation-avoider, says, "Mom, I'm sure she's not. Even so, we love Brian. And look, it's a beautiful ring." It's nothing special, and the gold washes out my skin. But I couldn't care less because it's mine. It's proof that I can stick with something.

"Thanks. Don't you like it?" I ask Mom, flashing it at her in case she didn't get a good enough look the first time.

"You'll have to give it back when you break up again, you know," she says with certainty that our breakup is inevitable.

"We're not breaking up! This is real." Lowering my voice, I add, "And no, I'm not pregnant, I'm in love." Who cares if I'm pregnant, anyway? I'd make a great mom. One of those easygoing, nonchalant moms who all the kids would call to pick them up from jail.

The bride, Elaine, comes to stand on Cori's left. She's radiant in her non-traditional maroon, lace dress, with her blonde hair pulled back by a pearl clip.

"Is everything okay, ladies?" she asks, and my stomach sinks for nearly causing a scene at her wedding.

I open my mouth to explain that everything is fine, but Mom beats me to it. "Sage and Brian are engaged. Can you believe it?"

Elaine's eyes widen as she brings her hands together. "Oh, congratulations! When did that happen?"

"Just now, out in the parking lot. Sorry, I didn't mean to steal your thunder." But Mom has to let the world know about her every inconvenience. I shoot her a pointed look.

Elaine waves me off. "Oh, I don't care about that. Weddings are to celebrate love, it doesn't matter whose."

Damn, Cori lucked out with her future mother-in-law. Brian's mom sucks worse than mine.

Although Mom sure is trying for first place when she adds, "They've been off and on again so often throughout the last year, I'd bet my own marriage on this one not lasting."

Cori and I share a look, silently communicating our joint frustration.

"Well, I won't claim to be an expert. My first marriage wasn't a good one. But he did give me Nick, so I won't say it was a mistake." Elaine chuckles, then clears her throat at Mom's glare. "But you've got a good community of women around you to help you through this transition. Don't hesitate to reach out if you need anything."

"Thank you for your *support*, Elaine," I say, glaring at Mom.

"Do you know when you'd like to have your wedding?" Elaine asks.

A winter wedding would be beautiful, but snow in Texas equals national disaster and wouldn't exactly match the other details I already have in mind. Summers are hell, but the faster I get it done, the quicker Mom shuts up.

Mom answers before I can. "She won't. She'll call off the engagement before the wedding happens."

Summer it is.

"Next month," I state.

Mom whips her head to me. "You are *not* getting married in a month."

"Why not? I don't want anything crazy." Nick's friend, Tyler, can officiate for us as he did for Elaine and Jonah, I can find a dress anywhere, and I'll grab some flowers from the grocery store.

Besides, getting it done before the summer ends would be better for my job. Or *jobs,* since my job description is a mile long. First and foremost, I draw. I draw coffee-related designs for t-shirts, coffee mugs, dish towels, keychains, bookmarks, and all kinds of random things. Next, I print out the designs or cut out vinyl and apply it to the physical item. Then I sell those items online and at vendor markets, along with bags of coffee grounds and whole beans.

When I'm not doing that, I help Cori out at her coffee trailer, making drinks and taking payments. Or, if you want full honesty, flirting with customers and upselling items they don't need to drive sales up.

Summers are slower, business-wise, but once school starts, the tired moms stop by for coffee after dropping off their gremlins. Fall means several fall festivals and markets that keep me busy almost every weekend. Online sales increase around Christmas, which means I'm busy packaging shipments. Spring involves more craft shows, then preparations for Mother's Day, so yes, summer is the best choice. Considering it's already July, I don't have much time to get this wedding over with. And I'll be damned if I have to wait a whole year before tying this knot.

One of the other guests calls out for Elaine, so she says, "Well, let me know if I can do anything to help," before answering their beckoning.

"I'll make a checklist of things we need to do when I get home," Cori starts. She's a planner. "I think the first thing is finding a dress and getting invitations-"

"Cori Lorraine, you are not instigating this. She cannot get married in a month."

"Mom. What did Dr. Phillips say?" Cori asks gently, as if speaking to an ill person. Dr. Phillips is the family counselor they've been seeing. I haven't met her yet, despite Cori's attempts at dragging me along, but I've heard about the advice she's given them. And it seems to be working. Cori's relationship with our parents has improved tremendously over the last year.

Mom takes a deep breath, letting it out slowly, not bothering to hide her rolling eyes. How embarrassing to be lectured by your own daughter?

"Sage, honey. I support you fully. This is your life, and whatever you want to do with it, I'll be here cheering you on. Because I love you." Her hands are raised as if in prayer. "But it's *because* I love you that I don't want you rushing into something you're not ready for."

"Thank you. But as I've already told you, I'm ready. So please hear me."

Her hands fall. "Fine. But your father's going to have an aneurysm."

I grab Cori's arm. "Then I'll take Cori with me to tell him. And she can throw Dr. Phillips in *his* face, too."

AS EXPECTED, DAD SIGHED AT THE NEWS AND DRAINED HIS GLASS before heading back to the bottles of alcohol. Now, with my own drink in hand and Brian a few feet away chatting with Nick, I stand with Cori as she wrings her hands.

"Out with it," I tell her.

She shakes her head. "It's nothing. Just... I keep asking you to come with us to counseling so we can avoid situations like this."

"Like what? Mom and Dad already know I'm going to do what I want. *They're* the ones with the issues. I don't see why *I* have to attend those sessions."

"Because the counselor needs to hear your side. And it would feel good to talk about it, don't you think?"

I wave my hand in dismissal. "Nah, I'm good. It doesn't bother me like it does you when they disapprove of my life." In fact, there isn't much that bothers me. At least not for long. I don't have the time to linger in the unpleasantness. If someone hurls an insult or doubtful comment towards me, I simply leave it and walk away.

Unlike Cori, who picks everything up and plasters it on her heart. That's just one of the many differences between us, like her brown to my—when it's not dyed—blonde hair, or her anxiety to my chill. Although, I have to admit that she's grown a lot in the last year since starting therapy and counseling. But I don't need stuff like therapy because I'm good. Really.

"Okay, but like..." She cringes, asking gently, "You didn't accept Brian's proposal because of Mom and Dad, right?"

"Of course not! I'm not stupid." I throw my hands in the air. "Why is it so hard to believe that I want to get married to Brian?"

"Because I know you," she states carefully.

I roll my eyes, but I see where she's coming from. When Mom or Dad tell me I can't do something, I have a tendency to say, *'Oh yeah? Well, watch this.'* I consider it to be my best and worst quality.

"Seriously. I want this. Because I love him, not because I want to prove anyone wrong—although that's a bonus. It's time, don't you think?"

"There's no correct timeline to follow except your own," she says.

"Exactly! And I want to do this now." There's nothing else going on in my life at the moment, so now is perfect.

After her own eye-roll and sigh, eerily similar to my mother's, she shakes her head and grins. "Okay then. When are we going dress shopping?"

I smile, throwing my arms around her.

2

ARE YOU CRAZY?

T he cake is finally cut, and the bride and groom are sent off for a weekend in New Orleans, exciting me for my own honeymoon. Different possibilities pop into my head, like a trip to Mexico. Except I don't have a passport and doubt I'd be able to get one in a month. I could go to Florida and relax on the beach. Or I could just save my money on the plane ticket and drive down to Galveston.

After the rest of the guests leave, Cori goes into the house to listen for Natalie, Nick's baby sister, asleep in her crib, and Brian pulls me into a dark corner. We're on clean-up duty along with Nick and his friends, Tyler and Callum, but with Brian's tongue in my mouth, the plastic cups and napkins littering the ground cease to exist.

"Hey, quit slacking. There will be plenty of time for that for the rest of your lives," Nick calls out. I pull away to find him and Tyler smirking in jest, but Callum scowls.

I wave them off and pull Brian back towards me.

I first met Callum around two years ago, but I can't fill two hands with all the facts I know about him. I know he's judgmental, grumpy, and that he keeps a beard because he looks alien without one. But with one? I'd be whistling if my lips weren't otherwise occupied. If only he had Tyler's personality, I might've thought twice about accepting Brian's ring.

The night we met, Cori and I were celebrating our twenty-third birthday at an expensive restaurant along with friends. Callum sat at the other end of the table, glaring at me, for reasons I'm not sure of. I can only assume he thought me to be too loud, too obnoxious, or both, but whatever his issues with me, they seem to have only worsened with time.

Which is why it's been my goal to be as annoying as possible whenever he's around. For example, at Nick's birthday party a few months ago, I was in charge of taking pictures. I made sure to capture Callum's every yawn, every scowl, several blinks, and all the awkward smiles, and plastered them all over social media the next day. He seems to be irritated by my presence in general, but he especially hates it when I ask if he's missed me or tell him how handsome he looks.

"Seriously. None of us wants to see that, and we'd all like to get home at some point," Callum says.

I break away from Brian's embrace. "Aww, Callum," I taunt. "Feeling jealous?"

It's only fun when he reciprocates, but this time, he doesn't. His intense gaze bores into mine for a second longer than is comfortable before he ties a trash bag too roughly, ripping it and spilling its contents.

I grab a new bag and head over to help pick it all back up.

"I got it," he snaps.

"Just let me help." We get about half of it in the new bag before I catch him staring at my ring. "Did you hear the news?" I ask, straightening my hand for him to get a better look at its shine. But he lowers his gaze and shoves a stack of cups into the new bag. "Yep. Congrats."

While Callum isn't mine or Brian's friend exactly, I'll still send him an invite; we've been around each other so often by this point, I think it'd be weird not to. Like how I was invited tonight simply for being related to Cori. I have a few single friends I could set him up with; maybe they'll warm his heart and get the stick out of his ass. I'm sure his presence could be pleasant after some work is put into him.

"Are you going to come to the wedding?" I ask sweetly.

"Do I have to?"

I roll my eyes. "Just for that, you're in charge of delivering chairs and tables to Mom and Dad's house."

"For what?"

My eyebrows rise. "My wedding? Isn't that what we're talking about?"

"You already know you're having it at your parents' house? Shouldn't you be taking some time to visit different venues?"

"Nope. We're having it in a month at Mom and Dad's."

The discarded plates and plasticware he held in his hand clatter to the floor. "Are you crazy?"

Static crackles between us in the dead silence of the building. Nick and Brian have already walked back to the house, carrying trays of leftover food, but Tyler lurks in the corner, taking a suspiciously long time untying a Mr. and Mrs. banner.

Tired of this pointless conversation, I tie the bag roughly like Callum did to the first, and barely avoid ripping this one apart too, before walking away.

"I've only been engaged for like two hours, and I'm already sick of having to explain myself."

He follows, hot on my heels. "That's just it, though. You've only been engaged for two hours, and you already have your wedding planned?"

"Not the whole thing," I reply, defenses up and swords ready. "But I want this wedding done in a month, and Mom and Dad's backyard is already available. And free." Why am I even bothering to explain anything to him? I don't owe him—or anyone, for that matter—any explanation.

I storm off to the garbage can outside, yank the lid off, and throw the bag in before slamming it back down. My skin prickles at his presence so close behind me, but I'm done with this interrogation. I turn and stomp off towards the house to collect Brian and get the hell out of here.

"Sage, wait." His voice is calm again, the only reason I stop in my tracks and whip around to face him.

"Why? So you can tell me I'm making a mistake like everyone else? I'm twenty-five. I think I know my own mind by now."

"See, I don't think you do. I think you're conflicted about your feelings for Brian and you figure this will solve it. It won't. It will only trap you and make things worse."

"What are you even talking about? You don't know me, you don't know anything." How did we get here? We were having a simple conversation about my wedding and now he thinks he can psychoanalyze me?

Anyone would be stupid to get married to someone if they were having doubts, but I'm not. I love Brian. I love his ability to erase my stress and distract me from any sad feelings. I love how he makes me laugh, love that I'm never bored in his presence. He's sweet and thoughtful and takes care of me better than any man I've been with so far. Who wouldn't want all of that for me?

He takes a step forward, his forehead pinched. "Look. Can you just promise me something? Can you just take this week and really think about what you're getting yourself into here? This is marriage. This is legally bound by law. This isn't a way to entertain yourself on a slow day; this is a life change."

"I know that." I won't bring up the fact that I could just get a divorce if the marriage doesn't work out. Something tells me that wouldn't go over well.

"So then you'll know it's not something you should jump into."

The stifling heat from the day is replaced with a warm, yet welcome breeze that blows away my fighting mood. "Why do you even care? We barely know each other."

"Because I'm a caring person." The voice in my head snorts. "And you're kind of a part of our friend group now, whether you meant to be or not." He sighs and runs a hand down his face. "I just don't want to see you get hurt."

I find myself itching for my colored pencils so that I can capture the moon and the truth of his statement reflecting off his hazel irises. I don't have much time for unrestricted creativity these days. When I'm drawing, it's usually merchandise for the coffee business, and there are only so many sayings and illustrations you can put on a coffee mug. Unfortunately, it's what pays my bills, so I can't just drop it and move on to something else like I do with most other things.

"Well, thank you for looking out for me. And maybe I'll take some time this week to think about it, maybe consider a later wedding. But I do know my own mind."

Truly. I pride myself on not wasting my time or sitting around wondering if I should or shouldn't do something. If desire strikes, I jump into action. And if it fizzles, I leave behind whatever's bogging me down. Life is too short to worry or doubt, and I'd rather spend mine living and experiencing whatever I can. Even if that means making mistakes.

But when Callum opens his arms for a truce hug, a wave of doubt slams into the shields in place specifically to prevent second-guessing. Callum hates it when I touch him. He jolts back as if disgusted anytime our arms have brushed or fingers grazed each other. But here he is, offering a hug of his own volition. No bribe, no begging on my part, it's just a free hug from Callum.

I take hold of this moment and jump into his wide embrace, nuzzling into his chest. His body tenses, but envelops me as the scruff of his beard scratches my forehead.

"I just want you to be happy, Sage."

Overall, it's a nine out of ten hug, the kind you could easily melt into. It's warm, enveloping, and his cologne nearly elicits a groan. The only hugs that deserve a ten are the kind that end in sex.

Annnddd, on that note, I need to go.

Pulling back, I return the sentiment, calling over my shoulder as I run toward the house, "You too. Let me know if you're coming to the wedding. I'll set you up with one of my friends."

He only grunts in response.

3

WHAT COULD GO WRONG?

With 'Bride' in silver, glittery letters across my chest and a plastic, silver tiara on my head, we step through the automatic doors.

"Welcome to Ross," a cashier calls. I smile and wave, herding my crew to the dress racks in the middle of the store. Cori and I closed the coffee trailer a few hours early today to dress shop with my best friend, Danielle, and Cori's best friend, Hailey. I couldn't imagine experiencing such an important life event without any of these women, but I'm already kicking myself for inviting Mom along.

"Remember when Stephanie got married?" Mom asks. "She made an appointment at a bridal shop in the city. They brought us champagne while we relaxed in plush chairs. And we got to see her in the most beautiful, floor-length, sparkling-white gowns."

I do remember. I also remember how they wanted a soul and a few arms as payment, and how they fucked up my older sister's alterations. She starved herself for a couple of weeks to fit into the dress and still walked down the aisle with her boobs spilling out.

"What do you even hope to find here?" Mom grabs the bottom of a short, neon-green dress, raising her eyebrows and scrunching her nose.

"Hey, that's actually cute." I pull it off the rack to examine it more closely, but the color would clash with the dusty-blue dress Cori's already purchased.

"Sage Marie, you are not getting married in a green dress."

"Quit being a snob. This is *my* wedding. I'll get married in my PJs if I want to." I gasp and turn to the girls. "Oh my God, a pajama party!"

Cori's face brightens. "Oh, please do a pajama party."

"I am not coming to your wedding in my pajamas," Danielle adds, with a similar expression to Mom's on her face.

Hailey shrugs, sipping her blueberry-vanilla latte from the *'Coffee Break'* cup in her hand.

On second thought, that's more Cori's style. I can see it now: reruns of her favorite TV show on a projector screen so she's not the center of attention. Popcorn and ice cream for dinner, like our grandparents used to feed us on Sunday nights at their house. Blankets laid out across the lawn, and books within reach, just in case.

No, I want dancing and cute dresses and everyone's eyes on me the entire time.

"Maybe for your wedding. Or the bridal shower. Speaking of which, we don't have much time to plan that."

"Already on it," Cori says. "It's in two weeks in the back section of the diner." The diner in question belongs to my dad after it was handed down. Cori and I used to work there, but Dad struggles with ideas of improvement that aren't his own. If you had asked me a year ago where I'd hold my bridal shower when the time came, the diner wouldn't have been anywhere near the list of options. But in the year since Cori and I quit, Dad's finally updated the menu and replaced the torn bench seats. It's still just a diner, but at least it smells like home-cooked meals and coffee, rather than mildew.

While I sift through the racks, pulling any white, champagne, or light pink dresses I see in my size, Cori holds up a knee-length, long-sleeved white dress. It's made of lace with rhinestones near the neckline.

"Oh, that would be perfect," Mom says. "Please get that one."

"I would die of heat stroke in those sleeves." Although I could cut them off, maybe alter the neckline, bring the hem up a little. I'm not a professional, but I know my way around a sewing machine.

I add it to the pile before heading to the dressing room. Cori has a folder open in her hands and takes notes about flowers, the cake decorations, music, while Mom gives her suggestions she 'would like me to seriously consider.' I exclaim my rejection of each idea through the door.

"Just grab some flowers from the side of the highway. Make it easy. And we'll just set up a Bluetooth speaker and shuffle a music station." I slip on a pink strapless dress with thin material that would be perfect for the hot weather.

Mom sighs. "If you'd just agree to wait a few more months, we'll have time to do everything properly."

"Nope." I open the door and hold my arms out. "What do you think of this one?"

"No," Mom states, closing her eyes.

Danielle turns her nose up. "It looks like a bathing suit cover."

Ignoring both of them, I spin and strike different poses while Hailey snaps photos; after I try on each dress, we can compare. I close the door again and choose a dress with intricate beadwork around the bodice and a tulle skirt short enough to give Dad a heart attack.

"I just don't understand the rush. I know work will be busy

over the next few months, but we're all here to help. Planning this wedding in a month is just chaos."

"Mom."

"I'm just saying-"

"Please stop *just saying*. Brian and I have set the date for three weeks from now. That's final."

The silence rings louder than when I came home from college and told Mom and Dad I'd dropped out. They blinked at me, waiting for me to declare, "Just kidding!" And Cori glared, ready to fly across the table to pummel me for wasting away a scholarship she'd have killed for.

"Fine. But when you wake up and realize this isn't what you want after all, don't come crying to me."

Her angry footsteps retreat before Danielle whispers, "She's gone."

"Good. She's ruining this experience for me."

"But... like, you've had the major conversations with Brian, right?" Cori asks. "About kids, or if one of you takes an out-of-state job opportunity, and finances, things like that."

"He knows I want kids, I can move my job anywhere, as long as you don't mind me stepping away from the trailer. And our finances are separate and will stay that way. Or, at least until we have kids." I open the door again and spin around.

"Okay, but what if he gets injured and can't work? Are you okay with paying for everything and supporting him? What if he gets sick? What if *you* get sick? Are you both willing to stand by each other? What if you can't have sex?"

"Okay, chill. We're not even having sex now. Not until the wedding night. We decided we wanted to have something to look forward to since there aren't any surprises between us." We've done every position in the book, had sex in all the exciting places, and it's always best after we've gone a while without.

"Yeah, you need the sex to look forward to because a marriage isn't exciting enough," Hailey adds, unhelpfully.

I roll my eyes. "You know what I mean. It's hard, though. It's only been two days, and I'm going crazy."

"Well, to keep yourselves busy so you don't cave, why don't y'all start having these serious conversations? You know, just to make sure you can make this last," Cori suggests.

I guess it's not a bad idea, so I don't reject the list of questions she texts me.

"Now, for the bachelorette party," I start. "I was thinking, what if we had a crafting party instead of the typical strip club, bar, whatever scene? I'll need help making the corsages and boutonnières, and probably my bouquet."

Cori gives me a strange look, and Danielle scoffs. "We're not going to a strip club? But the boys get to."

"Stop whining. We can for yours." Honestly, I'd much prefer to get a lap dance from some greased-up, muscular man with thick arms and wearing practically nothing. But I have too much to do before the wedding.

I close the door again while Cori jots down some notes.

"To keep things cheap, I have to do most everything myself. Which means I need help from you guys. And Stephanie, if we absolutely have to invite her." I love my older sister, just not her righteousness. "But only if she agrees to bring the babies."

"Okay, that leaves food, cake, you need to get your rings, Brian still needs to find what he's wearing, Danielle and Hailey need to find their dresses. Oh, and shoes! And then we need to give the final head count to the party rental place for the tables and chairs..." Cori's breath heaves faster and faster, so I open the door and pull her into the room with me.

Placing my hands on her tense shoulders, I look into her gray eyes beneath a pinched forehead. "This is *my* wedding, and there's no panicking involved in the planning of *my* wedding. Save it for your own." She nods but doesn't relax.

"Look, it's nothing to get worked up over. It's just a party. What could go wrong?"

THAT EVENING, I RETURN HOME WITH THE LACY, WHITE DRESS IN case I don't find anything better by the time the wedding arrives. Brian, still in his greasy uniform, plays video games with his online friends. I kiss him on the head as he pulls his headset off.

"I was thinking we could hang out with the guys tonight at the bar," he says, referring to his bandmates and their girl-friends. "They're meeting at Buffalo River in a couple of hours."

I adorn my best pout. "I was going to ask if you'd be up for a date night. We haven't spent much time together since we got engaged." He's been busy with his band, with practice almost every day after a ten-hour shift at a mechanic shop.

"Could we invite Corbin and Thalia? Make it a double date?" he asks, not removing his eyes from his game.

"No, you invited them last time, remember?"

Finally, he looks at me. "Then how about tomorrow? We can even go to that place I hate that you love."

It hits me then, as I stare into his oblivious brown eyes, how little time we actually spend just the two of us, not just lately, but *ever*. Date night usually ends up including at least one of our friends, if not a whole group of them. Anytime we push plans off to 'tomorrow,' those plans usually get cancelled. And anytime we are alone, our mouths are too occupied for any meaningful conversation.

"Compromise. Have dinner with me beforehand, then you can meet the guys."

He groans. "I was hoping you'd come. Everything is always more fun when you're there."

I mistake the warmth on my cheeks for delight in the

compliment, until I realize how tired I am of having to be the fun one all the time. There's a time for fun, but this isn't one of them.

"No, we have some things to discuss, and we can't put it off any longer. I need to work on the invitations anyway," I explain, as I head to the kitchen to pop some chicken nuggets into the oven.

He agrees, although reluctantly, and I take that as progress. While dinner bakes, I do a lap picking up various clutter: Brian's pile of socks underneath the coffee table, the collection of dirty cups on the counter, and the stack of mail on the table. Then, I start the load of laundry that Brian was supposed to start earlier and fold the clothes from the dryer.

As I stir powdered cheese into a pot of boxed macaroni, I wonder if we're too old to eat this kind of stuff. But that thought is quickly replaced by glimpses of my future. This evening is representative of most nights I've had and will have for the rest of my life. Is it enough? For me or for Brian?

Life with Brian is driving a sports car, pedal to the floor, on an open road. It's exactly what I wanted for my early twenties, excitement and thrill. But, eventually, we'll reach a road with speed limits and need a bigger car to fit car seats and haul strollers and sports equipment. Can he do the minivan with that mommy-finger song playing through the speakers and a 'baby on board' sticker on the window?

Once dinner is done, I set the table with plates and silver-ware, and call Brian over.

He lifts his headset but doesn't rise from the couch. "We're not going to watch a movie or something while we eat?"

"No. As I said, we have some things we need to discuss. Plus, we never use this table." Except for physical activities.

The thought of eating at the table instead of the couch is as revolting to me as it is to him. But if we're getting married, shouldn't we, at the very least, be able to eat our chicken nuggets and macaroni and cheese at the table like adults without the TV as a buffer?

His lip curls. "Do we have to?"

"Yes. Let's talk. Cori sent me a list of questions to ask your fiancé before the wedding. You know, just to ensure we're on the same page."

Brian finally shuts off the PlayStation while I get my phone and open up the list. There are twenty-five questions, some thought-provoking, but others, like *'What's your ideal date night,'* I'll probably skip because I already know his answer.

Wait. Does he know mine?

"Okay, question one. Your ideal date night. I know your answer—a concert or karaoke." He nods, taking a bite. "What's mine?"

He cocks his head, chewing and swallowing before admitting he has no idea.

"A picnic at night, stargazing," I answer.

His face twists. "That doesn't sound like you at all." I get why he would say that because I like fast-paced environments, like him. But that doesn't mean I can't also enjoy the intimacy found beneath the expansive dark sky, peppered with the windows to heaven.

"Moving on. How do you feel about starting a family? Personally, I think three kids is ideal. And I'd love to get started right away because I don't want my parents to be too old to play with their grandkids."

"Hmm." He shoves an entire dinosaur-shaped nugget in his mouth.

"What?"

"Nothing. I just thought you'd want to wait a while on kids. We're young, you know. We have a lot of life to live before we're ready."

"Well, I also don't want to be too old myself when our kids have kids." I wave it off and look back at my phone. "We can discuss that more later. Oh, okay. This is a good one. How do you suggest we handle conflict?"

Conflict isn't our strong suit. So far, our conflict resolution has involved breaking up anytime an issue arises. Then we get bored, miss each other, and brush our conflict under the rug.

"I think we should not have any from now on."

The laughter forming in my throat catches when I grasp his seriousness. "What do you mean? Every relationship has conflict at some point."

He shrugs. "But why? If we're mature enough, we can just decide not to argue."

I blink rapidly. "That's not how it works."

"What do you suggest then?" He focuses entirely too hard on stabbing a piece of macaroni.

I wait for him to finish before explaining. "Depending on the conflict, we communicate our sides, and if things get too heated, we take a step back and give each other some space. Then, we resume the conversation once we've cooled down." We never allow ourselves to walk away until our heads are clear, and we end up saying things we don't mean.

He lifts a shoulder again. "I guess that will work."

"Great! See? We're getting somewhere." Next on the list is, "How can I help you face your fears?"

He chuckles. "Don't bring snakes into the house."

I glance back at the list. "I think it's talking about deeper fears. Like failure or something."

Already finished with his food, he scrapes the cheese sauce left on his plate. The sound elicits an unpleasant shiver throughout my body. "I'm not really afraid of anything."

I scoff. Everyone's afraid of something. "Okay, well, how will you help me face mine?"

"What are you afraid of?"

Mom would answer that I'm afraid of staying in one place too long. Dad would answer the same, along with most of my siblings. But I'm not. I simply don't like wasting time on things that don't bring me joy.

Like with college.

Thing is, I know what I want and what I don't. I sound like a broken record, but why are women praised by society for knowing what they want, but torn down when they act on their desires?

That's a rock better left unturned.

"I guess I don't really have any fears either." I clear the gravel from my throat. "What about the division of house-work?" We've had this discussion before, but never seem to get anywhere.

I remind him of the laundry he was supposed to do once he got home from work.

"You don't like the way I fold. Or how I clean," he says.

"So fold and clean the right way. There is no room for weaponized incompetence here."

"But I don't know how to clean to your standards. Plus, how is that fair? Just because I do things differently from you doesn't mean I'm doing it wrong."

"Folding the towels your way means they won't all fit on the shelf. Putting too many clothes in the washer is wrong because the clothes don't get clean. Not using the vacuum hose along the wall means all the crap that accumulates there doesn't get sucked up. Not scrubbing the bottom of the cups-"

He closes his eyes. "Alright, I get it."

Once again, we don't reach a solution. But I'll be damned if I get stuck with all the housework just because I'm the woman. Heated, I jump right into the next question. "How will you handle it if I'm unable to have sex?"

His head snaps up. "Why wouldn't you be able to have sex?"

"I don't know. If I get sick or something."

His eyes move to the wall behind me, as he considers that possibility. "Well, would you be okay with sharing me with someone? Maybe Danielle? Just for physical needs? Marcus does it with his girlfriend's friend once a month, just to keep things fresh." His words spill faster and faster as if he knows what's coming. "But I'd only do it if you weren't able to-"

I jump out of my seat, and the chair hits the wall behind me. "Wrong answer."

"Alright, alright." He rises slowly, his arms out as if I'm rearing up.

"Put your hands down, Brian. I'm not a horse."

"Alright, I'm sorry. Now I know you're not okay with that. See? No arguing, no conflict," he says, gently.

I right my chair and fall into it, grabbing a forkful of food. "I won't put up with cheating."

"I wouldn't cheat on you, Sage. It was a dumb suggestion. I'm sorry. Are we done? Or are there more questions?"

I look at the list and the twenty-ish questions we didn't get to, including *'Do you think we're on track to still be in love in 15-20 years?'* I think we need a break before we can answer that one with a yes.

So I nod, and he leaves to meet his friends after a kiss to my forehead, as if he didn't just suggest having sex with my best friend. I take my uneaten plate to the counter, and get started on addressing envelopes for the invitations before I change my mind.

4

I'D NEVER DO THAT TO A POOR CAT

At 8:45 a.m., I knock on the door of the apartment next to mine, behind which a youthful voice calls, "Callum's here!" The door opens, and two sets of small hands reach for the plates in mine. Their mother doesn't get off work until mid-morning on the weekends, so I sometimes bring them breakfast. Today's meal is eggs, bacon, and apple pancakes.

"Thank you, Mr. Callum," the young boy, Logan, says.

Logan's sister steps up, handing me a foil-wrapped package. "Our mom made this for you yesterday in thanks."

"She didn't have to do that," I say, sniffing the foil—homemade bread. "Thank you."

After storing the bread in my kitchen cabinet, I walk downstairs and knock on Mrs. Browning's door.

"Just a minute!" she snaps from the other side.

While I wait, I straighten the number '1' above the knocker, but it shifts again when she wrenches the door open.

"Don't forget we have to stop by the pharmacy," she barks, slamming the door behind her.

"I remember, Mrs. Browning."

We walk at a snail's pace, her cane ready to trip me if I try to pass her. When we get to the truck, I pull out the stool I keep in the back so she can climb in. My truck isn't lifted, but she's only about four-foot-eight, hunched over.

I pull into traffic while she starts her typical rant. "I wish you'd get a smaller vehicle. What do you need with a truck anyway? You don't haul anything that I know of."

"I like my truck."

"Why? It's ugly." It's green; turf green, they called it at the small used-car dealership I purchased it from.

"I'm sorry, Mrs. Browning. Next time I get a vehicle, I'll keep your tastes in mind."

Her glare is terrifying, but that doesn't stop the grin from spreading over my face.

Despite it being one of my days off, Sundays are my busiest day of the week. Monday through Friday, I work at DCB charity, helping underprivileged children find funding for their extracurricular activities. Most of my college teammates earned football scholarships, despite their families being wealthy enough to afford the tuition without aid, my family included. And we earned those scholarships by paying for private coaches and summer camps to improve our skills over the years as we grew up. The kids who couldn't afford all the extra training rarely made it as far as us because they just weren't good enough.

I want to change that. Money shouldn't be the only path to opportunity that leads to more money. I understand that's just how things work, but only because society allows it.

But Sundays are for neighbors and other people in the community who need some extra help. Maybe if I give back enough, eventually it will make up for the pain I caused when I was younger.

If *anything* can make up for it.

I head into the pharmacy to pick up Mrs. Browning's medication before dropping her off for the early church service. Then I rush to the grocery store. If I don't make it back as she's walking out of church, and not a minute later, she'll lecture me the whole drive home.

I speed through the aisles picking up fiber-full and heart-healthy food, before racing over to Mr. Parsons'. After unloading his groceries and cleaning out his cat's litter box, I have just enough time to bring two cups of tea for our weekly chat to the recliners in his living room. I met Mr. Parsons at the shelter I volunteer at when he came to adopt a cat after his passed on. His wife loved cats, and he couldn't imagine not having one in his house, even if she was gone too.

"My daughter's coming tomorrow for dinner if you want to join us." He waggles his eyebrows.

For the hundredth time, I say, "She's married, Mr. Parsons." And ten years older than me.

"Yeah, yeah." He waves his hand dismissively. "But one of these days, she might not be. Better to start laying the foundation now."

Fred, the cat he adopted, jumps onto his lap and turns around a couple of times before finding the area acceptable enough for his nap.

"You don't have to make me family to keep me around," I tease. "I'll always be here if you need me."

Fred purrs.

"Not if you go off and start your own family."

I shake my head. "I'll still be around. I enjoy our tea-talks too much." I leave it at that. Explaining how I won't allow myself the joy a family could bring would only lead to questions I'm not willing to answer.

"Yeah, about that, do you think we could switch to beer? Something a little more manly?" He holds up the teacup, unusual next to his scruffy face.

"Not at 10:15 in the morning on a Sunday." Lifting my pinkie to play the part, I take a sip.

"Fine." He drinks his own with a scowl. "Now, about those damn panthers..."

The Panthers in question are the local college football team. As a former Panther myself, Mr. Parsons feels the need to lecture me when they play poorly. I didn't see the game yesterday, but I hear all about the 'shit defense' and that 'damn quarterback who couldn't throw a complete pass two feet away.' Before I know it, I'm running late for Mrs. Browning.

"Crap. Mr. Parsons, I've gotta go." As fast as I can, I wash my teacup and rush out the door.

My tires squeal to a stop in front of Mrs. Browning, arms crossed, face pinched in irritation.

I open her door and lay the stool down as she says, "You're two minutes late."

"I'm sorry. I lost track of time talking to Mr. Parsons." I get her situated and run around to the driver's side. "Hey, you'd like him. Why don't I take you with me one of these days?"

"I don't like cats."

"Well, why don't I bring him to you? Or we could all go to a neutral place. Maybe lunch? I'll buy."

"Of course, you'd buy. You think Social Security pays for extravagant purchases like eating out? But no. He'll probably have cat hair on him and smell like cats and attract all the stray cats around."

Alrighty then.

Once we get home, Mrs. Browning makes me lunch like she does every Sunday. She instructs me to sit at her small dining table covered with a clear plastic tablecloth to protect the delicate lace cloth underneath. Her apartment is minimally decorated, like mine, with a red and blue plaid couch, a small TV she sometimes has to smack to turn on, and a single painting on the wall of none other than a *cat*.

Photos of her grandkids and child-made drawings cover her mint-green refrigerator, and she points to them with the spoon in her hand, giving me the weekly updates on their lives. It's not long before she sets a plate in front of me and a glass, with lemons painted on the side, of unsweetened iced tea.

One of the reasons I suggested a restaurant is that we eat the same egg salad sandwich on stale bread, with a cucumber salad swimming in some dressing made with vinegar and mayonnaise. I gag my way through, but I'll never let her know how much I despise the taste. It might break the heart we picked up medication for this morning.

"I'm going down to the shelter now. Want me to put your name down for a cat?" I joke as I finish cleaning up after lunch.

"Do it and you'll never get another of my egg salad sandwiches."

Don't tempt me. "Just messing with you. I'd never do that to a poor cat."

That earns me another glare as she hands me a bag. "Here. Dog toys I made." I peek inside to find several pieces of braided rope. Besides wanting to be a good neighbor, I put up with Mrs. Browning's food because she spends a lot of her time sewing or knitting things for the shelter, at least when her arthritis allows her. When people donate, they think of the food and money, but not toys or blankets, which are just as needed. "I'll work on some cat toys next."

I kiss her cheek in thanks.

AFTER AN EIGHT-HOUR SHIFT AT THE SHELTER, I RETURN TO THE empty apartment I've called home since I graduated from college. The silence mocks me as I eat a lonely slice of that homemade bread over the sink, before a sharp note from my phone pierces the air. I take it out of my pocket and hang my head at the message on the screen.

SAGE

I haven't received a yes or no from you.

Right. The wedding. I've spent every second of the last couple of weeks trying not to think about it. And I sincerely hope she's spent every second thinking about what I said. But knowing her, she's still dead set on ruining her life by trying to prove to everyone she knows what she's doing. She'll marry him, they'll get joint bank accounts, and they'll live in happily married bliss until the honeymoon phase is over. That's if their relationship hasn't already aged out of that need-to-touch-each-other-constantly stage. Then, she'll wake up one day and realize what she's done. She'll panic, she'll pack her bags, she'll run away. Her parents will be disappointed, but Sage will have already moved on by then.

I received the invitation in the mail four days ago. It went straight into the trash can. But I took it back out and set it on the table next to the door, determined to torture myself with its intrusion into my life. At least, until I couldn't stop myself from angrily ripping it into a hundred pieces and stuffing it down the garbage disposal.

The exact moment I saw her bounce into the restaurant with Cori on their birthday two years ago was the moment my heart ceased being my own. My fall was instant, and it was painful. She batted her eyelashes in mock shyness, but I knew she was giddy to be the center of attention. And Cori was perfectly happy to allow her every inch beneath the spotlight. Except she wasn't just *in* the spotlight, she *was* the spotlight, and I wanted to lean my head back, close my eyes, and bask in her warmth. Instead, I spent the evening devouring every full laugh, every beaming smile, and hating myself for not being worthy of her.

My phone dings again.

SAGE

Are you coming or not? I need a final head count.

I don't have an answer. Of course, I want to be around to witness every single detail of her life, and that would include her wedding. But to watch her marry another man? I don't know if I can stomach bearing witness to such an event.

Because I can't seem to help myself, I log into my social media account to look at her page. She posted this afternoon, the first time since posting the embarrassing photos of me from Nick's birthday a few months ago, sharing the links to her wedding registry. Most of the comments are people sharing their shock. Either they didn't know she was engaged or didn't know she and Brian had even reconciled their differences from their last breakup.

There's a photo accompanying the post, a selfie of her showing off her ring. Her head is cocked, and her eyes look to the side in a coy manner, knowingly dropping a bomb on her followers.

Every single detail about her is beautiful. From her light brown eyes to her messily painted fingernails. I can barely stand to see another man's ring on her finger. How could I possibly watch her, wearing a wedding dress, walk down the aisle to Brian, of all people? He's nice enough, but nowhere near Sage's level. He has no idea what to do with a woman like Sage. Then again, neither do I.

I'm tempted to chuck my phone across the room when another text comes through, but it's Hailey this time.

HAILEY

Hey. Have you decided yet?

No. She keeps texting me, but I don't know what to say.

HAILEY

She asked if I knew your answer.

I've confided more in her than Tyler or Nick, including my past and heart-wrenching love for Sage. Life would be so much easier if Hailey and I had more than a platonic relationship; she knows my history and, despite being the person who should hate me the most, doesn't make me feel as if I'm dog shit on someone's shoe. However, despite connecting quickly after we met, we've never felt more than friendship. Not that I'd allow myself to feel anything more, anyway.

Running my hand down my face, I walk to the living room and fall onto the couch. The peeling leather crackles, but I refuse to buy a new one. I bought it from a woman whose husband had passed suddenly, leaving her alone with four small kids to raise on no income. She had asked for fifty dollars and I added a zero to the end. I should have given her more.

As if stalking Sage wasn't enough torture, I click off of her page and see the name, Jake Elliot, in my search history. I open his profile. No updates since I last looked, less than a week ago, so I scroll down, rereading the sparse updates I've already seen a million times. Three people wished him a happy birthday; he didn't respond. Some guy tagged him in a funny video about dogs; he didn't respond. And an old high school classmate of ours posted on his page, asking how he was doing; he didn't respond.

Since high school, he's posted a total of three times. Once, when he got a job as a busboy at some diner, and he asked if any guys had black pants they were willing to give him for his uniform. Once, when his bike was stolen and he asked if anyone had an extra he could have, or buy if needed. And once, when he was looking for the owner of a dog he'd found begging for food outside the diner he worked at.

I hope that by his few updates and lack of replies that life is keeping him too busy and satisfied to spend much time on social media. But I fear that his life is empty and there's simply not much to post about. Which is why I make sure mine is the same.

To punish myself further, I respond to Sage.

ME

I'll be there.

Then I decide that isn't enough.

ME

Let me know if you need any help.

SAGE

You can pick up and deliver the chairs and tables, like we discussed 🙂 And maybe alcohol? That can be your gift to us.

Instinct has me groaning at the amount of money this is going to cost me, especially since I know she's making a mistake. But knowing myself, I'll spend any amount she wants me to. And knowing her, to warn her she's driving towards disaster would only make her speed up.

5

OH, AND BRIAN

The sunset paints the sky a brilliant orange, as if the clouds are ablaze, as Brian pulls into Mom's driveway. Friends and family spent the day at the diner, showering me with gifts that now take up the backseat. Well, and Brian, but it's called a '*Bridal* Shower.' Even though Brian was there, it was *my* day. What started as a simple brunch with gifts, games, and funny stories morphed into an all-day affair, and now I'm ready for a relaxing evening with my favorite people.

It may not be a typical bachelorette party, seeing as we still have preparations for my big day, but it's exactly what Cori needs after a month of unnecessarily stressing over being a good maid of honor. And, I have to admit, I'm looking forward to a night of crafting, assuming I get assigned to the fun stuff rather than cleaning or something boring.

There's a lot to do, but I'm not the one worried; if it gets done, it gets done. If not, no one's going to remember. As long as there's food, alcohol, and me, that's all that matters.

Oh, and Brian.

For his bachelor party, he's going out drinking with his

friends tonight with strict orders not to hook up with any of the professional dancers. It's not the women I don't trust, but the large group of drunk, horny men. I've also given strict orders not to get too wasted that he doesn't show up tomorrow. How humiliating would it be to walk down the aisle to no one standing at the altar?

During the shower today, Mom told me not to take any gifts out of their boxes just in case the wedding doesn't end up happening. She also instructed Cori to put a sticky note on each present with the name of who gifted the item, so I'll know who to give it back to when this all goes up in flames—Mom's words, not mine. Ignoring her advice, I reach back now, grabbing the two bottles of champagne Brian's sisters gifted to us for our honeymoon.

Danielle was in charge of bringing wine, but if Mom is too much of herself tonight, I'll need these extra bottles. Brian won't mind. He takes my bags inside now like the gentleman he is, while I carry my dress in its garment bag, then I kiss him goodbye.

After hugging my niece and nephew, I run to the bathroom to change into comfy clothes, legging-shorts and a tank top. Then, I join everyone in the kitchen, taking the glass of wine Cori offers me.

"Your mom's already had a few glasses. You're welcome," Hailey says. One glance at Mom's flushed cheeks and goofy grin has me throwing my arms around Hailey in thanks.

Cori picks up a notepad and pen. "Okay, now that you're here, I have the stuff for the bouquets, boutonnières, and corsages in the dining room. The baking supplies are here,"— she points to the island cluttered with everything we'll need to bake my cake—"and the decorations are in the living room, ready to be hung up. So who wants to do what?"

"Oh, Cori. I love you and your lists." I wrap her in a hug, too.

Danielle speaks up. "I need dinner before you start ordering us around." She pats her belly where the image of Eeyore is depicted on her purple tank top. My stomach is grumbling too. We ate brunch at the shower, then cake, but that was hours ago.

Cori jumps into action, pulling a vegetable tray from the refrigerator and a platter of sandwiches. Stephanie sets out a pitcher of water to balance out the wine before asking, "So is everything else set for tomorrow? Food, the dress, whatever Brian's wearing?"

"I don't actually know what he's wearing. I told him he could choose, and he said he wanted it to be a surprise," I answer around a mouthful of sandwich.

Stephanie gapes at me. "What if he shows up in one of those stupid dinosaur costumes or something?"

Mom giggles, her eyes glassy with mirth.

"Okay, how *much* did you give her to drink before I got here?" I ask Hailey, not that I'm complaining.

She only shrugs and sips her wine.

I turn back to Stephanie. "Anyway, if he wants to wear a dinosaur costume, that's totally fine with me." After all, it's his wedding too, even if he wanted no involvement in the planning.

We take our time snacking and chatting, dreaming of the future and planning out everyone else's weddings. Cori seriously considers the pajama party, Danielle will have the most expensive wedding known to man because she's spoiled by her parents, but Hailey goes quiet, peeling the strands from a celery stick and avoiding everyone's eyes.

Hailey's parents, who have always been so loving and supportive of their daughter, and seemingly very happy in their marriage, divorced recently, shocking pretty much everyone. And leaving their already guarded and hesitant daughter, determined that love is a scam.

The four of us are sisters in a way—we aren't afraid to square up to one another, but fiercely protective of each other at the same time. So I change the subject for Hailey's sake. "Okay, enough making this about y'all. This is *my* night."

A knock sounds at the front door, and Mom calls for Dad to answer it.

"Dad isn't here," Cori reminds her.

My two younger brothers, Spencer and Solomon, are spending the night out of the way with Dad at the farmhouse. I considered having my wedding there. It'd be the perfect venue with so much open space and nothing but green fields for miles. But the house is too small. Even though our guest list is small as well, it's still too many people for one bathroom that doesn't have a lock on the door. I've walked in on Nick sitting on the toilet enough for three lifetimes.

"Oh, right." Whoever it is at the door knocks again. "Well, *someone* better go answer that then." Danielle and Cori both rise at the same time, but Danielle tells her to sit.

Just as I'm wondering if someone ordered a surprise stripper for me, Callum and Tyler round the corner, carrying boxes of glass bottles.

"What are *you* doing here?" Hailey asks, scowling at Tyler and his backwards baseball cap.

"We're the entertainment for tonight, and you're first on my list for a lap dance, H." His eyebrows flick upwards as his lips morph into a teasing smirk.

"We're dropping off the tables and chairs for tomorrow," Callum answers drily. He's speaking to Hailey, but his intense gaze holds mine. I take it he still doesn't approve of my forthcoming nuptials.

"And the booze," Tyler says, lifting the box. "Where can we put these?"

Cori directs them to a corner in the dining room, next to boxes of disposable dinnerware, before cleaning up the food. I watch the guys disappear once more through the front door to unload the tables and chairs, wondering what Callum's problem is.

He's always been the quiet one of all the men, partly why he gets along so well with Cori and Hailey. The three of them are perfectly content to play the part of wallflowers. While Cori is anxiously stuck inside her own head, and Hailey has too much trauma from high school to enjoy herself freely, I'm pretty sure Callum just hates fun.

"Okay," Cori begins. "Stephanie, I'm assigning you to Cake duty. Danielle and Sage, do y'all want to do the bouquets and stuff while Hailey and I decorate?"

"Sure," I answer at the same time Danielle grumbles, "If I have to."

"Mom, you can..."—Cori looks between her list and Mom a few times—"sit there and look pretty. Okay, everyone, get to work."

Before joining Danielle, I grab my Bluetooth speaker, turning on an upbeat playlist to bring *some* energy to my only bachelorette party. Mom moves to a chair in the dining room, bopping her head to the tune.

Mom smiles, a nostalgic gleam twinkling in her eyes. "Remember when you and Cori were little and would take turns marrying Sam? You'd get dressed up in my old prom dress and make Sam put on one of your father's ties. Then one of you would be the officiant while the other would be the bride, before switching." She hiccups.

"Yeah, that's a cute story and all. But Sam turned out to be a dick." Sam was our childhood friend, more so Cori's than mine, but still. Then he and Cori dated for a while before he cheated on her, manipulated her, took advantage of her low self-esteem, and basically drove her into Nick's arms. Not that she resisted.

"My point," she says, suddenly sober. "I don't want you marrying your Sam."

Brian is *nothing* like Sam. Sure, we spend a lot of time apart, as Cori and Sam did. But it's not because Brian is cheating on me. And sure, there's some disconnect, but it's only because Brian is a bit aloof at times, not because he's arrogant. Marriage isn't about being completely taken with each other all the time; it's about waking up every day and choosing to fight for the other person.

The front door opens, allowing Tyler and Callum back inside.

"Ready for tomorrow?" Tyler asks me. Brian and I asked him to officiate the wedding, so he'll be standing up there with us. Ironic, considering I almost hooked up with him once.

"Yep. Other than this crap we're working on tonight, I'm completely prepared. Mentally *and* physically," I add, waggling my eyebrows. Going a whole month without sex is probably the hardest thing I've ever done. Brian is incredible in bed. So much so that I only have one complaint: the lack of intimacy.

"Gross. None of us needs to know about your *physical* readiness," Hailey says, entering the room to hang some tulle and vines around the front door.

"And how are *your* physical needs, H?" Tyler asks.

If Hailey had the power, he'd burst into flames by the glare she gives him.

Smirking, he holds his hands in surrender as he walks backward into the living room, probably to say goodbye to Cori.

"Ugh. If he showed me an ounce of the attention he gives you, I'd have been on him yesterday," Danielle says.

Hailey's cheeks flash an angry red before she leaves the decorations to deal with later, heading back to the kitchen. But I don't have much time to wonder about her lack of a smart remark before Callum speaks.

"Is there anything else y'all need from us?" he asks, hand on the doorknob.

"No, that's it," I answer, rising from my seat to see if he'll let me hug him in thanks. But he's already opening the door.

"Hey, Callum." I grab his arm. "Thank you. I don't remember if I've said that yet, but thank you."

His eyes bore into mine for a moment too long before he suddenly nods and turns to walk out the door. "Yep. See you tomorrow."

"Wait. Did you want to say something?" Even if it's not something I want to hear, he should say it. Words left unsaid are opportunities wasted.

He turns to face me, but won't meet my eyes. "Nope."

"Yes, you did. What is it?"

Finally, he looks at me, defeat and sadness tainting his handsome face. "Nothing, Sage. I only wish you a... long-as-possible and... I guess, *happy* marriage." He says the last bit quickly as if the words might choke him on their way out. "Tell Tyler I'm waiting in the truck." Then he's gone.

"What was that about?" Danielle asks once I sit back down.

I open my mouth to answer that I don't know, but Mom sighs heavily before I get the chance. "If she wasn't in such a hurry to get married to what's-his-name, she could find out. Think of the beautiful babies you could have with Callum, Sage. I know you think I don't know what's best for you, and maybe I don't most of the time. But maybe I do once in a while."

What the hell does that mean? *Think of the beautiful babies you could have with Callum.* There could never be babies with Callum, there could never be anything. He can't stand me. And maybe I enjoy irritating him occasionally, but even when I'm nice, like tonight, he can't get away from me fast enough.

I gape at her for a moment, but brush it off; she's just drunk. Or maybe she's not drunk enough... "Hailey, Mom needs more wine!"

Tyler emerges from the hallway, but before opening the

door to leave, he turns to Hailey, who approaches from the kitchen with the wine bottle. "Oh, H. Guess what? I accepted a coaching position at your school last week. Looks like we're going to be coworkers." He smirks again, then disappears through the front door, leaving her staring at the space he just vacated.

"CAN'T SLEEP?" HAILEY ASKS ME FROM THE LIVING ROOM FLOOR. After completing most of Cori's list, we finally gave it up around one a.m. and turned on a crime documentary. Cori lasted about ten minutes before falling asleep next to Hailey on a pallet on the floor, and Danielle snores softly from Dad's recliner next to the couch I claimed.

"Nope," I answer.

"Nervous about tomorrow?"

A snort escapes. "When have you ever known me to be nervous?"

She levels me with a look that tells me she knows exactly what's on my mind. What Mom said earlier, about Callum, I can't get it out of my head. I'm not nervous exactly, but I'm eager. Tomorrow can't come fast enough because, after the vows are said and the marriage license signed, it'll be too late for any more doubts from my family members.

"Sage-" she begins, but I cut her off.

"You know what I want right now? A donut." I throw the blanket covering my lap to the side and stand. "Come on, I know a place that's open twenty-four hours."

She considers the offer for a minute, looking as if she'll decline. But the lure of sweet fried dough must overwhelm all reason, because she shrugs and stands.

"Should we wake them?" she asks.

"No, Danielle isn't pleasant when she's woken up. And Cori

needs her sleep. She's had a big day." And she'll have an even bigger one tomorrow, stressing over everything going according to her plan. I can't imagine the levels of anxiety she'll reach planning her own wedding.

I write a note to let them know where we went in case they wake up and stick it to Cori's forehead. We grab our purses, slip on some shoes, and I throw Hailey the keys to my car. "You're driving."

Thirty minutes later—because it takes at least that long to get anywhere in the Houston area—we sit at a table with a dozen donuts, each a different kind, and two bottles of chocolate milk in front of us.

"Okay, this one is not bad," I say around a mouthful of chocolate donut with bacon pieces on top. "It's nauseating to think about, but the saltiness complements the sweet."

I hold it out for Hailey to take a bite, but she turns her nose up. "Nope, that one's all you." She breaks off a piece of a boring blueberry cake and pops it into her mouth.

"So, are you really going through with this wedding?"

I shoot her a glare, but she only raises her dark eyebrows. "Umm... It's the night before the—no, actually, it's the *morning of* the wedding. If I weren't going through with it, I would have said so long before now."

"Yet I'm still not convinced. No one is."

"Why?" I ask, the question bouncing off the walls of the empty dining room. "Why is it so hard to believe that I might actually stick with something? Why is it so hard for everyone to see me making a commitment and actually *committing*?" One of the bakers pokes his head around the wall at my raised voice.

"It's not," she answers, unfazed by my outburst. "I don't mean that I'm not convinced you can commit. I'm saying I'm not convinced you want to be married to Brian."

"Why not? Brian's great."

"Sure. But is he *the one*?"

I take a deep breath of dough and coffee-scented air. "Brian is perfect for me. He's adventurous, he's creative, he's sweet." Who could be more right for a girl who loves spontaneity and colorful personalities?

"Look, if you want to marry him tomorrow and stay married for the rest of your life, great. If you want to marry him and divorce him a year later, I'll throw you a divorce party. And if you want to bolt now and hide until the smoke leaves your parents' ears, I'll help you pack." She reaches across the table to hold my hand. "I said something similar to Cori when she was considering moving in with Sam. As long as it's what *you* want, and not something you feel you have to do in order to prove some point, then do it. Whatever *it* is."

"And what point is it you think I'm trying to prove?"

"That you know your own mind. You don't. That's why you're so insistent that you know what you're doing. Because you're out here winging it just like everyone else. You don't have any more of a clue what you want from life than the rest of us do." She takes a sip of her chocolate milk. "You and Brian have been together inconsistently for a year. Emphasis on *inconsistently*. You never fully committed to *dating* each other, but now you're getting married. And your mom likes to bring up your tendency to quit things, like college. She thinks you bounce around too much in life. And I'm not criticizing you here, I'm just pointing out the criticisms you've heard that would lead you to agree to marry a man who doesn't seem to match you emotionally."

I shove the rest of the donut into my mouth and get to work on one with Fruity Pebbles sprinkled on top.

"You like to say you're this confident woman, Sage, and you are. But it's okay to not be confident about every decision in your life. Even if marrying Brian is without a doubt the right decision, it's okay to admit that you're nervous or scared."

I chug the rest of my chocolate milk despite the churning in my stomach before answering with the only thing I know to say. "I am confident in my decision. I love Brian. I'm insistent on marrying him because I love him." Even I struggle to believe it, but it's true.

Calmly, Hailey closes the donut box and picks up our napkins. "Then let's get you home so you can rest before your big day."

6

I DON'T

After sleeping in until the last possible second, I woke up to Stephanie icing the cake, lining the bottom with flowers, and topping it with a glittery *Mr. & Mrs.* sign I cut out with my vinyl cutting machine. Mom played with my niece and nephew, Cori ran around like a headless chicken, cleaning up clutter left behind last night, and Hailey stole fingerfuls of icing. I grabbed a cup of coffee and joined Danielle on the back porch, listening to the birds sing and the trees rustle with a warm breeze.

Now, chaos ensues behind me once again as I gaze at my reflection in the full-length mirror in Mom and Dad's bathroom. Hailey snaps photos, Stephanie wrestles her kids into their wedding attire, and Mom asks if she looks fat in the dark blue dress she wears. Danielle tries to finish curling Cori's hair, but Cori won't stay still, not yet having reached the end of her to-do list. As the bride, I don't even know what's on there.

I've spent the day sipping mimosas and lounging back while Danielle washed my face and applied my makeup. Half of my hair, dyed light blue a few days ago to match the bridesmaids' dresses, is pulled back and adorned with Baby's Breath.

I altered the sleeves of my dress, manipulating the fabric to hang off my shoulders. My long, slender legs, tan from the summer sun, end in the cutest pair of open-toe heels, white with rhinestones along the straps.

"I think that's everything," Cori says, stepping beside me in the mirror. "Are you ready for Dad?"

I've got a slight buzz, but that doesn't stop me from taking a shot of the Vodka I stashed in my purse this morning.

Our guests are already melting in the sweltering heat outside, and Dad waits just outside the door to complete the first look. I can't imagine his reaction. A bride expects her father to tear up at the sight of his little girl appearing suddenly for the first time as a grown woman. But a sinking feeling in my gut tells me he'll take a quick glimpse before holding out his arm and suggesting we get this over with.

Fanning myself with my bouquet, I ask, "Can I have a moment alone first? I just want to... You know, pray or something."

"Yeah, sure." She steps away, but turns to me one last time. "You look beautiful, Sage."

I smile, squeezing her hand. Then Mom takes her place as everyone else leaves us alone.

"My baby girl." Tears well in her brown eyes that match mine. "I don't say it enough, and I'm sorry for that, but I am so proud of the woman you have become. And I wish you a lifetime of happiness with Brian."

I get misty-eyed myself, this sweet moment with Mom springing up out of nowhere. "Thanks, Mom."

"You look so beautiful. I can't wait to see Brian's face when he sees you." She lifts on her toes to kiss my forehead before closing the door.

I stand there frozen for a moment, staring at that closed door. The door that leads to an aisle that ends in a lifetime with Brian.

A *lifetime* with Brian. Forever and ever and ever until I die.

Do I really vow to be his wife, through thick and thin, when I'm already nauseated from the highs and lows an ordinary day with Brian brings? I get high off sex with him, until he rolls over and leaves, either to play video games or meet his friends at some bar. I get in a loving mood and want to cuddle, until he turns and breathes his warm, stale breath in my face. I grow eager to get home to him, until I see a pile of his socks under the coffee table.

Do I vow to a lifetime of that? Yes, I do.

But do I really?

Yes, I... don't.

Brian's lazier than a man on football Sunday, and I have, what Mom calls, a short fuse. I call it an assertive and honest approach to life—piss me off and you're going to hear about it promptly so we can fix it and move on. But men don't change, no matter how much you tell them to. I may be the dumb twin, but I'm smart enough to know that.

Quickly, I move around the bathroom, collecting only the necessary items, including—and pretty much limited to—my sandals and the bottle of vodka.

I double-check that my phone is in my bra and hoist myself out the window. My tight dress makes this maneuver difficult, but determination and adrenaline drive my movements. Maybe all those times sneaking out of the house as a teenager were preparing me for this moment.

Creeping along the brick on the side of the house, I listen for the voices in the back. Easy chatter echoes toward me from calm guests, unaware the bride has just escaped.

I peek around to see the front door and jump at the sight of Callum with his arms crossed as if he's been waiting for me. "What are you doing?" he asks.

My blood runs cold. "Uhh..."

"Did you just sneak out the window?"

"No, I was just... I n-needed air."

He juts his chin towards the sandals in my hand. "Why do you have those shoes if you're already wearing your heels?"

"Umm..." I'm not sure whether I should confide in this man who repeatedly told me to reconsider this wedding. Giving him the satisfaction of knowing he was right is about as appealing as saying those vows after all. Except my car is blocked in the driveway, while Callum's truck is further down the street, free to leave whenever needed.

"Okay, fine. You caught me. You were right. Now, can I have a ride?" I smile sweetly and bat my eyelashes.

His expression doesn't crack.

With my blood pumping with urgency, I try harder. "Please, Callum?" Still, nothing. I playfully cross my arms. "Look, you can give me a lecture the whole ride if you want. But we need to go now."

He runs his hands down his face a couple of times before digging his fingers into his eyes. Finally, he starts moving, pulling his keys from his pocket. It isn't often I get to see Callum in clothes other than jeans and a t-shirt; he wears jeans even now, but his outfit is topped with a buttoned shirt and ends with a clean pair of boots.

"You look nice," I tell him as he walks beside me.

"Are you kidding me?" he snaps.

I flinch. "What?"

"*You look nice?* I look nice because I was attending your *wedding.* The wedding you're currently running away from, and you're complimenting me on my looks?" he asks incredulously.

We reach the passenger side of this truck, and he wrenches the door open.

I frown. "Why are *you* upset? You should be boasting about how you told me so."

I hoist myself inside, the pungent stench hitting me.

"Why does it smell like mothballs in here?" I ask, wrinkling my nose.

Callum gets in the driver's seat and starts the engine. "Well, I *did* tell you so. But any normal person would be feeling like shit right now, so I don't want to rub it in. *Yet."*

"Actually, I'm feeling pretty good right now." Instead of walking down an aisle towards a miserable life, Callum is driving me off toward freedom.

He breathes loudly through his nose as though trying to calm himself, then pulls away from the curb.

Rolling the window down, I close my eyes as the wind washes over my face. I turn up the radio and sing along to some country song. I don't really know the words, but that doesn't matter. What stops me is Callum shooting looks of apprehension my way every couple of minutes

"What is your problem?" I ask, turning the volume down with a scowl to match his.

He shakes his head. "You just walked out of your wedding. You're singing to music and sticking your head out the window like a dog. You're acting as if school just ended for the weekend."

"Yeahhhh? I don't see the problem." I find myself with a free evening ahead, who wouldn't be full of joy? Although I'm bummed about missing out on the Mexican food we had planned for the reception...

"Hey, can we stop for tacos after we get my stuff?"

"Tacos? And what do you mean, *get your stuff*?"

"Oh, we need to stop by my apartment and get a few things." After that, I'm not sure where I'll go. The farm is too far to ask Callum to drive to. I guess I could have Cori stop by Callum's and pick me up, but his apartment is in the opposite direction.

He rolls his eyes but doesn't respond. Ignoring him, I pull

my phone out of my bra to turn it off, but there are already a few texts.

DANIELLE

Sage!!! Where did you go?

You could have told me you were leaving at least!

Or taken me with you. Your mom is driving me crazy!!!

CORI

Sage, are you okay?

HAILEY

I'm filming your mom's head exploding. In case you want to see it later. It's hysterical.

P.S. are you okay?

I'm both looking forward to and dreading that video.

"Were you never grounded as a kid? Forced to take responsibility for the chaos you caused?" Callum asks, his jaw clenching and unclenching.

I side-eye him. "Why are you being such a dick? It's not a big deal."

"It is when people's emotions are involved." One hand runs through his hair in exasperation as he steers the wheel with the other.

Obviously, he means Brian, but for a moment I wonder if he's referring to someone else.

"Brian's getting his heart broken right about now. And your Dad spent a few hundred dollars on everything. I know you went cheap on the decor and stuff, but that's still wasted money."

"Hey! I don't know why you're stressing out. I'm the one who has to deal with the fallout."

"You made me an accomplice!" he protests.

A snort escapes. "Okay, we escaped my wedding, not prison." Although how different are they, really, when married to the wrong person? "And for your information, Mr. Morals, my dad only paid for the food."

"Which will now go to waste."

"Just because it's no longer a wedding doesn't mean no one can stay and enjoy the food and decor." I hold up the vodka, gesturing the bottle towards him. "You need to chill. Want a drink?"

"Not while I'm driving," he grumbles.

"Fine. Maybe when we get to your place."

His hazel eyes shoot to mine. "*My* place?"

"Oh, yeah. Can I sleep on your couch? Just until tomorrow." My lips spread into a grin as I add to sweeten the deal, "I'll pay for your tacos."

He rolls and stretches his neck before mumbling, "Why not?"

I should have found Tyler and asked him for a ride. He'd be singing along with me and telling jokes to make me laugh. Hell, even Nick would have been a better getaway driver than the stiff, grump beside me. But desperate times call for desperate measures, and I now find my good mood soured.

Oh well. At least I have a place to sleep where my parents can't find me. For now.

"Um, not to make things worse, but you may have to buy the tacos. I forgot my purse."

He nods slowly as he grumbles, "Figures."

7

ONLY THE NECESSITIES

I must hate myself. Actually, I know I do, because I RSVP'd yes to her wedding in the first place. But if anyone deserves the torture of watching the woman they love make the mistake of marrying another man, it's me.

Regardless, I can't help but thank God she left. My only concern is why she won't allow herself to feel the negative emotions that accompany a situation such as this. Not that I know for certain what someone might feel after escaping out a window, but I imagine they should feel whiplash at the very least. She should be walking down that aisle right now. Then, celebratory dancing to upbeat music before being sent off in a storm of bubbles.

Instead, she'll spend the evening bored in my shitty apartment, then she'll sleep in my bed while I lie awake on the couch thinking about her. She'll shower in my bathroom, her naked body just feet away from me, only separated from my own by a single door. She'll inhabit my space for too brief a time, allowing me a taste of unwarranted happiness. And she'll leave behind her fruity scent, like tart cherries, dancing in the air I breathe. A cruel reminder of what I could have if I were a better person.

One whole evening with Sage. We'll eat together, maybe watch a movie together, and sit together on my lumpy couch. Maybe her thigh will brush up against mine, maybe she'll get cold and lean into my warmth. Maybe we'll share a blanket.

Shaking my head, I dislodge the wishful thoughts from where they latch on like leeches, sucking all reason and logic from my brain. The woman just walked out on her wedding, for Christ's sake. Although she hasn't a single care in the world. Not an ounce of regret. Not a bit of shame.

How does one capture that wispy air and bottle it for later?

"You should have told Brian at the very least. Or Cori." I don't want Cori mad that I helped Sage get away without at least informing her of the plan. Cori likes plans. She doesn't function well without them, unlike her twin, who thrives on the unknown.

"They'll find out sooner or later. Besides, it's *my* wedding. I'll leave it if I want to." She begins humming some song and bopping her head.

"But-" I don't know what I start to say. What hasn't been said already? It doesn't matter because she cuts me off anyway.

"Callum." Her tone is firm. "I know what I did. But I never should have gotten to this point." A humorless laugh comes out sharply. "You tried talking me out of it, for fucks sake! I made a mistake accepting his proposal, but now I'm back on the right track. You should be happy that I have finally realized that. Now, can you please stop trying to ruin my day?"

Keeping my eyes on the road, I nod, giving it up for now. But sooner or later, she's going to need to cry, and I find myself dreading the moment while also hoping it's *my* shoulder she releases her emotions onto.

In between poorly belted lyrics, she guides me to the apartment she's shared with Brian for the last year or so.

"So what are you going to do now?" I ask.

"I'll probably stay with Cori for a while. Although if Nick's there all the time, I probably won't stay long. Point is, my name isn't on the lease, so I'm free to do whatever. I could move across the country if I wanted. Or I could marry someone else. Or I could move to Paris!"

I pull into a spot by their—now just Brian's—building and unbuckle my seat belt.

"You can wait here, I'm only grabbing the necessities," she says, hopping out of the truck.

I follow her anyway, not the kind of man to sit back while she carries her bag.

"ONLY THE NECESSITIES, HUH?" I STAND IN THE BEDROOM STARING at the pile of crap on the bed. A teddy bear bigger than Sage, four duffel bags stuffed full of clothes, a suitcase straining against its contents, and a box fan.

At least the pile of crap is distracting me from picturing Sage with Brian in that bed.

"Well, yeah. I need options for outfits, I can't sleep without the fan or the teddy bear, and the suitcase has some of my craft supplies. For my job?" She says with an attitude.

I grab what I can and make the first of many trips to my truck. When I return, she's added a box and three pillows to the pile, and I threaten to tie her up if she adds anything more.

A mischievous grin spreads over her beautiful, plump lips, and she says, "I'll get you the ties."

I swallow.

"Oh, wait, I need-" but I don't hear what she needs because she disappears into the bathroom to collect more crap.

After my backseat is bursting with Sage's belongings, I ask if she wants a moment to say goodbye.

"To whom?"

"I don't know, the apartment. A chapter of your life is coming to an end, that doesn't make you feel a little mournful?" Maybe she doesn't share my sentimentality, but I'd imagine moving out of a place one called home for a significant amount of time should have some sort of effect. Then again, Sage has moved out of this apartment a few times already. Maybe she thinks she'll be back.

She scrunches her pert nose. "Why would it? I'm moving on to better things."

I let out a sigh, probably my millionth of the day. If she doesn't allow herself to feel something, all her emotions will hit her at once. And it won't be pretty.

We climb into the truck and set off for the tacos she's requested.

"Text me what you want, I'll go inside and order," I tell her as I pull into the parking lot.

"I'll go. I'm paying, remember?" I glance over at her outfit. "And you're still in your wedding dress." It's not obvious she's a bride, with her short dress and sandals, now that she's ditched the heels, but it's still made of lace and covered in those gemstone jewel things.

"So? Maybe they'll give us a discount if we tell them it's our wedding day."

I rub at my chest and the stinging sensation currently causing me pain.

"Come on, it'll be fun. We'll tell them an elaborate tale about how we met." Her eyes turn glassy as she envisions the story, swiping her hands in the air like she's painting it before her eyes. "I accidentally sexted the wrong number, but one look at my boobs and you had to have me. We talked on the phone a few times before you arrived at my door to take me to a fancy restaurant, but seeing me in my red dress, you knew you wouldn't be able to sit through dinner where I'm not the meal.

So we passionately made love on my couch before finally going out for that steak. Only two months later, after our first fight, you dropped to one knee and proposed with a ring made from a condom wrapper. And when everyone's gathered around, chin in their hands, invested in our love story, we'll tell them how our parents don't approve. How they tried to keep us apart. And that's why we had to elope. And why we're alone for our reception, picking up tacos on the way to our humble home."

She blinks at me, waiting for a response. "I... uh..."

Patting my hand that rests on the center console, she grins. "Don't worry, honey. I'll do all the talking."

To my relief, she refrains from telling that ridiculous lie to the young woman behind the counter, but she does spend twenty minutes talking about her hair color. I'm caught between wanting to listen to her every word and telling her to wrap it up so I can get home and hide in my room until she's ready for bed.

Once we arrive at my apartment building, she insists on having all of her things brought inside, even though we'll just have to bring them back down the three flights of stairs tomorrow. Assuming she leaves tomorrow.

There's not much space left in the apartment, but we manage to sit side by side on the couch with her teddy bear taking up the third seat, and eat while watching *Friends*. I've never seen the appeal of this show, with its terrible acting and cheesy storylines. But I'd watch it every day if it meant listening to the sound of Sage reciting the lines along with the characters, and throwing her head back and laughing as if she's watching it for the first time. Her laugh is what I imagine the color neon pink sounds like, full and obnoxious. But beautifully mesmerizing as it demands every ounce of your attention.

Besides, a character on the show is going through almost exactly what Sage went through today. Maybe this is good for her.

There's a knock on the door, halfway through my second taco, and Sage meets my eyes. "I'm not here," she mouths, as she rises and hides in the bathroom.

Looking through the peephole, I see Nick, standing with his arms crossed. I imagine Cori is with him, but she isn't within my frame of sight.

Hesitantly, I open the door, and sure enough, Cori pops over from against the wall. "Can I talk to her?"

"Hello, Cori. Talk to... who exactly?"

"You know who. I just want to see if she's okay." I know Cori wouldn't bombard Sage with guilt, but I continue to play dumb anyway. "Just a tip for next time, maybe hide her stuff before pretending she isn't here." Cori points inside to where a few of Sage's bags sit by the door.

With nowhere to run, I open the door to invite them inside. "She's in the bathroom. We were eating tacos, so she might be a while." But she ignores my false warning, dropping a purse beside Sage's crap and barging through the bedroom.

Nick, still wearing his wedding attire, rocks back on his heels, hands in his pockets. "So, how'd you get roped into this mess?"

"Wrong place, wrong time." And yet, right place, right time. I was fetching my tie from my truck when I heard a noise from the side of the house. I went to check it out when my heart leapt at the sight of her escaping.

He nods, and I fetch us both a glass of water from the kitchen. "How's school going?" He's attending a school for aircraft maintenance.

"Hard, but good. How's work?"

"Same. We just helped a kid join a culinary competition for children over in The Woodlands, and he brought us a pie on

Friday. It was dark chocolate but had hints of orange and raspberry. I kind of want to hire him as my private chef, but he's only in junior high."

Nick laughs. "Sounds like something Cori would like."

I change the TV over to a preseason football game. "So, how pissed were her parents?"

"Her dad wasn't; he just broke into the food and reclined back in his chair in front of the TV. Her mom, though, went on a whole tirade, making sure everyone heard how she predicted this would happen."

I let out a low whistle, thanking God once again that I got to leave before all that happened.

"How's Sage?" he asks.

"She's acting like nothing is wrong, but I can't imagine she truly feels nothing."

"Yeah, well, that's Sage. Always looking on the positive side of things."

She's known for looking forward with an eager smile, whereas my head is turned around, frowning at the destruction I've caused. I can see the collision in my mind when Sage barrels into a stone wall of her ignored feelings. Yet, I can't help but wonder what it would be like to emulate her and drop the heavy guilt I carry around, if only for a moment.

Nick and I sit in silence for a while, both of us tired and unsure about what will happen with Sage and her parents now. I find myself desperate to talk about her, to share my feelings for her and how her smile could blind a black hole with its brightness. But Nick doesn't deserve the burden of that secret. A secret that can't ever be spoken aloud.

"I tried talking her out of the engagement, but she was determined."

Nick's head whips around. "You did? Why?"

I shrug. "Like everyone else, I knew it was a mistake." What I don't say is that everyone else thought it was a mistake because they can't imagine Sage sticking to anything. But I knew it was a mistake because I knew Brian wasn't right for Sage.

"The more you tell her not to do something, the more determined she is to say yes," Nick says.

That's what terrifies me.

"Brian was a piece of shit anyway. I mean, who proposes only to walk out on the wedding a month later?" He sighs.

I nod in agreement until I realize what he said makes zero sense. "Wait. What are you talking about?"

8

THAT MOTHERFU-

When the knock sounded on Callum's door, I assumed Mom stood on the other side of it, red-faced and ready to wag her finger at me. I am immensely relieved when it's Cori who steps into the bathroom. In the past, there have been times when Cori and I have struggled to understand each other. But she's my twin. She's always been there for me when it mattered. I hope I've been there for her too any time she needed me, but sometimes I get too wrapped up in my own stuff that I don't always notice other people drowning.

Without a word, she sits beside me on the edge of Callum's bathtub and takes my hand in hers. Both of us still wear our dresses, although I've added fuzzy socks and a salsa stain.

"How'd you know I was here?" I ask, breaking the silence.

"Callum's truck was the only vehicle missing from Mom's. And Tyler said Callum texted him asking for prayers for sanity." I should have known Callum would text Tyler.

"Are they mad?" I ask. I don't have to specify who I mean.

"Of course not. Mom got to play the victim, which, you know as well as I, is her favorite pastime." She meets my eyes, brushing a strand of my wayward hair behind my ear. "Mostly, they're worried about you. I convinced them to give you time as you did for me last year, and they promised not to bombard you with calls yet. But I'm worried too. Are you okay?" she asks, gently.

"I'm fine, actually. I didn't want to marry him. Mom was right. I stood there staring at myself in that mirror and kept thinking about how Brian is the perfect match for me sexually. But he's no match for me emotionally." Now, I sit here only thinking about Brian's expression when he found out I was gone. Maybe Callum's right, I should have been more careful with his emotions. I left a man at the altar and grabbed tacos on the way home to another man's apartment. What the hell is wrong with me?

"I only have one regret: not telling Brian before I left. Not letting him down gently. How devastated was he?"

Her eyes narrow, shifting to the side. "Hold on, I'm confused. He left *you*."

"What? No, I escaped out the window."

She's silent as her gaze bounces around my face. "You didn't know?"

"Know what?"

"Right after Mom left you in the bathroom, she went in to check on Brian, to make him promise he wouldn't hurt her baby girl. But he wasn't there. We called him, and he answered, but he only said 'Tell Sage I'm sorry' before hanging up. Danielle and I went to tell you that he was gone, but you were gone too. I just assumed you already knew about Brian and ran off to nurse your wounds."

"He *left* me?" I scoff. "That *mother fu-*"

"Really?" she asks, rolling her eyes. "You thought you left *him* at the altar. You have no right to be mad now."

I guess she's right. Good news is, now I don't have anything to feel guilty about.

Even as her twin, who's known Cori literally every second

since her heart started beating, you'd think I'd have her figured out. However, I have no idea how to read her stoic expression as her blue-gray eyes search mine once more. I imagine she feels similar.

"Why did you really accept his proposal in the first place?"

I sigh. "I don't know. I thought it sounded fun. And it would prove Mom wrong about my inability to commit. That may be true about some things in my past, but I'll have no problem committing when the right man comes along."

"But I asked you specifically if you were only saying yes to spite Mom. You assured me you weren't. And you should know that *fun* isn't a good enough reason to get married."

"Yeah, well, I'm human. I make mistakes. I make dumb decisions. I lie." The lies were to myself more than anyone else; I genuinely believed the lies I told everyone else. "You're not the only one Mom criticizes, you know. I'm bound to take one or two things personally now and then, causing me to travel too far down a road I never should have been on."

She squeezes my hand and lays her head on my shoulder. "Yeah, I guess. So? What now?"

"I guess I will get back to life. Oh, would you be willing to go get my car from Mom's for me?" I flash her a smile, hoping to sweeten the deal.

"I already drove it here." She pulls out my car keys from her back pocket. "Also, your purse is with your stuff. And the bag you left at Mom's is in the backseat of your car."

I pull her into a tight hug. That's basically all of my current problems figured out. It can only go up from here.

"Wait, so are you able to get your money back from your hotel bookings?"

My *honeymoon!* I forgot all about it. It's nothing fancy. Brian and I were going to lounge out on the beach and relax after spending a month planning a whole wedding. Then make the drive to San Antonio and eat dinner on the River Walk. It's not Paris, but it's still romantic.

"No, you know what? I'm still going. I mean, *I* planned and paid for it." I grab her hands again. "Hey, come with me. It'll be so much fun. We've never gone on a trip before, just the two of us. We've earned it, don't you think? After all the hard work we've done this year?"

She laughs but shakes her head. "I'd love to, but I have to run that trailer we worked so hard on. Nick still doesn't know the difference between a latte and a cappuccino. Plus, we'd get sick of each other after a couple of hours."

I let out a sigh. "Yeah. It might be good for me to go by myself anyway. Maybe I'll meet someone." Cori rolls her eyes when I waggle my eyebrows.

"Maybe give it some time. You haven't even taken off your wedding dress yet."

AFTER CORI INSISTS ON TRANSFERRING OWNERSHIP OF AN AIRTAG to my account, drops it in my purse in case I accidentally leave it somewhere, and personally double-checks that the tracker is enabled on my phone, she leaves with stern instructions to call and check in during my trip. I sigh in relief when the door closes behind her, and change out of my dress.

I take a quick shower, lathering myself in Callum's body wash, and slip into my pajamas, a tank top and a pair of silk shorts. Callum lounges back on the couch when I emerge, a totally different picture from his earlier knee-shaking and tense shoulders. Except his spine stiffens when he notices me, and he shifts further away when I sit on the couch.

"Do you not like me?" I ask. I already know his answer is no, but I want him to admit it. I want him to look me in the eye and hurt me with his distaste for my personality.

His forehead creases. "Yeah, I do."

Lies. "Then what is your deal?"

"It's just been a weird day. Outside of the norm." I meant his deal any time I'm around, not just today, but I leave it be.

"I never took you for someone who needed routine."

"I don't. It's just... it was a weird day."

If he doesn't want to talk about it, I won't force him. Yet. I change the TV back to *Friends*, and we finish eating in silence.

An episode later, the air conditioner kicks on, blowing directly above me. There's a blanket draped over the back of the couch; I pull it down and scooch closer to cover Callum, wanting his warmth, and ready to share the blanket if needed. My knee rests on his thigh, and I lay my head on his shoulder. It's an innocent touch. But he jumps up like he's been burned, quickly scooping up the trash from the coffee table.

See? Can't get away from me fast enough.

"Umm, I'll go get the bed ready for you," he says, walking towards his room.

"Thanks for the chivalry, but I'm smaller than you and fit better on the couch."

"No, you'll take the bed. I just need to change the sheets."

"You know, we're both adults. I think we can share a bed without your dick accidentally slipping into me." It's just sleeping, and we'll be fully clothed. Maybe it's because I have no revulsion to touch, but I've never understood the big deal with sharing a bed. If we can sit next to each other, why can't we sleep next to each other?

"No. Not on your wedding night. Too weird."

He disappears for a while, and I rummage through his cabinets for dessert while I wait. I missed out on the cake earlier, too, but I didn't think to get any from the store before heading to Callum's.

I munch on some expired Halloween candy when Callum finally emerges with a set of sheets for the couch. His neatly-cut hair is wet, and he changed into a t-shirt and gray sweatpants. I'm not exactly sleepy, but I rise from the couch anyway, grab Ben, my stuffed bear, and head for his bed.

As we pass each other, I touch his arm, running my thumb over the goosebumps rising on his skin. "Thank you, Callum. For today. You really helped me out."

He averts his gaze and nods. "Good night." He breaks free from my grasp and lies down on the couch, eyes closed and feet hanging past the arm.

I answer, "Good night," and close the door behind me. His bedroom is simple, with only a bed and a dresser. No night-stands covered in soda cans or dirty clothes all over the floor. I glance at his closet door, wondering if he shoved his clutter in there last minute, but I don't invade his privacy; if he has a jar of human teeth inside, I don't want to know about it.

I should be exhausted after the day I've had and what little sleep I got last night, but I'm wide awake. Climbing into Callum's fresh sheets, I turn the volume down low on my phone to keep it from disturbing Callum through the thin walls; the bear needs his sleep, so he's not so grizzly tomorrow.

Then I turn on a TV show. It's a drama depicting the impact of tourists on the lives of locals, but my focus won't shift from the happy couples vacationing in a romantic place. And how I'll be going on my honeymoon alone.

Danielle should still be awake. Despite what I told Cori, I don't want to go alone. No one would. A theme park, an interac-tive art show, a ghost tour; all entertainment meant to be enjoyed with someone. And who am I going to have romantic dinners with on the River Walk? The lights and the water, cheeks flushed from a glass of wine or two, the hum of chatter and dishes clanking around us... No, I won't be dining with no eyes to gaze into.

> **ME**
> Wanna go on my honeymoon with me?

> **DANIELLE**
> You're still going???

> **ME**
> Yep! So can you come?

> **DANIELLE**
> Can't I don't have any more days off work 🥺
>
> Are you really with Callum??? Is there something I should know?

> **ME**
> Nope, just a weird coincidence

I text a couple of other friends and some old coworkers, but no one can drop their plans for a last-minute, week-long vacation. Even Hailey has to get her classroom ready for school, and Tyler, although he's a PE coach, still has preparations to do before the school year begins.

I flop back on the bed, flinging my phone away. It bounces off the bed and onto the floor, but I don't bother picking it up.

Maybe I'll find new friends to spend the week with, a group in each city. They could turn into lifelong friends after making memories I'll cherish forever. And dining alone doesn't sound so bad. Maybe I'll take one of those spicy books Cori recommended; who needs a man when you've got smut and a vibrator?

Was Callum right today? Should I be feeling more than I am? What does it say about me that I only look forward to the freedom being single provides? Every other time Brian and I have broken up, I've felt the same way, a mustang let loose on a sandy beach. Then, after a few days, I start to miss him. But is it really Brian that I miss, or just a body? Is it really a body I want, or am I just bored? Am I really bored, or is there a hole deep down that I keep filling with temporary solutions because I'm too blind to realize that I'm unhappy?

Those couples in that TV show aren't as happy as they appear. Hidden behind their loving smiles and caresses are festering wounds they bandage with lavish resorts and over-spending. They pretend their rooted fears of failure, of loneli-ness, of the unhappiness they've already reached aren't there because they have everything they could want.

Do I do that? Ignore my issues by focusing on my next adventure?

Holy shit, I sound like Cori. Maybe I'm more tired than I thought.

Whatever, I'll think about that tomorrow. I allow the comforting cedarwood lingering from Callum's body wash to pull me into a deep sleep.

9

SAY A PRAYER FOR ME

Sage's snores saw through the closed door. I wish I could sleep as soundly as her after the day she's had. Instead, I lay awake as usual, with demons clawing at the walls of my brain to be let inside.

I almost caved when she offered to share the bed. I'd enjoy her curled up next to me, leg draped over mine. But I'd wake up, hard and ready, and that cannot happen. For several reasons, least of which is, she was supposed to be Mrs.... whatever-Brian's-last-name-is by now.

My phone rests within reach on the coffee table. I shouldn't give in to the impulse, the incessant voice urging me to just take one tiny peek. But if I do, maybe I'll relax enough for sleep to find me.

I open my social media app and click over to Jake's page. Still nothing. No new updates, no new life events to brag about, no new posts he's been tagged in. My thumb hovers over the 'message' button. I could just ask how he's doing. But it would hurt more if he never answered. If he left me on 'read,' or never opened the message at all.

I've been over this with my therapist. I've made my peace

with the situation and said goodbye to my guilt through a letter I mailed to a blank address. Yet, the torture I put him through still catches up with me, no matter how many times I leave it behind.

I was just a kid—that's what they tell me. I didn't know any better, and I should forgive myself for the mistakes I made then because I've gone through leaps and bounds to ensure I'll never be that person again.

But I'll always be that person to *him*. If he looked into my eyes now, he'd still see that fifteen-year-old kid who caused him so much pain.

Which is why I put the phone down. I don't deserve to reach out, to disturb the peace I pray he's finally found.

SAGE IS STILL SLEEPING BY THE TIME I NEED TO BRUSH MY TEETH and change my clothes. I'm supposed to go to work today, but I've already asked for permission to work remotely since I have an unexpected houseguest. My boss agreed, but only after I attend a meeting this morning.

I don't want to invade Sage's privacy by barging into the bedroom, nor do I need the image of her sleeping in my mind. Especially, if she took off any part of the silky pajama set she wore last night. But it is my bedroom after all, surely she wouldn't have slept naked in someone else's bed. Who knows with that woman?

Slowly, I open the door, averting my eyes from the bed as I fetch khakis and a polo from my dresser. But as I approach the bathroom door, my eyes inadvertently go to the angel in my bed, and my heart twists in pain. To my dismay *and* glee, the blanket is bunched at the foot of the bed, revealing her gorgeous body, still wearing her pajamas. Her blue hair is splayed around her on my pillow, and I vow never to change those sheets again.

The longer I stare, the harder it is to look away. She stirs, letting out a loud snore before flopping over onto her stomach. Even with dried drool on her cheek, she is the most beautiful sight I've ever seen. I reach for the bathroom door, but it creaks when I pull on the doorknob, and Sage's eyes flutter open.

"Sorry," I whisper.

She squints through the light from the window and asks what time it is in a gruff, yet sweet, voice.

"It's seven. I have a meeting at work, so I'm getting ready."

She pulls the pillow over her head and grumbles something unintelligible.

After making breakfast and leaving a plate for Sage with a note that I'll be back in a couple of hours, I head to work. Since school will be starting next week, applications flood our office requesting help with after-school clubs, sports, and even a few asking for help obtaining school supplies—those we send off to a sister charity. The meeting is to regroup, go over the procedure for denials, and discuss donors.

I arrive home around eleven, to the bedroom door still closed and Sage's plate still in the microwave. I take a seat on the couch and catch up on some emails until she finally emerges thirty minutes later, with her hair beautifully sticking up in all directions.

"Good morning," she sings. The hem of her tank top lifts too high when she stretches, exposing an inch of soft skin. "I'm starving. Do you have any Pop-Tarts?"

"There's breakfast in the microwave."

"Oh, five stars for you." She bounces to the kitchen and retrieves the plate without heating it. She could have sat anywhere on the couch, but she chooses the middle cushion, and her leg brushes mine when she sits beside me. "Ugh, it's cold. Three stars now."

"It's three and a half hours old."

She sets the plate on the coffee table. "Do you need a hug?"

"No."

When her arms wrap around me, she lays her head on my shoulder, and the scent of my body wash mingling with her skin suffocates me. It doesn't help that I'm inhaling deeply. "Tell me what's wrong."

"Nothing."

"No, there's something. Do you need a nap? A massage?" She rubs my shoulders. "I could go to the store and get some face masks and chocolate, and we can watch chick flicks from the early 2000s."

My face scrunches. "What? No."

"Well, what do you want to do then? It's beautiful out. Hot, but still nice. We could go swimming somewhere. We could have a picnic before I leave."

"The day is half over now."

Suddenly, she jumps up. "I know! You need a real *vacation!* Come with me on my honeymoon. We could leave around 1, think you can be packed by then?"

"Your honeymoon? I don't think so." Not only is that entirely inappropriate, but I'm barely hanging on after one night in her presence.

"Come on, it'll be fun. We'll go to the beach, play beach volleyball? Then we'll go to San Antonio, we can even visit The Alamo if you really want to."

"Sage, I'm not going with you on your honeymoon. Besides, I have to work."

"Call in. Tell them you have some horrible disease with boils all over your skin that spontaneously burst, shooting pus across the room. And the doctor put you on bed rest for a week. Besides, it's just a regular trip now that I'm not married."

I open my mouth to protest again, but she gets on her knees

74

in front of me and puts her elbow on my thighs, clasping her hands together, and I forget my own name.

"Pleasepleasepleasepleasepleaseplease?" she whines. The words spew from her lips in a desperate rush. "Don't make me go alone. It's scary for a young woman all by herself in unfamiliar places, especially Galveston, where you can't even walk alone at night without creepy men approaching, and the River Walk, where people get stabbed, and I'm just a tiny little woman who needs a big, strong man to protect-"

Her ringtone silences her, not that I followed any of that, and I help to haul her to her feet before I start drooling over that image I won't be able to banish from my brain anytime soon. I wait on the couch while she retrieves the phone from the bedroom before joining me on the couch.

"It was just Mom. No way am I answering that call right now."

Her phone rings again, and we both glance at her little brother's name on the screen. She snorts and throws her phone towards the other end of the couch. "Nice try, Mom."

"What if it really is Spencer? What if your dad had a heart attack from yesterday's events? Maybe that's why your mom was calling." I doubt very much they're calling for any other reason than to question Sage about yesterday, but the faster she talks to them, the faster everything is back to normal.

She considers that possibility for a moment before grabbing her phone and pressing the answer button. She doesn't say anything as she transfers the call to speaker, holding her breath until the voice speaks.

"Sage?" It's Spencer's voice after all. "Hello? Sage?"

Still, she doesn't answer.

"Mom isn't here."

Finally, she exhales. "Oh, okay. What's up, little bro?"

"I just called to warn you, Mom and Dad just left and are headed to Callum's to talk to you. Are you still there?"

She jumps up. "Shit! Yes, but leaving now. Thanks!" She hangs up, rushing to the bedroom, and I follow. I cringe when she throws her dirty clothes into the same bag that holds her clean clothes, but now's not the time for a lecture.

"They may not even know you walked out. Maybe they just want to check on you after being left at the altar. If they do know, why don't you just talk it out with them? Tell them your feelings, instead of running from the problem." Or, maybe meet them somewhere that isn't my apartment, so that I don't get caught up in this mess. Again.

"Nope, I'm good."

Too tired to argue, I drop it. "Do you need me to do anything before I take your bags downstairs?"

"Uhh, yeah? I need you to pack your own stuff."

"Why do *I* need to pack?"

"Because if Mom finds you here, she'll question you and you'll fold like a cheap beach chair."

"I'm not going with you on your honeymoon," I state with finality. "I just won't answer the door."

"If she thinks either of us is in here, a door won't stop her. She's going to want answers as to why you helped me yesterday."

"Your mother doesn't scare me." A lie. "I think I'll be fine." Another lie. "Besides, I can't just go on vacation right now."

She crosses her arms, raising her eyebrows. "Why not?"

"Be... because I just can't."

"Name one justified reason," she orders, holding up a finger.

My boss allows me to work from home whenever I need, as long as I let him know. I don't have any pets or kids. Honestly, nothing is stopping me from leaving whenever I want.

"I don't want to," I answer meekly.

"You don't want to go to the beach for a couple of days? To the River Walk in San Antonio for a few more? To a theme park, an art exhibit, a bar that sounds fun. You'd rather stay here and eat frozen dinners every night and do the dishes and fall asleep on the couch to the news?"

Okay, point taken. But it's still a bad idea. I tell her so, and roll my eyes, preparing for her toddler-sized fit when she throws her arms down and stomps her foot.

"Callum, please! You're making me crazy. We need to get a move on before my mom finds us. Do I need to get on my knees and beg again?"

For the love of all that is pure and holy, please do not get on your knees again.

What would it hurt, anyway? I can book another room, have my own fun close enough that she doesn't have to be afraid, but far away enough that my accompanying an ex-bride won't be weird.

My brain knows my heart is going to win this one anyway. All I'm doing by arguing with her is delaying the inevitable and risking a run-in with her parents. So I give in because I would never be able to resist her in the end, and pack my bag.

As Sage pushes me out the door, it occurs to me that I won't be home in time to take care of my neighbors on Sunday. Mr. Parsons has his daughter who can clean the litter box if I'm unavailable, but Mrs. Browning doesn't have another ride to church.

"Hey, go on to the car, I need to stop and talk to someone real quick," I tell Sage.

"Okay, but don't take too long. Mom and Dad are probably almost here."

I knock on Mrs. Browning's door, hoping she isn't napping.

"Who is it?" she shouts through the door; she can't reach the peephole.

"It's me, Callum."

I hear the lock click before she peeks out. "Why are you here? It's not Sunday."

"I'm actually going on vacation. It's a long story, but I wanted to tell you I won't be home until next Monday afternoon." She opens her mouth, probably to lecture me about the promise I made about her always having a ride to church, but I put my hand up to stop her. "Don't worry, I'll have my friend, Tyler, come pick you up and drop you off at church."

She closes the door to undo the chain and reopens it. "I wasn't worrying, I was going to tell you to have fun, you deserve it. And you absolutely will not have that Tyler come here. That boy is a menace." Tyler, like Sage, finds a thread and has to pull, or a button and has to press it. Despite only meeting Mrs. Browning once when I needed help moving some furniture around in her apartment to make room for her new recliner, he pressed every single one of her buttons.

"I'll tell him to be on his best behavior, I promise."

She sighs. "If it will make you feel better, I'll allow him to drive me. But one flirty comment out of his mouth and I'm smacking him."

"I'll pass along the message." Softly, so as not to break her tiny body, I hug her goodbye with instructions to call if she needs anything. "And if you could maybe say a prayer for me, that'd be great."

"Only if you say one for me," she grumbles.

10

THINK OF THE BED BUGS, CALLUM

"How did this happen?" Callum asks.

I look up from the game on my phone. I'd rather be sketching, but that's hard to do when he drives over every pothole in the road. "What?"

"How did I end up as your chauffeur? In your own car?"

"You said, and I quote, 'No way in hell am I getting in a vehicle with you behind the wheel.'" Maybe a part of me invited him so I could be the passenger princess. Another part wonders whether I can raise his tolerance of me up a level. The other part truly could not stomach the thought of vacationing alone. I'll see a movie or eat out by myself any day. But a honeymoon is not meant to be spent alone, even if the groom is not present.

"I just don't understand why we couldn't take my truck. Your car doesn't have cruise control, and the speakers suck." How dare he say a word against my baby?

"No offense, but your truck has a weird smell."

"Like menthol?" he asks knowingly.

My nose scrunches in disgust. "Like mothballs. Why would it smell like either of those things?"

"I drive one of my neighbors to church on Sundays. She puts mothballs in her closets and uses pain relief cream on her lower back, but I don't notice the smell anymore." I'm not surprised; Callum is one of those perfect people who volunteer and watch the news. He probably even invests in stocks and cleans his microwave.

"That's really sweet of you." But I wonder what kind of demons he has in his closet. Maybe I should have checked for that jar of teeth after all, before inviting him along on this trip. It's always the sweet ones who have the darkest secrets.

He shrugs. "It's not a big deal. She donates to our charity every year, despite not having much money herself."

The car jerks to the side.

"Shit!" Callum shouts.

My hand flies to the handle to brace myself, but instead of slamming on the brakes, he eases off the gas and pulls over to the shoulder. "What the hell was that? Did we hit something?"

Checking the rearview mirror, he opens the door and climbs out. "I think we have a flat."

Sure enough, the right front tire is in shreds.

"This is what happens when you offend Eleanor—she starts throwing shoes."

Callum raises his eyebrows at me. "What the hell are you talking about?"

He opens the trunk and unloads our bags, my box fan, more bags, and a couple of chairs. Finally, he reaches the bottom and pulls it up, revealing the spare.

"Eleanor, my car? You were rude to her."

He grabs the spare while I carry the jack and cross-thing to the side of the car for him. "Okay, but shoes?"

"You know, the headlights are the eyes and the tires are like the shoes," I explain, returning to the trunk for a lawn chair and flipping it out.

"Uhh, what are you doing?" he asks.

"I'm going to stay out of the way while you so chivalrously change a lady's tire." I wink at him, then snap some photos to document the moment when he finally accepts his task. The photos don't do the scene proper justice, but I can exaggerate the proper details if I draw him. I fetch my iPad and open the drawing app. Working quickly, I roughly sketch the proper shadows and lines to accentuate his masculine form.

While he fights to unscrew a tight nut-thing, one of his knees is on the ground, the other in the air, and the muscles bulge from his arms.

"Wait, hold that pose."

Shooting a look of vexation over his shoulder, he asks, "What are you doing now?"

"I'm documenting this moment." I have the photos for reference, but I make a mental note of the stark contrast of his burnt-orange shirt clashing against the blue sky. A detailed drawing can take me hours, sometimes days, and uses layers and layers of colors to bring out the highlights and form of the subjects. I have a feeling I'm going to return home with a hundred sketches waiting to be turned into works of art.

"I HOPE YOU BOOKED A ROOM IN ADVANCE," CALLUM ASKS, waking me from a nap I don't remember falling into. Sleepily, I raise my head and look around to the hotel parking lot where every single space is taken.

He should know this about me by now, but the planning I do in advance is minimal. Of course, I didn't book a room. Where's the fun in that?

He parks underneath the awning so we can unload, hoping a spot clears by the time we finish checking in.

While he starts loading bags onto a cart, I head for the concierge desk.

"Hi, would you happen to have any rooms available?" I ask the woman at the desk. She doesn't smile or greet me warmly, but I understand. A full parking lot means a hectic shift.

"Unfortunately, we're all booked," she answers, mock-pity twisting her face. She says something about a wedding, a bike rally, a conference, kids enjoying the last week before school starts, and parents staying after helping their kids move into their dorms at the local colleges. But I'm not listening as I bang my head on the counter.

Callum approaches behind me, and I cringe at having to tell him everything has to be packed back into the car. When I do, his face hardens like it's my fault or something.

The luggage is put back in the trunk, Ben is back in the back seat, and Callum and I park at a gas station and call every reasonably-priced hotel we find on Google.

"What about this one?" Callum asks, showing me his phone screen.

My eyes bulge. "300 dollars? I'm not paying that for one night."

"I'll pay it." When I shake my head, he pulls up a cheaper option. "Okay, this one?" He shows a sketchy motel with yellowed walls and brown carpet.

"Ew. Think of the bed bugs, Callum."

"Well, this is fantastic." Callum closes his eyes and lets his head fall on the headrest.

"Look, we'll make the best of it. Let's go take a walk on the beach, we'll find a sports bar to park at for a while, then we'll get some snacks, stream a movie from my phone, and have a slumber party in the car."

I can already see the illustration in my head, maybe more of a cartoon style with exaggerated details. Ben stuffed into the passenger seat with me, my eye mask pushing my hair up in a weird lump, and my feet on the dashboard. I have no idea how

Callum sleeps, but I imagine him sprawled out, hand down his pants, mouth open.

A realization hits me. "Oh no! How am I going to sleep without a fan?"

"That's what you're worried about? Not our phones dying, not asphyxiation, not wasting gas running the car all night? Not some stranger sticking his hands through the open window and unlocking the doors and killing us and stealing the car?"

"Your imagination is just as bad as Cori's."

There's that vexed expression again. "Says the one who created a whole back story for why you wore a wedding dress when we stopped for tacos yesterday. And, came up with an elaborate lie about an illness to get me out of work."

"Okay, look. We'll leave the windows parted just enough for me to hear the waves from the ocean, but not so much that someone can stick their hand in." If they really wanted inside, they'd break the window, but I leave that unsaid. "We'll run the AC in shifts if we get too hot. As for the phones, we can actually have a conversation instead of watching a movie. How does that sound?" I flash him a smile, but he doesn't look convinced.

"How do you do that?" he asks.

"Do what?"

"Find the upside to everything." I don't know what I expected him to say, but it wasn't that.

I shrug. "If there's nothing I can do about it, I'd rather not sit in my misery."

"But... how? We're four hours into this trip, and already we've had a flat tire and have to sleep in the car."

It takes me a second to find the right words. "I think about something else. Reroute my brain to focus on something new. For example, a walk on the beach," I say with emphasis. "Eleanor isn't driving around barefoot for now, and I'll think about the hotel situation tomorrow when I can do something about it."

He sighs as if that answer isn't good enough, but it's the only answer I have. I don't know how I stay positive, and I'm not always; even I have moments where I can't find the motivation to get off the couch. But if I allow them to be more than just moments, I'll never get off that couch.

"Think of it this way. We *get* to sleep in the car. We *get* to save money for a night. We *get* to... I can't think of anything else. Point is, just think of the things we get to do instead of the things we're missing out on."

He doesn't look excited at that prospect, but at least he nods. After he opens his door, we dodge traffic through the five-lane boulevard to reach the sea wall, then down the stairs to the packed beach. Since we can't shower tonight, we walk far enough away from the water so we don't get wet, or have to walk over mounds of dried seaweed.

The breeze blowing off the water tames the sweat already accumulating and the stress of the last few hours. I smile as a family plays with a beach ball to our right and a teenager builds a sandcastle to our left.

"There's a place just down the road, it has a deck we can sit on and eat and drink. And they have TVs. Want to go there in a little while?" I ask.

"Sure," Callum mutters, surly and unimpressed. He walks with his hands in his pockets, looking straight ahead, ignoring the laughter and fun around us.

Bumping his arm with my shoulder, I ask, "What's something you want to do on this trip?"

"Make it back home alive," he grumbles.

My head whips around to look at him. "What's that supposed to mean?"

"You're unpredictable, that's all."

I roll my eyes and try again. "Seriously. You *graciously* came along on this trip with me, so I want to make sure you have fun."

He sighs before answering. "I'd like to visit the Strand. Maybe that ghost tour you mentioned."

"Great minds think alike," I add, hoping to get a smile out of him.

I don't.

"We could see about doing a tour tonight. We probably won't sleep well anyway." I retrieve my phone from my pocket, snap a selfie, for which Callum scoffs, then search for tours. "Ooh, there's one in a cemetery. The earlier ones are sold out, but there are two available for ten p.m."

"Okay, that may be a little too creepy. I was thinking of a street tour where we're on the outside of the haunted residence."

I slap his arm playfully."Don't be a baby. I'll be there to protect you."

"Fine. Here, pay with my card." He pulls out his wallet, but I shake my head.

"My treat. You drove me here, then-" He snatches my phone from my hand and takes off running. "Hey! Callum Ridge, get back here!"

I trip on my shoes before deciding my pride is more important than my sandals. After flinging them from my feet, I sprint towards him, hurdling over a beach bag and cooler, then a woman laid out on a towel. He dodges a kid digging in the sand, almost colliding with a dog on a leash, its tail wagging with excitement. Even with my long legs, Callum runs far enough ahead, granting him the time to type most of his bank card number into the payment section. He lifts the phone out of my reach as I approach, out of breath, leaving me no other option than to climb. With my hands braced on his shoulders, I jump and wrap my legs around his waist.

Laughter overcomes us both, making our goals that much harder to accomplish.

Just as I begin shimmying up his body, he lowers his arms

and head, bringing his gaze level with my chest, and awareness of the awkward position hits us like a wave we didn't see building.

I would shift around to his back and request he carry me the rest of the way down the beach, a smooth way to transition from awkward to nonchalant. But he clears his throat, clearly disgusted with me latched onto him like a tree, so I hop down and fetch my sandals.

11

INSIDE THE IRON GATES OF AN OLD CEMETERY

S age has talked nonstop about anything and everything since the tension on the beach. But even if there was a second of silence where I could get a word in, I don't have anything to say.

She *climbed* me. Wrapped her legs around my hips and climbed until her breasts were less than an inch from my face. So close I could have reached out my tongue and licked one. It's a mercy she hadn't taken off her dress; if her bikini top were all that covered her, I would have dropped dead.

There's no break in her constant stream of words as the server delivers a margarita for her and a beer for me; I don't remember ordering one.

"- and that was during freshman year. Then, in sophomore year, I got grounded for coming home after curfew. Cori tried to cover for me, telling Mom I was in the bathroom. She even turned the light on, so you could see it under the door. Obviously, that backfired when Mom tried talking to me through the door, and I didn't answer."

I think back to what she's talking about now, but I come up empty.

"Anyway, that's when I started sneaking out. And I only got caught once. My little brother, Spencer, was making macaroni and cheese at one a.m. and somehow set the stove on fire. It was just a bunch of tiny flames, but the smoke alarm went off, waking everyone up and, well, they noticed I didn't come out of the room."

My gaze zeroes in on her lips as she sips through her straw. Their natural pink complements the blush on her cheeks. Her windblown hair, still flawless, is dyed a different color every time I see her; currently, the same shade as the sky behind her.

"Cori never really got in trouble. Neither did Stephanie." Suddenly, she gasps. "I've known you for like, two years, and I have no idea if you have any siblings."

"Oh, yeah, I have an older brother."

"Ooh. Is he hot? Do you have pictures?" Her brows bounce.

"He's married," I answer drily.

Her shoulders fall. "Damn."

The server returns to take our order: fish tacos for me, fried shrimp, cheese fries, fried pickles, and fried crab balls for Sage.

"What?" she asks when she catches my raised eyebrows.

"Nothing."

The silverware clatters on the table when she slams her elbow down and sweetly, yet terrifyingly, puts her chin in her hand. "You're not judging how much food I'm ordering, are you, *Callum?*" She hurls my name like an insult.

"No, ma'am." I don't know where the *ma'am* comes from, but I'm glad I used it.

"Because I may or may not eat all of it, but it's not your business anyway."

"I know. I was just wishing I had ordered fried pickles too." I may have been wondering how she stays so thin, eating the way she does, but I'd never judge anyone for something as minute as food. I learned my lesson years ago that you never fully know the details around the decisions anyone makes. And what or how much someone eats, just like what someone wears, or how someone looks, is none of my business.

"Oh." Her shoulders relax. "Well, you can share mine. We can share any of it." She smiles deviously.

"You want a taco, don't you?"

"Yes, please. Anyway, as I was saying earlier, the longest time I was grounded was six months." Oh, right. She was listing all the times she got in trouble as a teenager. "That's half a year. It's been eight years, and I'm still pissed about it. But I was suspended from school for fighting, and I popped off and said, 'I don't have to go to school? *That's* not a punishment,' in front of Dad, so..." She shrugs and sips her drink again.

"Why were you fighting?"

"You know." She shrugs again like I'm supposed to know what teenage girls fight about. I guess boys, maybe. Unless that's misogynistic of me to think boys are the only problem girls have. "This bitch wouldn't keep her mouth shut." She looks down into the blended ice in her glass, suddenly at a loss for words.

"About what?"

"It's not important now." She smacks her lips together, and I have an overwhelming urge to taste the watermelon flavor from her mouth. "Anyway, as I was saying, when I was in trouble, I was grounded from everything: the TV, the gaming console, outside." She ticks the items off her finger. "But when Cori was grounded, she only got her books taken away. How unfair is that?"

"Why are we talking about this again?"

"You got all awkward after I climbed you, and I don't do well in awkward silences. And I wanted to answer your question from yesterday when you asked if I was ever grounded or forced to take responsibility as a kid."

Oh, right.

"So, what about you? I bet you never got in trouble as a kid. I bet you were just like Cori—rule follower, wouldn't say so much as a cuss word, never skipped school."

If only she knew.

"Actually, I acted like you. I snuck out and partied a lot."

She snorts. "I don't believe that for a second. What the hell happened? How did you become..."—she gestures up and down my body—"you."

I don't tell the story to anyone. Hailey and Tyler are the only two who know my past, although Tyler and I haven't spoken about it since the night I told him. I should, though. I should announce it to everyone who approaches, or wear a sign above my head as a warning to stay away. Lord knows I deserve the judgment and scowls.

"I grew up."

Her glare ices over. "And you think I didn't?"

"No, that's not what I meant..." I peel at the label on my beer bottle. "Look, I don't want to talk about this anymore."

One of the reasons Sage is so likable, even if I don't under-stand it, is how easily she rolls with the flow. Instead of pushing me, she changes gears.

"Okay, how about we talk about what I'm thinking for my next wedding?"

OUR PLATES ARE CLEARED AWAY, STILL HALF FULL OF FOOD WE don't have room in our bellies for. Sage orders another margarita, but I stick with water, and she snaps more photos of us, the deck we sit on, the sunset. Before long, I retrieve her iPad from the car so she can draw, not realizing I'm the subject again. Every so often, she turns the screen so I can see the rough sketch of my unamused expression she seems to find comical, and my orange shirt blending with the sunset that frames my shoulders.

She doesn't talk while she works, but she does hum, and I find my guards softening without my consent. The crashing waves behind me, the breeze ruffling her hair, and her sweet, yet off-tune, melody flowing through my bloodstream. I could stay here and watch her draw, even listen to her ramble about nothing of importance, forever.

"Where did art come from?" I ask, realizing it's one of the few things I don't actually know about her. I've grasped onto every detail she's let slip in conversation, typically with other people, over the past two years, storing it for a time I might need the information. For example, I know she loves to stargaze, and her favorite wine is a raspberry Brachetto. She once sang to the tune of a song about *strawberry* wine, only she replaced the lyrics.

"What do you mean?" She doesn't look up from shading something on the screen.

"How did you get into drawing and stuff?"

She pauses, looking into the distance. "I don't really know. My Grandma was really talented and used to paint with me as a child, although I used cheap, washable paint while she used oil." She resumes sketching. "I guess that's where it came from."

"So where did sketching come from? Or... *graphic* drawing?" I don't know the right word, mainly because I don't know squat about art. I guess I figured sketching and painting were separate talents, and drawing on an iPad would be different from drawing on paper.

"They're just different styles of art. Some pieces need paint, some don't. And the modern world calls for modern skills, such as sketching digitally."

That's a good enough answer for me, so I let her draw in peace, until she sets her iPad on the table, glancing at me with uncertainty, dimming the light in her eyes.

"What is it?" I ask, concern washing over me.

"What do you think of how I make my income?"

"Umm, I don't?" If I had the slightest idea of what answer she was looking for, I'd give it.

"Do you think I should just forget about making designs and get a real job?"

Again, my mind scrambles for the right answer. "Do you enjoy doing what you're doing? And does it pay the bills? If so, then no."

She stares at me for a long moment, then grabs her iPad without saying anything.

"Why are you asking me that? You don't care what people think." At least, she pretends not to.

"I just wonder sometimes if there's any worth in it. I once overheard a person saying it's all just cheap shit I slapped vinyl onto as they were walking away, and that I wasn't a real artist. It didn't really bother me then, but what if they're right?"

"Well, you draw every design. It's not like you're just taking photos off the internet and profiting off someone else's work."

"Yeah, I guess you're right." There's definitely more to this than she's letting on. I don't want to push her, so I leave it alone for now. But I store it in the Sage folder in my brain, which pretty much takes up every inch of space, and make a plan to get her to open up at some point before this trip is over.

Eventually, the sky turns dark, the restaurant closes, and it's time for the ghost tour. A fifteen-minute drive puts us at the cemetery. I pull over to park on the side of the road, halfway in the grass. We climb out of the car, and I dig around in the trunk for the bug spray before meeting Sage by the hood.

"Here, put this on." I hold out the bottle.

She snorts. "Okay, Mom."

"I mean, if you don't mind the mosquito bites..." My arms itch already from the bites they took out of me at the restaurant.

"Fine." She snatches the bottle from my hands and quickly sprays her skin down. I do the same, then toss the bottle into the front seat of her car.

"So, do you think this will actually be creepy? Or more comical?"

"We're inside the iron gates of an old cemetery two hours from midnight. What do you think?"

Turns out, it's both. Twenty people gather around the tour guide, a man a few years older than me, dressed in Victorian clothing with a top hat. He has to be drenched in sweat underneath his frilly, long-sleeved shirt and pants. But he carries on, unaffected, gesturing with a walking stick to each tombstone as he describes the people buried underneath.

Anne Tabor, born in 1809, died in 1876, after marrying six different men during her life. Each of her marriages lasted almost exactly five years, and each husband is buried in a line, starting with her first husband and ending with Anne herself. No foul play was ever found in any of their deaths, most of them dying from natural illnesses, but she acquired property and wealth with each one. The guide claims the ghosts of each spouse currently haunt the cemetery. However, there's been no sign of Anne.

"How do they know?" Sage whispers beside me, her breath tickling my ear.

"I assume the descriptions of the ghosts match the descriptions of the men."

Earl Jetson, born in 1793, survived a gunshot to the face, a stabbing in his abdomen, and a poisoning incident, all three separate occurrences. Only to be taken out by what they thought was a bee sting on his sixty-sixth birthday.

While the guide tells the story of an older woman outliving her scheming relatives who were after her money, Sage admires a cement grave liner. Cracks line the bottom edge near the grass, big enough to peer inside. Crouching down, she lowers her face within inches of the cement.

"Sage," I whisper.

She motions with her hand for me to join her peeping.

"No, thank you. You're making me nervous. Come back here," I request urgently.

"What are you nervous about?"

"You're invading his privacy!" I don't admit that I'd also like to avoid a lecture from the tour guide for not following the rules; being respectful was the first rule he listed.

"The grave seems to be full of water. Do you think the casket's okay?"

"It's probably in a protective vault. You won't be able to see the casket," I explain.

Then she screams. The sound pierces the still and quiet night, and chills brush along my skin, leaving bumps in their wake. She stumbles backward in her rush to get away, crab-crawling on her hands and feet. Her chest heaves, eyes wide with terror.

Shaking my head and crossing my arms, I resist the urge to tell her I told her so. Again.

"Is everything okay? What happened?" The tour guide pushes his way toward us through the group, an expression of concern struggling and failing to replace his eager smile. "Did you feel a presence?"

"Everything's fine," I begin. "A frog jumped out at her from the crack in that grave covering, because she wouldn't listen and stay back."

He chuckles. "Yeah, that happens a lot. Mr. Wilson was an ornery old man. He's one of the last buried in this cemetery." While he continues with the tale of Henry Wilson, to whom the grave belongs, I hold my hand out for Sage. She shoots me an irritated look but grabs my hand anyway, and we get her upright again. She dusts off her dress and crosses her arms with a huff.

Supposedly, Henry Wilson loved pranks. He never answered a question with a discernible answer, but usually another question. He made announcements of fake events to town members, causing large gatherings for no reason. And he'd stand out of sight beside his house and jump out at people who walked by.

I lean down to Sage's ear. "Do you think this guy is just good at improv? Or do you think Mr. Wilson really did release that frog on you?"

She shudders. "I don't want to think about it."

The group moves on to more tragic tales of hauntings. Gasping sobs from a mourning mother, screams from a house fire victim, and wails from a war widow have been repeatedly reported. I'm not sure I believe in the idea of ghosts, but when something brushes against my left hand, despite no one standing on that side of me, I inch closer to Sage. She must experience some sort of energy as well, because her head snaps to her right as she mutters, "What the-"

She grabs my hand, holding it to her chest as she leans into me.

My skin crawls with fear, and I swear whispers drift through the air, raising the hair on my arms. I can't tell if it's simply the wind that picked up or if spirits are waking, and with every eerie second, I'm more ready to get the hell out of here. Yet, my dick doesn't get the message. Apparently immune to fear—or too stupid to care—it's alert.

I can't pull away, though; she needs me for comfort. And, admittedly, I need her.

Throughout the rest of the tour, one hand firmly grasps mine while the other holds onto my arm. It isn't long before my mind is consumed with her small, dainty fingers between mine, her touch around my bicep, and her face hiding in my shoulder anytime she hears a noise.

If you asked me what the tour guide said about the remaining tombstones, I couldn't tell you. I couldn't repeat a single word. But I could describe, in detail, the little squeak that escapes her throat when her body jerks. I could talk for hours about the desire to wrap my arms around her, to shield her from the world. And I could write a novel about the pain of knowing I'll never be good enough for her.

12

DON'T RUIN MY GHOST STORIES
WITH LOGIC

"Okay, so that was creepy," I say, closing the passenger side door. I press the lock button, the thump of the locks reverberating through the silent night and proclaiming to any surrounding danger that entrance is not permitted. Let's pretend that doors can stop ghosts.

"Do you think any of it was real?" Callum asks.

"It was entertaining, and that's all that matters." Like the dating shows I watch. I don't care if the lines or drama are scripted to increase ratings; it's captivating regardless.

"Yeah, I guess you're right."

Keeping his gaze on the road as he drives, pretending he doesn't notice me staring at him. At least, until his curiosity wins out and he turns his head, looking apprehensive at my devious smile.

"What?" he asks, his tone uneasy.

"You were scared."

He draws out the word, "Okay?"

"I'm telling everyone." I can't help the gleeful laugh that escapes.

"We were at a cemetery at night. Anyone would have been scared."

"Yeah. But you stood suspiciously close to me, like you wanted me to protect you from the little ghosts." My tone lifts mockingly, and he snorts.

"What about you? You held onto me like hands would reach up from the dirt and grab onto your ankles. And the frog?"

"Yeah, but I'm a woman." I may have been scared for like five minutes. But I love the thrill, the racing heart and goose-bumps, the ice skating down my spine, that horror provides. It's nice to experience a supernatural presence in a controlled environment, especially when you can brush it off as a 'script,' rather than reality.

"Oh, right, double standards. I forgot."

We drive for about ten minutes before he pulls into a convenience store and parks on the side of the building.

"We can use their bathrooms, brush our teeth, and get some water." He looks around the parking lot and at the sign advertising a twenty-four-hour operation. "I guess we can try parking here for the night. Hopefully, they don't call the cops on us for loitering."

An hour passes after we finish our business and get settled into our makeshift beds. I'm wrapped inside a blanket like a burrito, spooning Ben in the passenger seat, and Callum lies back in the driver's seat. But neither of us can sleep.

Not only did I sleep in late, but the ghost tour was scarier than either of us would like to admit, and sleeping in the car isn't exactly comfortable. I'm a glass-half-full girl, but only when I have cooperative company, and if he sighs in torment one more time, I might wack him.

I sit up and move Ben to the back seat, and Callum raises his brows.

"What's the most bizarre dream you've ever had?" I ask,

hoping he'll be receptive to my attempts at making the best of things.

"Why?" he asks, apprehensive once again.

"Because neither of us can sleep, and I'm trying to get to know you."

He pulls the lever to straighten the seat. "Okay, umm... probably one I had a couple of years ago. I was vacationing in Europe, but you could see America from the coast because the ocean wasn't as big as it is in reality. When you wanted to go back home, someone would pull the plug on the ocean floor, and we'd have to wait forever for the ocean to drain, but then we'd just walk across."

I tilt my head, scrunching my face. "That's the *weirdest* dream you've had? That wouldn't be in my top fifty."

"Well, it was unsettling standing at a port and watching the water spiral down into a huge drain, okay? A couple of ships got caught in it."

A snort escapes. "Mine would be the time I rode into battle on a pig, yielding a sword. I thrust my arm out to stab a gummy bear and, in real life, hit the wall beside my bed with my hand and woke myself up."

He blinks, allowing the words to sink in. "Okay, you win."

"What's the strangest food combination that you've tried and liked?"

"Grilled cheese and apples," he says without hesitation.

"Eww. What?"

"It's delicious, I promise. I'll make you one sometime." It's an innocent offer, yet he clears his throat and jerks his eyes to the steering wheel, where he runs his fingers along the curve. "What's yours?"

"Bacon and chocolate," I answer, thinking about that doughnut I ate with Hailey. I want another one.

His face twists. "You win again. That's nothing to be proud of," he adds, after I grin smugly.

My thoughts veer back to the events of tonight. "Have you ever experienced a ghostly presence?"

"Why would you want to do that to yourself after what we just went through? We already can't sleep."

I shrug in answer. "Ghost stories should always be involved in sleepovers."

"I don't think I've ever experienced anything like that. Except tonight, maybe."

"I don't really have any personal experiences either, but my grandma Lorraine swears she saw the neighbor who had passed away a few weeks before. She said he walked through her property on his way to his. For weeks, I was scared to visit."

"Was she high?"

"No, but remind me later to tell you about my other grandma. She smokes pot. Mom does *not* approve."

My eyes burn as a yawn escapes, but I'm enjoying this conversation. Callum is more relaxed than usual, freer from whatever ghosts follow him around all day. While it's alarming to see him so different from his typical surly nature, it's satisfying to know I'm the one bringing it out of him.

"Anyway, back to Grandma Lorraine, she swears her bedroom door would open sometimes at night, but no one would come through. And the lights would randomly turn off."

"That could be a simple explanation—electricity cutting off/flickering, or faulty wiring, wind blowing the door open, or an uneven foundation with a slope can cause the door to swing open-"

I shoot him a pointed look. "Don't ruin my ghost stories with logic."

He chuckles. "Sorry."

Unable to think of more questions, we sit in silence for a while. His voice is gravelly from sleepiness when he asks, "You want to try to get some sleep now?"

I nod and wrap my blanket around my shoulders once more before fetching Ben. Callum grumbles something when I accidentally whack him with Ben, but he accepts my rueful grin with one of his own.

We lean our seats back once again, yet my imagination starts going wild. What if that Mr. Wilson guy followed us? Is it even possible for a ghost to travel? What if, instead of an ornery ghost, an angry one followed us? What if I resemble a murderous wife and they want to exact revenge?

"Callum?" I whisper.

"Yes?"

"Will you hold my hand?"

He hesitates, but I try not to take it personally. Maybe he's taken aback by the request. It doesn't matter, because he finally says, "Yes," and reaches over to take my hand in his. My last thought is how warm and large it feels against my skin before I drift off to sleep.

A LOUD RINGING JERKS ME FROM SLEEP. I OPEN MY EYES, regretting it immediately when sunlight attacks my retinas, from where the sun shines through the windshield. Closing them, I blindly feel my way around the car for the source of the annoyance with no luck. Throwing Ben in the backseat, I feel under the blanket, my pillow, in the space beside and under the seat. Finally, I give up and open my eyes, light piercing my vision like a dagger, and find Callum holding my phone out.

"You could have said something," I grumble, snatching it from his hand. The ringing stopped, having run out of time, but I wasn't going to answer Mom's call anyway.

"I understand why you sleep with a fan," Callum says, with a scowl on his face.

"What do you mean?" I ask around a yawn, stretching my arms. Sleeping in a car sounds fun until you wake with a sore neck and aching back.

"You snore."

My hand flies to my chest as I scoff. "I do *not* snore."

"You do. And you did so at the apartment too, but it's much louder in such proximity."

"I've never snored a day in my life. It was probably you, and you're just blaming it on me." I pull the seatbelt across my chest. "Now, feed me breakfast and take me to the beach."

"Yes, ma'am." He backs out of the spot and pulls into traffic. My bossiness is playful, but I could get used to people blindly following my orders.

While he drives, I send a text to Cori.

ME

Do I snore?

She replies immediately.

CORI

Loudly.

Ugh. What does she know?

After eating breakfast at a diner similar to the one my dad owns, we head to the beach. Callum booked a hotel room yesterday during our frenzied phone calls trying to find a room, but we can't check in for another five hours. We spend the first couple swimming and lounging on beach towels I borrowed from Danielle, with not much energy after our poor night of sleep to do much else.

At some point, I doze off and wake sometime later to find Callum building a sandcastle just in front of our towels. The muscles in his bicep and forearm flex and move as he gathers sand. He digs a mote and shapes a bridge, and there are four tall towers connected by large walls, all shaped by his hands only. It's impressive, and I find myself wondering what else he can do with those hands of his.

Suddenly, a ball lands smack in the middle of his castle, destroying the masterpiece. He doesn't react right away, staring at the sand crumbling down, but after his brain catches up, his shoulders deflate.

"Hey, man. Sorry, it got away from me." A tall, sculpted man approaches, muscles flexing in his arm as he points to his ball.

Callum picks up the ball and tosses it. "It's alright, I get it."

The man catches it and juggles it between his hands, his inquisitive gaze bouncing between Callum and me. "Would y'all be interested in joining us? We could use a couple more players." He points behind him to three people separated by a makeshift net—a line drawn in the sand.

I hop up. "I'd love to. Come on, Callum."

"Um, no offense, Sage, but after playing with you last year, no thanks."

When we stayed for the weekend at Cori's ex's beach house, our game of volleyball might have gotten intense. But when your teammates aren't even trying to win, the captain is bound to lose their patience. Then Callum lost his patience with my yelling and threw me in the ocean.

"I'll just stay here and rebuild this," he says, gesturing to the sand with a perfectly smooth crater in the middle from the ball.

"Suit yourself." Holding my hand out to the tall, dark, and handsome stranger, I introduce myself.

"Jackson. Nice to meet you," he responds. As we walk, he points to each of his friends, telling me their names. "Kyle is the blond with the earring, Jasmine is the short-haired one, and Reagan has the mile-long eyelashes."

And when we approach, he calls out to them, "This is Sage, she's going to be playing with us. And based on what her boyfriend said, she might not be very good." I shove his arm playfully.

"First, he's not my boyfriend; we're just friends. Second, I'm just competitive. I played volleyball throughout high school and earned a scholarship to play at Sam Houston," I explain, leaving out the fact that I dropped out.

"Oh, awesome! You're on my team, then." He grabs my hand and pulls me toward the other side of the line. "Except we have an odd number now. How confident are you in your skills? Think we can play two against three?"

"I'm so confident that if we lose, I'll owe all of you *two* rounds of shots."

It's Jasmine who smiles and answers, "Okay, bet."

AFTER JACKSON AND I WIN BY A LANDSLIDE, HIS FRIENDS TAKE OFF for the water to cool off, while I join him by their towels.

"So, how long are you here for?" he asks before taking a sip from a water bottle.

"Until Thursday, then we're heading for San Antonio. I'm sort of on my honeymoon."

His head whips around. "You're *what*? I thought you said you and that guy are just friends?"

"We are. His name is Callum. He helped me escape my wedding." I wave my hand through the air. "It's a long story. Anyway, what brings y'all to the beach?"

"We grew up here and still live close by. Kyle's my roommate and Jasmine's my sister. Reagan and Jasmine have been friends since high school, so she's sorta like a bonus sister," he explains, looking fondly out at them splashing each other in the water.

"That's awesome. I'm not friends with anyone from high school anymore." Except Danielle, but we didn't attend the same school. I would consider myself to have a lot of friends. I could fill an entire page with their names and not have an inch of space. But most of those friendships are surface-level, people you call when you find yourself bored and in need of company, not who you'd call in times of need.

"Where are you from?"

"About an hour north of Houston, although I live a little closer to the city now. Oh, wait. Actually, I don't know where I live now." I forgot for a moment—I'm homeless. I could go to the farmhouse with Cori and Nick as I'd planned, but do I want to be a third wheel in their love nest?

Oh well, it's a problem for another day.

I run through the complicated situation to Jackson, and he smiles. "Sounds like you could move anywhere, huh?"

I help Cori run the trailer, but I don't have to. She has Nick now, or could hire an employee. And I don't have Brian's job to consider anymore. I'm completely free. Untethered.

"You should move here."

I snort. "That's a little fast there, buddy."

He laughs. "I just mean, you seem like the type of person who would enjoy living by the beach."

"Yeah, I would love it. Although if I'm going to move to live by water, it wouldn't be here."

He nods his agreement about the gray, murky water we have here in Galveston; it's not known for its beautiful beaches.

Callum appears at my side. "It's almost one, you wanna head to the hotel?"

I hop up and brush off the sand that clings to every inch of skin. "Yes, please." I'm dying for a shower and a nap.

"We're meeting some more of our friends tomorrow night at their beach house for a birthday," Jackson says, as we both stand. "They're having a bonfire, and there will be food and alcohol. Y'all should come by."

"I think we have plans already," Callum answers, raising his eyebrows at me. "Right?"

Ignoring him, I reply cheerfully, "Not that I'm aware of. We'd love to come by."

"Awesome," Jackson says, clapping his hands together. We exchange numbers while Callum crosses his arms and shoots me a glare that suggests we'll be discussing this later.

13

OVERWHELMING

"Y ou did catch my meaning, right? That I didn't want to go tomorrow?" I ask, knowing full well she understood the message behind my pointed look.

"Yes. But I think it will be fun. Jackson is cool, and I'd like to get to know him better. I liked his friends, too." Of course she did. She's too much of a people-person. I used to be that way. I used to love partying and meeting new potential friends. Now I'd rather stay home and wallow in my self-hatred.

I swipe the key against the reader on the door, but the light flashes red. I swipe it again, red. Red. Red. Red. I flip it. I try it faster. I try it slower. I flip it again-

Sage rips it from my hand. "Let me try." Still red.

Closing my eyes, I lean my head back and take a few deep breaths.

I leave Sage with all the luggage in the middle of the hallway while I go back to the counter, ask the lady for a new key, then try again. We're both exhausted and in desperate need of showers, and we're finally permitted entry into the room. Only to hit another roadblock.

"Didn't I make the reservation for two beds?" I ask, staring at the single queen-sized bed, neatly made with a sea-blue comforter. There's a single wicker chair with a cushion, but no couch, and my shoulders deflate at the prospect of going back to the counter.

"Yes, I'm sure there's just been a mistake."

"This whole trip has been a mistake," I mutter under my breath, setting down the fifty bags Sage brought.

"What was that?" she asks, knowing exactly what I said, but offering me the chance to rescind it.

"Nothing."

"Like I said at your apartment, we're both adults. All we're doing is sleeping. It shouldn't be a big deal." She stands with her hands on her hips.

I exhale a loud and dejected sigh. "It's fine, I'll just sleep here." I collapse into the chair.

Her foot connects with my shin, and I lurch forward to rub it.

"Ow. What the hell?"

"Stop being stubborn. Now, I'm going to shower. I suggest you get ready for yours, because as soon as I'm done, you'll get yourself clean, you'll have a snack, then you'll take a nap. I'm not dealing with your bad attitude the rest of the trip." She snatches a small bag from the desk and slams the bathroom door behind her. But *I'm* the one with the attitude.

AFTER A VIVID DREAM INVOLVING JAKE'S HEAD ATTACHED TO THE body of a shark, I wake from a restless nap. My mouth and head both scream for water, but I stay in the chair for a moment, listening to Sage's voice drifting from the bathroom. Or eavesdropping, whatever you want to call it.

"-and of course he's mad about it. He even napped in the chair beside the bed."

"Why are you complaining? You get the whole bed to your-self," Danielle's voice answers through the speaker.

"Because you know I'm a cuddler. And sure, I have Ben, but he can't exactly cuddle me back. Anyway, it's whatever. If he thinks I'm too gross to sleep next to, fine." I hear a spritz before a clack, and I conclude that she's fixing her hair.

"I can't believe he agreed to go with you. He's always been so... cold towards us. Thinking he's better than everyone." Is that really how I come off? After all the work I've put in at my therapy sessions to *not* appear arrogant and insolent, was it all for nothing?

Oh God, am I like Sam? Sam, one of my best friends from college, who fooled us all into thinking he just needed his ego taken down a notch, but in fact was a real-life bad guy. Sam, Cori's ex, who felt so entitled to anything and everything he wanted in that moment that he stomped over Cori's feelings and emotionally abused her. Sam, who betrayed us all when he cheated on her, forcing us to pick a side.

If I ever reach Sam's level without realizing it, just strike me with lightning or send a bus my way.

"Yeah, but other than the bed situation, it's been pretty fun. He's a little grumpy today, but he's just tired. He even held my hand while I fell asleep last night. If nothing else, I'm hoping to end this trip with a better understanding of how he works."

"Well, keep me updated. By the way, have you heard from Brian?"

"No, and I'm hoping I don't. At least not until I'm back home. I don't know what I'd say to him." I agree that they need some space away from each other before discussing their... break-up? Are they actually broken up if they haven't spoken yet?

"Keep me updated on that front, too. I've gotta run, some jackass parked over the line and I can't get in my car. Have fun tonight," Danielle says.

"Will do."

I rise from the chair and grab my water bottle from the counter across from the bathroom. Sage turns toward me through the open door, strands of hair locked in a curling iron.

"Hey, you're awake." Her face twists. "Oof, you didn't hear that conversation, did you?"

As I drain the bottle, I nod.

"Sorry. I'll be more discreet next time I'm talking about you." She smiles, indicating a joke, but I don't want to give her any more reasons to talk about me again. At least, not in that way. I make a mental note to be better. Although I'm not exactly sure how to accomplish that, considering I apparently have no self-awareness.

I don't want to share a bed because I don't want to wake up with a hard-on, having slept next to the sexiest woman I've ever laid eyes on. I don't want to share a bed because I don't want to confuse Sage further after having walked out on her wedding. I don't want to share a bed because I want to be respectful.

I can't exactly tell her the first reason. And if I tell her the others, she'll only roll her eyes and tell me I'm being ridiculous.

"I'm starving. How long will it take you to get ready?" she asks, putting the finishing touches on her makeup.

"Where are we going?"

"We're having a romantic dinner at an expensive restaurant," she answers, waggling her eyebrows.

I hope Mrs. Browning remembered to pray for me.

"Do you want my jacket?" I ask, once we're seated at the restaurant. A bucket chilling a bottle of wine sits atop a white tablecloth between us.

"No, it's warm in here. But that's sweet of you to offer, thank you," she answers with a sweet smile.

"Okay, but…"

"What?" she asks, when I can't find the words.

I settle for gesturing to her cleavage, hoping she gets my meaning. She looks down, then her head snaps back up.

"Are you serious?" Fire burns bright in her brown eyes, and I scramble for a way to undo what I just did. "Are you embarrassed of me because I'm showing a little cleavage? What the fuck is wrong with you?"

It's not at all that I'm embarrassed of her. It's just that my lungs struggle for breath at the sight of her temptation. But that's my problem, not hers. "You're right, I'm sorry. That was an asshole move. Feel free to throw some water at me, or something." I offer a playful smile, gesturing for her to bring it, hoping to pour some ice on the situation. Metaphorically, preferably.

"Maybe I will." Thankfully, her flames calm without drenching me in the process.

The server stops at our table, and Sage orders pasta with shrimp.

"That's what you ordered the first night we met," I say after placing my order, and I instantly regret speaking that observation out loud.

Her eyes widen. "You remember that?"

Of course, I remember. I remember every single detail of that moment, down to the loose thread on her dress underneath her right arm.

She scoffs. "What am I thinking, of course you do. You were probably judging me for ordering such an expensive dish on Sam's dime while you had that sad, tiny, cheap bowl of soup."

"For your information, I wasn't really hungry that night." That's not the reason for my ordering soup, but she doesn't need to know that. "And I remember because you kept dropping pasta onto your lap."

"Oh, right. So you were judging me for being sloppy." The

pained words contradict her light tone, the easy smirk gracing her lips.

"Do you really think I just go around judging everyone?" Sam did that, not me.

"Well, you were certainly judgy that night. You sat at the other end of the table with Cori and Hailey, glaring at me. I could only assume it was because you found me to be obnoxious or something."

"You are obnoxious," I say. "But that's one of the many lovable things about you."

She tilts her head and crosses her arms on the table, pushing her breasts further together. "Wow, an almost-compliment from Callum Ridge." She waves her hand. "Say more things."

"I just mean, being obnoxious isn't necessarily a bad thing. You're bold. You find good everywhere you look. You have fun everywhere you go." My beer arrives, thank God. I down half of it in one gulp.

"So, you mean to tell me you weren't glancing around the restaurant in embarrassment every time I laughed, or wishing flames would engulf me anytime I winked at you?"

I squint.

"What?" she asks.

"What are you talking about?"

"Well, when I first walked in, you had this look on your face like, 'what the hell is she wearing?' very similar to your face when you pointed out my cleavage earlier. Then, I was telling some story and I laughed, and you jerked your head around the restaurant as if you were embarrassed about how much noise I was making. I started telling another story about something—I can't remember what—and you rubbed your eyes and sighed as if you were tired of hearing me talk."

I'm still squinting, wondering how she has it so wrong when I say, "That's not at all what happened."

She leans back. "That's exactly what happened. But why don't you tell me how that night went? In your own words."

I fight myself every day to throw this memory into the abyss of my mind, never to be found again. Not that it works, but now I'm forced to purposely hold and stroke it lovingly, waking it to its full power.

TYLER AND I ARRIVED AT FRANCESCA'S, AN ITALIAN RESTAURANT TOO *expensive for us twenty-two-year-olds to be dining at, for Cori's birthday. After promising to foot the bill, Sam invited us along so that he wouldn't be the only man dining with four women. And to ease the tension between him and Cori's friend, Hailey, who wasn't fond of him.*

Cori and Sam had only been dating about a month, but they'd known each other since they were kids, having recently reconnected and taken their relationship further. Tyler and I had only met her once before this, but we were eager to get to know her better, maybe hear some embarrassing stories about Sam from when he was a kid.

Cori and a dark-haired woman I assumed was Hailey were already there, but Sam was running late.

"Happy Birthday, Cori." I handed her a card with a gift card to a bookstore inside from me and Tyler. All Sam said was that she reads, so I figured it was a safe bet.

She took it hesitantly. "Oh, thank you. You didn't have to get me a card."

"We wanted to," I said before turning to her friend and extending my arm. "Hi, I'm Callum, a friend of Sam's."

Just as hesitant as Cori, she slowly placed her hand in mine and said, "Hailey."

She and Tyler shook hands as well, but my attention was pulled to the entrance of the restaurant, the voices around me dissolving to nothing. A young woman with long, blonde hair laughed at some-

thing her friend said as they walked in the door. My eyes trailed down, admiring and drooling over the hot-pink dress hugging her slim body until it ended mid-thigh. But my gaze continued along her long legs to her black heels with straps. Those heels turned and pointed towards me, approaching closer with every step until they stood just a foot from my own brown, leather shoes.

My head was still tilted towards the ground when her hair appeared in my line of sight. She bent at the waist and waved her hand in front of my face, trying to get my attention. "Heeellooo?"

My back snapped up, suddenly aware of how creepy I was being. "Hey."

"What's wrong with you?" she asked, bluntly.

Cori rose and reprimanded her for being rude. "This is Sam's friend, Callum. Callum, this is my sister, Sage."

I took my seat next to Tyler across from Hailey, and for every second of the next half hour while we waited on Sam, I tried and failed to keep my eyes from straying to Sage. Hailey and I discussed our jobs and how she knew of a few students who could benefit from our charity, but she grew frustrated at having to repeat herself so often because I was too busy listening to Sage and her friend talk about the good-looking servers. Or some guy Sage had met at a club a few nights ago. Or them poking fun at Cori for some reason or another.

Her full lips had me hypnotized for long moments until her laugh would hit me over the head like a brick and I'd wrench my gaze away.

Finally, Sam arrived and ordered a bottle of wine for the table, but I stuck to water. My brain was already mush; it didn't need any help getting there.

I was too distracted to absorb any of the menu, so I just said 'same thing' to the server after Hailey ordered with no idea of what dish would be placed before me.

It was shortly after we placed our order that I noticed the thread. Sage was animatedly telling some elaborate tale about climbing out *of some guy's window after a less-than-stellar date, hopping his fence, and bumping into his hot neighbor's chest. She lifted her arm, and I saw it, less than an inch in length.*

I pictured myself pulling at it and unravelling it until there was no cloth left covering her body. When I was practically drooling over her, I ran my hands over my face, rubbing my eyes until they hurt, as if that would help erase the perverted images my mind had conjured without my consent.

Just when I thought I couldn't take it anymore, just when I was opening my mouth to give some excuse of a stomach ache to Cori, the food was delivered. The server placed a lonely bowl of soup before me, a bowl that wouldn't fill me up. But I'm not hungry anyway. I figured I'd scarf it down to be polite, then I'd allow myself to leave, to escape the clutches of this woman whom I had just met.

I was halfway done with my soup when Sage dropped a forkful of pasta in her lap. Instead of being embarrassed or running to the bathroom to desperately swipe at the stain, she threw her head back and laughed.

But it wasn't until she stuck two of the thin Italian breadsticks in her mouth and pretended to be a walrus that I fell. Not in love, but I knew I'd never be in her proximity again without giving her my full attention. I knew she'd be my first and last thought every day for who knows how long.

BEFORE I'VE SAID A WORD DESCRIBING THAT NIGHT FROM MY point of view, I say, "Okay, I see what you mean," I tell her. "But, I promise you it's not what you described. Occasionally, my face doesn't quite match up with my thoughts."

Her brows furrow in disbelief. "So what were you actually thinking in those moments when your face looked disgusted with me?"

My palms are slick, and sweat beads on my forehead.

"Well... do you think you could just trust me that it was only good thoughts?"

She scoffs. "What the hell does that mean?"

I let out a sigh. "It means that I was a little shocked at how beautiful you were, and how different your personality was from Cori's. I didn't know that you and Cori weren't *identical* twins, so I was expecting someone who looked like her. And not that she's not beautiful, but she was dating one of my best friends. And you know how quiet Cori is; to meet her sister, who laughed so freely and talked enough for both of you, it was..."—I shrug, looking for the perfect word to explain my face, but not wanting to give too much of my emotions away—"overwhelming."

By the way her face scrunches up, I assume I chose the wrong word.

"Overwhelming? That isn't much better than disgust."

I open my mouth to say... I'm not sure. But she cuts me off anyway.

"Just know this, Callum Ridge. You may think I'm too much, but that says more about you than it does me." She smirks before taking a sip of her wine.

Truth is, I do think she's too much, just not in the way she's insinuating. I think she's too beautiful, too smart, too worthy to be with a lesser man such as myself.

14

GOOD GOD, WOMAN! HAVE YOU HEARD OF SOCKS?

After dinner, I unwillingly followed Sage to a drag show and watched as several gay couples bought her shots to celebrate her calling off the wedding. Now, after brushing my teeth back at the hotel, I open the bathroom door, emerging from a warm, soft-lit bathroom into an icebox. I have gray sweatpants to keep my legs warm, but my shirt disappeared while I was in the shower, and my nipples harden from the chill.

Sage leans against the headboard, watching a scary movie completely unaffected, as if the characters sip tea rather than being mauled by some creature.

"Why is it so cold in here?" As I ask, goosebumps pop up on her arms.

"Because I don't have to pay the electric bill here."

That doesn't quite answer my question, but I shake it off. I have another question, anyway. She's wearing my missing t-shirt, and it's long enough that I can't tell if she's wearing shorts.

"Do you have shorts on underneath my shirt?" I ask, afraid of the answer.

She lifts the hem of the shirt to reveal a pair of pink panties with *'Friday'* written across the front. "Nope," she states, popping the 'p.'

Great. Now I'll never get that image out of my head.

"You realize it's Tuesday, right?"

Without taking her eyes off the TV, she responds, "Yeah, why?"

"Never mind." I turn off the lights, grab a bottle of water from the mini fridge, and get situated in my chair. Sage watches me for a moment before rolling her eyes and turning her head back to the TV.

"What?" I ask.

"Nothing."

"Just tell me."

"No." She changes the channel to Friends and turns over so that she's facing the windows.

I count to ten, wracking my brain for something to say to make it better. My main concern is waking up with a boner poking into her back and making her uncomfortable. I don't have much control over my dick when I'm asleep, and if I'm sleeping next to Sage, beautiful, tan, smooth Sage, I am guaranteed to dream about her. Which means I'm guaranteed to wake up erect.

No. It's better if I stay in the chair. As much as I don't want Sage to think I'm disgusted by her, I can't explain why I must stay out of the bed. Even with an extra pillow behind my lower back and my feet propped up on the ottoman, it's uncomfortable. But Sage is safer this way.

It isn't long before she snores softly, spread out over the bed. The comforting resonance mollifies the tension in my shoulders, and my eyelids grow heavy.

I look forward to tomorrow, when Sage and I will spend the day together completing some more items from the to-do list, like shopping. It's her bright smile, widening as she finds weird trinkets to spend her money on, like a jar of alligator teeth, that projects in my mind as sleep wraps its cold, malignant hands around me and pulls me down.

"I'm disappointed in you," Dad says. His hands are clasped on our wooden dining room table. "I thought I raised you better."

"It's my fault," Mom says through her sobs, hand pinching the bridge of her nose.

I sit drooped in a chair, growing familiar with the agonizing despair I'll spend the rest of my life with. A fog rolls in, and large purple vines grow along the walls toward the ceiling. Sweat beads along my temple, yet I shiver inside my letter jacket as I hear the hidden meaning within their words: "What a waste of breath and bone." Everyone would be better off if I weren't here, from all the torment and destruction I've caused.

The scene shifts, and Jake's face appears, eyes closed, slumped in a chair surrounded by his dad's liquor bottles and mom's pill containers. I'm unsure which ones were emptied by him or his parents, but it doesn't matter. Those same purple vines grow here too, smashing through the TV screen and ripping the faded wallpaper with large, gray thorns.

Regret.

I bang on the windows to wake him.

A whispered plea.

My name shouted with urgency. "Callum!"

A 9-11 operator asks what the emergency is.

"Callum!"

Police sirens blare past.

"Callum!"

Someone shakes my shoulders as Jake pleads for help in a feeble voice.

Heart racing as my chest heaves, my eyes pop open, focusing on a blue-haired angel here to save me, here to carry me away from everyone I've hurt.

"Hey," the angel says, meeting my gaze and stroking my hair. "I think you were having a nightmare."

It's not an angel after all, but Sage. I'm not sure if I'm relieved or disappointed.

Sitting up, I rub my face.

"What was it about?" she asks gently.

I shake my head. "It's not a big deal. Just a bad dream."

"You kept repeating 'I'm sorry' over and over."

I drink some of the water Sage hands me. As I set it on the nightstand, Sage climbs into my lap.

"Hold me. That was scary." Her voice trembles, and a weight sinks in my gut from making her worry.

I'm shaken, but she needs me to be strong for her. "Oh sure, no problem. I'm the one who had the nightmare, but you need consoling," I tease.

"Yes, it was. I didn't know what to do. I wasn't sure how to wake you without you lashing out at me." She lays her head against my chest just under my chin, my turn to stroke her hair.

"You're right, I'm sorry. They usually wake me eventually, so you don't have to worry about it if it happens again."

She raises her head to meet my eyes. "So you have these dreams a lot?"

I hesitate to tell the truth, but I've already partly admitted it. "Yeah. But as I said, it's not a big deal."

"Alright then, if you say so." She climbs back into bed. "I don't know how I'm going to sleep now, though."

My head falls against the back of the chair, wishing I wouldn't say what I'm about to, but not knowing how to stop myself.

Maybe if I sleep sitting up against pillows, I can keep myself from sleeping deeply enough to move without knowing it. Perhaps I can stop myself from spooning her and accidentally sexually assaulting her.

"Sage," I say, then wait for her to turn over.

"What?"

"My back is killing me. Can I sleep in the bed? I promise to do my best not to invade your side."

She sits up, her brows rising. "You fought so hard to sleep in that stupid chair, and suddenly you want to be in the bed?"

"As I said, my back hurts. I thought I could handle it, but first, I slept on the couch, then in the car, then in this chair. I'm getting old, and my back can't handle it like it could before."

She snorts. "You're twenty-five. But please." She pats the bed. "Come sleep next to me and keep my feet warm."

Slowly, knowing I shouldn't be doing this and also more eager than I have any right to be, I climb into bed beside her. Then my body jerks as ice-cold, bare feet curl between my shins.

"Good God, woman! Have you heard of socks?"

"Can't sleep with my feet being suffocated. That's what men are for anyway." Her eyes are already closed as she settles into her pillow and pulls the blanket to her chin. "Turn around. I'll be the big spoon."

"No. No cuddling. I'll sleep sitting up."

She opens an eye. "I thought your back hurt."

"It does. But my back is better supported in the bed."

"How much do you want to bet that you'll be cuddled up with me when we wake in the morning?"

"Nothing. As I said, I'll try my best not to pass over to your side."

"I won't mind. I'm a cuddler. I'll probably be the one invading your space because I'll unknowingly move towards your body heat in my sleep. Lunch tomorrow. Loser buys." She closes her eyes without waiting for my answer.

"Fine."

15

YOU ONLY HAVE ONE HONEYMOON!
OR SOMETHING LIKE THAT

"I win." I'm leaned back to whisper in Callum's ear, snuggled comfortably in his embrace. His left arm is underneath the pillow we share, his large right hand caresses my belly, and a third leg is currently reaching towards my ass. I almost regret the declaration of victory because I know he'll jerk backwards, depriving me of the coziness in which we slept.

He shifts, pushing his dick further into my back and groans, a low guttural sound that would make any sane woman feral, but he doesn't wake. I relax back onto the pillow when he snores softly, allowing myself to fantasize about his erection and how I could take care of it for him.

I'd turn over, placing my hands on his hard chest and pushing him back from his side. Next, I'd throw my leg over and straddle him, slowly rocking as I stripped his shirt off. Then I'd plant a trail of kisses down his neck, his chest, his abdomen, before pulling his sweatpants down and letting him free.

But this is Callum. He'll grab hold of my wrists before I can make our middles meet, stopping anything from happening. Either he doesn't think I'm good enough or smart enough for him, or maybe he's just simply not attracted to me, immune to the charms I can usually win over anyone else with. I mean, he wanted me to cover up my cleavage. What the hell? And I have small breasts, it's not like there was much cleavage to be embarrassed about anyway.

I've never thought of Callum in this way before, aware of his disdain for me from the second we met. He's attractive, sure. Okay, fine, he's fucking hot. I've always known it, but I've never allowed myself to lust over a man too blind to see what a prize I am. So why am I doing it now?

It's simply been too long since I had sex. To my dismay, Brian and I were able to uphold our deal of no sex before the wedding after all, and I'm not used to lasting this long before finding a partner.

Soft light barely penetrates the curtains, and I reach for my phone to check the forecast when Callum reaches full awareness of our current position. He jerks backwards and says, "Uhh..."

I force a small laugh and scooch back to my side of the bed, putting too much space between us. And yet, Callum seems to think it isn't enough by the way he shoots to his feet and disappears into the bathroom.

While I'm alone, I almost reach my hand down between my legs to soothe the ache. I'm desperate, my entire body heating as the blood pumps faster to my clit, calling for me to touch it. Maybe if Callum catches me, he'll join in. It's a nice thought anyway.

AFTER WE DRESS FOR THE DAY, CALLUM AND I EAT A FREE—IF WE ignore the technicalities—breakfast of Texas-shaped waffles and watery eggs in the hotel dining room.

"How would you feel about matching tattoos?" I ask around a mouthful of yogurt.

"I'd feel negatively about such an idea."

"But they'd be a nice, lifelong reminder of our adventures together."

His eyebrows lift. "Do we really want to remember this trip? Ow!" He exclaims after I kick his leg. "What the hell was that for?"

"We had a nice evening last night." At least, partly. "Don't revert to your grumpy self now. Anyway, we could get waves or something."

"How about you paint us both a picture or something instead?"

"Fine." It's not that I really want a tattoo, but I've never had one before, and I love experiencing new things.

The plan for today involves overpaying for souvenirs, such as sand in tiny bottles and cheaply made t-shirts that advertise Galveston. I'm hoping the rain holds off long enough for us to get through the necessary shops on the Strand, then we can find something indoors to keep us entertained. Like matching tattoos.

The Strand Historic District in Galveston is lined with beautiful Victorian architecture. Among the several gift shops, there's a confectionery, antique stores, restaurants, and boutiques, where I'll spend too much money on crap I don't need.

But you only have one honeymoon! Or something like that.

I buckle my seatbelt, an eager smile gracing my lips, but when Callum turns the key, the engine clicks, and his worried eyes meet mine.

He tries again, but it still clicks, and his head falls back on the headrest in frustration.

"Did we leave the lights on last night? Did a door not get shut all the way?" I ask. I was slightly buzzed after the wine at dinner, then the shots at the bar, but I distinctly remember hearing the locks click into place while we walked inside.

"The lights shut off after I closed your door. I know they did," he confirms, eyes still closed.

"Damn it, Cori!"

"Cori? What does she have to do with anything?"

"She drove my car from Mom and Dad's Saturday evening and rubbed her bad car luck all over Eleanor." I wave my hands around, acting out the very image in my head. Cori's dealt with every possible problem that can go wrong with a car. Her brand-new tires shred, she's had to replace her spark plugs more than anyone else, her lights randomly turn off, and there's a hole in her AC unit that causes it to blow whatever temperature it is outside. Oh, and the volume button on her radio controls her blinker.

I once had strict rules in place about her driving my car— don't. But I thought her curse had lifted since it's been a while since she broke down, or needed a ride because her car was in the shop.

"Eleanor's always been good to me. Cori drives her once, and so far, we've had a flat tire, and now she won't start." In high school, Cori and I shared a car with our older sister, Stephanie. The first time Cori drove by herself after passing her driver's test, the driver's-side door panel fell off, and the brakes started squealing. I started saving for my own car that very second.

Cori gets a lot of shit from her car, but she also gets a lot of shit from me for overreacting about things, and here I am, over-reacting. I take a deep breath and count to five while I exhale. "Oh well, a battery is an easy fix. We'll just get a new one." I dig through my purse for my phone.

"And how are we going to get there? It's raining," Callum says, gesturing out the windshield where, sure enough, the clouds have begun pissing all over an already shitty situation.

Another deep breath, and out for five.

"It's just a sprinkle, we can walk." As if to taunt me, the rain falls harder, turning into a downpour.

I have to shout to be heard over the drops pelting the roof of my car. "Or we can order a ride. Or wait until the rain stops."

"If we step out of this car, we'll be drenched before we take a single step. Might as well save your money and wait it out."

"But I'm going to be bored," I whine, allowing my head to fall against the headrest.

"Is that so terrible?"

"I don't like to be bored."

"I noticed."

And now I'm defensive. "What is that supposed to mean?"

His face softens. "Nothing. I've just noticed you enjoy things fast." I have another retort on the tip of my tongue, but he adds, "I'm not saying anything bad, Sage. Calm down."

Crossing my arms, I mutter under my breath, "*You* calm down." I don't know why I can't help myself.

He shakes his head. But he's right about the rain. Shopping in it isn't fun, so we hunker down and get comfy. Downpours like this don't usually last too long unless it's a hurricane, which it very well could be. My method of checking the weather involves peeking out the blinds, so naturally, I did no preparation for this week in terms of rain.

I want to double-check the forecast to see how much it changed in the last two hours, but I can't find my phone. I dump my purse in my lap and sift through all the junk while Callum types away on his, probably using this moment to catch up on any work he's been avoiding.

"Ugh," I complain. "I think I left my phone inside."

"I'm pretty sure I saw it on the floor next to the bed," he replies without looking up.

"Why didn't you grab it?"

"Why didn't you? It's *your* phone."

I don't know how to answer that.

"Come on. Let's race inside. Whoever gets the wettest is the loser. I know some ways you can entertain me afterward." I bounce my eyebrows for effect.

He groans.

16

HEY, YOU'RE ALIVE!

Twenty minutes later, I find myself sitting across from Sage on the green carpet of our hotel room, covered in bodily fluids only God knows about. My head lies back on the bed, face covered in vanilla-scented goo, while Sage clips away at one of my fingernails.

"Are you going to let me do your toes next?"

"Absolutely not," I state firmly.

"Ugh. Why not?"

"No one touches my feet." When we got up to the room, she gave me two options: model nude for a sketch, or let her take care of my cuticles and pores, which apparently have been driving her nuts since we met. Naturally, I selected pampering, expecting relaxation and comfort. What should be a peaceful moment is only painful as my muscles grow tighter with every second my hand rests on her soft, warm knee.

But I draw the line at pedicures.

"Ew. How gross are they?"

"They're not. They're just ticklish." I regret the admission as soon as it's out there. I lift my head slightly and peek at Sage, finding the definition of mischief painted over her features.

"You should not have told me that."

"Please don't tickle me," I try weakly.

She laughs evilly. "Oh, I'm gonna. You just won't know when."

I let out another groan, my millionth of the day.

"When can I take this stuff off?" I ask.

"Two more minutes. Do your pores feel cleansed yet?"

I don't know what that's supposed to feel like, but they smell nice. "Um... sure."

She tugs on my hand, needing it closer to better see whatever substance she scrapes off my nail. When my hand still isn't close enough, she scoots nearer to me, laying her knee over my thigh. It's innocent, just two people sitting close. But the way my heartbeat picks up, desperately pumping blood to places it shouldn't, shifts my focus to each point of contact.

Against my better judgment, I run my thumb over her skin, and my insides warm from the satisfaction of causing goosebumps to rise along her leg. She gazes up at me, a question simmering in her eyes. But she looks back down without asking it.

Instead, she asks again about drawing me nude. "I need to study the shadows and shape of muscles, and Brian didn't have many. You, however, have an excellent physique."

"Um, actually, I'm going to go ahead and get that battery." I stand and head to the bathroom, but Sage protests.

"It's still raining."

"A little rain won't kill me." But one more minute alone with Sage in this hotel room might.

AFTER BORROWING AN UMBRELLA FROM ANOTHER GUEST AND jumping Sage's battery off that same guest's car, I arrived at the auto parts store. Then, I changed the battery there in the parking lot, and with its impeccable timing, the rain stopped just as I closed the hood.

When I return to the hotel room, Sage naps with her mouth wide open and hair stuck to her cheek. While I wait for her to wake, I call Tyler.

"Hey, you're alive!" he says upon answering.

"So far. This morning almost took me out."

He laughs, but he doesn't understand the full extent of that statement. He doesn't know how I feel about Sage.

"It's just like you're hanging out with a female me," he says.

As terrifying as that thought is, they are both very go-with-the-flow. But she's a little more on the hot-headed end of the goofy/serious scale.

"We're sharing a hotel room."

There's a pause. "Like, with two beds?"

"Nope."

He whistles, shouts, and laughs all in the same breath. "Damn, you're lucky."

"Yeah. Lucky. I'm on a honeymoon that isn't mine but isn't hers either because she's not married, and she's hot, and we're both technically single, but it'd be the most idiotic thing in the world if we did anything physical. But I'm *lucky*."

"Are you kidding me? Like you said, you're both single, and you're both hot. Who cares about all the rest?"

While Tyler knows my past, we don't talk about it. He doesn't understand why I'm still caught up in the guilt and shame. So, instead of reminding him of my insistence on remaining single, I bring up more pressing reasons to stay away. "Why do I keep having to remind people she just walked out of her wedding?"

"But the groom also walked out. So, what's the problem?"

"Emotional turmoil, the messiness of rebounds, the chaos of dating someone who's ignoring their feelings..."

"None of that means anything to me."

I sigh. "I should have called Hailey."

"When you do, tell her I said hey."

AFTER ALL THE RAIN, I WAS HOPING THE PARTY WOULD BE cancelled. Or, after we finally went shopping, I was hoping Sage would be too tired to go tonight, maybe craving a night in instead. Unfortunately, neither of those things worked out as I'd hoped. As Sage gets ready, I struggle to keep my eyes on hers while she shamelessly changes out of her tank top and shorts in front of me.

"Do I have to go tonight?" Except, I don't want her to go alone, so I'm quick to add, "Actually, never mind. I want to go."

Her face lights up. "You do?"

"Well, I don't want you to be with a bunch of strangers by yourself."

Her eyes roll up. "That's not the same thing."

"No, but aren't you worried about showing up at a stranger's house after being invited by other strangers?" I know she's not, but I want to plant what little stranger-danger I can in her trusting brain.

Her lip curls. "No, why would I be? It's just a party. If anything, I feel safer knowing a bunch of people will be there, rather than one or two people. So, lots of witnesses in case something happens. Besides, I have you to protect me." She grins sweetly, then looks back in the mirror.

I guess she's got a point.

"Now, do you promise not to worry?"

"No, but I promise to try to have a good time." My fingers are crossed behind my back, but I do promise, mentally, not to ruin her fun.

Thing is, though, promises are made before all the factors

are accounted for. For example, the number of people invited to this thing. Or the tenacity of that asshole Jackson.

After we pulled up to a light purple house on stilts, we parked along the side of the road behind a long line of cars. Guests filled the deck at the top of the white stairs and spilled onto the sand behind the house, which is where we were headed when Jackson spotted us. He walked over to meet us with a bare chest and feet.

"Wow, Sage. You look gorgeous," he drawled, eyes traveling a little too far south. She does look gorgeous, though. But I'd think the same even if she wore a prison uniform rather than the white dress with blue flowers to match her hair.

"Thanks. I try," she said, giggling and flipping her hair.

"Can I get you a drink?" Jackson asked, eyes still on Sage's chest.

"Sure. I'm not picky."

He didn't ask me, but I called out as he walked away, "Soda for me, thanks."

"Don't be rude," Sage lectured me, swatting my arm.

"He's the rude one. He didn't even acknowledge me. How much you want to bet he forgets my soda? And did he lose his shirt?" My hands hid in my pockets before they found themselves possessively wrapped around Sage's waist.

"We're at the beach," Sage said with a roll of her eyes. "I thought you promised to have fun."

"I said I would *try*." But she was right. I had a problem with a guy not wearing a shirt at the beach; that's a new low for me. Although everyone else has a shirt on, why is he special?

He did remember my soda, surprisingly, yet delivered it without taking his excited, unnerving gaze off of Sage.

Now, I awkwardly sip my Coke while they talk—no, *flirt* —and I try not to barf. After telling some mournful tale about a friend of his losing their business after the last hurricane, he proceeds to brag about all the work he did with cleaning up and rebuilding.

"Wow, that's amazing of you," Sage coos.

He acts coy, waving her off, but clearly enjoying the praise. "It's nothing. If there's a need, someone has to fill it. Might as well be me."

I roll my eyes, then mentally reprimand myself for having an issue with someone who's clearly a good guy. I guess he's earned the right to brag.

"Callum is like that too, always willing to help out. I bet y'all would get along." But Sage's attempt at making us friends goes wasted as Jackson nods awkwardly before looking behind him for any reason to change the subject.

"Hey, come sit with me by the fire. I'll introduce you to some more friends of mine," Jackson suggests, already tugging her hand toward the circle of chairs around the bonfire.

"Sage, wait." I grab her other hand, and she halts. But Jackson halts too, glaring back at me.

Que the stare down until he gets the hint that I'd rather be alone during this conversation with Sage. He's either too stupid to get the hint or too determined to stand his ground until Sage waves him off.

"I'll join you in a second," she says, dismissing him.

He doesn't take his eyes off me when he answers. "Okay, take your time." Of course, she'll take her time. Sage follows no one's timeline but her own.

I jump right to the point the second he's out of earshot. "He's flirting with you."

"I know. He's so cute. And his arms?" Her eyes roll back in her head as she fans herself. That was not the response I was looking for. "I bet he'd have no issue with me drawing him nude."

"Seriously? Don't you think you should tell him to back off?"

She shoots me a look, suggesting she thinks I'm crazy. "No... why would I?"

Running a hand down my face, my mouth starts talking before my mind can catch up. "Why do I have to spell it out for you like you're five?"

She flinches back, brows shooting towards her hairline. "You did *not* just say that to me. Flirting with someone doesn't mean I'm going to sleep with them." She storms off toward Jackson.

Shit. "Sage, wait-"

But it's too late. Each of her footsteps slaps against the sand with resolve and stubbornness. She turns to ensure I'm watching before lowering herself into Jackson's lap, and my gaze zeros in on his hand, wrapping around and coming to rest on her waist.

The coke can crinkles from the jealousy in my grip. What am I going to do with this girl?

Sage throws her head back at something Jackson says, her laughter riding the wind in my direction before slapping against my cheeks. But after every word said, every chuckle, every playful smile, her eyes find mine. His lap may be the one she's on, but her attention is on me. And that gives me the strength to smile back before turning and walking away.

I head up the stairs with no plan in mind before claiming a spot in the corner out of sight from Sage. Then, because I don't know anyone and I don't want to stand here watching everyone like a creep, I pull my phone out to call... someone. Anyone.

I decide on Hailey; she'll have some sage—and Sage— advice for me on the bed situation. Instead of greeting me with a polite 'hello, how are you doing?' upon answering, she cackles evilly.

"Will you stop that? I need some help," I say.

"I'm sorry, it's just, you're stuck on the honeymoon of a

woman you're madly attracted to. I feel for you, I really do. But I don't have much joy in my life, just give me this."

I wish she could see me rolling my eyes. On second thought, I hit the FaceTime button and wait for her face to appear on the screen. Then, I roll my eyes.

"Really?" She asks, unamused.

"Seriously now, I need help." I switch the call back to voice so our conversation isn't overheard, and fill her in on the events so far. Including, but not limited to, the bed, the nightmare, the dinner conversation, the fact that Danielle finds me cold and Sage thinks I find her gross, and how I ended up sharing a bed with her. "How do I handle this?"

"Handle what exactly?"

"Okay, it's just... how do I not..." I don't know how to put into words my fear. Sage is touchy and cuddly. If I push her away, I run the risk of confirming Danielle and Sage's expectations and upsetting Sage. If I allow myself to relax and accept Sage's lack of boundaries, I run the risk of getting too comfortable. The risk of forgetting why I don't deserve her. "How do I get through this without my heart thinking I have a chance with her?"

"You do have a chance. You're just too stupid to allow it."

AFTER MY CONVERSATION WITH HAILEY, DURING WHICH NOTHING was made clearer, I peer over the ledge, careful not to let Sage catch me.

But our eyes meet, and a slow grin flashes on her beautiful, irritating face.

Fine. I crack my knuckles and look around, sending a thanks toward the sky when I find one of Jackson's friends from the beach within Sage's field of view.

"Hey, I don't think I got your name earlier. I'm Callum." I extend my hand, and she grasps it.

"It's Jasmine."

"Nice to meet you." I came up here with a plan, but my boldness washes away with the tide as I peer into Jasmine's dark, innocent eyes. She doesn't deserve to be played with, and I promised myself I wouldn't ruin Sage's fun, even if I don't like that she's having it with another man.

The silence is awkward as Jasmine waits for me to start a conversation. My body itches to turn toward Sage once more, to make sure she's safe and hasn't been carted off to some shadow to fool around with Jackson. But I don't want her knowing she still occupies my every thought.

"They look like they're getting cozy," Jasmine says, unaware that I'm trying to distract myself from what's happening in that chair.

"Yeah. I wish they wouldn't."

"Are you into her?" she asks bluntly, searching my face.

I decide to be honest. And pray the truth doesn't find its way to Sage. "Yeah."

I wait for the dreaded, *'Why don't you tell her,'* bullshit, but it doesn't come. Instead, mischief gleams in her eyes, and her eyebrow ticks up. "Wanna make her jealous?"

17

AREN'T YOU A LITTLE OLD FOR MIND GAMES?

What is Callum's problem? A little flirting is harmless. Besides, I just met Jackson. Despite what Callum thinks, I do understand I walked out of my wedding only two days ago; I'm not as stupid as everyone likes to believe. I *can* behave with propriety. When I want to.

However, with Callum and his superior uppityness, now is not the time. Now is the time to do the exact opposite of what his pretentious ass thinks I should be doing. And that involves running my hand up Jackson's chest and arching my back so that my breasts poke out, drawing his gaze once more.

I even fetch my phone from where I stuffed it inside my bra and snap some photos with my cheek against Jackson's.

"Send those to me," he requests once I'm done.

Despite finding no humor in his words, my head falls back and I force out a laugh.

It's only to take Callum down a notch. I find immense satisfaction in the scowl on his face, and even more when Callum crushes the can in his hand, the liquid splashing out and staining his shirt.

"Did I say something funny?" Jackson asks with a flirty smile.

"To be completely honest with you, my friend doesn't like that I'm sitting on your lap. I'm playing with him a little."

Both of our heads turn to find annoyance in Callum's glare. "I can certainly help with that." Jackson's arms tighten, pulling me further into him, while mine snake around his neck, and I drape my leg over the arm of the chair. But when I look back to see Callum's expression this time, he only grins before walking away.

With Jackson forgotten, I watch every step Callum takes across the sand and up the stairs until he disappears from view.

"Looks like we lost him," Jackson says, not loosening his grip.

Hardly hearing a word he says while he talks more about himself, my eyes remain glued to the railing surrounding the deck. Any minute, he'll look over to see if I'm still on Jackson's lap. And when he finally reappears, I don't know what guides me to smile and snuggle in closer to Jackson's chest. But it works. Callum jumps back, caught in the act of satisfying his curiosity.

Despite my smugness, I still can't peel my eyes away from his every move, as he approaches Jasmine, shaking her hand and probably introducing himself. Their conversation looks awkward at first, like neither of them is sure what to talk about. Good. That's what he deserves, the jerk.

But then Jasmine's smile twinkles a bit too much for my liking, as she takes a step forward and places her hand on his chest. She jerks her head toward the house before taking his hand and leading him inside.

"Oh, hell no!" Jackson and I both exclaim synchronically. I jump out of his lap and head for the stairs, because no one triumphs over me during emotional warfare. As I stomp past too many bodies on the deck, my phone rings. I silence the call with no time for conversation at present, but it starts ringing again before I reach the door to the house.

"Now isn't a great time, Cori," I exclaim into the phone upon answering. I stand off to the side of the deck, finger in one ear.

"Why? What's going on?" Worry laces her tone.

"Oh, you know. Mind games with Callum." Jackson, who trailed behind me as we marched up the steps, got sidetracked by an attractive woman in a bikini top and jean shorts. I can't blame him; she's hot.

Cori sighs loudly. "Aren't you a little old for mind games?"

"Aren't you a little too young to be telling me what to do?"

"You're only older than me by fourteen minutes."

"And don't you forget it, young lady. What do you want, anyway? I need to cock block someone." Cheers erupt when the pizza delivery guy rounds the corner of the house, causing him to jump and almost drop the stack of boxes in his hands.

"Where are you?" she asks.

"We're losing daylight here, Cor!"

"Fine. Mom called. She said she called you earlier, but you didn't answer. She wanted confirmation that you were alive."

When I finally found my phone, I had a few missed calls from Mom. But I'm still not ready for a lecture.

"I'm alive and well. I'll text you later. Bye." I don't wait for a response as I hang up and open the sliding door. It's a typical beach house with white wicker furniture and generic seashell prints on the walls. Liquor bottles cover the glass dining room table I imagine will shatter at some point this evening, and a few guests lounge on the couches watching a college volleyball game.

"Did you see a tall, surly man with a beard come through here with Jasmine?" I ask, betting they know who Jasmine is.

"Yeah, they went to Clark's room," a guy in shorts says without taking his eyes off the TV.

With no idea who Clark is, I thank them and head down the hallway. I open the first door, but it's an empty bedroom. The second door is the bathroom, complete with a man urinating. He nods his head in greeting before I close the door. I twist the knob on the third door, taking a step to enter, but I hit the door as it prevents entry. This must be Clark's room.

I raise my fist to bang on the door, but I'm cut off as Jackson approaches behind me. "Did you find them?"

"Yeah, no thanks to you."

"Jasmine, open this door right now!" Jackson shouts, banging on the door.

With my ear against the door, I listen for moaning or talking, but I only hear shuffling as someone approaches.

"What?" Jasmine demands, wrenching the door open. She holds a bathing suit to her chest, unclasped as if *someone* were in the process of taking it off. I push my way inside, looking around for Callum, but he's not here. Not in the closet, not behind the door. I crouch to look underneath the bed, but he's not there either.

"He's not in here," she says. I stand up just as Callum approaches from further down the hall, phone to his ear.

"What is going on?" he demands.

"You tell me." My hands rest on my hips, and Jackson crosses his arms.

"Well, I came inside to call my parents back, and Jasmine wanted to change into her bathing suit. And then y'all come in shouting and banging on doors. So I ask again, what is going on?"

I roll my eyes. "You know exactly what's going on." But does he? Do *I* even know what's going on? Or what exactly has fueled my actions, causing me to make a scene in some stranger's beach house?

And why does Jackson care if his sister hooks up with someone? And why did I automatically assume she and Callum were hooking up at all?

Maybe I *am* impulsive and possibly a little crazy.

"Didn't we talk about this?" Jasmine asks Jackson, mirroring his stance. "You agreed you'd relax on the whole *protective brother* act." She quotes the air with her fingers.

"And you agreed you wouldn't fool around with my friends anymore."

Callum squares his shoulders, intimidation radiating off him like heat from the sun. "Do you even know my name?"

"Okay, I think there's been a huge misunderstanding." I step between them, grabbing hold of Callum's thick forearm and pulling him away to diffuse this awkward situation before it's further blown out of proportion. "Jasmine, I'm very sorry for barging in. Super cute bathing suit, by the way. Why don't we go back outside?" I suggest to Callum. Thankfully, he follows without complaint, and I smile at the people staring from the couch as I wave and walk past like nothing happened.

We make our way back outside and find a quiet-ish spot by the water, allowing the breeze to cool the embarrassment on my cheeks. I don't get embarrassed often, but when I do, it's usually because of my own hastiness.

I plop down in the sand, immediately grabbing handfuls and letting the grains filter back to the ground through my fingers. Callum sits beside me and nudges my shoulder.

"What's wrong with you?"

"Oh, I don't know. Maybe the fact that you were flirting with Jasmine-" His laughter cuts me off. It's a grating sound at present, but still warms my insides. "What?"

"Relax. Flirting with someone doesn't mean I'm going to sleep with them."

I'm stunned into silence for a beat. "Oh, you have a lot of nerve, Callum Ridge."

"Yes, I do. Also, I won." He chuckles, confirming it wasn't all in my head like I thought.

"So I'm *not* crazy after all. You just make me feel like I am."

"Hey, you started it."

"You were the one who called me stupid!" I throw a handful of sand at his chest.

He flinches, then stills, mouth gaping as his mind catches up with what I just did. As he grabs his own handful of sand, wet enough to form a ball for better impact, I jump to my feet and take off down the shore. The sand-ball hits my back with a painful splat. While I scoop up more sand, Callum catches up with me, tackling me to the ground and straddling my hips.

A burning desperation to get away overcomes my instincts, at the same time that my muscles slacken from Callum tickling me. Between breaks in my laughter, I plead for him to stop before I pee on us both. Rolling off to lie beside me, he smiles.

"I win again."

That earns him another clump of sand.

"So you and Jasmine weren't really flirting with each other?"

"No. Apparently, Jackson has a history of interfering with her relationships, so she jumped at the opportunity to mess with him."

If I'm being honest, when I saw him and Jasmine walk into the house, jealousy sprouted in my gut, its sharp thorns grabbing onto my insides, poking holes in my sanity. I saw red, because if anyone is going to lead Callum into a house, it's me. For reasons I'm not quite sure of at this moment, but I won't overthink it.

The sharp ringing from my phone slices through the air, startling us both. I fetch it out of my dress with the intention of ignoring the call, but Brian's name on the screen has me pausing. Still reeling from the chaos Callum sent me through, I'm not in the mood to sift through the emotions of the past few days. I turn my phone off and put it away.

The sun sets to our left, just behind Callum. I motion for him to turn so we can watch what we can before it disappears behind the row of houses that block its descent. Cautiously, I wrap my hands around Callum's arm and lay my head on his shoulder, unsure if he'll be comfortable with this position. To my surprise, his head comes down on mine, and together, we watch day melt into night.

When the stars peek out from the dark sky, we search for constellations, ignoring the party raging behind us. And not once do I consider rising from this spot to join the laughter or drinking, to find Jackson and dance, or sit around the fire and get to know all the new people. Not once does Callum suggest we separate or find a different way to spend our evening.

It's my ideal date. But it's not a date.

18

POUT ALL YOU WANT, I'M NOT HAVING SEX WITH YOU

S age's head rests on my shoulder, and I don't know what to do. I laid mine on top of hers because my body refused to relax, and I thought maybe my head on hers would distract her from my tense muscles. I wanted to make her happy, keep her satisfied, and meet her halfway. But now my neck hurts from this position, and my stomach rumbles with hunger, and I don't want to move or upset her by pulling away.

"Why have I never seen you with a woman? Are you gay?" The questions catch me off guard, like an arrow to the heart of an unsuspecting innocent.

"Wow. Uh, how about we go back to the hotel and I'll post nude for you?" I would give my left lung not to have to answer.

She lifts her head, her expression softening to concern. "Do you think I'd care if you were? Are your parents homophobic?"

Shrugging her comforting hand off my shoulder, I open my mouth to assure her I am not gay. But how much easier would this be if I were? That could explain why I tense when she touches me, and it would stop her from trying to entice me. But no, I won't lie and reap the benefits of something I am not. I deserve every ounce of torture Sage could possibly give me.

"No, I am not gay. But I don't really have a reason for why you've never seen me with a woman. I just... have had a lot going on in my life. Too busy."

"For *two* years? When was the last time you had a girlfriend?"

My silence is louder than the roaring waves just feet away.

"Have you *ever* had a girlfriend?"

I'm quick to answer this time. "Yes, I have. A couple." One in high school, and one in college. But the first one doesn't really count, I guess, considering I was fifteen when we broke up. And the second... Honestly, I was in a fog for most of that relationship. I don't remember much, and she got tired of fighting for my attention. "Look, can we just drop it for now? Maybe one day I'll give you the full explanation, but now is not the time."

"Fine." She jumps up, startling me. "I'm starving. Maybe we should go find that pizza."

"Yeah. Or we could grab something and head to the hotel. Maybe watch a movie." I'd rather not return to the party and risk her falling into Jackson's lap again just to spite me.

"And cuddle?" she asks, waggling her brows.

I scratch my head, stretch my neck and back, stand, and dust the sand off my legs, all to avoid answering that question. Maybe I should reconsider lying about my sexuality after all.

She laughs. "I'm just messing with you, relax."

SAGE COULDN'T GET HER MIND OFF OF PIZZA AFTER BEING promised a slice at the party, so we picked one up on the way to the hotel. As we walked out of the shop, she asked, "Are you sure this is enough for both of us?"

I glanced at the eighteen-inch pizza in her hands, mainly to double-check that we saw the same thing. "Yeah, I think that's plenty. I doubt I'll be able to eat half of that." I lied. I could easily eat three-fourths of that pizza, but if she could put away more than half, I wanted her to have the option.

"Told you," I say now, gesturing to the two slices left in the box.

"But that's what we'll eat in the morning. And will one slice be enough for both of us?"

"The hotel has breakfast, remember? I assure you, we aren't going to starve." I refrain from mentioning that pizza is not a healthy breakfast. I don't imagine that going over well.

While she showers, I take advantage of the quiet and catch up on work emails. With the start of school, several kids are looking for help getting into football and band, which have higher fees. There are just as many applications for kids interested in joining various high school clubs, but their costs are much smaller and easier to acquire. That's one thing I love about this charity; while others have an amount requirement, we won't turn away a thirty-dollar organization fee that may be nothing to some families, but gas or grocery money for others.

My job is to check applications and ensure we have all the necessary information before handing the file off to my boss.

I love my job. That and my promises to my neighbors are the main things that keep me going each day. But it only makes me wish I could turn back time more, because Jake could have benefited from our charity. So much would have turned out differently if he'd had the help he needed.

With that thought in mind, my hands move on their own, checking social media like a fiend with no self-control. Still no updates.

I have a great job that helps people. Friends and neighbors, people who care and depend on me. I have money in the bank, more than I need. And I'm on vacation with a beautiful woman, enjoying myself.

And yet, all I can do is continue forward with no idea how

Jake's life compares to mine, and feeling guilty that I have it better than I deserve.

A SOFT, FEMININE MOAN WAKES ME THE NEXT MORNING FROM A blissful dream in which Sage and I were back on the beach. She laid perpendicular to me with her head on my stomach, talking about anything and everything. I just smiled, perfectly content to listen to her forever.

I slept in the bed with her again last night. I couldn't think of a good reason to stay in the chair, not one I could give to Sage anyway.

Now, Sage moans once more and arches her back, pressing her ass into me. If I lay here one second longer, I may find myself pinning her down with her wrists above her head and wiping that hint of a smirk off her face. Because she can pretend to be asleep all she wants, but she's not fooling me.

I rise and take much longer than necessary to brush my teeth, hoping she'll fall back asleep.

She doesn't.

I emerge from the bathroom to her waiting on me, sitting against the headboard, a devious grin etched on her face. As soon as she sees me, her hands teasingly roam over her breasts.

I freeze.

Knowing I'm caught in her trap, unable to look away, she continues, running her hands down her stomach and sucking her bottom lip between her teeth.

All the blood in my body reroutes to my dick.

"What are you doing?" My voice betrays me, giving away my pain and waning strength.

"I thought we could have some fun," she purrs. "I felt how much you wanted me."

How easy it would be to give in, to join her on the bed and

replace her hand now threatening to dip beneath her waist-band with my own. How amazing it would feel to sink my fingers inside of her, to coat them with her slickness.

I almost mistake my heartbeat for more thunder outside, but the morning sun shines bright through the windows.

Hooking my thumb over my shoulder, I say, "I'm starving. I'm going to find breakfast."

"Ugh." She yanks her hand from her shorts and crosses her arms across her chest.

"Pout all you want, I'm not having sex with you."

She hops to her feet. "Now who's the one playing mind games? What with the stroking of my leg yesterday, the spoon-ing, laying your head on mine..."

"Friends can do that sort of stuff. It doesn't always have to lead to sex."

"Why not? It's just sex. It's fun, it's not a big deal."

I can't have her thinking anything could ever happen between us. Especially not now.

I speak slowly the same words I've said about a hundred times already. "You are on your honeymoon with a man who wasn't the groom. After calling off your wedding."

She snarls. "You don't have to speak to me like I'm a child."

"Then quit acting like one."

That does it. She stomps over, stopping once we're toe to toe, and lifts her chin. Pointing her finger into my chest, she opens her mouth to give me a what-for, but I grab her finger.

"Yeah, yeah. Save it for later. I'm starving, and you have some self-pleasuring to get to." I turn and head for the door before I change my mind.

19

DAMN IT, SAGE, KEEP YOUR HEAD IN THE GAME!

After he leaves, I brush my teeth and change my clothes, before stomping downstairs to interrupt his peaceful meal. An idea pops into my head as I peruse the breakfast choices, and I head to the table with only a banana in hand. Maybe this will get him.

I sit down in my seat and lock eyes with Callum, willing his hazel eyes not to look away, before slowly raising the banana to my lips. But before I can blink, the banana is wrenched from my grasp and shoved into Callum's mouth as he devours my breakfast.

"What the hell?" I demand.

"Go eat a different-shaped fruit. I see some apples up there."

I cross my arms and lean back in the chair, glaring as he finishes *my* banana. I don't know when I started viewing him as a challenge, but I'm determined to crack him at some point. He may think he's too good for me, he may think I'm just a dumb blonde who can't decide on a hair color, just like all the other people in my life. But I guarantee he's not strong enough to resist me forever. I vow that by the end of this vacation, Callum will be inside of me one way or the other.

Neither of us takes our gaze off the other, except for the brief glances he gives his food when he's shoveling it onto his fork. And neither of us speaks until I remember the bet.

"I want to meet with Jackson one more time before we leave for San Antonio today," I say, hoping to elicit the green-eyed monster.

"Fine. Will that make you happy?"

"Your face as a seat would make me happy."

He rolls his eyes. "Let's say we *did* have sex. Let's say it was the best sex of your life." I huff a laugh at his shameless arrogance. "Then what?"

I shrug. "We do it again?"

"Wrong. Because that would lead to feelings. And, as I've said about a million times already, you. Just. Called. Off. Your. Wedding. You're in no place to be developing feelings for anyone."

"And, as *I've* said about a million times, I. Don't. Care. I wouldn't develop feelings for your grumpy ass anyway. Chances are, you'd develop feelings for me way before I did."

The fight leaves his eyes as he stares at me. I have no idea how to read his expression as he chews his cheek before saying softly, "And isn't that just as tragic?"

"No, because we both know there's no chance of that happening. So there's no problem."

He jams his fingers into his eyes. "Then can you just accept the fact that I don't want to risk it?"

In other words, he still refuses to admit that I disgust him. Maybe not physically, but otherwise.

"Fine."

AFTERWARD, WE HEAD DOWN TO THE BEACH ONE LAST TIME before we make the drive to San Antonio. Despite it being a

Thursday morning, beachgoers and all their crap already litter the sand. Callum and I lay our towels between a mom and her kids who dig in the sand with plastic shovels and a young couple reading a book together.

"Will you do my back?" I ask Callum, handing the bottle of sunscreen to him.

He shoots me a wary look.

"What?"

But he only shakes his head, taking the bottle without a word. I don't need a verbal explanation anyway, I know exactly what's behind the disdain in his eyes: he has to touch me. And we all know how horrible he finds that prospect. Not just *touch* me, a millisecond of skin clashing where he could wipe my germs off on his pant leg and no harm done, but *rub* my skin. Which he is doing now, and taking his time with, if I might add.

If I didn't know any better, I would say he's enjoying himself by the way his tender touch lingers on my shoulders before moving slowly to my neck. My eyes close, enjoying the feel of his massive hands on my skin. He moves to the middle of my back, slipping his hands underneath the strap of my swimsuit.

I imagine him taking one step forward, pressing his chest against my back, and wrapping his hands around my front.

What is wrong with me, lusting after a man who can't stand me?

He reaches my lower back, just above the waistband of my pink bottoms, and rubs even slower. For one torturous moment, I almost expect him to dip in. He hesitates, and my breath catches. But as he should, he moves his hands back to my shoulders before pulling away completely.

I turn around and hold my hand out. "Need me to do yours?"

"No." His quick answer unravels every second of the last few minutes.

"Fine. Suit yourself." I take a seat on my towel laid out in the sand, watching to see how he manages his back himself, which he doesn't. Taking pity on the man, I stand and wrench the bottle from his grasp.

"You did just fine touching my back. What's the problem with me touching yours?" I'd think that would be better since touch is more sensitive on the hands.

His voice is pained when he answers. "It's not a problem, Sage."

I decide not to stoke his moodiness and just let it go. I'm here to enjoy myself anyway.

After I finish coating his back in sunscreen, I ask, "Want to play volleyball?"

"Not with your competitive ass."

"You know I won't have to scream at you for missing the ball if we're playing against each other."

He thinks about that for a moment. "That's true. In that case, prepare to lose, Anderson."

I ENDED UP WINNING ALL THREE GAMES WE PLAYED IN BETWEEN swimming and lounging beneath the sun. Thanks to me, Callum doesn't end up sunburnt. But now I realize the missed opportunity. I should have let his stubborn ass burn, because then I'd be able to rub aloe vera on his back tonight in the hotel room.

Damn it, Sage, keep your head in the game!

Callum isn't thrilled by the idea of meeting with Jackson before we leave, but he perks up when he sees Jasmine accompanying her brother. Jealousy boils in my belly, but I guess I deserve it, considering the reason I invited them out for coffee was to irritate Callum.

"So what are your plans in San Antonio?" Jasmine asks, sipping her matcha as we get situated at a table by the windows.

"The only plan set in stone is an interactive art show tonight. I bought tickets three weeks ago. Other than that, I want to play at a theme park like I'm a kid again, maybe do karaoke or have sex with a stranger in a bar bathroom."

Callum rolls his eyes, and Jackson laughs.

"And there's a haunted bridge. Some say if you stand there and call the name of the ghost that haunts it three times, she'll appear. I figure we might do that tomorrow night."

"You're going by yourself," Callum says.

"Oh, come on. What if something bad happens to me?"

"I'll fetch your body in the morning and take it home to your parents," he states without empathy.

"What if there's nobody to fetch?" I ask, mistakenly thinking I've got him.

"Then I'll take your *fifteen* pieces of luggage home to your parents."

"Whatever. So what's the story behind your argument the other day?" I ask the siblings.

Callum whispers my name, probably to stop my prying, but I'm nosy.

"Kyle and I messed around a few times, and Jackson overreacted," Jasmine answers, bored.

"He's a known player, and I didn't want you getting hurt," Jackson says. "Then you and this stranger disappear, making us think you were going inside to do things together that my sister shouldn't be doing with men she just met."

Jasmine stands, rolling her eyes. "Whatever. I'm going to get a muffin."

"Me too," Callum says, pushing his chair back and following her to the counter. I watch their every step, ready to jump out of my seat if I see anything untoward. But what justification do I have for stopping any flirting that may happen?

Callum isn't mine. And, as he likes to remind me, I just called off a wedding.

Jackson chuckles. "You're into him."

My head snaps forward. "I am not!"

"You know he's into you."

I scoff. "No, he's not. He can barely stand to be in my presence. I'm working on it, though."

Jackson's lips flatten into a disbelieving expression. "No, he's definitely into you, but trying not to be."

"Then why did he reject me this morning?"

He shrugs. "Like I said, he's trying not to be. I don't know why, but no one looks at someone who's just a friend the way he looks at you."

I THINK ABOUT WHAT JACKSON SAID THE ENTIRE DRIVE TO SAN Antonio. Well, the hour it takes for me to fall asleep anyway. Then I dream about Callum and those muscles that bulged as he molded the sand for his castle.

Another phone call from Mom that I refuse to answer wakes me up around 7:37 p.m. Groggy and disoriented, I look around at the hundreds of blinding red taillights surrounding us. Callum's brows furrow as he stares out the windshield, one elbow propped on the door panel and supporting his head.

"How are we not there yet?" I ask.

He shoots a look at me. "You've been snoring away this whole time, and you're the one complaining?"

"What's going on?" I ask, gesturing to the traffic at a dead stop.

"I have no idea. I assume an accident."

"Ugh. One more thing to add to the list of crap that's ruining my honeymoon."

Callum's face twists into a confused expression. "I think

whoever was involved in the car accident has had a shittier day than you."

"But we're already pushing it for the art show. Any more delay and we're going to be late." The tickets are non-refundable, and I was looking forward to it more than anything.

"I'll buy you tickets for tomorrow or the next day."

That would be better anyway; I'd be able to enjoy it without sand in my ass crack. "Okay, that works. I'm going back to sleep. Wake me when we get there."

I almost don't hear his muttering. "Yeah, we'll see."

Turns out, my energy bar is full, and I can't fall back asleep. After a while, I give up and open my eyes to catch Callum, head resting back on the headrest, watching me, expression soft and eyes full of something I can't read. Only, he jerks his gaze forward to stare out the windshield once more. How long had he been watching me? And why? Is it just a coincidence that I happened to open my eyes the second he happened to look over? Or was he planning ways to drug me until Monday so he could spend the rest of the vacation in peace?

I don't know, but I have the overwhelming itch to get my iPad out and sketch the expression before it fades from my memory. After fetching it from my bag and turning on my stylus, I make sure to sketch the important details first, the slight crease between his brows and the conflicting softness of his stare. I have to guess at the folds in his clothing and the shadows on his face and body, but I get a good rough drawing by the time it takes us to inch through traffic and pull off the highway at our exit.

"So what do you want to do tonight?" I ask Callum, now that we've officially missed our check-in for the show. "There's plenty of nightlife here. We could find a place for karaoke, or we could go dancing. Live music..."

"I think I'm going to stop by a grocery store and get some sandwich stuff or something, maybe have a night in."

"Ugh." My head falls back against the headrest.

"I didn't say you had to join me. But I'm tired. In case you forgot, I'm the one who drove the whole way. Besides, it's late." It's just after nine, which is not late by any means.

I snort. "Okay, grandpa." My stomach growls, and my skin itches from the sand still dusting it. The more time that passes, the more I realize how amazing a long, warm bath sounds right now. "Alright, we can chill at the hotel and watch a scary movie or a crime documentary."

"Does it have to be a *scary* movie, though? We can't watch like a rom-com or something?"

"Aww." I rub the back of his shoulder. "Don't worry, I'll be there to protect you if you get scared."

20

WIPE THAT SMUG GRIN OFF YOUR FACE

Thankfully, there is no issue with the booking I made to avoid a repeat of Galveston. However, on our way up to our room, one of Sage's suitcases bursts open, throwing her underwear and bras, sweatpants with unicorns, an unopened box of condoms, a vibrator, and other embarrassing items everywhere. Of course, she feels not an ounce of embarrassment, but does curse at the loss of a suitcase. She asks to borrow mine and shoves as many of her things inside before carrying the rest in her arms. I refrain from pointing out the logic in packing light.

Our room is a typical hotel room, not much different than the one we stayed at in Galveston, except the color scheme involves dark blue instead of a sea-green. But my stomach drops at the lone bed.

I should have called to switch the room to a double-bed or booked a separate room for myself. I still could. But I can't get my feet to move.

What happened this morning, the situation in which I woke up, cannot happen again. Not only was it awkward, embarrassing, and inappropriate, but the longer I'm here with

Sage, the more my willpower flickers in and out, like the lights in a thunderstorm. One more gust of wind, one more night curled up behind her, holding her like I deserve to, and I'm sure to cave and make her mine.

"What is that smell?" Sage asks, nose turned up as she looks around. "Is there a turd somewhere?"

"I don't smell anything."

"Come over here." She motions for me to walk further into the room and points her fingers. "There is a turd in here somewhere."

"Oh." My own face contorts as the stench hits me. Sage is right, there's got to be human shit somewhere in this room.

Sage lifts the bed skirt and peers underneath, opens the nightstand, the dresser, the closet.

I suggest we go to the front desk instead of searching for it, because even if we find the source of the smell, there's no way we're staying in this room.

We gather our stuff and make our way downstairs. I realize as I'm approaching the desk that the opportunity to ask for that separate room has arrived, but the words don't come as I explain the situation to the lady at the desk.

She apologizes profusely and assigns us to a new room, even insisting on walking us to the door to inspect the room with us and ensure there is no smell.

Our shadows follow us along the floral wallpaper in the hallway. Unlike the hotel in Galveston that had no extra rooms, this one is eerily empty. I expect to hear a TV behind each door that we pass, but there's only silence.

I shake it off as we reach our door, this room exactly like the first, but only mustiness lingers in the air. Satisfied that we're satisfied, the lady leaves, and Sage closes the bathroom door to take a shower.

Then she screams.

Without thinking, I burst inside, not caring if she's indecent, only concerned about her safety. Once inside, I see her danger-ously standing on the side of the tub in her orange "Monday" underwear, and I grab onto her hips so she doesn't fall.

"It's back there!" She lifts her arm, pointing to a huge roach behind the toilet.

"Seriously?" I ask, body relaxing.

"Kill it!"

And that's how we wound up back in the car on our way to a much more expensive hotel. Before making a needless drive across town, I Googled and booked a room, then we stopped by a grocery store for sustenance.

We're climbing back in the car when she squints at some-thing across the street and points out the windshield. "Can you go over to that ice cream place? I'm craving cookies and cream."

"You just bought half the grocery store, including four different chocolate bars."

"I needed options. Now shut up and buy me ice cream."

I raise my brows.

"Pretty please?" she adds, batting her lashes.

"Let me stop and get gas first," I say, turning the key in the ignition.

"Get gas tomorrow. I'm exhausted and just want to eat and go to sleep."

"What if the world is invaded by aliens and we need to make a quick getaway in the middle of the night? But because we didn't get gas now, we have to stop while we're trying to escape, and we end up being attacked at the gas station?"

"If there is an alien invasion, I'll be on my back with my legs open."

My eyes widen, at first in shock. But they remain so while I question her sanity. And my own safety in close proximity to this madwoman.

"Cori's gotten me into reading lately. Turns out, I'm really into alien smut." I wish she hadn't explained further.

Once we arrive at the second hotel of the evening, I pop open the trunk to lug all our crap inside. But with all the grocery bags, we can't carry everything in one trip.

"Okay, now I need you to go check the whole room and make sure there aren't any bugs in this one," Sage says, stopping outside the door to our room.

With a roll of my eyes, I unlock the door and do as instructed.

After setting the grocery haul and suitcase down, I do a quick run-through, making sure to check under the bed and in the closet. No bugs in sight and no weird smell. Poking my head out the door, I let her know it's safe.

She gathers her pajamas and bag of bathroom stuff, but halts when I ask if we're going to get the rest of the stuff from the car.

"Let's just get it tomorrow. I have what I need for tonight."

"Did you leave anything valuable inside? What if it gets broken into?" I ask in my need to prepare for the worst possible scenarios.

She rolls her eyes. "It'll be fine. Quit worrying about everything, *Cori*."

While Sage takes a bath long enough to prune her skin, I fit what I can in the mini fridge and stick the ice cream in the freezer before it melts, then gather my clothes for my own shower. The stream of water, even with the door closed, is too loud, eliciting images of it cascading down Sage's skin. I turn the TV on to drown out the sound, but it's too late. The conjured images latch on despite my fingers digging into my eyes in a useless attempt at blackening my vision, and, like a starved man, my hand inadvertently veers downwards. I grip myself hard enough that it almost hurts, but the pain is still nothing compared to the want I feel for her.

It's not just her body that causes such desire, either. It's the way she impatiently rips into a bag of candy, sending pieces flying all over. It's the way she flings her clothes behind her when searching for something at the bottom of her suitcase. It's the way she barrels into a room, gracefully, yet giving anyone a start at the sudden disruption of peace. That's what she does to me.

While she is chaos, spinning through a room and creating messes wherever she goes, she's not a slob. She always comes back through, putting everything back in its place. But I'm afraid there is no righting my heart after the wreckage she's caused. The mark of her destruction will remain until I take my last breath.

When she's done in the shower, I quickly take her place without glancing at her; I can't run the risk of unravelling at the sight of her wet skin or hair. Until I'm standing in the same shower she was just naked in, and I realize how stupid I am.

I hate myself for doing it, but if I don't take care of the situation now, I might combust later. I take my cock in my hands again, pausing to give myself one more chance to back out. To just take a shower and get this night over with, without masturbating like a creep to the thought of the beauty just on the other side of this wall.

But I lean my forehead against that wall now, eyes closed tight, and my hand starts moving. More images flood my brain, of Sage, slicking her hair back with her hands while she emerges from the stream of water. She licks her lips and opens her eyes, smirking as they connect with mine. I follow a bead of water as it trails down her neck, between her breasts, and disappears into her belly button. Then it's her hand on my dick instead of mine, tugging at the tightness coiled around my insides until I'm releasing the pent-up need all over the shower floor.

After my shower, Sage finds a movie she likes, before grabbing a carrot from the veggie tray and dipping it in her ice cream.

"Ew. What are you doing?"

"Making the carrots taste better," she says, biting into it.

Shaking my head, I turn toward the TV, but remain standing.

"Are you going to stand there all night?"

Reluctantly, I sit, but still at the foot of the bed where I'm safe.

"Oh my God, get over here." Her half-eaten carrot hits me in the back of the head.

So I do, but I stay on top of the covers, snacking and squeezing my eyes shut at the gory parts until I'm shivering and can't stand the cold any longer. Because once again, Sage has turned the AC down to sixty. I shift, pulling the comforter over my legs, and I'm barely situated before Sage leans her head on my shoulder and entwines her leg with mine.

My body stiffens. "Sage."

"What?"

"You know what."

She looks up at me. "It's just cuddling, for fucks sake. It's cold in here."

"Which you have complete control over. We can easily make it warmer. And I know it's just cuddling, but I'm uncomfortable."

She scoffs and throws herself back to her side of the bed. "See? You hate me."

"I don't hate you, I just don't want-" I can't say it.

"You don't want what? Me touching you?" She holds her hands up. "Message received. My touch is gross. I'm disgusting."

"No, I just... I mean, yeah, but..." I can't find the right words to skirt around the reason to explain without explaining. Without risking her feeling insecure about herself in any way.

But she's a bold woman who needs a bold answer. "I don't want to get *hard.*" I whisper that last word as if it might make less of an impact.

The tension is sentient, snaking its way through the air and choking us both. I'd timed the admission perfectly with the movie as the characters move through a house, silently anticipating whatever lurks in the shadows.

"So let me get this straight. You don't want to sleep with me or cuddle with me or touch me because you might get turned on? Not because you find me repulsive?"

I swallow, wishing I could reel the statement back in like a fishing line. "You know that. You felt it yesterday and this morning. You even said earlier that you felt how I wanted you."

"Yeah, but then you rejected me, and I figured you were hard because of basic male anatomy. You know, REM sleep and nervous system crap."

I shrug. "I mean, that might have played a part. But-"

"And, if you're asleep, you could easily dream of holding whatever woman you find attractive. Like *Jasmine.*" She rolls her eyes and sticks her tongue out, as if the name has a bad taste.

"Or, like you."

She stares at me for a moment before one eyebrow lifts and her lips curl.

"Wipe that smug grin off your face," I say.

"No thanks, I'm feeling quite smug at the moment," she replies.

I swallow again, focusing on the TV screen. "I don't know why you're acting surprised. You know, I know, and everyone knows you're beautiful." I pick up the bag of pretzels, offering her one before I stick my hand in the bag. "Now, can we get back to this movie?"

"Okay, but my breasts are waiting for your face if you need

to hide your eyes from the scary monsters." She giggles and shakes her chest.

I let out a sigh, unsure of how to feel. On one hand, my admission will cause her to tease me mercilessly, making it even harder to resist her. On the other, the words spoken aloud brought a lightness to her laugh and mirth to her eyes. How could anyone be upset over that?

I chance a glance at her now, smile still pulling at her lips, until she catches me, and I jerk my gaze back to the TV. Right in time for a demon-horse-thing to jump out behind a tree.

I don't scream. I deserve credit for that. But I do jolt, throwing the bag of pretzels in the air and sending them flying all over the bed. Sage is silent, but her body convulses with laughter.

"Oh my God, you're such a weenie," she says through her gasps for air. "That was probably the tamest part in the entire movie. You're so screwed."

By the time we go to bed, I've covered my eyes three more times with Sage's arm while she laughed at me, and she's made at least ten more jokes about me getting aroused.

After the movie is over, she turns on *Friends* and locks eyes with me as she pulls my arm underneath her head, asking me without words if she can sleep on it. I don't answer, but I don't protest either, and she turns her head away while slipping her fingers between mine. I'm still sitting up against the headboard, not trusting myself to get close to her body. I fall asleep not long after her breathing deepens, holding her hand, and wishing I were a different person.

21

THAT'S EXACTLY WHAT A SERIAL KILLER WOULD SAY

Instead of waking with Callum wrapped around me, like the previous two mornings, I find him hunched over the desk, chin resting on his clasped hands. His eyes intently scan the screen of his laptop.

I know he works for a charity, but I wonder how he got into that line of work. Is that what he planned to do, or did he just apply for a job at random? In fact, the only things I know about Callum are surface-level facts, some of which I only just learned while on this trip. But what makes Callum, *Callum*? I don't know what his dreams are, or what he does in his spare time, or why he's so serious.

Maybe I'll focus more on getting to know him on a deeper level these last three days of our vacation. I may have only brought Callum along because he happened to be there when I needed to leave, but I want this time together to count for something.

I stretch and sit up, muttering, "Good morning."

"Finally," he says, lifting his head.

"What time did you wake up?"

"Around 7:30. It's ten now. You missed breakfast, but we have the stuff from the grocery store." He rises and kneels before the mini fridge, pulling out a fruit cup and yogurt. He brings both to me, along with plasticware and a protein bar.

"You're bringing me breakfast in bed?" I gush. "Five stars again."

"Yeah, yeah. I just want to get a move on." He's already dressed in a light gray t-shirt and black shorts. It takes me a minute to remember what day it is and what we discussed doing yesterday while waiting in traffic.

Friday. Theme park.

I hurry through my breakfast before completing my morning routine and dressing in a white tank top, athletic shorts, and tennis shoes. My hair is in a ponytail to keep it off my shoulders, my sunglasses are propped on top of my head, and I've applied sunscreen to every inch of visible skin. Ready to ride roller coasters and eat junk food like we're kids again, Callum and I head out the door.

It's the perfect day to get to know the less-serious side of Callum, to find out what his laugh sounds like when it's full force and shaking his belly. Or what his sense of humor is like after a carefree day of letting loose. I bet he's scared of the more exciting roller coasters, just like he is of horror films. And I bet he'll limit his junk food intake because he's *mature* or whatever. But hopefully I'll still get a good glimpse of him with his defenses down today.

I can already hear the laughter from children and the thunderous mechanics of the rides. I can taste the corndogs with a zig-zag of mustard, the funnel cake, the cotton candy. And the vomit in my mouth when I get sick from eating so much junk before being flipped around on the Cliffhanger.

It's exactly what I need. After a stressful month of planning a wedding and no sex, then being rejected by Callum time after time this week, I need thrill. I need to scream. I need my stomach in my throat before plummeting back down.

Which is exactly what I get when we walk outside to the empty parking lot. And I mean *empty*. Not a car in sight. Not even mine.

Shielding my eyes from the blaring sun, it takes a moment for the confusion to fade. I gasp, looking around in disbelief. "Eleanor!" But she's nowhere to be seen.

I grasp at my throat where, as I had wished for earlier, my stomach is now trying to climb its way out of. Caught in that moment between disbelief and begging God with my whole body to turn back time, the world stops.

"Are you sure we parked it here?" Callum asks, turning around as if we just overlooked her bright red body.

"We're in an empty lot, Callum. I don't think we misplaced her, obviously she was car-napped!"

Callum runs to look around the side of the building as if she could have moved herself. Not finding her—*because she's not here*—he comes back and says calmly, "Okay, first thing we need to do is call the police."

"First thing we need to do is hunt down whoever took my baby and rearrange their insides!"

"Sure, but how are we going to do that with no car?"

"Ugh!" Rage floods my body, overstimulated by the oppressive heat, the fly currently buzzing around my face, and the cars zooming past us on the highway. I don't often get angry, but when I do, it burns hot and fast. I stomp down from the curb and fall to sit in my defeat and heartbreak.

Why would someone take *my* car? She's nothing fancy, an old, cheap Kia, probably one of the last made that thieves are still able to hot-wire. But she's been so loyal to me—not including this week.

Callum hands me his phone. "Here. Call the police. I'll

head inside and see if they have cameras that would have caught it."

So I do. A man, with a bored voice, answers the phone. I give him the VIN and license plate numbers, make, model, color, and where it was last parked. He asks whether the vehicle has a tracking device installed just as Callum steps back outside.

"No, there's no tracking. It's just a cheap car. But it's my baby, so please do everything you can to find her."

I listen to his lack of emotion on the other end of the call, assuring me without assuring anything that they'll *do what they can*.

It's not just Eleanor, either. It's all the stuff that was in the trunk and backseat. When we came to the new hotel, we couldn't carry everything in one trip, and I didn't want to go *all* the way back downstairs to fetch the rest. My favorite purple dress with a slit on the left side. My favorite black pumps. Thank God I took Ben inside, even though I've ditched him for Callum.

But it gets worse; my purse. Callum told me not to leave anything valuable inside just in case it was broken into. Just like he told me to reconsider the wedding.

Why don't I listen to him? Clearly, he knows better than I do. I mean, I flunked out of college! Why in the hell would I ever trust my own instincts when I constantly fuck everything up?

But wait. My purse is inside that car.

"Oh my God, Callum!" I slap his arm in excitement. "There's an AirTag in my purse! I completely forgot. Thank you, Cori!" As fast as I can, I open the app on my phone to track it.

"What does Cori have to do with this?" he asks.

"She put the AirTag in my purse, assuming I'd lose it or something. She has absolutely no faith in me."

I show Callum the screen and the little dot, just a few miles away from our current location.

"Assuming they didn't discard the purse or sell it by now," he says grumpily.

"It's hidden underneath the passenger seat. Let's hope they haven't seen it yet." Regardless, I need everything inside the purse, so I'll be chasing down this dot, whether it's Eleanor or just the purse that I find once I reach it.

Callum suggests ordering a ride to a car rental place, but I don't have time to wait or sit through a bunch of paperwork. I need to get on the road now. Of course, Mom chooses this moment to call again, but I don't have time for this conversation, even if I wanted to answer.

"Not now, Mom. Eleanor was carnapped!" I yell into the phone before ending the call. Then, I run to the gas station beside the hotel, shouting out to anyone within hearing distance.

"Can someone give us a ride? My car was stolen, and I need to chase it down!"

Callum comes up beside me, calling my name. "You can't just ask a stranger for a ride!"

Ignoring him, I glance around at the few people who had stopped to listen, but most shake their heads and get inside their cars. But one man, maybe a few years older than me, dressed in Bermuda shorts and a t-shirt, gestures to his jeep. "I'll take you, hop in."

I claim the passenger seat, thanking him profusely, and Callum follows, climbing in the back seat and cursing under his breath.

"Where do we need to go?" The man asks. He has blond hair and bright blue eyes, and would totally surf if we lived anywhere near a shore.

I turn my phone so he can see the dot on the screen.

"There's a tracker in my car. They're headed NE on I-35." I have faith that we'll catch up. Surely, they'll have to stop somewhere without getting too far away from San Antonio.

"Got it," he says, reversing out of the parking spot. "My name is Grant, by the way."

"You better not be kidnapping us, Grant," Callum says, glaring at him through the rearview mirror. "Because I'm texting everyone I know that we're in your Black Jeep Wrangler, license plate JTY-8938."

"Be nice," I growl. "He's doing us a huge favor."

"I won't harm you, promise." He raises his pinky finger, and I wrap my own around it. Any man who makes pinky promises must be trustworthy, right? "I don't have much on the to-do list for today, so when you asked, I figured, why not have some adventure?"

"I like the way you think, Grant."

While he races down the highway toward my baby, Callum questions the man, as if we're in an interrogation room. I'm the good cop in this scenario, obviously. I don't take my eyes from the dot while we learn that Grant's last name is Peters, he's an oncology nurse, has lived in San Antonio his whole life, and is a father to a six-year-old daughter.

"Grant Peters, nurse at Methodist Hospital. Got it," Callum repeats while typing on his phone. He snaps a photo of Grant, for which he smiles, unaffected by the paranoia.

"I'm sorry about him. He worries about stuff," I say, gesturing toward the backseat.

"It's no problem. You can't be too careful these days," Grant replies.

A text appears at the top of my screen.

CALLUM

That's exactly what a serial killer would say.

> **ME**
> How would you know?

> **CALLUM**
> Why didn't your parents teach you about stranger danger?

> **ME**
> They tried.

"So, you're a nurse? That's amazing. You're like a real-life superhero," I say, mainly to take my mind off Eleanor, partly to make small talk and fill the awkward silence. But also because it's true, especially now that he's helping us rescue my car.

Grant chuckles. "Thanks."

Callum scoffs from the backseat

> **CALLUM**
> Now is not the time for flirting!!

I turn in my seat to gape at him. At what point was I flirting? *Unbelievable.*

Instead of stewing in my annoyance, I decide to use it. I lean my elbow on the center console and rest my chin in my hand.

"So, are you married, Grant Peters?"

He looks over at me, eyebrow quirked, and grins. "No, I'm not. Are you and... actually, I don't think I got your names. But are you and *he* not together?"

"I'm Sage, but no. Callum is just a friend. And it will stay that way because he doesn't want to risk catching feelings for me. So I'm completely available to flirt with whoever I wish."

"She just ran out on a wedding last Sunday," Callum says, looking out the window, unbothered by my retaliation.

Grant coughs and shifts in his seat. Rolling my eyes, I flop back into my own and watch the dot in silence.

"This is kinda fun, though, isn't it?" I ask after a while, smiling.

"Having your car stolen is *fun?*" Callum asks.

"Like my new friend, Grant, just said, we're on an adventure. A quest, if you will, to find my missing baby. Hunting down bad guys to rescue Eleanor. Hide and seek, but with a thief." My heart pounds with the thrill of the chase. As long as things don't end tragically, I'm a big fan of drama.

"You truly are amazing," he says with a bite in his tone.

My smile slips from my face as I wonder what the hell that is supposed to mean. Partly to save face and partly because my good mood is standing on rotten wood, I snap back, "I know I am, and don't forget it."

Callum glances over at me, softening his face. "I just mean that I admire your ability to see the *adventure* in such a shitty day."

As he should. Clearly, he could use some lessons on looking on the bright side of things.

"It's only shitty right now. Once we get Eleanor and my stuff back, we can resume our vacation. Maybe we can still go to the theme park today. Or hang out with Grant?"

Grant looks sideways at me. "Uhh, I'm probably just gonna go home after this."

Suddenly, the dot exits the highway. I sit up straight, heart thumping with excitement.

"They're going somewhere!" I watch as they pull into the parking lot of some building behind a BBQ place. Zooming into the map, I grin and slowly turn to face Callum. "Remember how I insisted last night that we wait until morning to get gas?"

"Yeah..."

"If we had gotten gas last night, like you insisted, they wouldn't be pulling into a gas station right now."

I watch with bated breath as we drive closer and closer to the stagnant dot on the map indicating Eleanor's location. Everyone doubts me and my intelligence and second-guesses my decisions, including me, as proven this morning. But so far, the choices Callum didn't agree with last night have worked out in my favor. Eleanor would have been taken whether I had left my purse inside or not, whether she needed gas or not. But because of both choices, we're getting closer to rescuing her.

Maybe I do know what the hell I'm doing after all.

22

HONESTLY? I JUST WANTED TO SEE YOU NAKED

"You know, they could have found the purse and ditched it. Or sold it. Or gone through it and thrown out the AirTag," I explain.

She frowns. "Can you quit ruining this for me? Why are you so negative? You just can't accept the fact that I was right, can you? Can't accept that I might actually be smart after all?"

My shoulders deflate. Why can't I explain anything correctly to her? "What? Not at all. I just don't want to get your hopes up and then have them crushed when we get there and don't find your car."

"*If.*"

"What?"

"*If* we get there and don't find her. You said *when.*"

Running a hand down my face, I sigh. "Sorry. *If.* Just be prepared for all the possibilities, okay?" I want to say more, like how I hate it when she's upset, or how I'd do just about anything right now to get her car back for her, just to prevent that bright smile from slipping from her face. But I don't.

"Well, I'm choosing to be positive. She's still at that store waiting for me. I can feel it."

I also refrain from saying it's just a car, because if Sage thinks she's feeling some emotional connection to a hunk of metal and oil, I'll let her have this moment.

When Grant pulls into the parking lot of the gas station, we can't miss Eleanor's—I mean the *car's*—red body parked halfway between two parking spots around the side of the building. Her—I mean *its*. What is wrong with me? *Its* door is wide open as if she'd been forgotten about. *It*. As if *it* had been forgotten about. I shake my head, trying to knock the pieces back in place. It's just a car.

As soon as we're parked, Sage throws open the door and rushes over, checking her car over for damages while I call the police station back to let them know we found it and find out what the next step is, if any. I'm told we need to wait here for an officer, so I relay the message to Sage, who is checking the trunk for all of her stuff.

Miraculously, everything is still there, including her purse underneath the passenger seat.

"Well, I'm gonna head home. Glad you got your car back," Grant says, backing away slowly from this shit show.

Sage throws her arms around his neck. "Thank you so much for helping us and not driving us off to some secluded cabin where no one could hear our screams," she says into his chest.

He pats her awkwardly on the back. "Uhh, sure. No problem."

After a police officer arrives to take note of any damages, or lack of, and to speak with the cashier about camera footage—which there is none on this side of the store—we're free from this nightmare of a morning.

Earlier, Sage called this an adventure. Every day is an adventure with her. One minute, you're driving along a peaceful road, the next, you're flying down a side street that's not marked on the map. And with a snap of her fingers, you're back on the road as planned, as if nothing had happened at all.

After the adrenaline calms from coursing through my veins, my stomach growls. I suggest grabbing some BBQ from the restaurant in front of the gas station until Sage lists all the food she'd rather fill her belly with at the theme park.

"After everything that has happened, you're not ready to leave yet?"

"Leave my honeymoon early? No! We still have so much to do. We still haven't seen the interactive art show, there's a popular bar with live music I wanted to go to, and a romantic dinner on the river walk."

I clear my throat. "Oh. So, bad news about the interactive art show. I couldn't find another show before we leave that wasn't already sold out." I checked while I was waiting for her to wake up this morning.

Her shoulders deflate. But they perk back up when she says, "Oh well. That just means I'll have to take another vacation soon to come back and see it."

"Sure. But do you really think the two of us should be having a romantic dinner?"

"Yes! I've been looking forward to that almost as much as the art show. Come on. We'll go to the theme park for the rest of today, have tons of fun, and just forget this morning. You'll see."

I'd rather just go back to the hotel room at least, maybe take a nap after all the excitement today.

As a child, I loved the behemoth roller coasters that drop you when you're least expecting it, or jerk you around until you puke. But I grew out of craving the buzz in my blood, wanting smooth and expected instead. I no longer enjoy the sound of my heart pumping with adrenaline, nearly beating itself to death.

Because I wish it had that day ten years ago.

WHEN WE WALKED OUT TO THE PARKING LOT OF THE HOTEL THIS morning, there was an eerie feeling as I looked out at the empty lot. Something wasn't quite right, but it didn't hit me right away as to what was awry. After pulling into the parking lot of the theme park, I get the same feeling; there's not a single car in sight.

"Where is everyone?" Sage asks, face twisted in confusion.

I spot a piece of paper taped to the gate, and after throwing the car in park, I run out to read it.

Closed for remodeling: 08-10 to 09-21.

Sighing, I rub my face, thinking of how I'm going to tell Sage. But I guess this is tiny compared to what she went through this morning, and not even that broke her spirit. So I man up, get back in the car, and break the news.

At first, she doesn't answer, staring out the windshield. But then, "You're right. We should just go back home." Her voice is soft and defeated.

If she had said those words earlier, I'd have packed my bags as fast as I could and jumped in the car without hesitation. But a dejected Sage is unnerving, not to mention heartbreaking. There's no way I can allow her to be so upset, not after all the work she's done at staying positive.

In the past—in fact, several times just this week—I've rebuked her for her disregard when it comes to negative emotions. But the theme park being closed is no reason to let your entire day, or vacation, be ruined. Such a minuscule problem can't be the thing that breaks her.

So I pull onto the highway without a word, acting like I'm doing what she suggested. Only when we get to the hotel room, I wait until she's looking at me before peeling my shirt off. Her eyebrow quirks upward, but she remains silent, watching. Next, I take my shoes off and kick them under the bed. I slide my shorts down, followed by my underwear, and I lie on my side, head propped up by my hand on the bed.

Sage's mouth hangs open as her eyes trail down my body, lingering on my dick.

"Draw me like one of your French girls."

She squeals with excitement, fists balled up and shaking in the air. The reaction I was hoping for.

I can breathe again now that there's light back in her eyes, life back in her voice. I'll probably wish I could have done something different to bring her joy later on, but for now, I bask in her warmth.

She rushes to grab her sketchbook and settles herself in the desk chair, now swiveled around to face the bed. But when she holds her phone, I snatch a pillow and cover myself.

"No pictures."

Her hands fall as her lips form a pout. "But-"

"No buts. I don't care how long I have to lie here. No pictures. And could you leave my face out of this, please?"

She smirks. "Fine. But I'm hanging it in my bedroom." Shoulders deflating once again, she adds, "Whenever I find a bedroom. Hey, why don't we both find an apartment we can rent together?"

"Sage," I groan.

"Not like that. We can find one with two bedrooms."

"Still not a good idea. Besides, who would take Mrs. Browning to church? Or take breakfast to Logan and Ari on the weekends?"

"Who? And who?" she asks, before sticking her tongue out in concentration.

As she draws, I give her a quick rundown of the reasons I can't leave my apartment and the neighbors who rely on me.

She looks up, lowering her pencil to her lap. "Oh, right. The reason your truck smells weird."

"Yep."

She holds my gaze for an intense moment before resuming her drawing. "Have you ever been a bad guy in your life? Ever been selfish, or done the wrong thing just because?"

I swallow. Hard. There are two options here. I could lie, doing the very thing she's asking me about. Or I could tell the truth, spurring questions about what I've done in my past that was so bad.

"Yes," I answer simply, despite it taking every ounce of strength to do so.

"Really?" She scoffs in disbelief. "Did you wear dirty under-wear or something? Put a plastic water bottle in the trash instead of the recycling bin? Leave your shopping buggy outside the cart return?"

I shake my head.

"Come on. Tell me. I'll tell you a secret if you tell me one."

"Maybe when I'm not naked and vulnerable," I reply, gesturing to my body. "Why do you want to draw me naked so badly anyway?" I know she's an artist, but I didn't think she was into nude art.

She smirks again, and it makes me nervous. "Honestly? I just wanted to see you naked."

I should have known.

"But also, because the human body is art. And like I told you, I need to reference shadows and contours of a male form. It's easier drawing from reference than it is from my bare imag-ination."

"I can testify that your imagination is not bare," I say. "You could sell your art, you know. Not just graphic designs, but whole paintings on canvas. Not this,"—I gesture to my body —"but maybe something from that vast imagination of yours."

"Yeah, I want to, but... I don't know." I'm not sure what I said that was wrong, but a crease forms on her forehead. And I'll do anything to smooth it.

"Why don't you?" I ask, gently coaxing the answer from her downturned lips.

The only answer she gives, though, is a shrug of her shoulders.

A truth for a truth. No matter how exposed I am physically, I'll peel off every layer of skin until she sees as much of my soul as she needs to feel comfortable confiding in me.

Here goes nothing.

"When I was fifteen, there was this kid I went to school with. His hair was always so greasy and speckled with dandruff. His clothes were dirty and torn, and he had holes in his shoes so big you could see his toes. The teachers kept having to offer him clothes from this closet they had in case any kids needed anything." She watches me, but I can't look directly at her while I spill these secrets.

"He was two years ahead of me, and a few other football players, who were on the varsity football team, made fun of him constantly. I didn't want to participate at first, but eventually it was expected of me if I wanted to impress my teammates. So I did. And that's why I am the way I am now. Helping out everyone I can, working for a charity. Because of guilt."

It's not the whole truth, but all she needs to know.

Her eyes narrow. "Bullies don't typically feel guilt. The ones that made fun of Cori and Hailey never did, until I beat it out of them. Even then, they only felt guilty that they were weak." She looks back down at her sketch, shading an area intently.

I think back to the first night in Galveston, when we were eating dinner on the deck of the seafood restaurant. *This bitch wouldn't keep her mouth shut.*

"That's why you were suspended from school. For standing up for them," I say, realization dawning.

"Anytime I got caught fighting, it was in defense of Cori and Hailey. But everyone, including Mom and Dad, assumed I got into fights about boys or something stupid. I just never corrected them."

"Why not?"

"What's the point? They can think what they want to about me. It's a waste of my energy to try and change everyone's minds. If they want to think I'm frivolous and impulsive, let them."

Neither of us says anything for a long while, our minds spinning with our admissions.

I find myself desperate to reach for my phone. To see if there have been any updates on Jake's social accounts in the last 2 days since I last checked. Maybe one day I'll gain the strength to starve the curiosity out of existence instead of feeding it by stalking a memory. Then again, I don't deserve to live without the hunger.

23

AS SERIOUS AS A HEART ATTACK

Callum glances down at his naked body and shifts uncomfortably, as if he's only just remembering how bare he is to me in this moment. Emotionally and physically, he's as exposed as he possibly could be.

He's an attractive man, I've always thought so. And sure, maybe part of me just wanted to see him naked. But I'm an artist too, and the human body is art. It's a painting itself of the person who inhabits it, by the permanent crease between his brows that depicts the turmoil within. Or the hunch of his shoulders, even the small scar below his bottom lip that he got in a four-wheeling accident.

I've always loathed him for being so mature, never making mistakes. Now I know he has, in fact, made a few that he had to learn from to become the man he is today.

I give up the drawing for now since he's uncomfortable, putting my sketch pad and pencil away and throwing Callum his clothes. Not that it matters much now, I give him his privacy while he dresses, and make us sandwiches for lunch. Once I'm finished, I join him on the bed and hand him his plate. He doesn't eat, though, only pulling at shreds of lettuce that poke out from beneath the bread.

"I'm afraid of failing." My voice is barely a whisper, but there's fear in admitting the fear out loud. He wants to know why I don't sell my own paintings. There's the answer.

He waits for me to elaborate, but I'm not really sure how to explain it.

"I took some art classes last year. While I've always been pretty good on my own, I wanted to refine my talent and actually learn what I'm doing. But what if, after taking those classes and learning everything I have, I still can't use it to earn a living?"

"Don't you already? With the coffee designs?"

I roll my eyes. "Yes, but I want to sell my art *because* of my art. Not because the cute coffee bean I drew and ironed on a coffee mug would make a good gift for some kid's teacher. I want my art hanging in someone's dining room and admired daily, not on a dish towel stored away in a drawer and waiting to dry dishes."

I let out a sigh, shifting my legs and curling them beneath me.

"When Cori asked me last year to partner up for her coffee business, I jumped at it because I wasn't doing so great on my own. I had quit the diner and was attending craft shows to sell my artwork. But I wasn't drawing in many customers. People would just walk right by my table, filled with all sorts of things. I think maybe they were overwhelmed by the variety, and that I should have had a specific niche. The other vendors in attendance had a single topic that would draw people in, like clothing at one booth, or salsa at another. My booth had abstract acrylic paintings, tote bags with graphics, tie-dyed crap, even candles.

"So when Cori suggested partnering up to sell coffee-related designs along with her bags of coffee, it gave me an area to stick with. Something for customers to recognize when they glanced at my table." Something for a shopper to say, *'You know what? I'm almost out of coffee at home, let me stop by here real quick.'* Or, *'Crap! I forgot to get a gift for Administrative Assistant Day. But a bag of fancy coffee and a mug will do.'*

He listens intently, stroking the back of my hand. While I wait for him to respond, the hum from the AC comforts me through the awkward silence.

"You want everyone to think you know what you're doing, or what you want, but you don't," he says. "It's why you're so positive all the time. Because admitting that you're sad about something not working out is admitting that you were wrong. Admitting that you *don't* know what you want out of life. Am I right?"

He seems to know me better than I know myself because that's exactly how I feel. Hell, Hailey even said the very words he just did, but I ignored her.

"It's okay." At first, I assume he's trying to coax away the tears that glide down my cheeks. But then he says, "Not knowing, I mean. It's okay. It's also okay that you're spontaneous and act on feelings in the moment. I wouldn't change that about you if someone had a gun to my head."

"But...why?" He tried to talk me out of the engagement, even tying the trash bag too tight in his frustration with me. He huffed and puffed the whole drive to his apartment when I ran away. He rolled his eyes and ran his hands through his hair, just like he's doing now, anytime I mentioned being perfectly fine after ending my relationship.

I don't know why that one line bothers me so badly, but it does.

"If you wouldn't change those things about me, why do you act as if I'm the most annoying person ever?" I sit up on my knees, adrenaline pulsing through my body. "You've always treated me as if you're so much better than me, so much smarter and more *put-together*. Admit it, you can't stand me. I was hoping that would change on this trip, and maybe it has a little, but don't sit there and pretend like you wouldn't change me into this perfect, polished woman who sits down and shuts up and does what she's told."

He closes his eyes for a moment before hanging his head. "I would never change you. I told you at dinner on Tuesday that I thought you-"

"*Overwhelming* is the word you used."

"Yes, but not-" he sighs. "After everything I just confided in you, don't you get it?"

"No, I'm stupid, remember?"

He shakes his head, breath sawing in and out like he can't catch it. "Don't put words in my mouth. I've never thought you were stupid. It's just-" He's cut off by his phone, ringing insistently.

Glancing at the screen, we see Nick's name, but he declines the call.

"I'll call him back later." But the phone starts ringing again before he has a chance to set it down.

Nick again. After he gives me a look full of alarm, he brings the phone to his ear. I move so my ear is against the back of it, but Callum brings the phone back down and puts it on speaker.

"Hey, what's wrong?" Callum answers.

"Where is Sage's phone? Cori and I have been trying to call her. Their mom had a heart attack."

"Sage, we have to leave."

"No, we don't." I move under the covers and cross my arms to further prove my point that I'm not leaving.

"Your mom had a heart attack. Do you know how serious that is?"

"As serious as a heart attack?" I joke.

His eyes widen in shock.

"But you don't know my mother like I do." She loves being the center of attention and plays the victim any chance she gets. "I didn't answer her calls all week, so she's trying to force my hand. I bet you a thousand bucks she's at home on her couch, bored."

"Are you kidding me? This vacation has been the worst anyway, let's just go home and see your mom." He starts gathering the few things he unpacked, like his laptop and the clothes that he wore yesterday.

Is it really only my 'glass half-full' personality that's allowed me to enjoy this trip? Because, unlike Mr. sees-room-for-improvement-wherever-he-goes, I have enjoyed every second— mostly. Even with his surly ass as my traveling companion. And there's so much more I was still looking forward to. "I didn't get to have the romantic dinner on the river walk. I didn't even have sex. Who suffers through a honeymoon without having sex?"

"People who aren't actually on a honeymoon," he mutters, shoving his dirty clothes into a plastic bag to keep them separate from his clean clothes. "And you can always come back at a different time to do all that other stuff."

I already planned to anyway. "Will you come back with me?" I don't know why I even ask. If I make a plan to come back, I should do so when Danielle, or even a group of my shallow friends, can come with me.

"That's not a good idea." Of course. That's probably why he's so eager to leave now. We may have had a tender moment earlier, but he can only handle so much of me.

When I still don't get up, he packs my things up as well, before disappearing into the bathroom to collect all of my skin-care and make-up products.

Once he's through packing, he stands by the door staring at me. But I don't move.

"Well, I'm leaving. And I'm taking your car."

"Fine. Bye." I don't know why he thought that would work on me.

"Sage, if I have to throw you over my shoulder and stuff you in the trunk, you're coming." Still, I refuse to budge. He drags his hand down his face. "Fine. I'll come back with you. I'll take you to the art show, and we can have dinner on the river walk. Although it's really not that romantic. It's overcrowded and kinda smells-"

His phone rings again. He pulls it from his pocket and points the screen at me after checking the name. Cori.

I hold out my hand, but Callum shakes his head, using this moment to challenge me once more. So I raise my eyebrows, crossing my arms, and grin in triumph when he stalks toward me, rolling his eyes.

"Cor?" I answer.

"Are you on your way yet? How far away are you? What time does the GPS say you'll get here?"

The panic in her voice has me rising from the bed, although reluctantly. "We haven't left yet."

"Please hurry."

I slip my shoes on and grab some of the bags piled by the door. While I wait for Callum to check out at the reception desk, Cori fills me in. Mom felt pressure in her chest and was lightheaded. She insisted she simply needed to lie down, but Dad called for an ambulance when she started struggling for air.

After assuring Cori that we're on our way and will get to the hospital as soon as possible, I end the call. On the bright side, if there is such a thing in a situation like this, they didn't wait to call, and Mom was conscious when the paramedics got to her house.

Of course, I want Mom to be okay. I just don't want to leave my trip early to go sit in a waiting room while Cori scratches at her wrists, or Stephanie demands an update from the nurses every minute, with the beeps from my little brother's game devices or the sighs from Dad.

I'm the positive one. The one who has to make sure no one else has an aneurysm. The *sage* to ward off the negative energy. The one who has to distract them all from their worry, while they tell me to grow up and have some class. I can hear Stephanie now. *'Will you stop clowning around? Mom just had a heart attack.'*

But what if this was my fault? If I had answered just one of her phone calls this week, could I have prevented this?

THE SUN BEGINS ITS DESCENT AS WE PULL INTO A PARKING SPOT AT the hospital. After driving straight here, I wish we had taken a few stops to delay this, but now that we're here and there's nowhere left to go but inside.

Callum turns off the ignition and asks, "I'd like to come inside with you, but do you think that would be weird? Since I'm not family?"

"You don't have a choice. You're coming inside whether you want to or not." I'm not sure why. You'd think I'd have grown tired of him by now, but the thought of him leaving me is not one I want to entertain.

He nods. "Alrighty then."

We make a stop at the gift shop. I'm sure everyone else has already bought her flowers, but I buy her the largest heart-shaped balloon I can find and a card with hearts all over it.

To no one's surprise, I find the exact scene I pictured when we reach my family in the waiting room outside the CCU. Stephanie stands at the desk, pestering the nurses for an update. Cori stares at a spot on the floor, bouncing her knee. Dad and Nick talk about Nick's schooling. And Spencer and Solomon are slouched in chairs, playing video games.

"The party has arrived," I announce, raising my hands in the air.

Cori jumps up, squeezing her arms around my middle. "Thank God."

Nick takes a relieved breath when his eyes lock with Callum's, and he stands to clap him on the shoulder.

"They're still running tests, but she's stable. They said they'd let us back there two at a time in a little while," Cori relays. We sit just as Stephanie comes over.

"Finally. Where the hell were you?"

"On my honeymoon?"

"If you didn't get married, you can't call it a honeymoon."

"Either way, I'm sorry you had to leave early. How was it?" Cori asks.

How do I describe these past few days? When so much, and yet nothing, happened? I give her a vague description of the better parts: the ghost tour, shopping, and the beach. I pull up photos to show them.

Then Callum speaks up from where he leans against the wall. "We also had to sleep in her car the first night, had a flat tire, got stuck at the hotel with a dead car battery during a storm, got stuck in traffic and missed the art show, had to switch hotels in San Antonio, Sage's car was stolen, and the theme park was closed for maintenance."

Everyone gapes at me.

"Why do you insist on focusing on the negatives?" I ask Callum.

His face falls, and he looks away, almost as if he didn't realize that's what he's doing. What he's done this whole trip. What he's done since I met him. "Sorry, I just wanted everyone to know the whole story, not just the pretty parts."

"Sorry, I don't think my woes need to be told to everyone. Not everyone enjoys throwing themselves a pity party." I'm not my mother, who wants everyone to know how miserable she is all the time. I'm not Cori, who used to marinate in her own misery before she finally acknowledged she needed a professional to talk to. And I'm definitely not Callum, who seems to be Cori in male form without the jittery anxiety.

Now the air is thick with awkward tension as Cori scratches at her wrists again and Nick calms her by holding her hand, and Dad and Stephanie shift in their seats. My brothers both shamelessly bounce their eyes at the stare-down between Callum and me, probably wishing they had popcorn.

But he shakes his head and looks away again, giving up.

To avoid the choking silence, I stand and pull on Cori's hands. "Come on, Cor. Dance with me." She hates dancing, especially in front of people. But if her mind is freaking out about people watching her, it won't have the room to worry about Mom's health issues. We could all use the distraction.

But she resists, eyes widening and shooting around the room.

"Stephanie?" I try.

"We're in a hospital waiting room. Could you act like a grown-up for once?" she replies.

I sit back down in my seat with a sigh and get out a pen to sign Mom's card with.

"Oh, good. You got her a card. I didn't think of it when I got here, I was just worried about getting to Mom."

Right. Ms. Perfect Stephanie was only worried about Mom, as a daughter should be. And I'm somehow the bad guy because I stopped at the gift shop.

"Sage!" Stephanie says, Mom-voice activated after I hand her the card. "That is entirely inappropriate."

"Are you kidding? That's hilarious." Inside the card, I wrote, *When they said 'follow your heart,' they didn't mean to the ER.* I repeat the joke out loud and laugh, while Stephanie and Dad glare at me.

Callum and Nick chuckle, but Stephanie throws the pen down. "I'm not signing my name to that."

"Fine." I pick up the card and pen and storm off, leaving them all soaking in their worry.

24

JUST HUG ME GOODBYE AND START PLANNING THE BABY SHOWER

After a stroll to the car to retrieve my sketch pad, I head to the cafeteria to work on some of the sketches I started this week. I'm refining areas of Callum's abdominal muscles when I sense his presence before I see him. Maybe it's his woodsy-vanilla scent, maybe it's the feeling of someone watching me. Perhaps it's chemical since I've spent almost every minute of the past few days in his presence. Like our bodies aren't quite right without the other right beside us.

Ugh! What is wrong with me that I feel the need to romanticize everything?

I look up at him now, standing in the doorway, thick arms across his wide chest. A crease in his forehead, like he's disappointed in the way I stormed out of the waiting room.

I roll my eyes, returning my focus to my sketch. But he approaches and pulls out a chair.

He watches me for a little while before quietly saying, "I don't really view it as self-pity, so I'm sorry if it comes out that way."

My eyes narrow and snap to his. "Then what do you call it?"

"I don't know, only talking about the good stuff feels like I'm bragging. Like everything is perfect in my life."

"Isn't it?"

"No."

Just because someone has it worse doesn't mean your own shitty feelings are invalid. But shouldn't we try to see the good in our lives and enjoy it before it's gone?

"You have a good job, a place to live, and you come from a good family. What is so wrong with your life?" I've always known he sees room for improvement everywhere he looks. Like Sam, Cori's ex. Nothing was good enough for him. That's what I loved about Brian, he's so similar to me in that he spends ninety percent of his day smiling and laughing. Crying makes him uncomfortable, leaving no room for sadness in our relationship.

Callum looks down at his hands, clasped on the table, knuckles white. "There's just some stuff. And I'm not complaining, I don't want anything to change."

"Talk to me about it. I can be a good friend if you let me in."

"Maybe I will someday. But right now, they're finally allowing visitors to go back and see your mom. Spencer and Solomon went back first."

On the walk back to the waiting room, Callum fills me in on what the doctor said. It was a minor heart attack, officially called an aborted myocardial... infraction? Infarction? I don't know, but had they not called 911 right away, it would have been worse. When we get back, Spencer and Solomon are already back in their seats. Dad's asked to go alone after me, so when Cori and Stephanie return, both teary-eyed for whatever reason, I head back to the room they tell me is assigned to Mom.

I stop before I get to the doorway and watch her through the window. They said she had to lie flat for a few hours, but she's propped up with pillows now. Emotion almost takes me at the sight of our matriarch, dressed in the thin, scratchy gown that matches every other patient. But I force my thoughts to move on to something else. Like another heart attack joke, or the fun I had this week. Because, regardless of Callum's pessimism and all the unfortunate incidents, I did have a lot of fun.

Mom picks up her phone from where it lies on the table and types, probably a social media post letting the world know her drama. Mom once posted asking for "Unspoken prayer requests" for herself because her sister's husband, who lives in another state, was sick with the flu. Another time, she was on the phone for four hours, telling anyone who answered her call about the bee sting on her finger. I know it's just how she processes unpleasantness, by talking about them, but she takes it a bit too far.

Once she's done, I enter the room. "Hey, Mom."

She smiles weakly, her eyes tired. "Finally. My Sage."

"How are you feeling?" I ask, tucking her blonde hair behind her ear.

"Like I had a heart attack," she chuckles, but winces. "You didn't have to come, you know. They said I came early, so it wasn't so bad."

"I almost didn't. Callum threatened to stuff me in the trunk, then Cori called, panicking."

A smile graces lips. "I like him." I don't know if she means generally, or for me. I almost scoff and make a smart ass remark.

Sure, he accompanied me on a last-minute trip and paid for half of it, but he clearly feels nothing but disdain for me. Then again, he did pose naked for me, simply to cheer me up. And he drove me around in my own car without too many complaints.

I grip my head in pain from all the conflicting, confusing emotions bouncing around up there.

"He's mildly irritating at times, but he's a good guy." I pull up the chair and take a seat.

"I called you. A few times."

"Yeah, well, I didn't want to hear a lecture about *acting rashly* or that *you were right* or *how much daddy spent on the food.*"

"We froze most of it, and he's delighted he didn't end up having to share it with anyone. But more so because you didn't lock yourself in a marriage you didn't really want to be in."

When I don't say anything, she sighs heavily through the weight of helpless desperation.

"I just wanted to know that you were okay. Sage, you're my baby girl. I love you more than anything in this world." Her eyes fill with tears. "You're supposed to come to your mother when your heart hurts, for whatever reason. But you and Cori both avoid me. And that makes me sad. Not for me, but for you. Because you should have a mother whom you want to curl up next to when you're hurting. But you don't."

"I could if you'd just let us live. Even if you think we're making a mistake, let us. If I want to marry Brian tomorrow, just put the dress back on that you wore to our first wedding. If I want to move to Europe, just buy a plane ticket to visit. If I want to walk out that door right now and head to a sperm bank, just hug me goodbye and start planning the baby shower."

Her eyes widen, and her mouth drops open. I don't think she breathes for a moment. The machine beeps alarmingly, so I rush to reassure her.

"I won't actually do that. I'm just saying."

She shakes her head, taking a deep, calming breath.

"So, have you got any sympathy comments on your post yet?"

"I'm not putting this online. No one needs to know I had a heart attack, so don't you dare tell anyone." She points a stern finger at me.

"Wow. Why not?"

"Because I don't want Cheryl from down the street telling me she told me so about cutting out red meat. And I don't want people thinking I'm getting old. I'm not. I only made a post asking for unspoken prayer requests, so nobody asks for details."

I roll my eyes.

"Is that for me?" Mom asks, nodding to the balloon and card.

"No, it's for me," I answer sarcastically, handing it to her. Suddenly, my palms are clammy. I didn't think twice about writing the joke, but everyone's reactions now have me questioning myself. This is Mom after all. Maybe I should be in here speaking soft words of love and shedding tears like my sisters instead of... well, being myself.

I hold my breath while she reads the card. "Sage Marie," she says, eyes rising to meet mine. But her lips tip up into a grin before relief loosens my shoulders and laughter overcomes us both. Once again, I've uncharacteristically doubted my own judgment for no reason.

Mom winces again, bringing our moment to a screeching halt, and a nurse steps in, shooting me a glare before asking Mom if she needs more pain management. Mom nods, and I take that as my cue to leave and let Dad see her again.

MY SHOULDERS DEFLATE AT THE SCENT OF MELTED CHOCOLATE when we get back to Eleanor. I had forgotten about the chocolate bars I bought yesterday at the grocery store in the back seat. Fortunately, the chocolate that oozed out of the wrapper stayed inside the grocery bag without staining the leather. *Un*fortunately, I have no comforting treat to make me feel better about today.

And what a shit day it was. I'm tired. I hate being in a bad mood, but especially when I have no chocolate to make it better. Letting my forehead fall against the window, I wait for Callum to turn the key and get the air flowing. Despite the night sky, the air is still thick and humid, and my legs stick to the seat.

"Where to now?"

Good question. I could go back to Callum's and stay, or drop him off and go somewhere else. My brothers will be home alone, so it will be quiet there. I could make the drive to the farmhouse to stay with Cori and Nick.

But who says the vacation is over just because we had to come home? We've already visited two major tourist places in Texas, and we live in the suburbs of Houston. Why not take these last two days and do tourist-y things in a city we should know better than we do?

"Your apartment," I state firmly. "This honeymoon isn't over."

Confusion settles over his face, so I tell him of all the things we could do. A picnic at the Water Wall, dinner at the aquarium, the Space Center, a comedy or magic show.

"Hell, we may have to extend our vacation just to fit everything in!"

Am I stalling so I don't have to face my life without Brian, my homelessness, or those fears I keep ignoring? Possibly. But I think I deserve more of a break after the events of today.

"Sage-"

My hand flies up. "Don't. Don't tell me it's a bad idea. You keep saying that, and I don't really know why, but I need this. And I don't want to force you, so if you truly don't want to continue our trip, then we won't. But give me an actual reason that isn't, 'it's a bad idea.'"

He looks into my eyes while he thinks, then nods and says, "Okay. We can continue the vacation."

"Great. Now feed me before I get cranky."
He chuckles. "Yes, ma'am."

25

WHAT ELSE WOULD I CALL IT? A FRIEND-MOON?

I t takes longer than normal for the haze of sleep to clear and to remember where I am the next morning. The window in my bedroom allows soft light through, as I run through the last events I remember. We left San Antonio because Sarah was in the hospital. After picking up burgers and a chocolate milk-shake last night, we came home, ate, and passed out not long after. My head snaps to the other side of the bed, where Sage slept, but it's empty. Now I'm even more confused; Sage is never out of bed before me.

The stream of water turns off from the bathroom, and Sage walks through the door, a towel wrapped around her body and hair dripping all over the carpet.

"Good, you're awake," she says cheerfully.

"I can't believe you are already." I sit up and rub my eyes.

"Yeah, well, I'm excited. Dad called, Mom should be released from the hospital in the next hour. So after that, we should go to the Water Wall. We need some good pictures from this week that don't involve fixing the car or being stuck in traffic." Somehow, she manages to maneuver her short, purple dress on without taking the towel off until she's covered. She wraps it around her head next, before shimmying her pair of pink 'Tuesday' panties up her long, tan legs.

And I'm staring. Creepily.

I look away, searching for my phone or literally anything I can distract myself with. I find it and read the message waiting for me:

> **TYLER**
> You're back? Does this mean I don't get to take the lovely Mrs. Browning to Church tomorrow?

> **ME**
> I mean, if you're gonna cry about it, by all means.

> **TYLER**
> That was sarcasm. She's all yours.

She climbs up onto the bed, her dress barely covering her knees, when she curls her feet underneath her. "But the afternoon and evening are open. Any ideas?"

I open my mouth, but she continues before I can answer.

"We should have dinner at the aquarium either tonight or tomorrow, and possibly find a comedy show or something."

She takes my phone to search for ideas as I rise from the bed to dress. I have to dig through Sage's clothes to get to mine at the bottom of *my* still-unpacked suitcase.

"Ooh, there's a 90s R&B-themed bike tour through Houston!"

"What the hell is that?"

"I don't know, but it sounds cool." She gasps. "A booze and boos ghost tour! We could do that tomorrow to bookend the honeymoon."

"Would you quit calling it a 'honeymoon?'" I ask, pulling a gray t-shirt over my head.

"What else would I call it? A friend-moon?" She nods once, decided. "It's now deemed a friend-moon."

THE WATER WALL WOULD BE SO MUCH MORE PEACEFUL IF IT weren't littered with other people, but I guess I can't fault them for flocking to the sight. The 64-foot-tall, semi-circle wall of cascading water not only drowns out the sounds of the city, but is mesmerizing to watch. A perfect spot to sit in introspection, staring blankly while the mist of the water tames your stress.

After visiting with Sarah for a little while, then helping Stephen get her in the car and sent home to rest, Sage and I headed for the popular spot for couples' engagement photos, apparently. There are at least four couples here with photographers risking their expensive equipment near the water.

Sage carries hers on a strap around her neck, pointing and shooting it at me every so often.

"Okay, now go stand there," she says, pointing and readying her camera. "Hurry, before that other couple comes."

I do as instructed, but I don't smile when she snaps a few photos. The heat is oppressive, and I'm ready for a nap.

Finally, she relents, having captured my same expression in enough photos to please her, and we claim a bench off to the side beneath a neat row of trees. I pull out the sandwiches I packed before we left this morning, and hand one to Sage.

We eat in silence. Well, I do; Sage hums while she chews and bobs her head to melodies that don't belong to any song I'm familiar with. Then she points out a woman she believes she knows from college, a man who looks like an ex of hers, and has to pet and coo at every dog that flounces past us.

I know she doesn't like to talk about her feelings much, but so much has happened to her in the past five days. I didn't push the subject last night because so much of it was fresh, but I think we should clear our emotions a bit before continuing this *friend-moon*. This sunshiny exterior of hers has to be covering up a thunderstorm inside.

"So," I begin carefully. "Do you want to talk about your mom?"

Her brows furrow. "No, why would I?"

"Because she had a heart attack. And I know you've been avoiding her calls all week. I just want to make sure you're not blaming yourself, or anything."

"Do I look like I'm beat up about it? Besides, it was just a minor one."

"Because she got help in time. It could have been much worse. And it could happen again."

"You're ruining this beautiful day," she says, waving her hand around all the sunshine.

I grab hold of that hand, pulling it into my lap and softly running my thumb over her skin. "Just talk to me, Sage." Regardless of her tough exterior, I know she needs to.

For a moment, I don't think she will. Her lips are curled between her teeth, closed off to my attempts at lightening her load. Yet, like a frozen pond cracking in spring, so does her resolve as tears well up, threatening to spill.

I try not to stare, but the gentle brown hue of her eyes, glossy and raw, hypnotizes me. Following the trail of a tear broken free as it glides down her cheek, I reach up and stroke it away.

The floods burst forth, their flow quickening. I pull her head onto my shoulder as sobs wrack her body, and run my fingers through her hair. She smells like an orchard, brightened by fresh rain.

Sitting up, she takes the hem of her dress and dabs at her cheeks. "Shit, I really needed that. Thank you." She clears her throat and takes a drink of water.

I fall back against the wooden bench, jarred from the

whiplash this girl sends me through with almost every word out of her mouth. "You didn't talk about anything," I point out.

"I told you, I don't need to. Sometimes, all a girl needs is a good cry."

I can't understand how, but maybe she truly isn't bothered by everything that's happened. Maybe I'm wrong about her and her denial of authentic emotions.

"Could we at least continue our conversation from the hotel room? About your fear of failure?"

"Nope," she says, popping her lips on the 'P.'

"How about how I wouldn't change you?"

If looks could kill, everyone within a mile of my body would be dead.

"Fine. But your positivity is a bomb waiting to blow. And they always blow at the worst times."

She rolls her eyes, dry and clear.

AFTER WE LEAVE THE WATER WALL, SAGE DIRECTS ME TO AN interactive art show Sage discovered online, smaller and less elaborate than the one in San Antonio, but similar enough. I have no idea what interactive art is, but it must be exciting if she's so desperate to visit.

We show our tickets at the door and are directed inside a large, dark room with glow-in-the-dark structures and images. Sage's white sandals shine underneath the blacklight, and appear as if they're floating above a floor so black, it's invisible.

"It's a maze," Sage exclaims, reading the sign in front of us. "The clues for the way out are found in the environment. Whatever that means."

Next to the sign, a sculpture of a woman reaches her hand towards the ceiling, where I find a mirror. The tops of mine and Sage's heads reflect back, along with an image just beneath our feet. But when I look down, I only see the black sea of nothingness. Glancing back at the mirror, there's definitely an image somehow beneath us, partially blocked by our bodies. I keep my eyes on the ceiling as I pull Sage to the side to reveal the full glow-in-the-dark design, depicting an intricate bow and arrow knocked and aiming to the right of us. That must be the direction we're supposed to go.

I grab Sage's hand and follow a wall covered in more artwork, paintings, sculptures, shaped and painted abstract metal, all facing or pointing the direction we walk, until we reach a fork in the path.

"This is so cool!" Sage squeals, bouncing on the balls of her feet. She wraps her free hand around my arm and squeezes it to her body, and I have to ground myself. My pulse throbs in my ears as sweat beads along my forehead. I've been in such close proximity to this woman all week. Why does she still have this effect on me?

The clues are all some variation of the first few, all giving some direction of where to look next, yet they're still intricate and beautiful. At least, the pieces I actually notice. Sage eagerly does most of the work to get us through the maze because I'm useless. She pulls me along, into secret rooms off the typical path, one filled with unique art made with recycled material, one with sensory art we're allowed to feel, and one with mirrors so you're made to feel as if you're the art.

But the real picture of perfection is the woman whose hand I hold throughout the entire exhibit. The clues to her are the only clues I want to reveal. The opening to her heart, the only path I want to find. The awe on her face, the wonder in her smile, the faint mediocrity in her hard swallow when she admires something she doesn't think she could accomplish, or the mock confidence when she squares her shoulders after moving on from each masterpiece.

I've seen what she's capable of, creatively. I know she's brilliant, and while she may have some idea, she doesn't understand the extent of her power. No one would guess that she wasn't the very definition of conviction. Except me.

It takes us an hour to reach the end, and we emerge into another room, this one all white except for the images painted directly on the walls. "*Add your own art!*" the sign instructs above a table of brushes, paint, cups of water, sponges, stencils, a hairdryer, and other supplies.

A woman at one end of the wall paints a face within a tree, while a couple at the other end adds their handprints to a self-portrait of both of them. There are several faces with special flair to make them unique, paintings of beloved pets, and abstract symbols of whatever the artist was feeling in the moment. It's a mural of various souls all connected by this one place.

"Okay, so what do you want to paint?" Sage asks, rubbing her hands together and looking for a free spot.

"I don't know, you're the artist."

"But it's *our* piece." She walks over to the table and squirts different colors onto a palette. She returns to where I stand, tapping her chin with the handle of a paintbrush and studying the other sections of the wall for inspiration. "How about I just paint the background, and you can add whatever you want when I'm finished?"

The background sounds like it would require the most skill and time, so I agree, taking a step back and slipping my hands in my pockets to watch. She dips the brush into a dark green color, then collects the tiniest bit of white, mixing the colors in between and swiping the brush back and forth a few times before putting it to the wall.

When she's laser-focused on her task, the vision of the finished project tuning everything else out, I pull my phone out to snap a photo. The brush fits so naturally in her hand, like it's an extension of her arm.

Oblivious to the phone just a few inches from her face, her tongue pokes out from between her lips. I end up snapping at least fifteen photos, each one capturing her, enchanted by her own creativity, and make one my background photo before I can stop myself.

I get lost in the hour it takes for her to finish before she holds out a paintbrush. Taking it, I admire the beautiful scene of a meadow with a clear sky and brilliant sun shining above. Then I ruin it.

26

DO IT AND SEE WHAT HAPPENS

A tornado. Callum ruins the vivid colors with strokes of gray and white, funneling down into the grass and barreling towards the simple, yet pretty, flowers.

I say *ruins,* not in the traditional sense, but because that is what a tornado does. It's actually brilliant, and exactly what I was picturing when I painted the serene foundation. I had hoped he'd add an oxymoron, something to completely contradict the background, and he did just that.

But now that I'm thinking about it, he's called me overwhelming and chaotic just this week. Is that how he sees me? A tornado ruining his beautiful day and wrecking his peace?

"Is that supposed to be me?" I ask, hands on my hips and ready to fight.

He narrows his eyes. "No, why would you think that?"

"What else am I supposed to think?"

Tilting his head, he studies the tornado. Then he laughs. "It does kind of make sense."

And just like that, the flames licking at my cheeks die out, and I bust out laughing too. It's simultaneously the last thing and the exact thing I expected him to say, but his delivery was just what I needed to realize how ridiculous I'm being. Which is *not* something I admit often.

An employee takes a photo of just our art, and then one of the two of us posing beside it. After the ingenuity we were treated to during the maze, then leaving behind an insight into Callum's and my creativity combined, this was the highlight of the entire week. And desperately needed after yesterday.

We reach Eleanor, but with no set plan in place, we stay parked, discussing the options for dinner.

"What about the Aquarium? Everyone says you have to eat there at least once in your life." Danielle says the food is good, but the real treat is the massive aquarium that takes up the whole wall with hundreds of different fish swimming around as your dinner companions.

"I'm not sure I'm comfortable eating seafood with fish eyes staring at me," Callum answers with a shudder.

"They have other things besides seafood. I think."

"Still. Why don't we cook something? At the apartment."

"Together?" I ask, perking up.

"Um, sure." Apprehension covers his face. "Do you... Do you know how to cook? Because I've had Cori's food, and she tends to forget she's even cooking."

I wave my hand dismissively. "That's because she either gets lost in a book or her freaky mind. I, on the other hand, have a *clear* head."

"Because it's empty?" he deadpans.

The air heats faster than I can blink. "You did *not* just say what I think you just said."

He elbows my shoulder. "I'm just joking, relax. Friends joke around, don't they?"

Sure, they do. But when you grew up being the 'dumb' twin, and dropped out of college because you failed nearly every class, jokes like that tend to hit a little harder than you'd think. Especially when coming from someone who most likely doesn't mean it as a joke.

An hour later, Callum holds out a black apron and unloads the grocery sacks.

"I don't know a single man who owns an apron," I state, slipping it over my head.

"Yeah, you do. Me."

Any normal woman would be embarrassed by the snort that escapes, but life's too short to care about things like that. "Obviously, I mean besides you."

"Mrs. Browning made it for me. I don't usually use it, but figured you might not want to get meat on your dress."

We're making meatballs because I made an inappropriate joke about them in the grocery store. I'm not sure if, by having us eat meatballs, he's punishing or rewarding me for the joke. Either way, the recipe for the soy sauce and honey glaze we'll smother them in sounds amazing.

After the usual preparation—washing our hands and fetching bowls and utensils—Callum and I mix the meat and start forming the balls.

"How big would you say yours are? I know I saw them, but I didn't get to feel." I ask, holding up two for him to compare.

He glares in answer.

"How come it's balls, anyway? Why can't we do other shapes?" I ask.

"Because anything disk-shaped is a hamburger, and anything else would probably be more of a nugget situation."

"Do you have any cookie cutters?"

"Do I look like I bake cookies?" With his scruffy beard,

broad chest, and permanent scowl, he looks like he'd be better chopping trees.

"No, but you don't look like you cook breakfast for the kids across the hall, drive your elderly neighbor to church, or own an apron," I point out. "It's fine, I don't need them anyway. How about some friendly competition?"

"Doing what, exactly? Making different shapes?" When I nod, he continues with the questions. "What is the challenge, though? Who makes the best? Or weirdest? And who would be the judge? Because you'll just vote for yours, and I'll just vote for mine. Not to mention, different shapes would probably require different baking times."

I sigh. "Never mind, you take the fun out of everything." We end up making boring balls, though I poke smiley faces in mine. I have no idea if they'll survive the baking process, but I had fun, and that's all that matters.

Next, we start on the glaze. "Stir the whole time, don't let it burn," Callum instructs sternly.

"Or what?" I ask, quirking a brow.

His face scrunches. "Or...we'll have to start over?"

I was hoping for a threat involving bending me over the counter.

Callum steps up beside me, flooding my senses as he spoons two tablespoons of soy sauce into the pan. His sweet scent fills my nose, his arm brushes against mine, and I can't look away from admiring every inch of his face.

"So we're *friends* now?" I ask, partly to distract myself from lunging at him and risk being rejected. Again. And partly because I almost scoffed when he called us friends earlier. I've had to pull his reluctant, snooty ass around on a leash this entire week.

"Haven't we been?"

"It feels as if it's been one-sided."

He releases a hard sigh and searches for an escape from the

question in the glassy black liquid. "The only reason I've been hesitant to do *anything* with you is because..." But he shakes his head, changing his mind.

"No," I demand, grabbing onto his shoulder to hold him in place. "You're talking. Right now."

His shoulders fall in a dejected slump. "I guess I'm a little afraid I can't match your energy. That you'll find me boring. And that insecurity sorta keeps me from being able to relax around you." Is that really all it boils down to? All the irritation with me, the jerking back when I touch him, the annoyance— it's insecurity?

He grabs a bottle from the counter next to the stove, and I watch as he pours honey into a measuring cup, mesmerized by the smooth, sensual flow of the golden syrup. Callum has flecks of gold in his green eyes that match the honey perfectly, and I know exactly which colors I'd blend to copy the shade.

As the honey nears the edge of the measuring cup, Callum lifts the bottle and swipes the last drop with his finger from the spout before closing the lid. His hand moves toward the towel, as if to clean off his finger, but before I can stop myself, I find my hand on his wrist, tugging it toward my mouth.

Every interaction between us for the past two years is now painted in brighter colors. Well, *some* of them. I have questions, so many questions. But I latch on to the suggestion that I may have misunderstood his animosity towards me, if for no other reason than I want him in this moment. And if I'm wrong, maybe I'll regret what I'm about to do later. Or maybe I'll simply appreciate the ride.

He searches my face for an explanation before locking his gaze on my parting lips. I expect him to wrench his hand away, avert his eyes, and say, *"We shouldn't."* But he doesn't.

Instead, he says, voice deep and dangerous, "Do it and see what happens."

My lips spread into a smirk. "That better not be an empty

threat." His gaze darkens, zeroing in on my lips closing over his finger and licking the sweetness off. From his point of view, I imagine the wet warmth of my mouth, and hope he's picturing himself inserting a different body part.

Come on, Callum. I will him to let go with a flick of my tongue.

The crease between his brows, the slight shake of his head, indicative of the battle waging inside. He's strung too tightly, but with the slow roll of my eyes back into my head, his control snaps.

"Fuck it." His body shoots forward, pinning mine against the cabinet. His tongue replaces his finger, no warning given, yet no warning needed.

Somehow, he's still alert enough to our surroundings to reach over and turn the burner off before lifting me onto the countertop. He centers himself between my legs, flush against my middle, not once removing his mouth from mine. He doesn't just kiss me, he claims me. Devours me. Declares that no other man will ever be enough for me in one stroke of his tongue along mine.

His hand wraps around my neck, tilting it back for better reach, and my back arches, pressing me into his erection. Our teeth clash, and I think I scratch him by accident, shamelessly digging my nails into his back. I yank at his shirt until he disconnects just long enough to pull it over his head before his lips return to mine. But only a second later, they're gone again, trailing along my jaw this time.

The straps of my dress fall down my shoulders before being wrenched off completely and tossed to the floor along with the apron. There's no bra between him and my chest, not that it would stop him from me. My breasts are small, and he practically takes the entire thing into his mouth, biting just enough to bring me to the line of pleasure and pain. I almost come from that alone, but he's just as desperate as I am for his touch on my clit.

He lowers himself to his knees before me, which—with his height—puts his head right where I want it. He slides his hands through the legs of my underwear, pulling until I'm completely exposed.

Then he feasts.

A feral moan escapes my lips at the intensity, and my hips buck of their own accord. I have no control over any part of my body, but I would take this feeling over any other. He slips two fingers inside me, while his other hand reaches up to palm my breasts once more. Meanwhile, my own latch onto the first thing I find—the knob of the cabinet door—and the other grips a fistful of his hair. It doesn't take long before I'm tensing, screaming his name at the exact second the timer for the food starts wailing.

Callum continues lapping me up, carrying me through until I return to Earth and realize I broke the cabinet door off. It fell behind me, pulling my arm into an awkward position. He chuckles and takes the door from my grasp, leaning it on the floor against the other cabinets. Then he keeps his eyes locked on mine while he sticks his fingers in his own mouth this time and licks me off of him.

I expect him to carry me to the bedroom now, or lean back against the counter so I can finish him off. But he steps away and grabs a pot holder.

"What are you doing?" I ask, breathlessly.

"I have to take the meatballs out of the oven."

"Let them burn." Electricity still buzzes low in my belly, and I'm not yet done with this man.

"Not when a cow gave its life so we could eat." It takes four seconds for him to retrieve the baking sheet from the oven, and one more to throw me over his shoulder.

We reach his bedroom in ten long steps, his bed in five, and after I'm thrown down, I unbutton his jeans as quickly as I can. I grab his length in my hand, lowering my head to return what he gave me, but he tips my chin up and shakes his head.

Even though he hasn't had his release yet, his movements this time are leisurely and careful. Like we have all the time in the world. Or maybe because we don't, and he doesn't want it to end.

27

OR WHAT?

I step out of the remainder of my clothing, unable to take my eyes off the beauty leaning back on her hands and panting on my bed. Her hair, pulled loose from its ponytail, now lies over her shoulders. How long could I last if it were tight in my grip and her lips around my cock? I don't have the patience to find out, though, because I need to be inside her. Now.

But I'm torn because I can't rush this. When she sucked on my finger, my sanity shorted, and who knows when I'll regain it? Her tongue licked away every excuse I had given for why I had to resist. The yearning has bubbled up inside me for too long, and my strength has been tested too much just this week alone. There was nothing else to be done except let go.

I pump myself, not that I could be more ready, before climbing over her exquisite body.

"So beautiful," I growl against her skin. The warmth of her flush against my body elicits a groan that I release into her neck before scraping my teeth over her pulse. Running my fingers through her hair, I meet her lips once more, overwhelmed by the taste of her, unable to get enough. My hands savor every inch of her soft skin as they trail downwards, over her shoulders, her breasts. *Fuck.* Her hips. Her thighs. I grab onto one, hooking it over my back, and grind into her. This position alone could finish me, but wouldn't leave either of us satisfied.

With feeble restraint, I roll off, leaving her whimpering in displeasure, and dig around my nightstand for a condom. I don't remember how old they are; it's been two years since the last time I allowed myself the company of another woman, but I bought them long before that. I cherish connection and doing things the right way instead of just doing what feels good in the moment. But I don't allow myself to have either of those things. My hand is it.

The expiration date on the box claims they're still good, thank God, so I rip off the foil and slide it on. Sage holds my gaze as she runs her hands down her body, squeezing her breasts and coating her fingers in her wetness.

Lining myself back up with her entrance, I push in gently. Her tight walls clench around me, bringing me to the edge embarrassingly fast.

"Don't. Move," I choke out, already out of breath.

"Or what?" she whispers, her breath tickling my ear. With no regard for my lack of control, she writhes beneath me, searching for whatever friction she can find and taking what she wants. And I love her for it.

Slowly, I start moving too, matching her rhythm. I may be the one on top, but I'm not the one in control. I wrap my arms beneath her and roll until she straddles my hips, immediately taking off riding as if her life depends on it. My vision blurs, mind dizzying, as I buck beneath her. She falls against my chest, hands tugging at my hair.

My name from her lips, like the call of a siren, is all it takes for me to fall overboard into oblivion. Her mouth slams onto mine, feeding me her scream, and stays there for... I don't actually know how long. Neither of us moves for a long time, and when she finally does pull her face away, it falls into the crook of my neck.

I just had sex with Sage Anderson. The joy that truth brings ignites my arousal once again, and I repeat it back to myself over and over.

She climbs off of me, nestling into my side and curling her leg over mine.

Then, like a blanket smothering flame, the shame settles over me.

My body only views happiness as stolen bread. When it's eaten, it only tastes of guilt before sinking like a brick in my gut, threatening to come back up in the most violent of ways.

"Do you find it ironic that of all the places we could have had sex this week, we ended up doing it in your apartment while cooking dinner?" she asks, breaking me out of the fog of self-hatred.

"Considering it's you? Yes."

She sighs contentedly. "That was good."

"Just *good*? Ouch."

She playfully slaps my chest. "It was definitely in my top five. I'm just... surprised at how good it was."

Top five? Surprised? "Again, ouch." But this is Sage. She's more experienced and skilled than I'll ever be. Honestly, I should be thankful she had sex with me at all.

She sits up, curling her knees beneath her. "Oh, shut up and take the condom off. I'm ready for round two."

Hoisting myself up on my elbows, I ask, "Already? You're not... hungry?"

"Nope."

"You know, the glaze could probably be salvaged, and the meatballs are probably still warm. Why don't we eat first, then revisit the idea after the food digests?" I suggest. I'm not surprised that her stamina beats mine, especially since it's been so long for me, but I'm still out of breath from the first round.

She grins knowingly. "Callum Ridge, you're not too tired, are you? Because I could easily go another three or four hours."

Lord, help me.

28

I THINK YOU TWO SHOULD COME TO CHURCH WITH ME

Of course, I have questions about last night, but I ignore them for fear of scaring Callum back into his moody self. I told him our rendezvous was in my top five; I lied. Sex with him certainly took the number one spot. His strangled growls, his hard body, his muscles tense like he'd die if he kept touching me, but also if he *stopped* touching me. I'm experienced in the bedroom, but with Callum, it felt like my first time.

And my appetite isn't satiated yet. I fling the covers off, revealing our naked bodies entwined together, and throw a leg over his hips until my slit meets his erection.

But that's not what I want to play with.

Climbing until I'm straddling his defined abs, I lean down and drag my tongue up the column of his strong neck, feeling his pulse thrum beneath his smooth skin, and ending with a nibble on his earlobe.

He groans, running his hands up my thighs.

"Do you want your breakfast in bed?" I whisper, letting my breath tickle his ear.

I've been called selfish in bed before, but I love giving as much as I do receiving. And, like the real man he is, Callum smiles, eager to please, and tugs my hips forward. Therefore, he shall be rewarded afterward.

Holding onto the headboard for balance, I position myself over his mouth, my clit already swelling. My eyes roll back in my head as his tongue slides up my seam, slow and torturous, and his beard scratches my thighs. He massages my breasts, twisting my nipples, and sparks dance in my vision as my hips start grinding of their own volition.

I fuck his face with no control over my body and no concept of how to be gentle. He urges my fervent movements by palming my breasts, the entirety of each covered by his large hands, while I claw at his hair.

My patience balances on a needlepoint. I don't want to wait until I'm finished when I can use the power of him filling my mouth to fuel my own orgasm. So, as much as it pains me to do so, I lift off just enough to turn around.

"What are you doing?" he asks, disappointed by the space between us. I let my movements answer him as I lower back down onto his mouth and lean forward. With my tongue trailing along his shaft, he moans and plunges his tongue inside me.

Pleasure takes over, forcing my instincts to drive my movements. There's no room for thoughts about last night or how we ended up in this position after my failed attempts all week. No room to contemplate what had changed in Callum or convinced him to give in.

Repeatedly, I'm brought to the edge, but I want to time my orgasm with his. My hand moves in tandem with my mouth, stopping every so often to cup his balls, and together, we grow desperate as the sensation becomes too much.

Finally, I feel him tense, his tongue moving erratically, and I allow myself to fall over just as my mouth fills with his cum.

Swallowing, I sit up slightly, riding the last wave of pleasure as Callum slows his tongue.

Turning back around, I fall against his chest.

"I want to be woken up like that every single day for the rest of my life," he says through quick breaths.

"I can make that happen," I offer, grinning into his neck.

"Calm down, you just got out of an engagement." He strokes my hair, and I close my eyes, savoring the sensation.

"Don't remind me. I still need to find somewhere to stay."

"Why don't we do that today? Figure out where you'll live and get the rest of your things."

"Because I'm still on my honey- sorry, *friend*-moon, and I would like to enjoy it."

Who knows what will happen with Callum and me after this weekend? Would he want to continue whatever this is? Would I even care if he didn't? I don't know, but I'm perfectly content in this moment with absolutely no desire to move an inch.

As if he read my thoughts, he rolls my body off his chest. "Where are you going?" I grumble.

"I'm taking Mrs. Browning to church."

"I thought Tyler was going to do it."

"No sense in making him come all this way when I'm here already." He pries my hand where it's latched onto his arm. "Go back to sleep. I won't be gone long."

"Can I come with you?" I sound whiny, but I'm not ready to be apart from him just yet.

I admire his sculpted back as he walks naked to his bathroom. "Yeah, I'd like that. But be prepared; she's grumpy."

"I've handled your grumpy ass all week. I'll be fine."

I rise from the bed once he has the water warmed up and join him in the shower. With my thirst for this man apparently unquenchable, my hands are all over him, and before I know it, he's holding me against the wall as he pounds into me until we're both shuddering in each other's embrace.

CALLUM SLOWLY DESCENDS THE STEPS TO THE BOTTOM FLOOR OF the complex while I bounce around, eager to meet this Mrs. Browning I've heard about.

"Come on, Grandpa," I joke.

"Which door is hers?" He points to the green door with the crooked number one. I knock with an avid rap, and Callum steps up beside me, leaning his head on my shoulder and closing his eyes.

"Stay still, I'm just gonna nap while we wait."

I lean my face against his, stopping myself from shifting the couple of inches between our mouths. Mrs. Browning might not like opening the door to us banging against it. And I don't mean with our fists.

I distract myself by straightening the number one, but it's useless as it swings against the door when she wrenches it open.

Upon seeing me, she freezes. Callum lifts his head, but doesn't make any introductions.

"Who are you?" she asks, eyeing my pink sun dress and white sandals.

I extend my hand. "I'm Sage, a friend of Callum's."

"A girlfriend?" she asks, raising her brows.

"I don't really know. It's complicated. Last week, I was getting ready to marry someone else, but then I ended up in bed with Callum last night. I think it's better if we avoid labels for now."

Callum rocks back on his heels, scratching his head. Mrs. Browning turns her nose up at my hand. She's cute. Short, with white, curly hair, like a cloud on top of her head. She reminds me of my grandmother Lorraine, only with a scowl instead of a bright, homey smile.

"I think you two should come to church with me," she states, finally closing her door as if the plans are decided.

"You know what, that might be a lot of fun," I answer.

We didn't go to church a lot growing up. If we did, it was to my grandma's church, where they sang hymns loudly and completely off-key. No one cared if you stood still and sang softly, like Cori, or clapped your hands and danced, like me. Obviously, I'm not the pious little Christian girl typically associated with church, but I do like the idea of a higher power being in control. It helps me to stay grounded and not spiral out of control—again, like Cori—with fear of "what next?" Or going insane with worry or regret with "What if?"

What's meant to be will be, and if it's not, it won't. A more specific, "Hakuna Matata."

And I believe in loving people regardless of where they come from or what they believe. I think that's what a Christian is supposed to be, whether or not that's how they actually act.

We walk at a snail's pace to Callum's truck, with Mrs. Browning examining me through her peripheral vision.

"I like your suit," I offer with a smile, leaving out the comment that her gray and white tweed skirt and matching jacket look much too hot for this weather.

"Thank you. While I'd never wear it myself, I like your dress as well."

I think that's a compliment, so I smile and hug her. She tenses, just like Callum would do earlier this week. You know, *before* I fucked it out of him.

"Sage, you said your name was?" she asks, after we all get situated in Callum's truck. Her in the front seat, me in the middle back seat. Callum starts the truck and backs out of the parking spot. It's cute seeing him take care of Mrs. Browning. Setting the stool down, pulling her seatbelt out for her, then running to the driver's side to latch the belt into the lock.

"Yep. Like the herb that cleanses negative energy, or wards off evil spirits."

She side-eyes me again. "And how do you two know each other?"

"My sister used to date a friend of Callum's, but he was an ass, so she left him for his roommate, who is also friends with Callum. They're not friends with the ass anymore, thank God. Anyway, Callum was in charge of bringing the chairs and alcohol to my wedding last Sunday, but after I jumped out the window, he helped me escape. Then we went on my honeymoon together."

Callum flashes a sheepish grin at her horrified expression.

"Well, you've certainly had... an eventful week, haven't you?"

"Oh, very. First, we had a flat tire. Then, we had to sleep in the car, and I'm sure you can imagine how much fun that was with Mr. Grump here..." I spend the rest of the drive to church taking her on an audible tour of the past week. I show her a few pictures too, and discuss the plans I have for turning a few into paintings.

When we arrive, Mrs. B. makes her rounds, saying hello to her fellow church-goers, introducing Callum as her neighbor, and me as "his... *friend,*" always ensuring there's a long pause between the words. But when it comes time to pray, Mrs. B takes my hand in hers, holding it tight, and even offering me an approving nod before closing her eyes.

I don't feel judged by her, but I do think she's confused about me. Maybe hesitant because she doesn't know what my intentions are with her *neighbor*, who clearly means more to her than just a neighbor.

But Callum, since entering the building, has returned to the guarded man he was before yesterday. The crease between his brows stands at attention while he wars with himself against whatever the hell makes him so tense.

29

A NAP IN GOD'S HOUSE IS A HOLY ONE

I went to church regularly with my parents growing up. I guess I enjoyed it; there was a good-sized youth group and fun activities planned every Sunday. But you grow up and start to fall asleep during the sermons, eventually not bothering to make the effort to attend. It's the same message anyway. Don't sin, love your neighbor, give to others.

I do most of that. Now, anyway.

The preacher wears jeans and a polo shirt that's a size too big for his thin frame. His voice shakes every so often, from nerves, I assume. But he leans forward on the tips of his toes, eager to share his message about forgiveness. Not just of others, but of ourselves. I don't want to hear a word of it, so I distract myself by looking around the room at all the people who showed up today.

The man in the front row with his arm around his wife; does he go home and scream at her, or does he make love to her with gentle hands? The older man in front of me with glasses bigger than his face; does he tip at restaurants, or shout in anger when his order is wrong? The middle-aged woman with short hair who types on her phone; does she mumble under her breath about kids throwing tantrums in the grocery store, or does she lean down to help the stressed mother by validating the kid's strong emotions?

I may not go to church, but I live by the same code of morals. And not because it's what I'm supposed to do, but because I genuinely care about people. How many of these Christians can say the same?

Sage sits next to me, listening intently. Or, appears to be listening anyway. On her other side, Mrs. Browning's hand is poised to take notes from the sermon but slowly tilts as she snoozes.

Last night was a mistake. I know that, and yet, I can't seem to stop Sage anytime she kisses me or strokes my dick, after waking it from its hibernation.

I catch myself looking towards the door constantly, as if Jake might come barging through any moment, reprimanding me for taking what I'm not owed.

The pamphlet we were handed before finding seats sticks out from Sage's hands. I take it from her, simply to have something to do. Inside, there's a list of songs we sang for worship, along with various groups that meet throughout the week for bible study, upcoming events, and a list of charities this church supports.

Just this week, members of the outreach committee will visit the nursing home to spend time with the residents there. Then, they'll take over donations of diapers and formula to a homeless shelter that houses single moms and their children. And on Saturday, they're going down to Houston University, my Alma Mater, to hand out welcome baskets, with gift cards and snacks to the incoming freshmen.

As the preacher gives his spiel about Paul, the "Apostle of Grace," and his self-acceptance, my knee bounces faster and faster with my self-hatred.

Who am I kidding? What was I thinking, going along with

Sage this week, pretending I'm worthy of an ounce of her attention? And what is wrong with me, sitting here as if I'm better than these people?

Guilt. It's my middle name. It's my entire existence. And I don't know how to escape it.

AFTER WALKING MRS. BROWNING TO HER DOOR AND DECLINING her lunch invitation so I can stop delaying the inevitable, I hug her goodbye.

"You should come with me again soon. I think you might need to hear the sermons more often."

"What about you?" I tease. "You slept through most of it."

She points her finger at me. "A nap in God's house is a holy one."

Sage throws her arms around Mrs. Browning, catching her off guard once more. After recovering, she pats Sage's back. "It was nice to meet you, Sage. I hope to see you around more often."

"You too, Mrs. B. But I saved your number in my phone so I can call you anytime."

Mrs. Browning doesn't look too sure about *anytime*, but nods anyway. As her door shuts, Sage grabs hold of my hand and walks with her head on my shoulder all the way to my apartment.

"So what do you want to do today?" she asks when I close the door, and starts massaging my shoulders.

My skin itches to visit the animal shelter or to clean Mr. Parson's house. I'm already planning a visit back to Mrs. Browning's church to accompany them to their outings this week, if only to make sure they give like they promised to.

"We should probably get the rest of your stuff from Brian's and find a place for you to stay."

"But our honeymoon doesn't end until tonight. We have the rest of the day." I could at least give her that. I've already lost hold of my self-restraint; surely I can make it out alive after one more night.

"Friend-moon," I correct her, grabbing a glass for water.

"Right. So I was thinking..." A devious grin spreads over her face.

"Matching tattoos?" I ask drily.

"No, but we could do that after! I was thinking we could see if they need any extra hands at that animal shelter you volunteer at."

I gulp half the glass, then lick my lips. "Wow. That wasn't at all what I was expecting."

"Yeah, I think you've tamed me. Like a stray cat." She shrugs. "I don't hate it."

There really wasn't anything we did on this trip that was all that crazy, except jump in a jeep with a stranger to chase down a car thief. Sage is known for her impulsiveness, but maybe she's only that way around people she feels the need to entertain.

"Let me call Diana, she's the volunteer coordinator. There's an application process, but she may let me vouch for you." There's also a schedule we follow, but that doesn't mean they don't need extra help.

AN HOUR LATER, WE'RE AT THE ANIMAL SHELTER, WALKING AND playing with dogs. Well, Sage is playing, I'm scooping shit. She rolls around in the grass in hysterics while five different breeds lick every inch of her they can find. I'm jealous.

"Should I get a dog?" she asks from beneath all the canine love.

"I think you should find a home first."

"My dog and I could stay with you." She sits up and scratches each dog behind the ear before rubbing bellies.

"That's not a good idea, Sage," I say, cowardly fiddling with the scoop instead of looking her in the eye.

She stands, dusting herself off. "I know, but if we only did things that were *good* ideas, you and I wouldn't have..." I meet her eyes as she bites her lip. Then she gestures to all the dogs. "I can't say it around them."

Somehow, despite the conversation, I find myself smiling. "You're a dork."

"How about this? I spend the night with you tonight, I go to Cori's tomorrow, and we just hang out every once in a while. We're not making any sort of commitment, we're not saying we are or we aren't, we're just spending time together when we want."

I want this. Hell, I deserve this. I've changed myself for the better, I've put in so much work to be strong, be helpful to my community, and earn a place in this world. All I'm asking for is Sage. She may be everything to me, but I think a little happiness with her is a small ask in the grand scheme of things.

Besides, as she said, it's not as if we're getting married, it's just...hanging out and *not* pushing her away. It's *not* looking over my shoulder for judgment that I'm living above my means. It's *not* allowing my self-hatred to keep me from making her happy.

And doesn't it count for something that I've introduced her to the world of volunteering at the animal shelter? What other good deeds can I rope her into? She could find her own Mrs. Browning and Mr. Parsons. She could donate proceeds of her paintings to charity, or donate lessons to kids who can't afford extra lessons outside of school.

"Why don't you have a dog?" She asks, grabbing a rope to throw.

"I've thought about it. I don't have a yard, though, or much space for them to play." What I don't say is how I prefer to suffer in loneliness and silence.

But now that I think about it, isn't that selfish of me? I could provide a home for a dog, a senior dog, one that doesn't need a lot of space to run.

It's decided. I'll get a dog and *hang out* with Sage. It's only a matter of time before she gets bored with me anyway. I'll be her rebound to help her move on and distract her from going back to Brian.

And that, ultimately, will serve as my punishment. Denying myself Sage pales in comparison to having her and losing her when she finds something better.

30

WOULD YOU LIKE YOUR DESSERT FIRST?

T hree glorious weeks pass, and I have yet to spend a single night away from Callum. We sleep every night entangled in each other. It's usually around this time that I start getting antsy, cause a fight, break up, only to make up a week later, all to keep things exciting. So far, I only look forward to the minute he comes home, and I can serve him dinner in an apron and nothing else. Not because he expects it, but because when you really like the man, you just want to feed him. Whether it's food or pussy.

Then we eat together on the couch—he doesn't have a table—without the TV and talk about our day or plans for the weekend. We paint together, cook together, browse dog beds online for when we get a dog, and joke about what we'd name our kids. Boring things can be fun and exciting with the right person. Doing it in Callum's kitchen was hotter than the time I fucked that tattoo artist in his chair after he pierced my belly button when I was eighteen. And I get more of a thrill hearing the doorknob turn when Callum arrives home than I ever did with Brian.

I don't even mind waking up early to drive the hour-long

commute to the coffee trailer. I spend that hour jamming out to the radio and singing at the top of my lungs.

Today, Nick helped Cori open the trailer before leaving for his own job. When I arrive, she manages the customers on her own. She may not be the most chatty or cheerful person, but customers return because she's quick and efficient, moving about the trailer as if she's made coffee her whole life. And her timid smile and soft 'thank you,' to each customer is cute.

"Morning," I greet her, immediately jumping into taking orders and payment, allowing Cori to melt into her zone without having to break her concentration to socialize.

After the morning rush is over, we clean, prep some more, and have a cup of coffee ourselves.

Today is the day to finally have the discussion with Cori about pulling away from the business. I've been avoiding it because, contrary to what I like to present, I'm not all that confident in my ability to make a living off of my art. I know I'm good enough; that's not the problem.

More than half the population drinks coffee. And the designs I make are funny sayings, like 'Mom fuel' on a practical mug, things a lot of people could relate to and would buy without thinking too hard about it. My art is my own random creativity that would be overlooked unless someone who happened to have an eye for it walked by my table. Now, without the security the 'Coffee Break' brand provides, I'll be vulnerable, hoping the right people come across *and* understand my artwork.

"I'm taking a step back from coffee," I say before I can chicken out. "I can still work at the trailer, but I don't want to do the craft shows anymore. At least, not for coffee stuff. I want to sell my own creations, completely unrelated to coffee." I'm not so worried about her reaction. She might spiral a bit at first, anxious about her business succeeding, but that's just her process. I've learned that she needs to embrace the worry before she can see clearly. Even if I don't work that way, I can accept that I simply don't understand her process.

"I think that's a great idea, Sage," she says, pausing from wiping the counter.

"Me too. Let's just hope I can make a livable wage and can eventually quit being your employee. No offense, but having your little sister as your boss sucks."

She rolls her eyes, but bypasses my joke. "Why would you be worried? You made money off the coffee designs with no problem."

"Yeah, but this is completely different." We've already rolled out our fall menu, which means I can have my favorite iced pumpkin latte. I drizzle the pumpkin sauce into a large cup before pouring coffee and syrup inside.

"You could ease into it. Sell coffee stuff and your own, until you're out of the coffee stuff."

"No, that was my mistake the first time. I need to pick a lane and stick to it."

I glance over at her after a beat. She bites her cheek, her nervous tick. "Are you going to be okay? Mentally, I mean."

She waves off my concern. "Yeah, I'll be fine. The trailer generates enough revenue to sustain itself, and we sell plenty of coffee through the website. We only did the merch side to get our name out there, and we've done that now." It doesn't sound as if she's telling me, but *herself.*

But then she grabs my hand and squeezes.

"Thank you for helping me start the business. I couldn't have done it without you."

Before the tears blur my vision, I force a laugh. "I know. You're welcome."

THE EVENTS OF TODAY CALL FOR A CELEBRATION. SO WHEN I GET home, just a few minutes before Callum is due, I wash the coffee smell from my skin, and lie in a provocative position on the bed. A minute later, he walks through the bedroom door, halting when he sees what's waiting for him.

"Welcome home," I purr, legs wide open and showing everything.

"Oh, man." Without taking his clothes off, he climbs on top of me, kissing my neck. "As much as I want to finish this, I'm starving."

"I was thinking we could have a date night." I can't help the flashback of asking Brian the same thing, and I prepare my heart for disappointment.

"Actually..."

Here it goes.

"I made reservations at Francesca's earlier. I figured I could give them to Tyler if you didn't want to go."

"Eek!"

"But I'm regretting that now,"—he kisses my neck again, sending shivers down my body—"because we have to get ready now if we're going to make it on time."

"No problem," I say, bouncing off the bed. "I can be ready in five minutes."

True to my word, I emerge from the bedroom five minutes later in my favorite purple dress with the slit up the thigh. His gaze gets caught on my chest, and his mouth hangs open. I already know the effect I have on him, but the pleasure it brings to see it in action hasn't waned a bit in the past month.

"Would you like your dessert first?" I ask, sliding my arm up the door frame.

Shaking his head, he says weakly, "No, we're already ready. Let's go ahead and go. I'll be fine."

I lift my other shoulder enough so that the strap falls. "Are you sure?"

His throat bobs as he swallows, and his mouth opens, but no sound comes out.

"Callum?"

"What-uh, what'd you ask?" He squints his eyes, trying to think through the haze.

Without answering, I straddle his lap. My dress rides up my hips, and I feel the moment he realizes I *forgot* underwear.

"Yep, we're going to be late," he says.

31

I'M SO GLAD YOU'VE WARMED UP TO ME

S age sits in front of me, hands curled around a glass of red wine, smirking because she knows I'm already anxious to get her home and back in my bed.

This past month has been the most exhausting, entertaining, busiest, and best month of my life, and somehow we've barely done anything at all. Nightmares haven't chased me in sleep, no living ghosts haunt my thoughts, and I've had no desire to check for updates on social media. And I'm okay with that. Maybe it's the selfishness talking again, or maybe I'm healing. Either way, Sage is to thank.

Once you've grown familiar with the darkness, you have to make a conscious decision every morning to leave it behind. No matter how far ahead you run during the day, it always catches up, so that by the next morning, you have to make the choice again. But with each morning that I wake beside Sage and imagine myself shrugging it off, it grows easier to do so.

"So, where do you want your copy of the tornado? And how big do you want it?"

"What do you mean?"

"I mean, I finally got the prints of our tornado in the mail.

I'll frame and hang it for you. Unless you'd rather have a large painting of you naked." She waggles her eyebrows.

I can't stop myself. "I'd rather have one of you."

She laughs. "That can be arranged."

As for the tornado, I'm not sure I want a reminder of the feelings I've evaded for the past three weeks.

"You should tell Cori this week that you want to take a step back." I grab her hand over the table.

She smirks. "I already did. Just today." But her expression softens, her cheeks blushing. "Do you really think I'm good enough to make it on my own? You don't think it's too impulsive or stupid?"

"It's not really about being good enough. It's about determination, and you definitely have that. So if it's what you want to do, I know you can."

She shakes her head. "That doesn't answer my question."

"You're the most talented artist I know."

"Still doesn't answer it."

I laugh. She's never needed someone to tell her she's good enough. But maybe everyone assumes that, so it never gets said to her. When was the last time she received a compliment that wasn't '*you're confident*' or '*you don't need validation,*' which aren't really compliments anyway?

"You are good enough. No, you're more than good enough. The only reason you wouldn't be good enough is if you never decided to do it."

Her expression softens. "Yeah?"

Rubbing my thumb against her skin, I say, "Definitely."

"I'm just worried that my own creativity will be too much for other people. What if I paint something, and no one buys it? Like that piece I did last week with the sun inside the face?" I love that one. When she told me about it over the phone on my drive home, I expected to find a creepy, Teletubbies sun. But it depicted a woman with golden hair, and the sun shone through faded strokes, almost like holes, of her face.

"I'm sure you don't have to worry about it. If no one buys your paintings, which they will because you're amazing, I'll buy them all."

"What if they're expensive?" she asks, raising a neat brow.

I lift a shoulder. "I'll get a second job."

Her cheeks flush pink, and her eyes sparkle as a smile widens from each ear. "I'm so glad you've warmed up to me."

I don't know what she means, so I open my mouth to ask when she perks up.

"Ooo, there's a chef," Sage whispers, attention focused behind me. "I don't know why, but I love seeing them. It's like seeing the artist of a piece you've admired." As she watches his movements, I watch her and the fascination gleaming in her eyes. It's exactly how I feel inside when I look at her or her paintings. Even her colorless sketches are breathtaking.

"Do you think it'd be weird if I said hi?" she asks, watching his every step as he passes our table to shake hands with a guest behind Sage.

I watch as well, but not for the same reason. I watch because his hair, free from his hat, is neatly styled and shining beneath the soft lighting. I watch because his skin is clear and glowing. I watch because the holes in his pants and shoes are missing, and it's confirmation that he's doing better, that I didn't completely ruin his life.

I watch because it's Jake.

32

HOLD THAT THOUGHT. I NEED TO KILL BRIAN

I don't eat at restaurants often where the chefs aren't preparing meals from frozen ingredients, partly because there's no one to accompany me, partly because my budget doesn't allow for frequent fine dining. The only other time I've been here at Francesca's was when Cori's ex covered the bill.

Callum and I currently sit only a few tables away from where we met, where I'm positive I embarrassed him by the horrified look on his face anytime I laughed or spilled my wine. I still have questions about that night, but I'm not ruining the connection we've finally found together. The past will stay in the past for as long as the present will allow.

The chef, after receiving compliments from the table behind me, walks back toward the kitchen.

I turn around to face Callum, whose face has blanched as if he's seen a ghost.

"Are you okay?" I ask, alarmed as his chest heaves.

But he doesn't hear me as the chef passes by our table, slowing when his gaze lands on Callum. The tension hatches with a sudden crack as they hold each other's stare, and I hold my breath. A crease appears on the chef's forehead as he takes in Callum, our table, me.

He has dark hair, a slender figure, and blue eyes that narrow the longer he stares at Callum. I assume he knows him, but neither makes any move to acknowledge the other. A chill moves through the air, and bumps rise on my exposed arms.

Wanting this weirdness done with, I ask hesitantly, "Do you two know each other?"

Callum doesn't answer, and I don't think the chef will either. Until a rough, "No," comes from his deep voice, and he stalks off.

I wait for an explanation from Callum, but he stares at the ground, mouth agape. Reaching across the table, I grab his hand, and he latches on, squeezing as if his life depends on it.

I'm proud of how far our relationship has grown over the last three weeks, and I look forward to seeing what's in store for us. Maybe we'll become more than what we are even now. Maybe we won't, and we'll remain friends. Either way, a deeper understanding of the other has rooted itself in our friendship, and I'm happy to have him on my side and glad I can be here to comfort him over whatever just happened.

I'm patient as he slowly comes back to himself, clearing his throat and evening his breath. The color doesn't return to his face just yet, but he meets my eyes.

"Who was that?" I ask softly.

"No one. Could we just go? I've lost my appetite." He grabs his napkin from his lap and throws it on the table.

"Wait, just talk to me. Or we don't have to talk about it, and I can distract you. Here." I grab two breadsticks from the basket and stick them in my mouth. But my walrus act only brings out the Callum I met that night two years ago.

His eyes dart around the room. "Stop, now is not the time. I just need to get out of here." I can't help the sinking in my gut, the familiar reactions to Callum's rebuffs.

"What is your problem?" I ask loudly. A few heads in the vicinity turn our way, but I'm only trying to help. If he'd just communicate, we could solve the problem and get back to enjoying our evening.

But once again, he looks around the room like my reaction is embarrassing him. "Please stop making a scene. I just want to go home."

He wants me to stop making a scene? No problem. There's just one more thing I need to do first.

I stand abruptly, allowing my chair to crash to the ground, then grab my glass of ice water and throw it in his face. I don't linger while he gasps at the shock of the cold, or swipes at the water dripping down his face. I don't right my chair either, though I do feel bad about the mess I've left for the waitstaff.

I command my tears not to fall, but they don't listen. I tell my lips to smile the anger away, but they quiver. I tell my body to relax, that it's not a big deal, we've been through this before, but it trembles. With shaky hands, I open the door to the restaurant and walk around to the side of the building, out of sight for whenever Callum comes outside. Then I reach into my bra for my phone and make a call I don't want to make.

"Sage?"

And with a weak, desperate voice, I ask a question I don't want to ask. "Can you come get me?"

He agrees, and I tell him where I'm at, but I guess my voice lacked the appropriate desperation to properly relay the emergency because I'm still waiting fifteen minutes later when Callum rounds the corner.

"I figured you'd left."

"And how would I have left, Callum? We came together in your truck."

"Right," he says, sounding as if he's miles away.

"What the hell was that in there?"

He shakes his head instead of answering, as if he can't or

won't talk about it. But I need answers as to where this sudden shift came from.

"Just talk to me, Callum. I can help you work through it." I step in front of him and run my hands up his chest. "I can help make you feel better."

But he recoils as if my touch is revolting.

"I think we need some space. I've got my own shit I need to work through. And you need to take some time to think and just be by yourself. Figure out what you really want out of life."

Where is this coming from? "I know what I want. And it's you!" I take another step forward, and his back hits the wall.

He erupts. "You don't know what you want, Sage! You don't have a damn clue. Stop lying to yourself for once and just admit that you keep fucking up your life because you jump into things without thinking first. Like an engagement, or jumping into bed with me."

I flinch, his words a slap to the comfort I've found in him.

"This past month has been a mistake."

Tears blur my vision.

"Shit, I... I'm sorry. I'm so sorry, I didn't mean that. Or, at least I didn't mean to be such an ass about it."

My fists ball up as embarrassment from crying over this asshole blasts my cheeks, like the heat from a hot oven.

"Fuck." He runs his hands through his hair, his breath increasing. "See, it's not you who's the tornado, it's me. I'm the one who would wreck your life. Wreck any peace you find, destroy any happiness, darken your sunshine." What the hell is he talking about? "Do I need to go on, or do you finally get it?"

I may not understand, but that doesn't mean I deserve another insinuation that I'm stupid. Maybe it's this restaurant that brings out Callum's distaste for me, and I'll have to spend another two years training his tastes for my personality once more.

Except I won't be doing that. I'm done. In a matter of

seconds, the past month has gone up in smoke. I've been humiliated enough by this ass, and I have too much pride and dignity to allow myself to go through that again.

A car pulls up along the curb, and I wrench open the door with the parting words, "Pack my stuff and have it ready."

A MONTH AGO, ALMOST DOWN TO THE HOUR, I WAS EATING TACOS on Callum's couch after running away from Brian. Now, I'm eating tacos on *Brian's* couch. What a strange turn of events.

Neither of us has said much besides greetings and *'What tacos do you want?'* At some point, soon, I need to ask him nicely if he'll drive me to Callum's and help me get my things. I'm not ready to face Callum by any means, but I need my car. And Ben.

"This is awkward," I say, breaking the ice.

"Why? It doesn't have to be. Neither of us wanted to get married. We probably should have gone about things differently, but it's in the past." He shrugs, leaning his head back on the couch. "So there's nothing to be awkward about."

That's exactly what I thought too. I guess he's right, there's nothing for us to talk about then. At least, not involving us.

"Cool. In that case, can you turn your ex-fiancé brain off and act like a friend for a minute?" I ask, turning to face him.

He wads the foil from his first taco and throws it on the coffee table. "Sure, what's up?"

I waste no time. "Callum's an ass."

"Is that who that was? I didn't get a good look at his face before you shouted at me to floor it." He bites into his next taco.

"Yes. I've sorta been staying with him."

I rub my temple and meet Brian's eyes. He doesn't appear to be bothered by anything I've said so far, so maybe I can spill the full truth.

"Okay, look. Full honesty, I didn't set out to get involved with Callum. It was just a series of strange events. Callum used to hate me, you know? Or still does, I'm not really sure. But we were having fun together this past month, and I thought we were actually getting along. Anyway, we slept together about a week after our wedding. A few times. But it was just physical. At least, at first. But then we sort of settled into this comfort, and I ended up staying there way longer than planned. And we were having date night tonight, you know, to celebrate some things, and because we actually enjoy each other's company." I don't know if he catches the hidden jab, but I continue anyway. "But then he had some awkward encounter with one of the chefs at Francesca's. And then he just switched back into hating me." That only covers about half of my confusion, and might be too much information for an ex-fiancé, but I needed to get it all out before the emotions boiled me alive.

He thinks for a minute before taking a deep breath. "It sounds like you've had an eventful time."

I blink a few times. "That's it? That's all you have to say?"

"I wish I could say more, but I don't know Callum. Or what his issue with you is, or what the weirdness with the chef was. I only know you. And maybe you've tried to do too much in the month following your escape from our wedding."

"Well, what have you been up to?" I'm surprised to find the apartment well-kept. When we were together, he never cleaned, but his usual pile of socks is missing from beneath the coffee table. The sink only has one cup inside. And the stove is sparkling. Which probably means he's eaten out for every meal, but I don't see any take-out containers littering the surfaces either.

"Uhh, let's not talk about me."

His sidestepping that question isn't comforting. But would I really care if he were already seeing someone else? Nah.

"Don't you think you should just..." He shrugs. "You know, cool off for a little while?"

"I have been *cooling off*. I went on the honeymoon to relax, and I've been *cooling off* with Callum."

"It doesn't really sound like it."

I nod in understanding. "So what you're saying is, I need a *second* honeymoon? I like the way you think."

He laughs. "No. I think that's the last thing you need."

My phone rings. I roll my eyes, expecting it to be Callum, and prepare to yell into the phone to leave me alone before dramatically throwing it across the room. But my stupid heart betrays me with disappointment when Cori's name appears on the screen instead.

"Hello?" I answer, walking into Brian's room for privacy.

"Where are you? I'm coming to get you and your car."

"Why?"

"Callum called. He told us what happened. Please tell me you're with Danielle or someone else who's not Brian."

"I'm at Brian's." I sit on his unmade bed, with no top sheet and the blanket halfway on the floor.

"Sage," she says pleadingly. I picture her closing her eyes in exasperation.

"We're just talking about Callum." I know I should have called Danielle. Though, I didn't really want to explain the situation to her, or to Cori, for that matter. I didn't want the whole, *'Well, what'd you expect after having jumped into bed with him less than a week after your wedding?'*

"Okay, well, keep it that way. I'm coming there after I get your stuff from Callum's."

That reminds me, I have a few things here I still need to pack up.

"Are you okay?" Cori asks after I don't respond.

I fetch my leftover clothes from the closet and throw them

in a pile on the bed. "I'll be fine. No need to worry about me. How much did he tell you, by the way?"

She begins listing events, and turns out he told her pretty much everything. "Nick is going to stay and talk to him."

I take one last walk through the bathroom to make sure I don't leave anything behind, like my favorite coral-colored nail polish that I find in the cabinet. Or my music box Grandma gave me when I was five, with all my jewelry inside, that sits on the counter. Or the clothing items in the corner of the bathroom that I don't remember leaving there.

"Anyway, you should come back to the farm with me. Nick can stay at his apartment for a little while, and we can have girl time. You probably know this already, but the land is very healing—"

"Hold that thought. I need to kill Brian."

"Why, what happened?"

I hold up a familiar purple tank top with a depressed donkey graphic. "I think he slept with Danielle."

33

BENEATH THE STROKES

C ori said the land on the farm is healing, and so it is. One week later, and I barely remember who Brian is. Or Danielle. It's quiet this far out from the highway; the honks and squealing tires don't reach the peace found on the land barricaded by stalks of corn.

Callum, on the other hand, has invaded every thought. Just when I'm humming along to my speaker, smearing my creativity all over a canvas, not a care in the world except for how to get acrylic paint off Cori's t-shirt I borrowed, Callum appears in my mind's eye, just as unwelcome as finding Danielle's clothing in Brian's bathroom.

In the week since I stormed out of Brian's apartment after throwing the shirt at him, not bothering to see where it landed, I haven't spoken to him, Danielle, or Callum. I wasn't upset that Brian had slept with someone else, not really; even if it was my best friend. How could I when we were over, and I'd done something similar and just as stupid? What had me running down the stairs and waiting in the sweltering heat for a half-hour for Cori to arrive was embarrassment.

Had they been messing around behind my back the entire

time? Did other people know and look at me with pity? Is that why Brian left the wedding, thinking he got away with his unfaithfulness? And if he wanted my best friend, why propose to me? After all, he did suggest her as his sexual partner if I were ever unable to have sex.

Danielle texted me later that same night, the only reason I deleted her contact from my phone when I should have blocked her.

DANIELLE

Sage, I'm soo sorry. It just happened, it wasn't planned. We ran into each other at Buffalo River and things got heated.

We've only seen each other a couple of times since, but were waiting until the news was worth sharing.

Sage, please talk to me.

I thought you were happy with Callum, I really didn't think you'd mind.

Sage won't mind, she's easygoing, go-with-the-flow, down for whatever. I guess they forgot I'm also quick to hit the delete button on my phone.

The piece I've been working on is a rendering of myself without any depiction of my face or body. I guess you'd call it a portrayal of my personality, rather than a self-portrait. I painted the canvas a solid color before adding bright orange and pink flowers, with different textures and patterns. At least, it's how I see myself—a fan of variety and brightness. Or simple on the surface, but with a deeper meaning when studied.

The past week has been full of stress, while simultaneously being the most boring week I've ever lived. I went to work, I came home to the farmhouse, I painted some, I ate dinner with Cori—occasionally with Nick—and I went to sleep before repeating the same routine the following day. Doing anything to distract myself from thinking is how I've spent my time in between. Especially about Callum.

Why do I miss that jerk? And what is there even to miss? I mean, sure, he seemed to know me better than Brian—or I—ever did. And he smelled nice and made me feel seen, and I didn't feel like I had to beg or act out for his attention. But it's not really Callum I miss, it's that one version of him that I don't know if I'll ever see again. And I can't waste any more time hoping to.

As crazy as it may sound, the only person I want to talk to isn't Kiersten, or Tiffany, or Mikayla, or Brooke, or Miranda, or any of the other so-called friends I only see when we're doing something fun. Not even Cori or Hailey. I want to talk to my mom.

For reasons I think are obvious, I kept my living arrangements private after my honeymoon. As far as she and Dad are aware, I've been at the farm with Cori. But now, there's some twisted part of me that wants Mom to roll her eyes and scoff when I tell her the more pearl-clutching details of my current situation. I'm in a funk and I need someone to kick me into action, and hearing Mom tell me I'm doing everything wrong should light the fire under my ass. It might help me unlatch this regret that's clung to me since Callum yelled at me outside the restaurant.

Or, it might help me to come to terms with what he said about allowing oneself to embrace the sadness. Because beneath the strokes, the canvas is painted solid black, and covering up the darkness with pretty, vibrant flowers doesn't make it go away. It only seeps through all the bright layers painted over it, ruining the image.

I PLANNED TO VISIT AND TALK TO MOM BY MYSELF, BUT chickened out when I climbed into my car, and bumps rose on my skin from the ringing of the eerie silence. Turning the radio up to an ear-bleeding volume only brought on the anxiety, so I went back inside and dragged Cori out to come with me.

Once we pull onto the highway, a pop station plays softly through the speakers, but Cori tries to change it to rock until I slap her hand away from the buttons.

"What are you even going to talk to Mom about?" Cori asks, adjusting the vent so the air isn't blowing directly in her face.

"Just some of the things that happened with Callum and Brian. You keep validating my feelings, and it's not making me feel better."

She scrunches her nose. "I'm...sorry? I guess?"

I know people are right when they say I jump into things without thinking, but I've never considered the fact that I should change. I like my life, and I don't regret my actions often —I simply drop it and move on. But now, I'm wondering if I should take the advice Mom and Dad always gave me growing up: 'Why can't you be more like your sister?'

"How do you control yourself enough to think through your actions?"

She turns the radio off, preparing for a serious conversation. Or, maybe just using this moment as an excuse to stop listening to my favorite music.

"I don't really choose to. It's more like I'm scared to act."

I sit up in my seat, grabbing onto the steering wheel with both hands. "But how do I be more like you?"

There's a pause before she answers. "You've given me shit my whole life for being the way I am."

"I know, but clearly I only know how to fuck up my life." Like with college, my wedding, and now I can add Callum to that list.

"Umm, same." Neither of us says anything for a while. "You know, I think you're scared to act too."

"No, my problem is that I act too quickly."

"Yeah, but only because you're scared to do what you really want, so you jump into something else. Or you're scared something won't work out, so you sabotage it before it proves your fears correct."

That's exactly what I did when I quit Dad's diner. I wanted to sell my art, but was scared I wouldn't make it and would have to go crawling back to the diner begging for my job back. So I jumped into the safety that Cori's business provided.

"You've been making more merch for the fall markets instead of pulling back like you wanted," she says softly as if I didn't already know. "Because you're scared."

"Okay, so? How do I be more like you?"

She huffs a laugh. "You *are* like me, that's what I'm saying."

"Ugh." I find a balled-up napkin in my car door and throw it at her. "You're not helpful."

"Just for that…" She turns the radio back on and switches it to the rock station to punish me.

CORI AND I WALK A FEW STEPS AHEAD BEFORE WE REALIZE MOM had stopped in her tracks at my words. "You *what?*"

Under orders from her doctors to take better care of her heart, she's had to stick to certain foods in her diet. She's adjusted well, but Dad hasn't. In order to be a loving husband and support her through this change, he's refrained from eating his typical bacon cheeseburger every Thursday night and supreme pizza with extra cheese every Saturday. They've also gone for walks every morning and evening around the block, and Mom has discussed stress-relieving exercises with her therapist.

It just so happened that Cori and I arrived for her evening walk, and Dad was all too happy to let us accompany Mom instead while he snuck something high in fat and cholesterol. I figured that would be a good time for this talk because if it gets too heated, I could just run away.

"It's not a big deal," I say, defensively.

"You slept with Callum less than a week after your botched wedding?" Mom clarifies.

"Yes, but again, not a big deal." She's reacting exactly as I expected. Exactly as I wanted. Still, my body can't help but square up.

She turns on Cori. "Did you know about this?"

"Uhh, I can't remember," Cori answers, as she starts walking again with brisk steps.

"Also, I stayed at his house for the three weeks after. And I'm going to start selling my own artwork instead of merch for Cori's trailer." Maybe if I dump it all on her at once, she'll want to take a nap from all the different thoughts frying her brain.

"And, last thing, I found Danielle's tank-top at Brian's."

Mom stops walking again. "Is that why you walked out on the wedding?"

"No, it was after I had him come pick me up after I threw water in Callum's face because he pissed me off."

Traffic rolls through as people arrive home from their day jobs, and we pass by other neighborhood residents out for their own evening strolls. Mom is quiet for a long time, allowing us to both enjoy the evening breeze, apologizing for a scorching day, and grow concerned about what she'll say when she finally speaks.

"Okay, I can't take it anymore," I say, coming to a stop. "Lay it on me."

"No," Mom responds simply, continuing forward.

"What do you mean?" Cori asks, just as flabbergasted as I am.

"I've been told I meddle too much in your lives, by you two *and* Dr. Phillips, so I have nothing to say. In fact, I apologize for reacting so badly earlier. It was just a shock."

Cori and I share a look in which both of our brow lines meet our hairlines.

"Although," Mom says, suddenly stopping and turning to face us. "I assume that's completely over since you threw water at him? And why did you wait so long to tell me? You've come over a couple of times since then, and we talked about everything you did on the trip. You even showed me pictures. And why the blatant lies about staying with Cori at the farm?"

I mean, the answer is obvious, but I choose to say nothing rather than be lectured about my attitude.

"She needed time to process some things," Cori answers for me as her hair snags on a branch hanging over the sidewalk.

Mom helps her untangle the strands while her forehead pinches for me. "That's not like you. You don't process, you just act."

"Yeah, well, like you, I've also been told the way I handle things isn't the best way."

Once Mom gets Cori's hair free, she wraps her arms around us both and steers us back home, where she makes us lemonade like we're five. We sit side by side on the couch, and I tell her the rest.

After I'm finished, Mom updates Cori and me on her latest doctor's appointments, and how it's affected her mental state. Deep down, regardless of how minor, her heart attack scared the shit out of her. Out of all of us. Mom's never been the worst mom in the world. Sure, she has her flaws, and has said hurtful things that have affected me more than I'd like to admit. But I fall asleep on Mom's shoulder, feeling safe and loved for the first time in a week.

34

WITHOUT SAGE TO WARD OFF
THE EVIL

There's a knock at my door, but I can't convince myself to move from the couch to answer it. The remote is in my hand, but I don't remember grabbing it, nor turning on the weather report. While my eyes have been glued to the screen, I haven't absorbed a single word.

In fact, the only reason I know today is Saturday is because Mrs. Browning called to ask if I was going to be late again tomorrow morning, or if she just needed to find another ride to church. When I told her I'd be there on time, she suggested, once again, that I attend the service with her. I agreed since I can sit and disassociate there just as well as here on my couch.

The second my eyes locked onto Jake, a haze thicker than I've ever known settled around me. I moved through the motions, going to work, falling asleep without eating, and waking every night by some variation of the same nightmare. I have no further explanation for what happened. The strength it took to shrug off the guilt simply gave out, reminding me why I don't deserve love or happiness.

The knock sounds again, pounding this time, before the

door cracks open. I mute the TV when Hailey sticks her head in the opening, asking if she can come in.

I motion for her to enter, and she appears, holding a take-out bag from our favorite Chinese restaurant.

Irritation rings in her voice when she asks, "Did you not hear me knock the first time?"

"Yeah," I say, turning back to the TV.

"Yeah, what?" She sets the bag on the coffee table and sits beside me.

"Yeah, I heard you."

She sighs, but doesn't press further. Digging through the bag, she lists everything she ordered and asks what I want.

"I don't care." I won't taste any of it anyway.

She hands me two boxes, one with beef and broccoli, one with lo mein. I don't want to eat, but I force the food down in half-chewed lumps.

"I'm changing this. Life is scary enough without seeing this." It registers what I'm looking at on the screen. A category five hurricane barreling towards the east coast of the U.S. Their only hope is that it weakens before making landfall.

She changes the channel to a show compilation of funny videos people have sent in, mostly of people falling or pets doing silly things. Hailey laughs freely for one episode, leaning back with her feet propped on the coffee table.

After I've picked through half the container of lo mein, she sets her food down and turns to face my stony expression.

"Talk to me."

"There's not much to say," I answer, without looking at her.

She doesn't care. "Talk to me about what happened with Sage."

When I don't answer, she shakes her head. "Callum. *Something* happened. Cori told me Sage is still pissed at you, and while she may be hotheaded, she doesn't hold grudges."

"I don't even know how to explain what happened, okay?

We were at Francesca's, and suddenly, Jake was in front of me, wearing a chef's coat."

"*Jake?* The *Jake?* You mean he works there?" She lets out a sharp laugh. "That's great, Callum. Now you know what he's up to. And a chef? That's amazing!" She shakes my arm.

But I don't share her enthusiasm. Yeah, I'm thrilled that he's not taking after his parents, that he's healthy and fed and feeding other people for a living. I should be happy. I should be on my knees thanking God. But when I saw him that night, my guilt awoke with a hunger from the slumber I'd allowed it to fall into. It's thrashed around inside of me ever since, shaking my heart like a chew toy. And now, without Sage to ward off the evil, my nightmares have returned.

"He still hates me. That was obvious." The glare he gave me, full of burning hatred, branded my face with shame because I know he saw the teenager who hurt him sitting in that seat, rather than the man I am today.

"Okay, but what did that have to do with Sage?"

"I never should have gotten involved with her, and now things are so much worse than they were."

"But why?" she groans, growing tired of pulling answers out of me.

My brows rise. "Besides the obvious answer?"

She tucks her legs beneath her, preparing for a long conversation. "Quit being dumb, Callum. You're so intuitive and good at giving advice to other people, why can't you do the same for yourself? You know you can't live the rest of your life this way, closed off from people because you think they're better off without you. All because you made mistakes when you were younger."

I can, actually. And that's exactly what I plan to do. "Jake almost didn't have a life at all."

"And that was his doing. I know you feel guilty, but *he* made that choice. And you're not the only factor that led to that choice," she says impatiently.

"If I can't turn back time and take back all the damage I've done, the very least I could do is take the blame so he doesn't have to."

She sighs. "I know it's often used as a metaphor, but guilt and blame are not actually backpacks you can pass along or carry around for someone else."

The whir of the air conditioner kicks on, and she wraps up in the blanket on the back of the couch. So different from Sage, who'd snuggle up next to me, making me sweat with her body heat.

"Do you remember the joy you felt when you found out that one bully of yours was getting a divorce at twenty-three?" I ask. "Or the despair that Nick felt when he found out that football player who broke his leg got signed by an NFL team? I'm just trying to give Jake that same feeling when he discovers how empty my life is. Or save him from that shitty feeling he probably had when he saw me dining with such a beautiful woman."

"Okay, I was being petty. Yeah, that guy bullied me, but I should never have been so giddy over another person's misfortune. As for Nick, he was feeling jealous."

That's just it, though. All I'm trying to do is balance out the unfairness of the world and give myself what I deserve. Or deprive myself of what I don't. And Sage deserves someone who loves themself, because my self-hatred rages inside like a caged animal, and look what happens when it breaks free?

"From the sounds of it, Jake has a great career now. We may not know anything else about his life, but we know that. Nothing about the way you're living now is affecting his quality of life," she explains, gesturing with her hands around my empty apartment. "Sure, it may bring him an ounce of happiness to know you're unhappy, but that's a spiteful reaction, just like mine was."

But this is more about me than it is Jake. It's about my inability—or refusal—to forgive myself. Jake shouldn't and probably wouldn't forgive me, so I won't either. I don't deserve it, but most importantly, I don't want to. And now, throw everything I've said to Sage into the mix.

"I just want to die, Hailey. I want to stop existing. Not because I want to escape the pain, but I don't deserve to be here. I don't deserve to draw breath or take up space. I'm broken beyond repair, I've ventured into territories I can't come back from. And someone who feels that way cannot be romantically involved with another person."

Her eyes fill with tears to match mine as I talk, and when I'm out of words to describe my anguish, she wraps her arms around my shoulders and squeezes.

"Please don't," she whispers into my neck. "Promise me."

I wouldn't do that, not to her or my parents. There are too many people in my life I care about who also care about me for some reason. So no matter how much I think they're all better off without me, I would never actually consider not being here for them.

I just need everyone to understand that this is more than feeling guilty about unkind words once said ten years ago, this is about a man who should be locked up behind bars with photos of his victim on the wall of his cell so he never gets another second of peace.

ON TUESDAY, MY SAVING GRACE COMES THROUGH IN THE FORM OF a message on my social media page. From Jackson, of all people. At first, I didn't bother looking at it; what could he possibly want from me? However, by evening, the notification by the message icon starts grating on my nerves.

After finally reading it, I pack my bags.

JACKSON

> Hey man, hopefully you remember me from Galveston? I'm heading to the East Coast with a crew to assist in cleanup from that hurricane that came through. They're desperate for help. I was wondering if you wanted/were able to come since you said you do this kind of stuff?

I called my boss to ask for permission to work remotely once more, told my parents where I was going, and sent a vague text to Tyler, Nick, and Hailey, asking if they'd be able to take care of Mrs. Browning, Mr. Parsons, and the siblings across the hall. Then I rode in one of two minivans with eleven other people and no idea how long I'd be gone.

35

WHAT WOULD CORI DO?

There's been no word from Callum. No 'how are you,' no apology, nothing. With no one around to distract me, I'm forced to think about my life instead of jumping into my next adventure. And since I'm homeless, that's first on my list of improvements I need to make.

"Hey, I have the greatest idea ever," I say into the phone. It's Sunday. The trailer is closed, and I stood in front of my easel earlier with only varied designs for coffee cups coming to mind. So I gave that up and spent the rest of the day searching for apartments, only to find out how much rent has gone up in just one year since I moved in with Brian.

"Oh, jeez," Cori groans teasingly.

"Shut up, it's a great idea." I pause for effect. "How about I take over Nick's rent and move into his apartment?"

There's only silence.

Unable to handle the nausea Cori and Nick make me feel with their inability to stay away from each other for more than a few hours, I've stayed at Mom and Dad's since crying on Mom's shoulder. Mom and I have stayed up too late watching ghost-hunting shows, then we wake up and have our morning coffee together—decaf on Mom's doctor's orders. And while it's been nice, I need my own place.

I'm currently pacing Mom's kitchen while she boils the chicken for our dinner. Another instruction from her doctor: avoid sodium and eat lean. And another reason I need out of here: if I don't get a damn cheeseburger soon, I might die.

"Nick spends every night with you anyway, so why not? It solves my problem, and Nick will be able to save the money he spends on rent."

Crickets.

"Why are you freaking out? This is a great idea."

Still nothing, and I wonder if she's been thrown into a horrible memory, paralyzing and trapping her in fear.

"Are you having flashbacks to when you moved in with Sam?" I start gently. She didn't want to, but didn't see any other option at the time. And Mom and I sorta pushed her to agree, too focused on our own agendas that we overlooked how unhappy she was. "Because I could understand that, but Nick is nothing like him. And this is a completely different situa—"

"No, it's nothing like that. Sorry, you were on mute because —" She squeals and lets out a high-pitched giggle. She whispers, "Stop it."

"Ew. What is Nick doing to you right now?" Mom looks over her shoulder, nose scrunched in disgust.

Cori laughs. "Nothing, he's going to behave now. Both Nick and I think that's a gr—"

"Gotta go, Sage," Nick says.

"Wait, is that a yes?" But they've already hung up.

WHEN I WENT TO COLLECT MY STUFF FROM THE FARMHOUSE, Nick all but threw his apartment keys at me before slamming the door in my face and attacking my sister with his mouth.

That may be an exaggerated account of the events, but that's how it felt. I opened my arms to hug Cori, but was left standing alone on the porch instead.

However, a smile grew on my face at the prospect of living by myself for the first time ever. I hadn't realized it until now, but I've never lived alone. I went from my parents' house to a college dorm, back to my parents' to an apartment with Cori, then to Brian's, and here we are: on my way to *my* apartment at twenty-five.

Now I walk around the dreary place, taking note of where I want my things and how I'll brighten the place up. Nick left his furniture behind, a blue couch probably older than me, a TV and stand, and a bed and dresser. There's also a small dining table that I'll most likely use as a desk; I don't plan on having many dinner dates.

The first task I start with is setting up my Bluetooth speaker, turning on music, and lifting the blinds to allow more light. Fluffing out my pink and yellow comforter across the bed provides a nice break from the tan walls and carpet. I set out photos of family and friends, but the apartment needs more of me. The windows need curtains, and the brown cabinets with brown countertops won't suffice for a space I'll call home.

After getting my clothing unpacked and taking inventory of the dishes Nick left in the kitchen, I grab my keys and set out for the store. But when I return to the empty apartment, I lose all motivation to apply the pink contact paper. Who decided DIY projects should be 'do-it-yourself' instead of 'do-it-together' anyway?

ME

Come entertain me and help cover these ugly cabinets.

ERIN

Yes! What cabinets? And what can I bring?

ME

I have my own place now.

HAILEY

Are you going to feed me in exchange for my labor?

CORI

I can't, Nick and I have plans.

ME

Then come after. I'm your sister. I should take priority. I'm in crisis!!

On second thought, bring Nick. We can sit back and watch him work.

Erin, another friend of Callum and Tyler's from college, turned coworker of Hailey's, isn't high on my list of friends, but if we spent more time together, she could easily replace Danielle. She's a junior high cheer coach, which means she's bright and sunny and much more on my level than Cori or Hailey. She brought the wine we're currently sipping while we watch Nick apply the temporary contact paper to my cabinets, fix the ice maker he broke, and hang curtains.

"Has anyone heard from Callum?" I told myself not to talk about him tonight, but I can't help myself.

Hailey answers. "Yes, he actually went on a trip to the East Coast with someone named Jackson?

"Jackson?" I ask in disbelief.

But Hailey misunderstands my confusion. "He said you and him met a Jackson in Galveston."

"Yeah, we did. But where would he have gone with him? Why is he on a trip at all?" I sit up on the couch as question after question pops up in my mind, like why is he having fun, and who the hell does he think he is?

"Jackson was putting together a crew to go help the victims of that hurricane that came through a couple of weeks ago. They're cleaning up and handing out food, things like that."

My body relaxes, knowing he's not having fun, but doing something meaningful instead. Although I think that is sort of his idea of fun.

"I don't understand what happened between us. Everything was great. We were talking about him buying my paintings if no one else does. How disgustingly sweet is that?" So much for not talking about him. "And then, like someone flipped a switch, he just... changed."

After talking it through with Mom, it's apparent he knows the chef somehow. But what beef could he have with someone who cooks it for a living?

Hesitant and careful with her words, Hailey says, "It's not my past to tell, but can you just trust me that there's more to the story? And that if you knew, you'd understand?"

"No. If there's more to the story, then he should explain it to me. Otherwise, I can only form my thoughts and opinions based on the parts that I'm aware of."

"And I agree with you, and you definitely deserve an explanation. But it's such a fragile subject." The concern and sorrow in Hailey's expression have me worried.

"Should I call him? I've given him space, but I could-"

"Don't you think you should take some time to just... chill?" Cori says, rising and fetching her purse.

"What is that supposed to mean?"

She reaches inside the small black bag, pulling out something she keeps hidden in her hand. "Just what we talked about the other day. You asked how I control myself enough to think through my actions after giving me shit my whole life for overthinking everything. But overthinking would have prevented me from going, in a little over a month, from dating Brian, to being engaged to Brian, to walking out on a wedding, to sleeping with, then heartbroken over Callum."

I already know this, which is why I asked her for advice on how to control oneself in the first place. *But I sure am grateful for the lecture*, I think, with an eye-roll.

"You and Callum need distance and time to think and heal. And maybe at some point in the future, you'll both be better at the same time. Or, maybe you'll be better, but Callum will still need time. At which point, you can do all this fussing then."

"But it was so easy and nice," I whine.

"What? That *one* month you spent with him?" Hailey asks. But I've since realized that I don't have to pretend around Callum. He sees through all the layers of paint I use to cover up my own brokenness, and doesn't shy away from it. He doesn't ask me to stop crying to make himself more comfortable, or suggest I forget my troubles for a time when he doesn't have to deal with my bad mood. I do that on my own because I'm so used to people expecting it of me, but he seemed to accept whatever version I gave him.

I know I can bring that back out of him. I just have to find a way to make it permanent.

"Here," Cori offers, reaching out her clasped hand. Inside my own, she drops a bracelet. "I made these for us."

I turn it around to read the letters, 'WWCD?'

"It stands for 'What would Cori do?' and I have one with your initial," she explains. "So you can remember to overthink a little more, and I can remember to overthink a lot less. Maybe we can come from our opposite sides of the scale and meet somewhere in the middle."

Erin sits up straight. "Look, why don't the three of us— sorry, Cori, but you're excluded since you have a man—make a pact? No men. If we're feeling lonely, we'll go on a girls' date with each other."

I roll my eyes, letting my head fall back onto the couch.

"Are you even able to go without a man?" Nick asks me, popping his head over the countertop.

I shoot him a glare. "Of course, I can go without a man in my life. Now, hush and get back to work on my cabinets."

"Prove it. I bet you'll cave within a month."

I rise and reach over the counter to shake his hand. "Fine. But if I win, you clean my apartment for two."

He snarls, but accepts.

NOW THAT I HAVE A PLACE TO LIVE, THE NEXT STEP IN GETTING MY life together is to pull back from coffee. After the next farmer's market, Cori and I plan to run a discount for whatever inventory is left over, then switch to a print-on-demand service from which Cori will still pay me royalties, since they're my designs. Honestly, I'm not sure why we weren't doing that in the first place.

Work ended an hour ago for me, and I now plant heavy feet on each step toward my apartment, dreading the blank canvas that awaits me. I have my social media sites set up with a strategy in place for marketing and tons of ideas for new pieces. But anytime I try to film myself painting, my creativity flows right into a dam, blocking anything besides coffee art from appearing on the canvas. So far, I've created a coffee mug shape by gluing coffee beans to canvas, a painting of a coffee bean using old coffee instead of paint, and writing the word 'coffee' over and over until it formed another coffee mug. I might need therapy after all.

I've never had this problem before. Even when I dropped out of college, I poured my emotions into my art and came out with some masterpieces—at least, in my opinion. I have all of those listed on my website for sale and will take them to a craft show in a couple of months if they don't sell online. But the motivation to paint any more of them is nowhere to be found.

I take the last step to my floor and turn the corner with a sigh. But a bouquet waiting by my door has me pausing.

Vibrant orange and pink carnations bloom from a black vase. I can't remember the last time I received flowers from anyone, and in my excitement, I almost drop it on the way inside. I set the vase on the counter and check the card. There's no name, but I know exactly who they're from after reading the note:

> Congrats on the new apartment. Your easel would get the best light by the window in the dining area. You could put your cutting machine on the table. You eat on the couch anyway.
>
> I'm sorry for the things I said.

Since I already had my easel in the dining room by that window, I set the flowers on a little table beside it, and am immediately overcome by an idea. Without changing out of my work clothes, I grab a blank canvas and cover it with strokes of celery green and sable brown to match Callum's eyes.

36

I'LL BE RIGHT BACK. HOPEFULLY
WITH YOUR HOT DAD

U nlike yesterday, when I dreaded the thought of coming
home to my empty apartment, I rush up the stairs after
closing the trailer, eager to continue the painting of Callum.

Only when I do, I scare a cat who'd been roaming the hall.
It turns and runs the other way, stopping just beyond the
neighbor's door to watch me.

Patches of its dark fur, speckled with orange and tan, are
missing from its thin, bony body. There's no collar, indicating
it's owned by someone, but I should ask around just in case. I
bend down and call it over, but it just stares. Snapping a photo
with my phone, I think of how I can get this animal into my
apartment to keep it contained.

An idea strikes, but I'm not confident it will work. I run the
risk of it running away when I quickly, but quietly, unlock my
door and race inside to pour the last of my milk into a bowl.
When I open the door again, the cat has inched closer, but
halts at the sight of me. Slowly, I lower the bowl down just
inside the door and take a step out of sight. But nothing
happens. The cat doesn't come to drink, and I can't see it either,
to know if it ran away or not. I don't want to scare it off by

peering around the wall, so I mentally prepare myself for a long wait.

Maybe the owner of this cat is a tall, hot doctor or a muscular handyman who will want to thank me for rescuing his baby. Maybe he'll ask me out and we'll have a romantic dinner before doing it up against his front door because we're too impatient to walk to the bedroom.

While I'm fantasizing about the possibilities, Callum's face keeps merging with the handsome stranger's, and I have to shake my head to clear the image. I look over at my easel and the bouquet next to it, itching to get back to work before I lose the inspiration I've finally found after a month. But it'll have to wait.

Finally, the cat slowly inches toward the bowl. My heart beat picks up at the excitement, and when it's finally inside the door, drinking the milk, I close the door as swiftly, yet quietly, as possible. The cat whips around, then crouches as if preparing for trouble.

"It's okay, little one. I'm just trying to keep you safe. You don't understand my words, but maybe my tone will comfort you?"

My soft, gentle tone does nothing for its nerves as it glances around the room and darts toward my bedroom.

"Please don't pee on anything," I say a little louder. "I'll be right back. Hopefully with your hot dad."

But after knocking on nine doors, only one of which answered, I still haven't found the owner. Behind the tenth door, however, I luck out; a beautiful, green-eyed, blond man answers. He's tall with large hands that remind me of Callum's, with broad shoulders. And he's wearing scrubs!

"Can I help you?"

"Hi, and hopefully. I found a cat wandering around outside my door, and I'm looking for the owner." I show him a photo, but he shakes his head.

"Sorry, I don't have a cat. I've been thinking of getting one, but haven't yet."

"Oh? Do you, or your girlfriend... know anyone around that owns one?" I ask, twirling my hair.

His teeth are perfectly straight and pearly white when he smiles. "I don't have a girlfriend, but no. I don't know anyone else around here."

"Me either. I just moved in a couple of weeks ago. I'm on the floor above you."

"Yeah? Well, it's nice to meet a neighbor. I'm Owen." He extends one of those large hands, and when I place mine inside of it, I'm thrown back in time to when Callum's hands were on me.

Lost in the memory, I almost forget what I'm supposed to say. "Sage."

"Sage. I like that." My panties should be melting from his grin. One more thought about Callum and they would be. But any attraction toward Owen dissipates as quickly as it came. "Would you wanna grab a coffee sometime?"

"Um, sorry, I'm sorta taken." I don't know where the lie comes from, but I don't feel bad about it.

"Oh, okay." A pinch forms on his forehead in his confusion.

"Sorry, I should get going. It was nice meeting you."

"Yeah. You too." He shuts his door, leaving me alone with my own bafflement. I can't be with Callum, but somehow that doesn't stop him from interfering with my love life. Or, maybe my judgment has just gotten better. Maybe there's some sort of sixth sense I didn't know about that warned me against falling for Owen's good looks alone.

Whatever it is, it looks like I'm adding a litter box and cat food to my shopping list.

After setting up the litter box in the bathroom, I set out a few of the treats I got from the store earlier in front of me, hoping to lure the cat out from beneath my bed. While I wait, I post the picture on a couple of lost pet sites, hoping no one claims it. I sort of like the idea of having a pet. I discussed with Callum the idea of getting a dog, but a cat is just as good. Someone, anyone to keep me company, I'm not picky who—or what —it is.

Half an hour passes before the dark nose appears, sniffing the air. But it slinks back into the shadows after our eyes meet.

It's all good, no worries. It takes time. Patience. I don't have much of that, but now's a good time to learn. Shaking my head to clear it, I rise.

Except it's not all good. My emotions are quick to form, whether they make sense or not, whether they're justified or not. It doesn't help that I'm confused as hell about Callum and whatever's going on with him. Hailey said there was more to the story and that I should trust her. Fuck that. I'm tired of being patient.

A truth for a truth—that's what we did when I was drawing him. I pull out that sketch now. I completed the most important areas when he was in front of me, but I should be able to finish the shading and smooth out some of the areas alone.

I'm always alone nowadays. It felt so liberating moving into this apartment by myself, but it's too quiet. Even with music or TV to drown out the silence, I find myself missing the man in this picture. And the most frustrating part is, I don't even know why.

Laying down my sketch book and drawing pencil, I fetch a sheet of lined paper and a pen and write a letter instead.

Callum,

How are you? I don't know why I decided to write a

271

letter instead of texting or calling you, but it seemed easier. I also don't know why I decided to write to you at all.

Maybe I should stop while I'm ahead. For some reason, though, my hand keeps writing, even though I'm not really saying anything. Who knows, I may not even send this.

I just remembered, you're not even home. Hailey said you're with Jackson? That's weird. I guess I could email it.

Things are changing in my life. You already know—thank you for the flowers—that I took over Nick's apartment. I'm spending more time alone and getting to know myself better. And I know you and I have our issues, but for some reason I can't explain, all I want to do is tell you about it. So here it goes.

Like I just said, I moved into Nick's. I've never lived alone, and it's so boring. How do you do it?

I've been trying to paint more. I'm having trouble focusing, but I'm hoping writing this letter will help.

I found Danielle's clothes in Brian's bathroom and freaked out. My instincts are at war with each other. On one hand, what the hell? On the other, I miss my best friend. But the truth is, I'm not mad about the situation at all. I'm not actually mad at Brian or Danielle, I'm mad at you. I'm using them as a focal point for my frustration because I don't even know what happened between us.

So, what's the deal? Hailey says there's more to the story, but no one will tell me what.

You know what? I am sending this because I want some answers, Callum Ridge.

Your move,
Sage

I wasn't positive I'd receive a response, but he replies the next day. I get the notification as I'm once again sitting on the floor with a trail of treats leading from beneath my bed, waiting for my charms to work on the cat.

> Recipients: pinkhairdontcare@lwb.com
> Subject: I'm sorry.
>
> Sage,
> I'm sorry you're struggling, especially because of me and my mess. This is exactly what I wanted to avoid—dragging you into it.
> The chef we saw at the restaurant was Jake. When I saw him, I couldn't breathe. I needed air, and I needed out of the restaurant, but...well, you know the rest.
> As Hailey said, there's a lot more to it. But I'm not sure you'll understand. And I'm not insinuating that you're dumb or anything, I know you're not. It's just that we deal with things in different ways, and the way I'm dealing with it may not make sense to you.
> I'm not in the right mental space to be in a relationship right now. And probably never will be. It has nothing to do with you or your personality. Sage, you're amazing, but you don't need me to tell you that. Our time together was more than I could have dreamed of, and I'd love to have more time with you. However, not only am I not in the right headspace, neither are you. You just admitted that.
> But sending me this was a good idea. Let's keep this going.

Callum

Thousands of questions arise from what was supposed to make things clearer. Like, what the hell does Jake have to do with him not being in a relationship? Why would seeing him elicit such a reaction? And what more is there? But also guilt, because I should have realized that he was struggling to breathe instead of pushing him to talk about it right then. He asked me not to make a scene, most likely from panic rather than embarrassment, and I only made it worse for him.

I look down at the 'WWCD?' on my bracelet. Cori would give him time before pestering him with questions, and maybe I'll do that. But I still need to talk to him, to have him in my life in some way. All this time, he was already in my life, but wasn't really part of it. And now I don't know how to live without him.

> Recipients: callumridge@lwb.com
> Subject: (no subject)
>
> *I'm full of great ideas, but no one believes me.*
> *I'm working on a new piece. It's not done, but I've got a rough outline. It's a portrait of you. Don't worry, it's just your face. Your face when you look at me, actually. I'm working from a few photos from our trip as a reference.*
> *I'll give it to you when you get back. How is your trip?*
>
> *Sage*
> *P.S. I'm sorry for the way I acted at the restaurant. I shouldn't have thrown the water—metaphorical alcohol onto an already burning flame. I'm working on not acting as rashly.*

> Recipients: pinkhairdontcare@lwb.com
> Subject: Can't wait to see it.

Jackson is an alright guy once you take you and your shenanigans out of the equation. It's rewarding work being here and helping. In the grand scheme of things, I know I'm only one person and can't make much of a difference for the amount of destruction caused by this hurricane. But I'm trying.

I can't wait to see the portrait. Not that I'm excited about seeing my own face, but I'll love anything made by you.

Even though it wasn't what I needed at the moment, I wouldn't change the way you reacted because it's just who you are. You won't accept being treated in any way less than what you deserve, and I wish I could give you that. I just can't right now.

Callum

37

GUYS LIKE ME DON'T DESERVE HAPPY ENDINGS

D evastation shrouded the community of too many towns, and there weren't enough hands or resources to make much of a difference. But I was trying. I kept my body busy enough that my brain didn't have time to think too hard about things, I ate just enough to keep me going, and I slept on the floor on a pile of old sheets in the sanctuary of a local church.

No one wants to go without the luxuries they've grown accustomed to, such as eating whatever, whenever they desire, a cushioned mattress that doesn't kill my back, or hot showers. But among all the loss and destruction, I have it so much better than many of the people we're here to help.

Upon arriving, I started with clean-up and rescue, finding lost pets, and searching through debris for anything salvageable. I helped a young couple, newly married, as they dug through the rubble that was once their home for anything not broken beyond repair or covered in mildew. Once we were done, they could only fill two suitcases. But despite their circumstances, they smiled, took their belongings, and joined other families to help search.

Then, I handed out supplies for a few days, such as

toiletries and clothing, to people who had lost everything and were staying in pop-up shelters. A man took four bags, one for him and one for each child that stood behind him in dirty clothing they'd been wearing for days. He smiled and shook my hand.

Next, I worked with a food pantry to help restock food that people had lost with power outages. A tired mom with two teenage boys whose refrigerator had gone out four months prior, spoiling their entire food supply, hugged me tightly. "I didn't know how I was going to replace everything a second time."

Now, Jackson and I, along with the other volunteers, work on clean-up in preparation for rebuilding. The work is hard, but it's been more healing than anything else.

My days are chaotic and full of sadness for those impacted by the storms, as well as compliments and good wishes I don't deserve from the people I help. But they're also full of light and hope. Seeing the good in humanity and the love for fellow humans, despite being strangers. Most importantly, I'm pulled out of my own head enough to stop the cycle of dark thoughts I'm constantly caught in.

Nights, however, are sticky and hot in this building packed full of bodies that generate enough heat to overpower what little air conditioning we get. I lay here unable to sleep, panting for breath, and desperate for morning when my demons can't reach me.

I miss her. She was my knight, shielding me from the nightmares, from myself, from past misgivings. Life was enjoyable when she was part of it, if only for a month. With the way I treated her at the restaurant, I've dug myself an even deeper hole where I deserve to stay forever, far enough away that I'll never hurt her again.

I'm due back at work in a couple of days, and I'm not sure what will happen after life settles down. I want to see her, and I know she wants to see me, but I don't trust myself with such a fragile, beautiful grenade.

"Callum," Jackson calls from his own pallet on the floor next to mine.

I grunt in answer.

"I just wanted to say thanks for coming with us, I've really enjoyed it. Well, maybe not *enjoyed* it exactly." He chuckles, gesturing around. "But I'm glad I came out here and was able to bring such a large crew with me. You're a good man, Callum Ridge."

My skin crawls at the sound of those words; they couldn't be further from the truth, and I don't do stuff like this for praise. In fact, if I could do without a single 'thanks,' I would. But to explain why would take too much time and too many details that no one wants to know.

WHEN I LEFT FOR THE EAST COAST, IT WAS FOR SEVERAL reasons. One of which was to keep myself from doing the very first thing I do when I get back home. I don't even stop at my apartment first before parking my truck between two shiny black cars in the parking lot of Francesca's. I take a deep breath to prepare for the confrontation I'm hoping to have, then make the trek to the tall double doors.

Now that I'm here, I can't remember why I thought this would be a good idea. I can't remember what I hoped to accomplish when I exited the highway for here instead of home.

My plans are derailed anyway when I see a blond man emerge from the restaurant, his girlfriend latching tightly—almost possessively—to his arm.

"Callum," he says in surprise and stops in his tracks.

I want to hide behind the bushes and pretend like I'm not

here. But bushes don't stop a man like him. "Sam. What are you doing here?"

Last I heard, he had gambled away his trust fund and was unemployed. But I guess with rich parents, you're never actually poor.

"We were having dinner with my parents," he answers. Figures.

Kenna flashes her hand at me, adorned with a large, glittering diamond. "We announced our engagement to them." She wields the news as a sword, like it should hurt that I'm only just now finding out. If we were still friends, I probably would have helped plan or set up the proposal, instead of finding out an ex-best friend is engaged while passing him on a sidewalk. But for once, I'm not the reason things went to shit.

Sam lowers his gaze to the ground, almost guiltily. He *should* feel guilty.

"Wow. Gross," I say. I have no desire to be cordial to either of these people. After the way he treated Cori, emotionally abusing her, manipulating her, crushing her self-esteem, and cheating on her throughout their entire relationship, Tyler, Nick, and I wanted nothing to do with him. And I've never wanted anything to do with Kenna, considering she cheated on Nick before stealing Sam away from Cori. It's a whole mess in which I'm not directly involved, but still affected nonetheless.

Kenna scoffs. "Oh, get off your high horse, Callum. Stop looking down your nose at everyone and get a life." If only she fucking knew.

Sam glances awkwardly between us before holding out his car keys. "Can you wait for me in the car?"

"Fine. But don't keep me waiting long." He flinches, grimacing when she kisses him hard on the mouth. I cringe as well, imagining it was painful.

After she's gone, I take a step, intending to leave him here. "I don't have anything to say to you, so bye."

"Wait." I jerk back when he grabs my arm. "I just... how's Cori?"

"She's great now that you're out of her life. Even better now that Nick is in it."

"Who'd have thought, huh?" He chuckles. "Her and Nick. I never saw that coming."

"Yeah, well, I'm glad it did. He knows how to treat her." I struggled with how to react towards Sam when I learned the full extent of how he mistreated Cori. On one hand, he's an ass who doesn't deserve anything. But on the other hand, so am I. Not sure if I was being hypocritical or not wanting to separate myself from him, I sort of sat back and let Tyler take control. He spoke for both of us, assuming it was what I wanted, when he pulled away from Sam.

Now that he's in front of me, I feel only betrayed that I struggled with those feelings at all. Even though Sam and I have more of a history than I do with Cori, no good person would ever side with him. And I'm ashamed that I ever wondered if I was allowed to leave his friendship behind. Ashamed there's someone out there who hates me as much— possibly more—as we all hate Sam.

"It's funny. Cori sat at home falling in love with my room-mate while I claimed I was at work, but really was with Kenna. Now, I sit at home, wondering if Kenna is really with someone else when she claims she's at work. Except I have no one else to fall in love with."

Does he think I'll feel bad for him? "Looks like you're getting exactly what you deserve." I push past him, but halt when he speaks.

"Are you? Getting what you deserve, I mean? I hope so."

My mind spirals, wondering what he knows. I never told him of my past, and I don't hear any malice in his tone, but what else could he mean?

"You're a good guy, Callum, and even though I lost you and

Tyler the day I lost Cori, I never stop hoping you all are happy. Never stop wishing the best for you."

Maybe he is better than me, because I don't wish the best for him. Especially, now that he's said that right before I walk inside and beg a man who probably wishes me dead for forgiveness.

But because I've been there, I can't stop myself from asking, "Why are you going to marry Kenna? You clearly don't want to. Are you punishing yourself?" Not that he doesn't deserve it, but why waste the life you're given by continuing down the same bumpy, miserable road instead of taking a more pleasant drive?

He looks off toward his car and shrugs. "Guys like me don't deserve happy endings. I guarantee Cori has wished ill on me since everything went down."

"Does that sound like her? Besides, I doubt she's thinking about you at all." Maybe Jake hasn't thought about me either. Maybe he'd forgotten about me until I ruined his peace that night a month ago.

"I hope you're right."

"If you want to turn your life around, the only one who can is you. And if you don't, the only one who will suffer is you. Just don't ever treat anyone the way you treated Cori." I don't know if men like him can change, but maybe he's seen enough of it from the opposite point of view to be a better man.

"You're a good man, Callum Ridge," he says, slapping my shoulder before walking away.

I roll my neck, resisting the urge to shout at him. I'm not a good man; I'm the furthest from it.

The chill nips at my cheeks as I stand there, alone. My feet, as if stuck in the cement sidewalk, refuse to move toward that door. Nothing Sam did was directly toward me, yet look at how I reacted to seeing him in person.

I can't go inside now. So, like the coward I am, I chicken out and leave.

Recipients: pinkhairdontcare@lwb.com
Subject: Don't tell Cori

Sage,

Don't tell Cori, but I ran into Sam, and I need someone to talk to about it. He doesn't look happy. In fact, I'd wager he's miserable. It was a jarring experience, and I'm not quite sure how to feel about it. Not that I miss him, but I miss my old friend, the man he used to be. Well, the man I thought he was, anyway. I didn't realize how much until I saw how miserable he seemed.

Would Cori hate me if she knew I told him not to marry Kenna? Oh, they're engaged, by the way. I asked him if he was punishing himself. Which is ironic because that's sort of what I'm doing. It's one of the many reasons I need to stay away from you. I shouldn't even be telling you this because I know you'll just try to talk me out of it. Or try to make me feel better. But I don't want to feel better, I just want to feel pain.

Callum

Recipients: callumridge@lwb.com
Subject: (no subject)

I've typed and retyped this email so many times because I have so many emotions, and I'm not sure what you need from me right now. I don't want to make things worse like I did at the restaurant. So tell me what version you need of me, or what personality you want me to put on to help.

Sage

Recipients: pinkhairdontcare@lwb.com
Subject: I just want you

I emailed you instead of the various other personalities in our friendship circle because I love yours the most. I never want you to try to be someone else. Not for me, not for anyone.

Callum

Recipients: callumridge@lwb.com
Subject: (no subject)

Okay, you asked for it.
Who the FUCK DOES THAT ASSHOLE THINK HE IS GETTING ENGAGED TO THE DEVIL BEFORE CORI AND NICK?!?!? Cori won't hate you, but I might. I'm sorry you miss your friend. I understand what that feels like. I miss Danielle. And I miss the version of you that I knew during that month we were... together? Hanging out? Whatever we were, I miss it. But I don't know if I'd get that same version back.

Anyway, Sam deserves to burn in hell for the pain he caused my sister.

Sage

Recipients: pinkhairdontcare@lwb.com
Subject: (no subject)

Do I?

38

I OFFER YOU MY CONGRATULATIONS AS WELL AS MY SYMPATHIES

The only reason I agreed to dinner is because Tyler and Hailey said they had something to ask me. And the fact that they have a question *together* piques my curiosity enough to pull me from my apartment, where I've burrowed since I returned home a week ago.

Tyler brought burnt hockey pucks he keeps referring to as hamburgers he made on his new grill, and Hailey brought fruit salad, a vegetable tray, chips, and brownies. After we eat, they wrap everything up and stick it in my fridge so I'll have dinner for the next couple of days, and I begin to wonder if feeding me was the real reason they came over.

"What did y'all want to talk to me about?" I ask, unable to take the suspense. "Or was that just a guise?"

They share a look before returning to the living room. Hailey sits on the coffee table and clasps my hands in hers, while Tyler sits beside me. Now I'm worried.

Tyler begins. "First, we have reason to celebrate. Our favorite English teacher here finally got an assignment she's been begging the school for."

Hailey rolls her eyes and her shoulders. "I was told that I'd finally be allowed to run our no-bullying week this year after two years of asking. Only, the year they finally say yes just so happens to be the year that Tyler Borseth joins our coaching staff."

Tyler smiles proudly, as if he accomplished some devious plan. "They didn't want her to get too overwhelmed with teaching and all the planning, since someone from the school board usually plans the activities, so they assigned me as her partner. I'm absolutely beside myself with glee."

"And I'm absolutely beside myself with disgust. But,"—Hailey shrugs—"what can you do?"

"I offer you my congratulations as well as my sympathies."

Tyler laughs, but clears his throat when Hailey glares at him. "Anyway, Hailey and I were wondering... would you consider talking to the kids toward the end of the week at an assembly?"

"Don't answer right away," she adds quickly. "But think about it. Normally, with things like this, the speakers are people who have been a victim in some way. But you've seen it from the other side, and I think having that unique perspective might help."

After the last time I saw Hailey, how could she think I'd want to do this?

"It's a lot to ask. And it will most likely be emotional for you, so we completely understand if you don't want to do it. But we wanted to give you the opportunity," Tyler finishes.

Ahh. There it is.

In other words, they think it will help to heal the broken parts inside of me. And maybe it would. Spilling my regrets to a bunch of kids in their prime bullying years might bring some relief if they actually take my advice. If I can't give the apology I carry around to Jake, maybe I can hand it off to the kids in the audience who won't get one from their own bullies.

"Just think about it, okay? If you're not comfortable, don't feel bad for declining. We have a bunch of other options." Hailey squeezes my shoulders before saying her goodbyes—a hug for me, an eye roll for Tyler—and leaving for home.

Once she's gone, I ask, "Do you really think this will make any difference?"

"Honestly? No. Kids will be kids, and they're not going to listen to a bunch of adults. But they do this thing every year, and Hailey is so desperate to have it make an impact. And she already hates me, so I'm not going to be the one to tell her it isn't going to work."

"But even if it helps just one kid, that will make it worth it, right?" I ask, just as desperate as Hailey.

He nods hesitantly, leading me to believe he's just telling me what I want to hear.

What would I even say to these kids? I can't exactly talk about what happened with Jake. They'll have nightmares, then their parents will be pissed at Hailey. And I don't know if bringing them down a notch, telling them they're not as cool as they think, will work. I could pull the empathy card, or the "bullies are just insecure" card, but these are preteens. As Tyler said, they don't listen to anything adults say.

INSTEAD OF GOING TO BED AS I SHOULD, I FIND MYSELF GRABBING my keys and driving to my parents' house. They still reside in my childhood home, despite it being much too big for just the two of them now that my brother and I have moved out. It's a 3,400 square foot home with more bedrooms than we ever knew what to do with. That size is small for this area of Houston, but growing up, my brother, Connor, and I had every opportunity handed to us through Dad's wallet. That meant football for me and medical school for Connor to follow in Dad's surgical footsteps to an OR.

When I arrive, I walk in without knocking like I always do and find Mom and Dad in their pajamas at the breakfast table. They each have a glass of milk in front of them with a plate of cookies in between.

"Uh oh," Mom says at the sight of me. "We've been caught."

"What are you doing here, son? It's late," Dad says, dunking a cookie in his glass. Mom shoots him a look as she stands to retrieve a glass for me, so he quickly adds, "Not that I'm not glad to see you, I'm just curious."

"It's fine, I know you just don't want to share your cookies." I bite into one, but it tastes awful. Scrunching my face, I look around for a napkin. "Eww, what is this?"

"It's a cookie, Cal," Mom says, setting the glass of milk before me. I take a sip and almost spit it back in. Coconut milk.

"It's made with coconut flour and oil," Dad explains.

I should have known. Dad's a surgeon and has never allowed much junk food in the house. I guess I thought—or hoped—that by their guilty expressions, I would be treated to a sweet chocolate chip cookie. Instead, it's gritty with an earthy taste.

"So how was the trip?" Dad asks.

"Fine. Depressing, and I wish I could have stayed longer, but fine."

"We've kept up with the news. We're just heartbroken for those people," Mom says, hand on her heart. "We're proud of you for going and helping. You turned out to be such a good boy." She strokes my cheek.

"So?" Dad asks.

His face doesn't give anything away. "So what?"

"Well, it's nine o'clock at night. Not that we don't love surprise visits, but what are you doing here?"

Mom swats at his arm, but it's a valid question. I'm an adult, I shouldn't be running home to Mom and Dad. I want to talk to Sage, but I've bothered her with enough of my shit lately.

"Well, I almost did something the other night that I'm not sure if it would have been stupid or not. And I felt myself itching to try again tonight, so I came here instead. I found out where Jake Elliot works and I almost went inside to talk to him."

Dad shifts in his seat, shooting a look at Mom. We haven't spoken about Jake since I moved out. "Do you really think he'd want to see you?"

"No. But I have something I need to ask him."

"I doubt very much he'd forgive you, son."

"That's not it. I need to ask how he'd feel if I talked at a school assembly about bullying." So many unknowns, too little headspace for all the possibilities. Should this decision be up to Jake? No idea. But I'd feel weird agreeing without his approval. "Tyler and Hailey are running it at their school this year, and they asked me to speak." Before he can ask, I add, "They think it would be a unique take to hear from someone who's caved to peer pressure before. And they think it might help me get some closure."

"I'm not sure if that's a good idea, but it's up to you. Don't bother Jake with this, especially if he's doing well," Dad says.

But Mom squeezes my shoulders, forcing me to turn towards her. "I think it's a great idea. If anyone could actually make a difference, it'd be someone who's been on that side."

Dad shakes his head. "I'm just worried they'll see what a great life you live and think it won't matter what they do in their youth. They need a deadbeat or someone who's seen the impact of bullying."

Yeah, I'm doing great. I *don't* lie awake at night thinking about him or how lucky he is that he made it out. "You think I haven't?"

"Of course, you have, just not in the way I meant. I meant someone like Jake."

Is this all in my head? I know it is on some level, but now

I'm questioning the validity of my feelings, or wondering if I'm just some loser who's creating problems for himself. Like Sam.

Perhaps I should do the speech and be honest about how one unkind word will stick with you far longer than you'd expect, frying your brain until you don't know the difference between being selfish and working towards a better version of yourself. It might not make any difference to these kids, but Hailey and Tyler are right—I need this.

39

MRS. BROWNING WOULD BE HONORED

nother awkward silence. I don't know how many more of
these I can take, especially with a person who's been like
a sister to me since high school. After hearing from Callum
how much he misses his old friend, no matter how shitty of a
person he turned out to be, I asked Danielle to meet for lunch
so we could talk about things. But neither of us knows where to
start.

She sits across the table from me at a cafe in Houston,
tapping her finger against her glass of water and avoiding eye
contact. I glare at her, arms crossed, but it's not her I'm really
mad at. I feel bad for the way I reacted because none of my
anger was about them anyway. Sure, I was shocked and
confused about the timeline of events, but there's no sense in
throwing away a friendship when I don't want Brian anyway.

I've missed her. It would have been nice to have her around
after everything that happened with Callum. Although she
probably would have pushed for me to find someone else to
use to get over him. And for once in my life, I'm glad I've used
this time to think, to heal, rather than act.

Her face may not be as round or soft as when we met at

fourteen, but I still see that youthful sneer when I look at her. We were on opposite teams at a volleyball game. Emotions were heightened, and words were exchanged between the two teams, and Danielle just happened to be the girl closest to me. After the game was over, I found her on social media to continue the trash talk, but based on her profile, we had too much in common not to end up friends.

Sighing, I reach over, grabbing her hand in both of mine. "I'm sorry."

Her eyes widen. "*You're* sorry? No, *I'm* sorry. I've *never* been interested in Brian. He's always been... ew, you know? And yours, and I've never once had any interest in him whatsoever." She takes a breath. "But, I don't know, when we ran into each other at the bar, something sparked. I can't explain it. Anyway, we've only hung out, we haven't slept together at all. My tank top got left there because we went swimming in the pool at his apartment complex, and I had it draped over the tub to dry."

The story checks. The top was by the tub as if it had fallen off the side, forgotten about. It was on top of other dirty clothes, but those belonged to Brian. It's news to me that they haven't slept together, though, and I feel even worse now.

"It's okay. We both walked out of our wedding for a reason. There's no point in denying yourself love if you can find it."

"Well, it's not love, just attraction. Like I said, we've only been hanging out. Seeing where things go. And if we decided we did want to start dating officially, we were going to talk to you about it, break the news gently and make sure you were okay with it. But we also wanted time to pass because it's so fast after your wedding." Her voice still holds a hint of desperation, trying to convince me.

I shrug. "Yeah, but it feels like it's been so much longer." If he's ready to move on, he shouldn't hold back just because he thinks it's the right thing to do.

"It'll be so weird to see us together, you know."

"Yeah, I know. But the weirdness won't last long, and it'll be nice having Brian as a friend." Honestly, he makes a better friend than boyfriend/fiancé anyway. "Just tell me if he's treating you like shit so I can pummel him."

Her shoulders relax as her lips break into a smile, and she squeezes my hand. "Thank you."

While we eat our salads, I fill her in on everything that happened at that restaurant with Callum, and how I ended up at Brian's in the first place. Then I invite her over to see my apartment, where we stay up too late watching scary movies, and it feels incredible to have my best friend back.

But I still miss *him*.

IT'S USUALLY ABOUT THIS TIME THAT I START ITCHING TO CALL Brian, to brush whatever issues we have under the rug and have make-up sex. But this time, when I reach for my phone, it's not because I want him back in my bed.

He's taken now anyway, and I have a bet to win. I won't even mention that he's not the man I want.

ME

I'm sorry for getting mad. Just know it wasn't about you.

I think I was using you as a punching bag for my anger and disappointment over how everything ended with Callum.

This isn't one of those things Callum would accuse me of covering up. Brian and I just weren't meant for each other. He was my scapegoat because I didn't know how else to spend my time. And when my family made bets about my relationship, well, there was nothing to do except lock him in. At least, that's what I thought.

BRIAN

It's all good, no worries.

It's not all good. Not yet. But for the first time in a while, I feel like it could be soon.

> *Recipients: callumridge@lwb.com*
> *Subject: Some questions*
>
> *What do you mean, 'Do I?'*
> *I'm a cat mom now. I took her to the vet to check for a chip and posted all over the internet to find the owner, but no one has claimed her. I guess she's mine now. The vet said she's around 2 years old, and is considered a tortoiseshell, based on her coat. She was so skinny and skittish, but her fur already looks better after a couple of weeks. I need a name for her. What do you think about Sage Jr?*
>
> *I saw H and T the other day. Hailey asked if I'd talked to you and how you're doing. Tyler asked if you've given any thought to what they asked you before Hailey smacked his arm and told him not to rush your decision-making. What were they talking about?*
>
> *Sage*
> *P.S. Actually, what is Mrs. Browning's first name?*

Almost as soon as I send the email, my phone dings with an incoming text message.

CALLUM

Edna. Why?

Edna it is. I reply with a photo, a newer one of Edna and me with her cheek against mine.

ME

> Meet Edna. I've won her over with bowls of milk.

CALLUM

> Mrs. Browning would be honored. I can't really picture you with a cat, but I'm glad you're giving her a home. Don't give her any more milk, though; it's not good for cats.

My heart sinks. With my breathing increasing, I press buttons in a rush to dial Callum's number.

"Hey," he answers. I can't even enjoy the sound of his voice after all this time because I'm a horrible cat mom.

"What do you mean it's not good for cats? Cats are known for loving milk," I say into the phone.

"Yeah, but they're lactose intolerant."

My hand flies to my forehead as my stomach drops. "Oh, shit. I've given it to her every day. What else don't I know about cats?" I look at her now, nibbling on dry food out of the small ceramic dish I bought for her. It's pink with a little white paw print on the bottom, but I didn't think to check if the paint they used was safe for food. Would that be required for them to sell it, or could the manufacturer just sell anything they wanted as a pet bowl?

"I can get you some pamphlets from the animal shelter," he says, but they can't fit all the information needed to keep an animal safe inside a pamphlet.

Once again, I've jumped into something without thinking it through. "What if I accidentally do something to hurt her because I don't know what the hell I'm doing?"

"I'm sure you'll be fine. Everyone has to learn how to be a pet parent."

"No, I won't be fine." I pace the living room, pinching my forehead with my free hand as a tear falls down my cheek. "What was I thinking, anyway? I'm so stupid. I can barely take care of myself, how am I supposed to take care of another being?" I absolutely will not be fine; what a dumb thing to say. Suddenly, I don't trust myself to keep her because of how easily I could unintentionally poison her or bring her harm.

Edna jumps onto the couch and licks her paws, and I sit beside her before scooping her into my arms. She meows in protest, but doesn't try to escape my loose grasp. I can't keep her, but how could I give her away?

"I gotta go, Sage." The call ends, and I pull it back to look at the screen in shock.

"What the fu-" I cringe. "Sorry, Ed." I nuzzle my face into her fur. I know she doesn't actually understand curse words, but it seems wrong to use them around her—she's my baby.

But seriously, he hung up on me in the middle of a crisis? What an ass. I'm done with this back and forth, begging him for his attention. No more. I open my contacts and delete his number from my phone. I'm half tempted to block it too, but I'll save that one for the next fit I throw.

Edna and I curl up on the couch while I crash out and Google the side effects of dairy for a cat and distress signs I should be looking for. Along with other common cat allergies, illnesses, and any possible harm that could come to a feline.

I message the vet, asking if I should go ahead and make an appointment, if there's anything they can even do for Edna since I've given her so much, or if it's too late.

Once, when Cori and I were nine, we found a baby bird in our yard, so tiny we could barely make out its facial features. It was alive, its heart visibly beating through its translucent, featherless skin, and opening its beak for food. There were no trees around from which it could have fallen, so we assumed a predator of some kind had carried it off before dropping it in the thick grass.

Cori made a nest from an empty box of tissues, and we went hunting for bugs and worms to squash into baby food. Mom sternly shook her finger at us, saying we absolutely would not be bringing it inside her house. But we slid the box underneath our bunk bed anyway when Mom wasn't looking. Cori and I went to sleep, taking turns waking to check on our new baby throughout the night.

It was around one in the morning when Cori shook me awake.

"I think it died," she said, eyes welling with tears. I rose out of bed and found a trail of ants leading to the tissue box. They swarmed the baby bird's lifeless body, its heart no longer beating.

Cori and I held each other and cried, the confusion at what we did wrong more hurtful than anything. We fed it and kept it warm. What did we forget? And what if I wake up to find Edna in the same way because I don't have a damn clue what I'm doing?

I've always known I'd be a good mother, but based on what? Delusion? Simply because I want to be? I can't manifest skills or knowledge from determination.

A knock on the door calls me from my thoughts and sends Edna running for my bedroom.

I stand on my toes and look through the peephole, but duck when I see Callum standing on the other side of the door. I have no idea what my face looks like, or my hair, and I'm wearing ragged clothes with paint stains and a hole in the armpit.

Glancing behind me, there's a bra slung over the counter, paint supplies everywhere, and half my closet in the living room from my indecision on what to wear the other day. I don't have time to clean up the place or myself because he knocks again. But then I remember that I'm mad at him, and he doesn't deserve to see me at my best.

I open the door and cross my arms, struggling to keep my

face stoic and my body from jumping and clinging onto his. The feelings of my heart and brain aren't synced.

"Hey," he smiles, holding up a bag. "I got some stuff for Edna."

My expression almost cracks, but I resist the temptation until I get an explanation. "You hung up on me."

Surprise flits across his face, as if he didn't realize what he'd done. "Yeah, I'm sorry. I got an idea in my head, got excited, and hung up before I ruined the surprise. I got some cat milk that Edna is able to drink, and it's good for her teeth and bones. Also, some salmon oil that's good for her skin. You just squirt it onto her food."

Ugh. So much for being strong. I lunge at him, nuzzling my face into his chest. I missed him. "Thank you." My voice is muffled, but he grunts his response as he squeezes me back.

After we hold each other for far longer than is appropriate, I pull back and take the bag from him. As I pull the items out, he explains the benefits and dosage of each one and hands me a couple of pamphlets on cat care.

When we're done, the silence is thick. Like I learned in my Color Theory class about atmospheric perspective, the more distance between objects, the more blue in the air. The more sadness, the more courage it takes to cross the bridge that separates us. Ironically, the space has always been there between us, but after our friend-moon, the distance feels lonely and terrifying.

He might not want to talk about it, but I can't handle the quiet any longer. "You never answered the rest of my email."

He looks off into the distance. "Right. Umm..." He scratches his beard. "They just want my help with the no-bullying assembly in November."

"Oh." I get the feeling there's more to it.

"Yeah. Dad doesn't think I should, but Mom does. And I

think I'm leaning toward doing it, but I don't even know what I'd say."

Twisting the bracelet on my wrist, I grab a pen and notepad, motioning toward the couch. Cori would look at every possible reason something may or may not be a good idea, so that's what we'll do. "Why don't we list the pros and cons?"

He bites his lip hesitantly, but slowly makes his way to sit beside me. And because I'm a cuddler, and not all because I missed him, I throw a leg over his and snuggle up to his side.

"Okay, so, pros." I wait, pen poised, for him to answer.

"It might help me mentally. It might make a difference for a kid or two. It would make Hailey happy."

I jot those down and ask, "And cons?"

"It might destroy me mentally. I don't know how Jake would feel if he knew I was doing it."

I stop writing and look up. "Wouldn't he like that you're participating in something like this?"

"Maybe. Or, maybe he'd feel the same as my dad, that I have no right to inspire kids not to bully." He mindlessly traces the hem on his jeans.

"Can you answer that question now? The one where I asked what Jake has to do with us?"

He closes his eyes and opens his mouth to protest, so I add, "I know you're not ready for a relationship. I'm simply asking what Jake has to do with it."

But he shakes his head.

"Can you answer the first question I asked in my email? What you meant by 'do I?'"

Still, he's unwilling, or unable, to answer.

"Okay. That's okay." I pat his leg and turn back to the list. "No worries."

Suddenly, Callum's voice is soft and cooing as he says hello to Edna, who stalks, low to the ground, into the living room.

Her cautious gaze doesn't move from the strange man invading her living room. We watch silently while she eats a few pieces of food from her bowl that I've moved into the kitchen now that she's more comfortable here. And we hold our breath as she jumps into my lap and bathes herself.

"Do you have to do that here?" I ask. "It's kinda weird."

"Don't even. You know if you could bathe in my lap right now, you would," Callum says.

Edna jerks when I laugh at the unexpected joke. It's true, though. During our month together, I came home a couple of times to a candle-lit bathroom and Callum holding two wine glasses in a bubble bath. What I wouldn't give to go back.

When Edna settles down, so do Callum and I, into each other. I turn on the TV and find a movie, a rom-com in which two people who hate each other are forced to work together on a project. It reminds me of Hailey and Tyler, and that's my last thought before I drift off to sleep in his warm embrace.

AFTER WE WOKE IN THE MORNING, TANGLED IN EACH OTHER'S limbs with Edna snoozing on top of both of us, he kissed my forehead and left.

A week passes with no contact between us. Torn between wanting to reach out and wanting to give him space, wanting him more than breath and wanting him to want me back, I write another letter.

Dear Callum,

There was this girl who hated being sad. Anytime she cried, it made her head hurt, her eyes puffy, and her nose ran. It would ruin her entire day, so she decided she just wouldn't cry. Being the middle sister between two drama queens—Stephanie, who's like Mom and lets the world know about every inconvenience, and Cori, who's in a bad mood so often that she walks around like a zombie—made me never want to be sad again. Obviously, I know that's not how life works, but to a little girl who doesn't have it all figured out, it seemed like a fantastic idea.

I proceeded to take care of problems promptly if the answer was clear, or if it wasn't, I simply chose not to worry about it.

For example, the girls at school who sniggered mean things and spread rumors about Cori and Hailey. At first, Cori gave as much as she got, like I would have done. But she hated getting in trouble and upsetting our parents, so she stopped fighting it. She gave up and fell into a hopeless, depressed state she couldn't get out of. So I decided to be proactive and do something about it. I've already told you this, but anytime I overheard anything said about them, I beat the shit out of whoever was speaking. Maybe not the best course of action, but what else was I supposed to do?

Anyway, like I said, I was suspended several times for fighting. And my grades suffered, causing Mom and Dad to have several parent-teacher conferences in which my 'performance' was discussed. Mom and Dad didn't know how to handle the situation other than by comparison. 'Can't you be more like your sisters? They get good grades and follow the rules.'

They developed the assumption that I made poor decisions, which we all know is true, but I didn't want to embarrass Cori by telling them the reason why I got into fights at school. And I didn't want to embarrass myself for the reason why my grades sucked: I was dumb.

My grades were just good enough to allow me to play volleyball, and I never intended to go to college, but was somehow skilled enough that I earned a scholarship. I was so proud of myself for accomplishing something Cori didn't, and my parents were just proud that I was doing something with my talents.

But if I struggled with high school curriculum, I'm sure you can imagine how college went. I failed nearly every class that first semester. The worst part is, I actually tried. If I had been failing because I spent too much time partying or with boys, then it wouldn't have hurt so badly. But I worked my ass off, staying up late, joining study groups, reading until my eyes bled. But you can't fix stupid, so I dropped out.

Again, my parents, and everyone, for that matter, berated me for such a dumb, impulsive decision. I told them school was hard, but I didn't elaborate on the real reason: I was scared. Assuming I would lose my scholarship or my place at college altogether, I left before I could be humiliated by being kicked off the team or kicked out of school.

I already told you why I joined Cori's business venture—because I was scared of failing on my own. So before I could, I jumped ship and climbed into hers.

This is the one decision I made that I don't regret. Not only did I learn a lot, but I also helped Cori by accompanying her on her journey.

Then Brian. It was fun at first, but that was a relationship that had no business turning serious. But when your family doubts your ability to commit and starts taking bets on how long your relationship will last, you take drastic measures.

And when I found the tank top in his bathroom, my mind spiraled out of control with the possibilities that something was going on while he and I were still together. The reason why you don't go back to your ex-fiancé's apartment less than a month after walking out of your wedding is so your brain can adjust to the change in relationships. Physically, we were separated. But mentally, I didn't know where I belonged, or with whom, and my gut reaction was to be upset, when really, I'm relieved I'm not the only one walking out of weddings and jumping into relationships with other people.

I've had a lot of time to think about all of this since I left you at the restaurant. You were right when you told me I don't have a clue what I'm doing. I try different things out, then leave before I can get burned. On my own terms. And that's all I really know how to do.

You caught me off guard that night. I'm not used to being hurt that way because I'm usually the one causing the pain. It was a shocking experience, to say the least, but it may have been what I needed.

And right now, I'm in a weird place where I need to

'chill' (as Cori put it), but I don't know how to be by myself. And I think it's because I don't really like myself either.

Once again, your move,

Sage

40

WHAT WOULD SAGE DO?

A week after I sent the letter, I receive a thick envelope in the mail from Callum. I rip it open there by the mailboxes.

Dear Sage,

There was this girl who completely destroyed my world. I first met her when she walked into Francesca's, wearing a hot pink dress and I struggled to keep the drool in my mouth. I was so lost in my sudden attraction for this woman I knew nothing about that it took her waving her hand an inch from my face for me to realize she was talking to me.

She asked what was wrong with me. The answer was her.

Then, for the remainder of dinner, I had

to sit there being tortured every time she laughed, but not for the reasons you think. Not because I found her to be obnoxious. Or maybe I did, but in the best way. Her laugh was the sound of pure, unfiltered joy. A ray of light completely innocent of any evil in the world.

You think I was looking around the room in embarrassment. I was. But not because you embarrassed me. I was looking to see if anyone noticed how distracted I was, how creepy I was being, or how gone I was. I had to rub my eyes because of the perverted images that kept popping up in my brain.

And when you stuck the breadsticks in your mouth that night at dinner, it reminded me of when you did the same thing the night we met. It reminded me of how strong my feelings for you are. It reminded me of why I don't deserve you.

I told you the chef we ran into was Jake, but I haven't told you the rest of his story. Why it hurts when I look at you. Why I'll never be able to be with you.

It wasn't just my teammates and I, no one liked him. No one wanted to be around him because he wore the smell of cigarette smoke and his roach-infested house on his clothes. He was the topic of online forums, he was the target for stink bombs, he didn't have a single friend at school.

His dad was in and out of jail, and his mom was too high to remember she had a son. And apparently, he had tried out for the football team at one point before I was there. He made it, but had to leave because he couldn't afford the fees. And they didn't have any program for kids in need, since it was just an extracurricular.

I found out all of that after this one particular day. A girl I was dating had broken up with me and I was in a mood to hurt someone. So I followed him around school, saying every mean thing I could think of, just begging him to punch me so I could go at him. But he never did. Instead, he went home, took a bunch of his mom's pills and drank his dad's alcohol, trying to kill himself.

Halfway through, he changed his mind and, thankfully, was still alert enough to call for an ambulance. I was at football practice when this happened, and I came home to my mom and dad, having already found out through the vine of gossiping parents—some kids had told their parents about witnessing me pestering him that day at school. I'll never forget the look of disbelief in their eyes. They didn't recognize their son in my body.

When I saw him in the restaurant, all of that guilt came back at once. I couldn't handle it. And then you tried to cheer me up and I lost it. You don't deserve what I said to you or how I treated you. But that's just why I can't be with you. Why I can't be with anyone. I can't risk hurting you or anyone else because I hate myself.

Now that you know all of that, do I? Deserve to burn in hell for the pain I've caused, like Sam?

I love you,
Callum

I was standing when I started reading the letter, but when I look up from Callum's heartbreaking words, I find myself on the floor. Tears blur my vision and smudge the ink on the page that shakes in my hands.

All this time. All this time, he had feelings for me, but thought him to be the unworthy one. I had it so wrong.

Cori's initial on the bracelet on my wrist weakens my legs before I can stand. What would Cori do? She'd dissociate and avoid making a decision at all. But I can't sit back and do nothing while he's hurting like this, because, no, he doesn't deserve to burn in hell. But I can't go to him either. He'll just turn me away.

Imagining the initial is mine instead of Cori's, I ask myself, what would Sage do? The answer pops in my head immediately: whatever the fuck she wants. Not to boast, but everyone should wear a 'WWSD' bracelet on their wrist.

So without thinking it through before I can talk myself out of acting, I jump to my feet and take off. And it's the best decision I've ever made.

I'M TOO EARLY AND THE DOORS AREN'T UNLOCKED YET. HE'S probably busy prepping, but this won't take long. The faster he agrees, the faster he can get back to work. With my face against the glass, I spot a man just inside stacking menus, but he ignores me when I knock. He still pretends I'm not here when I start banging on the door, so I shout, "I just need to talk to Jake! Chef Jake!"

That gets his attention. He studies me, probably assessing my crazy meter, before disappearing. A minute later, Jake, in a white t-shirt and black pants, peeks around the corner and cautiously steps outside. His dark hair looks the same, if not a tad shorter than the night I was here with Callum. I try picturing the scrawny teenager with holes in his clothes that Callum described, but I can't. The man in front of me is broad-shouldered and healthy, although still slim.

"Do you remember me, by chance?" I ask.

He tilts his head, studying me. "You threw the water in..."—he gestures inside—"his face."

"Yes. Do you have a moment to talk about him?"

Looking behind him, he wrings his hands. He faces me again, swallowing hard, and nods.

"Look, he told me everything. I know he did a terrible thing. I'm so sorry for all that you went through in school. I can't even begin to imagine the emotions you must have felt to make a decision like you did." I pause, unsure of how to ask what I came here for. To ask someone to forgive a person who hurt you in such a way... honestly, I should just leave.

Instead, I ask, "Would you be open to getting to know the man he is now?"

He doesn't answer right away. His brows furrow as he glances around the parking lot. "Why?"

"Because I want you to forgive him, but I understand that would be difficult if you don't know all the good he's done with his time since. If you don't understand the guilt he's felt, or the time he's spent praying that you're okay. Also, he's been asked to do something, but he doesn't want to without knowing you'd be okay with it."

"Honestly, I don't even remember his name. I remember his face and a few of the shitty things he said to me, but not much else. Why exactly does he feel guilty? It was ten years ago. I don't think bullies typically remember being bullies, let alone feel guilt over it."

I blink, unsure how to answer that. "His name is Callum Ridge, and he thinks he's solely responsible for your suicide attempt."

He scratches his head. "Well, he's not."

I'm not sure if that's a good thing or not. On one hand, Callum has wasted all this time worrying over something Jake doesn't blame him for. On the other, there's less for Jake to forgive. "So, would you be open to getting to know him, then? Having a beer or cup of coffee with him and reassuring him that he's not a horrible person?"

His blue eyes narrow. "Uhh, I'm not sure if I really want to take on the burden of having to comfort some guy who used to bully me. He may not be the reason behind my actions, but he was still a jerk."

Shit. Not the reaction I was hoping for. "Okay, I get that. But I think it might do you both some good to reconnect and get some closure on that time of your life." I hand him the paper with Callum's number and address scribbled hastily. "Here's his info, just in case. Don't you want to talk to him about it?"

He takes it, but his forehead creases. "What is there to talk about?"

When he turns around, I begin to panic. But what else is there to say?

He reaches for the large door handle. "No, that's a time of my life I'd rather just forget about completely. And *Callum* is responsible for his own feelings, not me."

My shoulders deflate as he disappears inside, leaving me locked out here, unsure what else I could try to help Callum. Because I *have to* help him.

He did something awful. Unforgivable, even. But I'm selfish. And when I want something, I'll get it. And I want Callum to realize how amazing he is.

WITH THE JAKE ROUTE BEING A DEAD-END, I CHANGE TACTICS with my portrait of Callum. I had put it on hold when I sold my first ever commissioned piece. Mom's the customer, but it counts because Mom isn't easily impressed.

She asked for 'something pretty' to hang above the couch in her living room, so I painted bluebonnets, our state flower and Mom's favorite, around a red anatomically correct heart. She was mortified at first, unappreciative of the reminder of her heart attack, and uninterested in hanging an organ on her wall. But, in her attempts at being a better mother, she rolled her eyes and hung it on the wall anyway. After a few compliments from friends and neighbors, she appreciated the praise and directed them to my website. She's much freer with the praise she gives after she gets some first.

Instead of writing his name everywhere, I'm making a list of words to describe him, and using quotes he's said to me. For example, the singular words include: kind, humble, and admirable, but also words like breadsticks, tornado, friend-moon, and love. And even names such as Mrs. Browning, Mr. Parsons, the names of our friends, mine.

Around his eyes, I'll write the words, *'Her laugh was the sound of pure, unfiltered joy.'* For the other, *'You are obnoxious. But that's one of the many lovable things about you.'* And for a lock of his hair, *'I don't want to get* hard.' Then, I'll cover those words with the color of his skin, hair, eyes, a layer of paint thin enough that the words create the shadows and contours of his face.

I see the entirety of our friend-moon in a new light. Every pained look, every touch he didn't want, every sexual comment that made him squirm. He wasn't disgusted with me, he wanted me. He wasn't judging me, he was judging himself. He wasn't pushing me to behave, he was pushing me to stop ignoring my feelings.

And I now know why I was so hurt by his dismissal and our separation. Not because of pride, but because I'm falling for him for real. Not as a rebound, not as someone to *hang out* with. I may be selfish, but I want that version of him back because I want to cook and paint for him and fall asleep next to him every night. I want to wrap him in my love and make him feel like he made me feel: safe.

41

DO YOU REMEMBER OUR DISCUSSION ABOUT STRANGER DANGER?

"Are you sure you don't want lunch? You haven't let me fix you lunch in a few weeks. I'm worried about you," Mrs. Browning says as we reach her door. "You've been quiet, too. Is it Sage? You know, she's called me twenty times just this week to ask about you. And to tell me about that damn cat she named after me," she adds with a scowl.

I smile. "It's not really about Sage. Well, not *just* about her, anyway."

I've attended church with her a couple of times since returning from the east, and started visiting Mr. Parsons on Saturdays, mainly to keep myself busy. I only have an hour before my shift at the animal shelter, and I might end up going early and staying late.

"Okay then. If you change your mind, or if you want supper, just knock."

"Yes, ma'am." I hug her goodbye and head up the stairs to my apartment. Only when I get to the top and see who's waiting for me, I can't seem to take another step.

He stills when our gazes lock.

Neither of us says anything for a few minutes, both of us

avoiding eye contact and shifting our feet. He mirrors my stance, slipping his hands in his pockets, and I clear my throat.

Finally, he sighs. "Um, that girl with the orange hair, she gave me your address." Of course she did.

I nod.

"She said you needed closure or something, I don't know. Suggested I get to know the '*man you are now*.'" He makes air quotes with his fingers, and his tone drips with condescension.

"Why did you come? You clearly don't want to be here." I don't mean it as harshly as it sounds. I intend to let him know he doesn't have to be here for my benefit. But, like with Sage, my words are too gruff.

"I don't. Honestly, I was curious. And wanted to rub it in your face a little how well I turned out, despite everything."

"You did. You look great. Healthy. And a chef... that's so impressive." What else can I say to give him the validation he seeks? To keep the attention on him, I avoid any 'I' statements, like 'I'm proud of you,' or 'I'm glad,' despite the itch to tell him so.

"Also, I find it ridiculous that you feel any guilt over the... situation. If you remember me so well, then you'll remember how horrible my home life was, and how there was half a school that wouldn't leave me alone. It wasn't just you. It was a million different things all pressing down on a teenage boy. It was just,"—his voice cracks—"too much."

I nod, begging tears not to well in my eyes. "I know, but I was ashamed, still am, that I was ever a factor. No matter how small. Because, really, it was never about you at all." I shake my head. "That sounds shitty, but I was pressured by my teammates, and I caved under that pressure. I mean, how fucking weak was I when you were handling everything you were, and I couldn't do something as simple as *not* bully someone?"

"I'm happy for you that you had a true, American high

school experience. I didn't." He shrugs. "But it's over now. There's no point in beating yourself up over it anymore."

Therapy didn't help, time didn't help, punishing myself didn't help. And I doubt this discussion will help. "I don't really know how not to."

But what *would* happen if I simply... dropped it? My punishing myself isn't helping Jake in any way; all I'm doing is punishing the people in my life.

Standing at another impasse in the conversation, he rocks back on his heels, glancing around at the cracks in the siding and the paint peeling off the door.

"That woman said you wanted my permission before doing something? What is that about?"

I point to my door. "Do you wanna..."

He nods, and I unlock my door

He walks in slowly, taking in the place, declining any offer of coffee or water. He sits on the couch, but I remain standing. To join him, even with a whole seat between us, is too close.

"So, my friends, Tyler and Hailey, are teachers at a junior high. They're running a no-bullying week, where the kids dress up each day, and there's activities. At the end of the week, there's an assembly. They asked me to talk to the kids about how bullying is wrong."

"Why would you need my permission for that?"

"I don't, I just felt weird accepting considering I'm going to be convincing them not to do the very thing I did in school."

He looks down at his hands, pressed together. "Which school is it?"

"Simon's."

He raises his head. "Hm. That's where my little sister goes."

I don't recall him having a sibling. "Your what?"

Did he have a sibling in that house that relied on him? God knows if his parents didn't care for him, they wouldn't have cared for another child either. And after what happened, he disappeared. We assumed foster care, so he and his sister were probably separated. I never thought I could feel worse about the situation, but the walls close in.

"My little sister. She's twelve. Seventh grade."

"Is she your... biological sister?" I ask gently, hoping it was a foster sibling he took in after aging out.

"Yeah. She was two when we were put in foster care, but I was able to get custody of her a couple of years ago." He takes a loud breath. "As for the assembly, I think it'd be better coming from someone who's done it. You don't want to hear from someone about how drinking excessively is bad for you from someone who's never had a drop of alcohol in their life. It'd be more effective coming from someone who's suffered with alcoholism. Same concept."

A thought occurs. Maybe it could be the most effective with both of us up there. "Would you want to speak with me?"

He shakes his head immediately, as if he read my mind before I asked. "Hard pass on that."

"Would you come?" I hate how vulnerable my voice sounds, or the hope blooming in my chest that he accepts.

"Hard pass again." He stands, clapping his hands together. "Was that it?"

I don't know what I expected to happen if he came inside, but it wasn't for him to leave after five minutes. It's not like we'll ever be friends, so it'd be too much to hope for forgiveness.

"Yeah, that's it." I walk him to the door, but stop him before opening it. "Actually... look, I know you said I shouldn't feel any guilt, but I do. And I don't know how this will make you feel, so you don't have to say anything. But... I'm sorry."

He stares at the ground for a beat before nodding. "Have a nice life, Callum."

Recipients: pinkhairdontcare@lwb.com

Subject: Thank you.

So Jake showed up at my apartment. Do you remember our discussion about stranger danger? He's not exactly a stranger, but handing out my home address to a guy I used to bully was a bit of a risk. Not that I'm complaining, but if I'm ever murdered, I have a feeling you'll be involved somehow.

Never in a million years would I have done half of the things you've done. But it's time to admit that I don't always know everything. You and your perfect wildness has brought so much healing to my life.

Anyway, I wanted to thank you. The conversation was short, painful, and made me feel silly for holding onto everything for so long, but I think it helped.

Callum

42

MY EVEREST

My heart pounds in my ears as I stand off to the side in the junior high gym. It smells like sweat, peanut butter and jelly sandwiches, and farts that I'm not at all certain aren't mine.

No one likes public speaking, but it's never been a big deal to me. Not that I do it often, but high school speech class and presenting during meetings at work aren't anything to get worked up over. But standing up in front of a bunch of kids who aren't kids but aren't quite teenagers, who can find fault in anything and turn their noses up at everything, might be my Everest.

Hailey stands in the middle of the gym, opening the assembly, telling the kids to be on their best behavior, and introducing me. After she calls my name, I somehow end up taking her place, with the microphone now in my hand instead of hers and no memory of walking here.

I am terrified. Terrified of saying the wrong thing and disappointing Hailey, terrified of sounding dumb and being laughed at by these kids. And terrified this won't help at all to ease my own suffering.

I raise the microphone, but can't get my mouth to open or my brain to retrieve the words I had planned to say. Just when I start wracking my brain for a way out of this, considering faking a fainting spell or a heart attack, I see her. Sage.

I may have that heart attack after all from the sight of her long legs extending from her maroon dress, which somehow clashes with *and* perfectly matches her orange hair. She waves excitedly and blows a kiss, and it's exactly what I need to start.

"HURT PEOPLE HURT PEOPLE," I SAY INTO THE SEA OF PRETEENS. "And what I mean by that is, when someone bullies another person, the real problem lies within the bully. They're insecure about something, and instead of handling those insecurities like an adult, they're projecting them onto the victim. I know this because I did it myself.

"I was so terrified of being ostracized by my fellow teammates-"

A hand flies up from a boy with dark, messy hair.

"Oh, uh..." I look to Hailey, unsure if I should call on him or tell him to wait until after I'm finished. I take her shrug to mean that it's my decision. "Go ahead," I tell him, hoping I don't forget what I was saying.

"What does that 'ostrich' word mean?"

"*Ostracized?* It means... Well, I didn't want to be rejected by my fellow teammates. Or excluded. I wanted them to like me."

He nods, understanding, so I continue.

"I wanted them to like me so badly that I joined them in the bullying of a kid who didn't deserve any of it. One day in partic-ular, I was feeling sorry for myself. I wanted to make someone else feel as bad as I did because I couldn't handle the emotions I was feeling. I was hurt. I was dumb. I was immature. And I dealt with it as a hurt, dumb, immature kid would, by bullying."

I have no idea if I'm handling this appropriately, but it's too late to change anything now.

"When I was in high school, I was on the football team and wore my letter jacket every single day so everyone would know exactly which group I belonged to. I ate lunch with the cool kids, I went to parties, and I talked down to every person I thought was beneath me." Holding my hands out, I gesture to my clothing. "Now look at me. I dress like this every day, I eat lunch alone in my car, and I go to bed at nine-thirty most nights after watching the news. Because when you grow up, you look back at your younger self and feel only guilt that you cared so much what the 'cool kids' thought of you.

"When you're in junior high, you think being popular is the most important thing, and that not being popular is a death sentence. And it's okay to care what other people think of you to an extent. But life is so much bigger than wearing name-brand tennis shoes or having the right hairstyle. You may not know that yet because you spend your life within these walls and with these people, but I want you to know how serious this topic is. The reason you have these assemblies every year. I know you all dressed up in fun clothing all week and did activities, but this isn't just some boring agenda being pushed on you by a bunch of adults who forgot what it's like to be your age. Bullying has a lifelong effect on the victims. But also on the bullies.

"And I want you to go home today realizing how much of a privilege it is to worry about homework and these boring assemblies. Because some kids don't even have food. Or running water. Some kids have health problems they can't get cures for, or parents who don't care. And some kids are just different from you and have different priorities and hobbies."

I need to rein it in because I'm rambling and boring even myself.

"The point is, you never know what the person next to you

is battling in their life. Chances are, you'll *never* know, and you have to decide how to treat them based on the only information you have about them. Which might be that their hair is dirty and greasy, maybe their shoes have holes in them. Whether all of that is because of circumstances they can't control, or because they like appearing that way, how childish is it to bully someone based on their appearance? And what is it that you're covering up about yourself by making fun of someone?"

There's sniggering in the audience, and I feel like a dad reprimanding a kid who only thinks it's funny. But I'm not just doing this for myself or Jake, I'm doing this for Hailey, who will never get an apology from the people who hurt her in school.

I don't know if I'm allowed to do this, or even if it will work, but I have to try. "If you're comfortable doing so, raise your hand and tell me a reason you've been made fun of." Then, I pray at least one kid raises their hand to participate.

Hands go up all over the bleachers, and I look over at Hailey who gives an encouraging smile.

"Wow, okay." I point to a girl with a brown ponytail. "Go ahead."

"I get made fun of because I'm in band," she says softly.

"Because you're in band? Because you enjoy making music with an instrument? How dumb is that? The amount of energy wasted on making fun of someone because their hobbies are different could be spent learning how to play an instrument. And maybe that's just it—maybe they're jealous because they don't know how to play one." I doubt that's the case; band kids were always lowest on the totem pole in terms of 'coolness,' but they tended to be the ones who cared the least about what others thought of them. They were free in a way to be who they wanted, but also bullied over the dumbest reason.

I return the smile she gives me and I move on to another girl wearing a cheerleader uniform.

"Kids make fun of me because of my size."

"This is the perfect example of tearing other people down to make yourself feel better." Meeting the girl's eyes, I say specifically to her, "I guarantee the people who make comments to you about your size are insecure about their own looks, so they shift the attention to you. Your size is no one's business but your own. So the next time someone makes a comment, you should feel flattered that they spend so much time thinking about you."

She nods, and I can only hope the other kids in this gym, the ones who have made fun of this girl, hear my words.

I point to a boy wearing a graphic t-shirt with dinosaurs. "People give me mean looks when I try to talk to them." He looks down suddenly, shaking his body and flapping his hands, an action I think is called stimming. He sits low in the bleachers with a group of children with special needs and a couple of teachers on each end.

I walk closer to where he sits and kneel down. "What is your name?"

"Nathan," he answers without meeting my eyes.

I rise and speak to the audience again. "Y'all are missing out because I imagine Nathan here is an amazing friend. And anyone who makes a face at you for just trying to talk to them isn't worth your time, Nathan. You know, my favorite person in the world can walk up to anyone and strike up a conversation. It's my favorite thing about her. Don't ever let any of those inse-cure people change that about you."

We hear from a couple more kids before Tyler motions for me to hurry. Hailey slaps his arm down, then proceeds to move her hand in a 'wrap it up' gesture, agreeing with Tyler that I need to finish, but wanting control of this assembly.

"I'm getting orders to stop talking now, but I have one last thing to say. You'll have to live with your actions for the rest of your life. Don't say something you can't forgive yourself for. Because that self-hatred doesn't go away, it clings like cancer of the mind. You might not care now, but you can't hide from the guilt of hurting another person. And when it catches up to you, you'll end up a loser, just like me."

With that done, I pretend I'm Sage for a moment. I envision myself unstrapping a heavy bag from my shoulders and dropping it. Then I walk away.

AFTER THE SPEECH IS OVER, I STAND OFF TO THE SIDE BY TYLER while Hailey gives a closing message to the kids and tells them to head to their last period of the day.

"Good job, man," Tyler says, shaking my hand and pulling me in for a 'bro' hug.

I wipe the sweat off my forehead. "Were we that terrifying at that age?"

He chuckles. "Now you know how I feel every day." He slaps my shoulder in goodbye and heads to the locker room.

Feeling like I'm being pulled by some invisible magnet, my head turns, and Sage floods my senses. She stands just a couple feet away with her back to me, her fruity perfume hits me at the same time as her laugh at whatever Erin said as they hug each other goodbye. Sauntering toward me, her smile beams bright, and I can't help but smile back and open my arms. She fits so perfectly against my chest.

"That was a damn good speech, Mr. Ridge."

"Thanks. I didn't know you'd be here."

"Of course." She looks at the floor, toeing the tile with her black heel. "I didn't know if you'd want me here, so I didn't tell you beforehand. Sorry."

"That's okay. I'm glad you came." I want to ask how she's doing, what she's been up to, besides what she's told me in her emails, but I can't get the words out. Like I don't know how to talk to her in person anymore, now that she knows everything.

"Did you see who else came?" she asks gently, as if afraid of my reaction.

I shake my head and look around. Then I see him. My stomach dips, whether from joy that he heard or fear that he heard, I'm not sure. A young girl—a mini, female version of him—does some sort of elaborate handshake with fist bumps and funny faces, then runs off towards a group of her friends.

"So he came after all," I say.

"Yep."

My heartbeat picks up when he looks my way. I want to shy away from the eye contact, but hold it because he deserves to have his bully face him head-on. Instead of spitting in my direction or flipping me off, he nods and shoots a thumbs-up in my direction. Then he slips his hand in his pocket and leaves. And that's the best I could hope for.

43

I'VE GOT A FOOT AND IT'S COMING DOWN

I 'm nervous. I don't get nervous, but the soup and salad combo I had for lunch gurgles in my gut. My palms sweat all over the painting in my hand, and I've never been more glad I work with acrylic instead of oil paint. Not that I'd be carrying the canvas the way I am if it were oil, but—*focus, Sage.*

I knock meekly on his door. Time feels different on this side, but it's only seconds before he's standing in front of me, still in the jeans and buttoned shirt he wore to the assembly.

A gentle smile graces his lips, and I almost forget what I came to do when thoughts of pouncing cloud my intentions. "Sage. What are you doing here?" It's a question that could be asked in a hundred different tones, implying a hundred different things. But he asks as if he's pleasantly surprised that I'm standing, uninvited, on his doorstep, rather than annoyed.

"I wanted to bring you the piece I've been working on." I've never been shy or insecure about showing my artwork like some people. Selling is a different matter, but revealing a finished product to simply be admired? My ego could stand to be taken down a notch.

Now, however, revealing Callum's face to him, after everything we've been through, my hands tremble as I turn the canvas around.

Upon first glance, his eyes widen, the corners of his lips curling upwards. The sight settles my nerves and enrages the butterflies in my belly all at once.

"Like I said, it's what your face looks like when you look at me. Now, I know it's a yearning sort of look, but originally I thought it was disgust. You really should vary your expressions a little more," I joke, a poor attempt to lighten the mood. "And I must admit, my reasons for choosing your face were petty at first. But if you look beneath the strokes of your skin, you'll see who you really are: the most wonderful man."

He doesn't respond as he reads the words that make up the shapes and shadows.

"At first, I was just going to write your name however many times it took to create your face. But then I changed it to words that describe you, or things you've said, or"—I point to the words *frog* and *tornado*—"memories that only we'd understand." I didn't plan on using the surface paint either, but I wanted him to know that I see beneath his surface now.

"This is amazing, Sage. Truly, I knew you were talented, but I'm still blown away anytime I see your work." He carries it inside, immediately searching for the best spot to hang it.

"Thank you."

"No, thank *you*. And I'm paying you for this. How much is it? I don't care how high the number is." He inspects a bare wall in his bedroom and leans the canvas against it.

My arms cross over my chest. "No, it's my gift to you. My thanks for helping me escape my wedding, coming with me on my honeymoon, and for helping me see parts of myself I hadn't before."

He pulls me into his chest, his hands clasping behind my back as if he's afraid to touch me too much. I nestle into him, but my heart bursts with more to say.

Pulling back, I kneel down to the canvas. "I know there are parts of *you* that I still don't know yet, but this is you on canvas. All of you that I know. Your looks, but also what makes you, you. Your selflessness," I say, pointing to *Mrs. Browning* and *volunteer*. "Your heart, your intuitiveness." I point to one last word—*safe*. "You."

I thought he'd made me question my intelligence, my confidence, even my worth, but those insecurities were already there. He just forced me to realize what I was hiding by pretending I'm more confident than I truly am. He challenged me in ways I didn't know I needed to be challenged, and made me better for it.

Some complementary colors cancel each other out, neutralizing their vibrancy and turning them gray. And while I feel more settled and grounded, I definitely don't feel gray; I feel safe. I can be the vibrant, wild one who jumps into cars with strangers, but I can also be the one who spends all evening gazing at the stars without boring him to tears. Callum is the kind of complementary color that enhances my brightness and dimension, and I can only hope I do that for him, too.

"Can we start over?" I hate how pleading and desperate my voice is, but I want him. Not because I'm bored, not because he's hot, not because sex is great. But because he's home. He's soft and gentle, but has no problem handling me or telling me off if I need it. Not that I'll listen, but I like my men strict. He's the man for me in ways Brian never could be.

But he turns away. "It doesn't work like that, Sage."

Sometimes, I really just want to smack him.

"Because *you* won't let it. The only one standing in our way is you." My face blazes with frustration.

"I don't want to hurt you again." My heart breaks for how little he thinks of himself. And maybe this is a bad idea, but I fully believe we can tackle this together.

"Then don't. It's that easy. I know it doesn't sound like it, but it is. Literally, all you have to do is accept the love I so desperately want to give you." Besides, I've probably done more damage, said more hurtful things to him than he has to me. But the guilt hangs onto him like a clingy, defiant toddler he refuses to stand his ground with.

Well, I've got a foot, and it's coming down. The only way I'm leaving here without his acceptance is if he hauls me away.

Even if our relationship ends badly... well, frankly, I don't give a damn. I make decisions quickly, I don't always think things through, but I've never had a problem with living that way—the issue is with other people whose personalities could never allow them the freedom I have. Callum included. But Cori thinks every decision to death, and she's still made plenty of mistakes. I just want to live.

I look down at the bracelet now. What would Cori do? Cori would want me to be happy.

"Besides, you said it yourself. I have issues. And you have issues. We're kinda the perfect pair. Let us take our issues, throw them together, and who knows? Maybe they'll cancel each other out." Two negatives make a positive, I know that much. When it comes to relationships, that might mean burning us to a crisp, or it could mean an inferno of passion and happiness. Since I'm an optimist, I choose to ignore the former possibility.

"But you deserve someone who loves themselves, so that they can love you properly." My heart breaks as tears well in his eyes.

"I can love you and me enough for the both of us." He starts to shake his head, with 'that's not how it works,' on the tip of his tongue, so I add, "But since you're stubborn and won't listen, how about this: do I not deserve to be with the man I love?"

His expression softens. "Do you really love me?"

"I do." My voice is soft and seductive, and I bite my lip, hoping this ends the way I want it to.

He's quiet for a moment while he ponders his answer, rearranging the fibers of the carpet with his foot. "What if you get bored of me?"

"Well, first off, I'm saying let me love you, not marry me. That would be nuts." I smirk at the irony. "And two, you're going to get fed up with me way before I grow bored of you."

"It's fast." At this point, I think he's just teasing me, urging me to say more nice things, like I did when we talked about selling my artwork.

I laugh. He should know by now I don't follow anyone's timeline except my own. "I like things fast."

He nods once, decided. "Alright then. Go home and pack your bags."

"What? Why?"

"Friend-moon redo. Although we need a different name. Again."

"Seriously?" I ask, waiting for the punchline.

"Seriously." He looks up in thought. "Are you able to disappear for an entire week again? Let's redo San Antonio. And Galveston, if you want, although the water will probably be chilly. Or we could go to Dallas this time. Or Louisiana. Or we can just drive and see where Eleanor takes us."

Just like that, I've found the man who will speed down the open road with me, destination unknown, but who can also handle a slow cruise to enjoy the ride. My squeal erupts, piercing the silence, and I jump into his arms.

44

MAKE SOME COFFEE, CALLUM.
BECAUSE I'M NOT DONE YET

After Sage gives a quick goodbye to Edna, promising *'Auntie Danielle'* will be by to spend the week with her, we climb in my truck, ready for the hours-long drive to San Antonio. Sage was disappointed, missing the romantic dinner on the River Walk, so it only makes sense to start our journey there. Or here in my truck, if she doesn't quit looking at me like that.

Her eyes are soft, trailing down my chest, and pausing on my crotch. She bites her lip and quirks a brow before running her hand over her neck and down her chest.

"Touch yourself and see what happens."

She grins, nearing the waist of her shorts.

"I will bend you over this console," I threaten. But it only makes her smile wider as she slips her fingers into her shorts and arches her back. I'm torn between carrying out my promise and watching; I'm sort of curious anyway, what it looks like when she plays with herself.

So I watch as her eyes roll back in her head, as she rides her fingers, as she reaches back and grabs the headrest. And I enjoy the melody of her moans as she reaches orgasm.

All it takes to spur me into action, pushing my seat all the way back and unbuttoning my jeans, is watching as she takes her hand out and sticks her fingers in her mouth. My own groan escapes, a desperate, pathetic plea.

She shimmies her shorts and panties down her leg, climbs over the console and into my lap, and is moving before I'm fully inside of her.

Her ass hits the horn, causing us both to jump and her to bonk her head against the roof.

"Are you okay?" I ask, concerned.

She only laughs, nodding, before clashing her mouth against mine, and the taste of her lingering on her lips almost sends me over the edge. I reach one hand up to block her head from hitting the top again, while my other enjoys a handful of her ass as it begins moving again.

This woman. I want to breathe in the air she exhales, swallow her moans, and bathe myself with her wetness. Too much of a good thing is usually a bad thing, but I'll gladly live the rest of my life hypnotized by her beauty if it means causing her hand to slap against the window or her eyes to roll back in her head.

People who haven't hated themselves or gone through depression say to just be happy. But when you don't think you deserve it, that's impossible. It's a vicious cycle, a rip current you can't swim out of as it carries you further from shore. And the further out you go, the less likely you'll ever make it back at all.

I'm not in the clear. I'm still trying to find my way out, but instead of letting it carry me off like I'd been doing, I vow to start making that conscious decision, once again, every morning, not to haul my baggage around all day. And maybe eventually, I'll forget where I set it. For Sage.

FIVE HOURS LATER, SAGE SWIRLS A GLASS OF RED WINE, CHEEKS already flushed beneath soft lighting. Neither of us has said much, but not from discomfort or awkwardness. After we fastened our buttons and put our shirts back on, she talked the entire drive to San Antonio and has probably run out of events to inform me about. I, on the other hand, can't focus enough to string two words together because her cleavage, displayed above a low-cut, purple dress, demands my attention.

We've already been to the hotel, checked it for bugs and weird smells, and unpacked some of our stuff, although I don't see us needing a lot of clothes.

Despite the chill in the November air, I requested a table outside by the river. Of course, she didn't bring a jacket, but I don't mind giving her mine. It looks better on her anyway and lets every male in our vicinity know she's mine. She leaves it open, though, to taunt me. And I love her for it.

She looks toward the sky.

"I know it's not a picnic, and you can't really see the stars here, but is it enough?"

Her eyes snap to mine. "How did you know what my ideal date was?"

"That night we met, you talked to Danielle about letting one of the male servers take you on it. You mentioned riding him on the blanket laid out after you ate."

"And you remembered all this time?"

I lift a shoulder. "Of course. I've spent the last two years trying to keep my thoughts from drifting into a daydream in which it's me you're riding instead."

She smiles and reaches for my hand. "What's your ideal date?

The answer slips from my tongue, not requiring any thought. "Literally anything as long as it's with you."

She smirks, and I prepare myself for her taunting. "What

about jumping into a stranger's jeep to chase down a car-napper?"

The stress I felt in that moment as Sage threw herself into motion, determined to get Eleanor back with no consideration for how reckless she was being, is not something I ever want to feel again. However, her take-charge attitude, her passion for the things she loves, only made me love her more. "As long as you're not flirting with anyone else, and as long as you come out of it unharmed, I'd do *anything* with you."

I shouldn't have said that.

Her brow quirks up. "Or what?" Her teasing voice moves over my body like a mist, sliding down my spine and raising the bumps on my skin. Just then, our server approaches, and Sage watches me, her smirk still painted in red on her lips.

Before she can test me by shrugging my jacket off her shoulders and batting her eyelashes at the poor unsuspecting man, I rush to request the check. "And a to-go container for my... *girlfriend,*" I add, pointedly. The smile that breaks out over her face sucks all breath from my lungs.

She stands abruptly, sending her chair to the floor, and squeals, running around the table to jump in my lap. Her arms squeeze my neck while mine wrap lightly around her waist, and I breathe her in, hardly believing this is real. Am I entirely sure I didn't collapse in front of those kids and split my head wide open? Because this is exactly what I imagine heaven to be.

"Thank you for bringing me here," she says softly, her breath hitting my ear.

"Thank you for bringing me along on your honeymoon."

She laughs, pulling back to look at me. "It was more like I *dragged* you along, but sure."

"Only because I was afraid of getting my heart broken by having to watch you smile and hear your laugh, or smell your perfume, but not getting to touch you."

"What about *taste* me?" she asks, running a finger over my lips.

"Huh?"

"You listed every sense but that one."

It wasn't intentional, but now that I think about it, not being able to taste her would have been the most heartbreaking. I'm having withdrawals even now, despite the faint teasing from her lips in my truck earlier.

I grab her hips and lift her off my lap. "On that note, we need to go."

THE DOOR IS BARELY CLOSED BEFORE I'M SLIDING HER DRESS OFF her shoulders in a hurry. There's no bra or underwear covering her.

"Are you telling me there was nothing else but that dress covering you while we were at dinner?"

A devious grin takes hold of her lips.

Turning her around so her stomach is flat on the bed and her face in the sheets, I lift her hips in the air and run my tongue up her seam.

"I missed this so fucking much," I growl into her wetness before plunging my fingers inside. It isn't long before she's squirming, grinding against my face, then begging for release. I give it to her, but she gets no rest before I'm unbuttoning my pants and sinking deep inside my favorite place to be. It's warm and soft, and I never want to leave. But no matter how hard I try to make the moment last, I can't stop my hips from moving. The sheets muffle her screams, but I want anyone on either side of our room to hear my name on her lips.

I pull out just long enough to flip her over before sliding back inside. Her legs wrap around my waist, and her hands fist my hair. My forehead falls to hers, our heavy breath mingling, and my movements slow, wanting this moment, with my chest flush against hers, to last forever. She matches my movements, and we stare into each other's eyes while our pleasure builds. Reaching between us, I palm her breast with one hand while gripping her thigh in the other.

Our orgasms are separate, but it feels like we share one as she moves with me, legs tightening and hands tugging on my hair. I could not love her more if I tried.

Each time my lips meet hers is a silent vow to be better than my best in order to make her happy. Each stroke of my hand against her soft skin is a promise to forgive myself solely because she deserves better. And as I roll off of her, pulling her into my chest, I think about how I won't survive another separation, and that I will do anything it takes to keep her here with me.

"I miss Edna."

"Huh." I kiss her hair. "I'm not sure how I feel about those being the first words out of your mouth."

She pokes my ribs. "Well, she's my baby now, so you'll have to get used to sharing my attention with her. Also, I think we should finally get that dog. But one we know will get along with cats."

"The dog could live with me."

"Yeah, for now. But when we move in together, they'll both be there." She says it so certainly, like she has no doubts about this happening soon. Surprisingly, I don't either.

She rolls away to drink some water from her bottle on the nightstand. "When do you want kids?"

I choke. The nonchalant way she asked that question clashes with my inability to breathe. She offers the bottle of water to me when I'm unable to get control of my coughing, and I gulp down half of it.

I've never allowed myself the dream of having kids. I'd fuck them up, I know it. A family to come home to, kids to play with in the backyard, a loving wife to fall asleep holding. I've always wanted them, but I've never deserved those things.

But I can finally accept that I'm not that guy anymore. And now, instead of telling myself to stop thinking about it because I'm a piece of shit, I tell myself to stop thinking about it to allow some dust to settle before I pull Sage on top of me and start making that family I can now picture so clearly.

"Soon," I answer. "Not now, but soon." First, we need a dog or two. And a house with a yard for them to play in. And more counters for Edna to knock things off of. And an extra room for a nursery.

She smiles and takes the water bottle back. "That's an acceptable answer. What do you want to do tomorrow?" she asks, a droplet of water dribbling down her chin.

"I bought tickets for that interactive art show we missed last time."

"You did?" She squeals, capping her water bottle. "That was so sweet of you!"

A yawn delays my answer. After driving and having sex twice today, I'm beat. "Of course. Anything for you."

"In that case, make some coffee, Callum. Because I'm not done yet."

Where does she get her stamina from? I look over at her, already on her knees and ready to begin again, while I'm still winded and my heart still beating wildly.

"You don't want a snack or dessert or a nap or anything?" I try weakly.

"Nope," she says.

Then she pounces.

EPILOGUE

"You don't think it's too fast?" Callum says, his concerned gaze aimed at the whiskey in his glass.

"Oh, Callum," I groan. "Not this again." Hailey, Tyler, Callum, and I stand in a circle waiting for the fun to start after spending all day decorating. We're back in Nick's step-dad's hangar, only this time, white Christmas garland and fairy lights are wrapped around the rafters.

"I just don't want a repeat of your wedding to Brian, or any brides escaping out the window," he says, as if that happening *again* is entirely realistic.

"Considering the people involved, does that seem likely?" I ask.

"Yes," he states with certainty.

Actually, now that I'm thinking about it, I guess it is entirely plausible.

"I think everything is going to be fine. A happily ever after, if you will," Hailey says.

"What about us, H?" Tyler asks, his mischievous grin teasing his lips. "Are we going to have a happy ending?"

"Not if you don't stop talking to me," she states drily. I guess their working together on the no-bullying week didn't improve things between them.

Tyler chuckles while Callum shakes his head.

Since our trip to San Antonio, we haven't spent a single night apart. Slowly, I moved Edna over, hoping I wouldn't introduce too much change at once. We did get that dog, though, and he and Edna sleep together when we're not looking. We named it Henry, after Mr. Parsons. He's just as old, but still playful, and a great cuddler.

We attend church every Sunday with Mrs. Browning, who still hasn't warmed up to the idea of having a cat named after her, but she sewed Edna a blanket with her name on it anyway. We visit Mr. Parsons after lunch with Mrs. Browning, and I'm officially on the list of volunteers for the pet shelter now. I won't be able to do that for much longer, though.

Danielle and Brian are officially dating now, and are around here somewhere. I look around for them now, but don't see them. A thought hits me, and I start sniggering.

"What's so funny?" Callum asks.

"I can't find Brian and Danielle. I was just wondering if maybe they're in his car getting engaged."

Hailey snorts, and Tyler's head snaps to hers, his eyebrow flicking upwards. "That was a cute noise," he says playfully.

Her smile slips and she rolls her eyes, walking away from us while Tyler tracks her every step.

"Will you leave her alone? It's been two years of this merciless teasing," Callum lectures.

Tyler cracks his knuckles, as if preparing for a challenge. "Not until she finally warms up to me. I have all the patience in the world. And I don't know if you know this, but she has *no* patience. I'm sure to win any day now."

Erin steps up, resuming Hailey's vacated spot, and looks at my hand clasped in Callum's. Tilting her blonde head at me, she asks, "Didn't we have a pact?"

"Oh, right! I forgot about that."

She laughs, shaking her head. "Well, I'm happy for you anyway. Although I think that means you owe Nick."

Suddenly, Mom's voice rings out over the small crowd gathered in the building. Her voice, high-pitched from excitement, commands, "Okay, everyone, time to hide!"

Jonah switches some of the lights off, so only one glows in the center, casting shadows on everyone backing against the wall. While Nick wanted us all to witness the moment, he knows—we all know—Cori would not appreciate the attention on her. So we're hiding. There aren't many of us, my siblings and parents, a few aunts, uncles, and cousins, Nick's mom and step-dad, and the friends that are more family than friends.

Cori and Nick's voices grow louder until the door opens and they step inside.

"Where is everyone?" she asks. She was told Jonah and Elaine were throwing a Christmas party.

"The party starts a little later than I told you," Nick explains, stopping beneath the light and grabbing her hand.

"What do you mean?" she asks, concern in her tone.

"I mean, I love you."

Her lips spread into an unsure grin. "I love you too."

"I know we haven't been dating a full year yet, but when you know, you know. And I know, without a doubt, that I will never love another woman for as long as I live the way I love you. Marriage is a lot of work every single day, but I promise to wake up each morning and choose you." He gets down to one knee and pulls the ring, our grandmother's, from his pocket. "So, Cori... will you choose me back?"

I look up when Callum squeezes my hand, saying with the gleam in his eyes that he agrees with everything Nick just said, only for me. Sharing this moment with him, the moment my twin gets engaged, means everything to me. But having our own romantic moment in secret is kinda thrilling.

Cori's not one for showing much emotion on her face, almost like it seizes control of her body and paralyzes her features. She stares at the ring, expression blank, for a long while. And what Callum was saying earlier comes back to me. I know it's not too fast, Cori and Nick are perfect together. I'm completely confident that she'll say yes. And not because she's a people pleaser, but because she loves him.

But she and I are so much more alike than anyone's ever considered. We're both passionate, just about different things. We're both insecure, we just show it in different ways. And just like I was with Brian, when we're presented with a ring, we're stunned into silence. Again, just for very different reasons.

Callum and I hold our breath as she finally looks up at Nick, tears shining in her eyes. The emotion has such a hold on her, all she can do is nod and hold out her hand. With shaking hands, Nick slips the ring onto her finger, then she disappears in his embrace. He kisses her long and passionately. It's so hot, I'm sure our dad is shielding his eyes somewhere.

When they finally break apart, cheers erupt, echoing off the metal walls of the building. Jonah flips the lights back on, and I laugh at the look of betrayal on Cori's face. When her eyes catch mine, she joins my laughter, sauntering over to show me the ring and escape the commotion as family members close in to slap Nick on the back, offering their congratulations.

She whispers, "He proposed!"

"I saw, genius."

"With Grandma's ring." She admires it on her finger, more tears building. Grandma loved all of us equally, but I'm sure she's sighing in relief somewhere that Cori was the one who gets to wear her ring.

She leaves to show it off to her future mother-in-law, and Callum's hand lands on my back.

"Would it freak you out too much if I told you what ring I want when you propose?" I ask

He smiles and shakes his head in exasperation. "No, go ahead."

"Okay, I don't want a diamond. I want something unique. You could go more elegant with a sapphire like a royal, or you could do an uncut gem."

"What if I propose without a ring, and then we make a date for you to pick it out?"

"Actually, yes, that's exactly what I want. But don't propose in a cheesy way." Except I know that this man could propose to me in his pajamas in the bathroom with a keychain ring. I probably wouldn't even notice the ring until I pried my mouth from his and rolled off his body in exhaustion hours afterward.

I don't even realize we're gazing into each other's eyes until he breaks contact to look at my mouth.

He leans in, and even though it's a gentle kiss that leaves me wanting more, goosebumps erupt all over my skin. "Would it be rude if we left?" he whispers against my lips.

Glancing over at Cori and Nick, completely infatuated with each other and probably wondering the same thing we are, I shake my head.

"Let me go say goodbye real quick," I say, with a kiss to his cheek.

I remove the bracelet from my wrist and interrupt Cori and Nick's moment.

"Can I borrow your fiancée for a moment?"

"Only for a moment," he says, jokingly. At least, he'd better be joking.

After he walks away, I turn to Cori. "Callum and I are going to go home. I'm going to tell him the news tonight." She already knows the news because she was with me when I found out.

Her face lights up. "Oh, tell me how he responds. Like immediately after."

I laugh, taking her hands in mine. "Will do." I swap out the bracelet on her wrist for the one she gave me and pull up my sleeve.

"What are you doing?" She studies the bracelet, the little white beads that read '*WWCD?*' And I slip the one with my initial onto my wrist.

"You've gotten better at overthinking anyway, and I wouldn't change who you are for anything. I may not have shown that in the past, but it's true. And my crazy side may have landed me in an engagement I had no business being in, but it also led me to Callum. So,"—I shrug—"I think we should embrace our instincts instead of trying to stifle them."

Hailey told me it's okay not to be confident all the time. Callum has said something similar. But I am confident. Confident in my ability to not always know the right direction to go, but going anyway.

With that in mind, I hug my sister goodbye and head back to where he waits, grinning and looking down my body like he wants to devour it. Then, whether we'll go up in flames or end like a princess movie, I rest a hand against the secret in my belly and follow Callum toward the rest of our story.

Acknowledgements

I GET ASKED OFTEN how I wrote a novel (now two) with twin boys. Honestly, it's easier than you think; I set them up in the dirt with their construction trucks, and type away at my laptop in a chair a couple of feet away. Thing is, I don't think I would have written my first novel without them. They are the entire reason, the whole point, my everything. I write for them. To show that your dreams are worth reaching for.

Thank you Mom, for watching my kids so I can write, and for being the worst beta reader ever because you're so supportive. I could hand you absolute trash writing and you'd still tell me it was amazing.

Thank you to my husband, who tries to sell my book to his male, blue-collar coworkers who don't read romance. Thank you for bringing me coffee and attempting to make dinner so I can write, even though you can't boil water, and you almost burned the house down cooking ground beef once.

Extra thank you to my BETA readers, Jessica Aranda, Alex Flores, and Lauren Squindo. Your feedback was such an important part of this process because you gave it with so much encouragement and enthusiasm during a time when I really needed it.

About The Author

Amanda Courtney is a chronic daydreamer and writer of emotional love stories with flawed characters.
She published a collection of poems in 2022, some of which are featured in her first novel, WHAT HURTS THE MOST.
She resides in Texas with her husband, twin boys, and a herd of pets.

Follow along for updates on Hailey and Tyler's story, coming up next!